MY FATHER'S FUNERAL

A novel

Rebecca Worl

DROPHAT PUBLISHING
SEATTLE

PUBLISHED BY DROPHAT
Seattle, Washington

ISBN 978-0-692-37508-2

Printed in the United States of America

December 2014

Dedicated to:

Brad Hill, the prolific writer, committed missionary, dedicated father - although African dirt runs deep red in your blood, please don't ever ask me to bury you in The Congo.

Table of Contents

PREFACE

My father's casket was precariously lowered into the ground, a rough shallow hole dug with ebony arms and inhabited by a thousand red ants. The muddy crimson earth poured over the metal beaten from a long journey. I lost track of time, staring blankly as the hole filled slowly by the shovel full. The hypnotic rhythm of the digging, the hollow thump on the crate, the drums in the background and the roar of the rain left me numb in a trance of grief, relief and a great deal of fear.

"*C'est fini.*"

"*Madame, nous avons finis.*"

"*Madame!?*"

"*Oui*?" I came up for air and managed to respond in French. *Oui* always seemed to be the appropriate thing to say in French.

"*C'est fini mademoiselle!* - We are finished."

The Congolese man pointed to the haphazardly piled dirt. "Bury dead," he said in broken English, wiping the dirt off his hands. He threw the shovel on the pile and stood there. I smiled at him.

"*Merci mingi mpo na mosala…*-thanks very much for the work." He looked carefully at me without a flicker of a smile. I wanted to take a step back but held my ground.

"*Boye, likambo nini sikawa?*- so, what now?"

I was confused. I understood the words just fine but the implied meaning escaped me. I had already given the thirty francs for payment to the village pastor. It wasn't about the money.

He continued to fix me with his gaze, then to my relief he just turned away…

A strong hand took my arm. "Let's go Anna. It's over."

I realized I had been holding my breath, and let out a long sigh. Yes. Dead. Done. Finished. Buried. It's over. *J'ai fini.* I finally felt the cold, the rain dripping down my nose and soaking through my socks. I had been holding my breath for weeks and now I stood alone in the middle of Africa, staring at my father's grave, and I truly realized that he was dead. I had finally granted his last wish.

But my journey was *far* from over.

CHAPTER ONE

Two Weeks Earlier

I know Africa better than one might expect. I was born there, I grew up there, I was white there. Dad on the other hand, was mostly black. Not in skin tone by any means. A tall pale Swede, he stood out amongst anyone even slightly sun-kissed, but he was African through and through... I am becoming more certain of this since his sudden death.

It's backward that we can learn more about a loved one after they've died than when they were alive with us. We fail to take advantage of living moments. We somehow deceive ourselves that death is not imminent for all of us, and that our loved ones will "always be there" to teach us, talk to us, love us. We assume that there will be plenty of time to complete an unfinished conversation, to one day resolve a long-standing argument...to reconcile. Perhaps it is the sudden loss that propels us to anxiously grab onto whatever memory, writing, picture, or testimony of the person we can find in an attempt to sustain their life.

Life is 100% fatal; one out of every one human dies. You can quote me on that.

Americans sterilize death. Surgically clean it up, wipe away the blood, perform a little bit of magic with makeup and *voila* - the dead look ready for their red-carpet entrance into eternity. We dress cadavers in pretty gowns, comb their hair, place them inside velvet memory-foam-lined caskets, all while keeping our latex gloves sealed to our skin. We wear appropriate black clothing for the funeral, sit in the back pew, stare at a closed casket (or worse, an open casket), graze off of meat and cheese platters with toothpicks, carefully balance champagne in our left hand, shake hands with our right, maintain dignity and composure while presenting creepy statements like "I'm just glad he's in a better place," and "would you care for some olives?" Olives. Indeed… placates grief every time.

Death is not ignored in the Congo, nor can it be waved away with sleight of hand and a triple bypass surgery. Death looms, hovers - just one venomous snake bite away from bringing you to the other side, one malaria infested mosquito nip away from lifting your blood stream into the light. In Congo, death doesn't snicker discreetly in the corner, it laughs openly in your face.

My youngest, most vivid childhood African memory is of a funeral. Dad once took me to a *Kufa,* or death, in the village. Even now I can hear the wailing over the roar of the Land Rover as we near the village. We park near the circle of people gathered around the makeshift palm-branch awning that provides some shade. The mother who lost her little baby continues her keening for hours, her throat an open grave of grief. The women around her wail no softer. The entire village - relatives or not - join whole-heartedly with crying and moaning. The baby is passed around and clutched tightly by all. There is no embalming, no casket, no make-up, no gloves. The dead baby is handled, touched, kissed, caressed. The designated fly swatter waves the palm branches continually over the tiny body. Tears drip over the baby, making small rivulets down the dusty cheeks. She has no name. Why bother naming them until they prove their survival?

I inhale the smells. I can smell them still. The smoke of the fires mingles with the astringent aroma of roasting coffee. The Ngbandis are passing around *kwanga*, a fermented manioc dish that makes my nostrils twitch. And penetrating it all is the smell of death. The cacophony of sounds also cascade over me; goats bleating, the incessant pounding of corn and manioc, a radio blaring something from Kinshasa in staccato French.

Later in the day, we all get up. The child is carried on a woven mat to the edge of the village where a hole has been dug. They suspend the mat on ropes and lower her gently into the ground. The keening rises to a new level. Another mat is placed over her and then the filling begins. It doesn't take long for the small hole to fill up. Soon it is a mound. The mother throws herself onto the grave, swallowing the earth, dirt lodges under her fingernails. Nobody tries to restrain her. They just wait and watch. When her grief is spent, she will get up, go inside, and cook dinner.

In my bunk bed that night, up on the hill a mile away, death invades all of my five senses...no, all six senses. I feel the vibration of the drum's mournful message pounding in tandem with my own heartbeat. I hear the groans of the grieving, palpable in the thick air around me. A bleating pig is led to the edge of the jungle and its throat slit. The feast screeches in pain. The bleats fade away as the blood pumps out. I can picture it dripping red and turning to black as it dries and sizzles on the coals beneath. I inadvertently lick my lips; my taste buds salivate imagining the pork marinating in fatty palm oil. I can smell the traditional peanut dust and pili-pili pepper rub. When the food is ready, a massive feast begins, there is dancing, eating and mourning, simultaneously. I feel the complex mixture of immeasurable sorrow and acceptance. I sense the baby girl's departure.

In the village, there are no polite smiles, no please-and-thank-you's or meaningless apologies. When Death visits, He is entertained, but when the visit is over, He is ushered out the door.

There is no word for denial in the Congolese language, but across the Atlantic it's more than a word, it's a lifestyle. The front door is never open for Death's visit in the first place; His presence is not acknowledged. We turn a shy eye, look the other way, and commence with booting up our Blackberry. The dead don't even look dead, why should it seem real?

Our procedure for handling death is antiseptic, and we miss a crucial, key moment in our steps to recovering from the loss of a loved one. Opportunity for acceptance passes. We have more than just a thin latex layer of protection between us and the dead and our entire arsenal of self-preservation is launched, attacking any glimmer of reality. Of course, two years later, we slap down $150 an hour to talk to a shrink, consume a steady diet of Unisom and Prozac, and purchase the latest Dr. Phil book all in attempt to process the fact that someone we love is now on "the other side." Wherever that might be.

Which process wins the prize? On one hand, embracing the dead, literally, leaves traumatic marks. It's gruesome. On the other hand, denying it all together is more expensive. Pick your poison; neither package is pretty...

"Anna, would you like a re-fill?" I heard a faint voice that elbowed me out of my musings and back into the present.

"Anna?"

I begrudgingly acknowledged the offer and lifted my glass for more wine with just a nod. I had to snap out of this morbid reverie. Yet it was reverie that kept me from the present, which is what I wanted.

"Lovely service, really lovely... so many wonderful things that people said about your Dad, he looked so peaceful, so handsome....you look like him...he had such a strong faith...I wonder if he's looking down on us from heaven..." My friend Lilly poured me round four, and continued to yammer meaningless nothings about the memorial service. "I'm so sorry for your loss. I'll totally be praying for you. God works all things together for good you know!" Her voice nearly squeaked with forced spiritual enthusiasm. *He does, does He? Really? Since when?* All I know of life is pain and loss and loneliness, pain that sits heavy and cold, a paperweight on the soul anchoring me down tight. Lilly was going to have to do better than spiritual platitudes to open me into conversation. She continued on oblivious to my disinterest.

"I didn't even know your Dad spent so much time in Africa, and your Mom too... how much do you remember about her? What was it like being missionaries there? Do you remember much?" Lilly rambled awkwardly and shifted about in her Christian Louboutin stilettos. Grieving people always make others nervous.

"I remember the funerals." I placidly stared out the window. The rain was relentless but appropriate. The Space Needle was visible from this high-rise apartment, delicate and glowing bright against the night sky. I could see the elevators ascending and descending inside the Needle's slender legs. Lilly was kind enough to organize and host the memorial service after -"party," from her condo on Alki Point, Seattle's only sandy beach. She tried to be a friend to me, I appreciated the effort. But I don't do friends very well, obviously, since she didn't even know I lived in Africa for most of my life.

Lilly just nodded and coughed nervously to my peculiar response. She considered probing for further conversation but instead raised a platter in front of my face, "More olives? Pigs-in-a-blanket?"

"Yes please." I picked up my toothpick and imagined it was a massive spit with a rotating pig, I imagined eating with dirty hands and nails, I imagined burying my mouth into a greasy piece of meat, I imagined drinking till I was freely dancing, I imagined drums in the background, bare black feet pounding the earth, I imagined wailing. I nibbled politely at my appetizer, slowly sipping my wine and admiring my just-for-the-funeral manicure - French whites. I swallowed hard and heard the "ding" "ding" "ding" of a knife against a crystal glass - and we raised a toast to Dad. Seattle never felt so sterile, life never felt so dead.

"Here's to James."

Here's to you Dad, wherever you are…

"Anna, when you have a moment, we need to discuss your Father's will, there is something in here that greatly concerns you." A man sidled up next to me and whispered fateful information into my ear. I instinctively pulled back, my space and the comfort of my reverie violated.

The last conversation I had that night was with Ian, my Father's lawyer, my tax-lawyer…and occasional boyfriend when the occasion warranted. Great combination.

CHAPTER TWO

Lilly's shiny pot of French-press coffee sat on the large oak desk in her study, waiting to be pressed. The coffee grounds gathered magnetically together underneath the nylon mesh.

"Aren't you going to press that?" I am deeply annoyed by the little disturbances in life. My therapist calls it an "excessive need to control my outside environment." Whatever that means. She gets paid too much.

"Oh, yes, I forgot entirely, to, um, push the um, the…" Ian fumbled around from behind his open briefcase and stacks of legal papers and envelopes, leaned over and reached for the pot. He knocked a pile over onto the floor and papers scattered everywhere, dangerously near to the fire. Ian frantically scrambled to pick them up and restore order, muttering apologies and curses under his breath. Amazing, how this man could be mistaken for Daniel Craig, yet lack all the cool prestige and suave demeanor typical for a 007. At least they shared the same accent. Ian was the clumsiest lawyer I have known, maybe he could be a 001. License to annoy.

"I'll do it." I rolled my eyes, impatiently grabbed the press and slowly pushed my hand down on the top of the lid, watching the grounds sink to the bottom of the stainless steel floor. *Something so satisfying about that.*

"I asked Lilly to make us some, I figured we might be in for a long night. I'll pour you a cup?" Ian offered. He looked tired and awkward around me. Fidgety. The feeling was mutual. Neither of us ever knew what to expect of the other. On or off? Oil and vinegar, or cream and sugar… it all depended on the day and the mood. To be fair, *my* day and *my* mood. Lately, thanks to a recent shutdown of mine, it was oil and vinegar and we were not "on" so to speak. I hated the swiftly shifting tides of our relationship, yet could never settle on one wave.

"No coffee for me thanks." I tried to imagine Ian successfully pouring a cup of coffee without spilling. I had to decline; Lilly was infamous for buying cheap coffee, Folgers. Gag me. Such a disappointment, I can only drink the good stuff, Starbucks Pike Roast. Plus, I didn't want to be "in for a long night" with Ian, again. Not tonight at least. Also, I did not want the nice buzz I had going from my many refills of "consolation" wine to be interrupted by a sharp slap of caffeine. I swirled my merlot and made no attempt to hide my annoyance.

Ian cleared his throat and obviously tried to compose himself, putting on his best professional face. I almost snickered. At least he was perceptive enough to know this was not the time engage me as a girlfriend, or an ex-girlfriend, or whatever we were.

11

"Let's get down to business. Anna, I need you to pay close attention. There is a letter your Dad left that is addressed to you." Ian held up a plain folded note. *Intriguing...*

"And this isn't part of his will?" I asked.

"No, something else. Some... um... instructions. See here, it's addressed to you." He repeated himself uncomfortably. Ian waved the letter a little bit more in front of my face.

"Of course it's addressed to me Ian, I am all he had left." The letter made me bristly. I didn't want to open it.

"Yes, of course, I'm sorry, Anna, what I meant is, you see here, there is this letter..." He flapped the note around again, like it was a tasty tidbit before a pet. I was no pet, and this didn't look like a kibble. I narrowed my eyes at Ian and reluctantly snatched the letter from his fingers before he could loose his apologetic British tongue with more nervous words. The silence was palpable as I read the letter; the kind of awkward silence like when you accidentally open your front door and didn't know it was a religious evangelist who had knocked. I wished I hadn't opened this letter. I swallowed hard trying to maintain composure.

"Ian, are you sure this was addressed to me?" My voice wavered.

"You just said yourself that everything - "

"I *know* what I just said! Is this a practical joke, *Ian*?" I snapped, rising to my feet, blood rushing quickly to my face. Ian leaned back from the verbal sting.

"Don't shoot the messenger, *Anna.*"

"I'm sorry," I quickly offered. I regretted lashing at him, but I just couldn't digest what I was reading. I had just made a new year's resolution to reduce my profanity by 50% as a form of self-improvement. Bad timing. These were not the moments where remarks like "Oh my stars!" and "Goodness gracious!" were useful.

I clenched my hands into fists by my sides and tried to take a deep breath and count to 10. I was instantly furious with my father, not an entirely new emotion, but being dead and all, the closest person to take out my anger on was Ian. Poor Ian. How is it he always accidentally winds up in my cross hairs? Anger management classes had been a great waste of my time and money. However, self-defense and kick boxing were fantastic.

Ian cautiously reached his hand across the table and touched mine, as one would carefully approach a stray dog. Again with the unsocialized pet nuances. *Was I that hard to approach?*

"I'm sorry. I'll leave you alone for awhile..." he paused and dared to add more, "You know, just because he's gone, doesn't mean he can tell you what to do." Ian shut the large door behind him, leaving me all alone with my friend, merlot.

Dad wasn't telling me what to do, he was asking, begging...

I read the letter again.

> *Dear Anna Marie,*
>
> *I know you are just beginning to go through the early stages of dealing with the fact that I am dead. I know I am not in the ground yet, as this note was*

marked "urgent," to be opened immediately upon my death. Anna, here's why I'm writing, I need you to do me one last favor. I need to be buried in Goyongo. I need to be buried in the Congo, for various reasons you may not understand yet, but you will discover, I assure you. This is of the utmost importance. I want my whole body to return. Just take the path past the water source about a mile. There is a little gravesite there, you'll find it. This means the world to me; it means your world too... You are the only one who can and would do this for me, you must do this for me, take me home - for both our sakes. Please, sweet daughter, you may be all I have left, and I am all that you have left - I will be with you for the whole journey, just another couple weeks of me, and then you can move on with your life. Find a way, I'm sorry. Please, have faith.

  Your Father,
  James Landan.

I closed the letter and let my head fall on top of the table with a thud. *Oh dear god! Can he be serious?* "Have faith?" I mused. *Have faith? In what, Dad, in my abilities to get your stiff, dead body to the Congo? Have faith in your ridiculous motives for needing to go there? What kind of Heart of Darkness - Gorillas in the Mist - Out of Africa -*

Poisonwood Bible, B.S. is this? What could you possibly mean by, 'for both our sakes?'

I wadded up the letter, tossed it aside and returned to the very important business of drinking, alone, well aware of the promised hangover hungrily waiting to greet me in the morning. Hopefully nothing that a good hour of meditation, yoga, and a shot of wheat grass couldn't kick. It was worth it. I slowly finished my merlot. Yuck again. Probably Sutter Home. Lilly obviously had no taste for fine drink. I had a nice bottle of Carlos Basso Dos Fincas Malbec 2002 waiting for me at home. Aged six, oh well, it was enough to keep the tears at bay.

It was only Sunday…what a week, and it had only just begun.

I thought about the mile past the water source and wondered if that was where Mom was…I wondered if I would survive such a visit to my past…I wondered if returning would in fact, "mean the world to me."

I stared at his handwriting and suddenly felt grabbed by sorrow. As much as I held resentment toward my father, I still felt grief from his sudden departure. We were close when I was kid, very close. But then…we hadn't talked in so long. There was still so much to resolve. I would never have another chance. I swallowed my tears back hard and fought to regain control. Now was not a good time to cry. There never is.

CHAPTER THREE

The Monday morning sun was more gracious to my poisoned head than I had anticipated. The term "sun," a rare, exotic, three-letter word is not commonly heard on the streets of Seattle. I debated about doing hot yoga, but instead I shoved my head deeper into my feather pillow and imagined a handsome, young, Columbian Coffee Lord percolating me a cup of joe and serving it to me in bed, shirt off. His shirt, that is.

"¿Quieres café?" He asks, with a nod and a wink.

"*Oui, s'il te plais.*" Of course, I only respond in French. I also have a residue of Lingala in my head somewhere but it doesn't surface easily Then we both switch to English, naturally. "Why so sad senorita? You are way too pretty to be so sad, oh so pretty…"

"Pretty, who, me? Well, ok, if you insist…" I shrug and run my fingers through my counterfeit blond hair. "I'm not sad, just hung over." The piercing headache was hard to ignore.

"Why does senorita drink so much?" He is now gently tipping the coffee cup into my mouth, stroking my hair lovingly.

Between slurps I answer him, "I drank too much wine because my Dad died. Yup, dear Dad went and died on me, and then left me with a dying request to bury his body deep in the heart of the jungle. Not his heart, not his ashes, nope - the whole freakin' body, from head to toe!"

"Oh, you must be so disturbed, do you need some loving, senorita?" Columbian man inches nearer to my face, my heart is pounding.

"Yes, oh yes, please." The Columbian man reaches for me, takes my face between his hands, lowers his mouth to mine, and then of course he spills the boiling coffee all over my brand new, overpriced, white Pottery Barn sheets. I said some things I shouldn't have, he said some things he *really* shouldn't have and then he faded away...I couldn't even day dream about pleasant things, much less experience them in real life.

I stumbled out of bed and into my kitchen, which doesn't take long, a small benefit to living in a 600 square foot studio apartment. The other benefit to this miniature lifestyle is that I am literally across the street from Pike Place Market. I traded in square feet, a yard, privacy, children, and a husband for a very urban lifestyle. To be honest of course, the husband and children were not entirely my choice or "trade," they were just simply not on the menu for my life. Perhaps I am not selfless enough. Yes, I'm sure that is it, sacrifice and a halo was also not on the menu. I began to make coffee, like I do every morning, but living right above the original Starbucks café wreaked havoc on my culinary-beverage ambitions. I meandered down in my bathrobe to drink the magic, life-giving potion.

The Market was buzzing and pulsing with enthusiastic selling energy. Pacific salmons were already flying through air to the cadence of the handler's yelps and shouts, an ancient Seattle crowd-pleaser. The mandolin player had taken his morning spot on the corner and was strumming out a few cheesy fisherman tunes. Kids were riding the bronze pig and posing for the paparazzi, commonly known as – mothers. Fog was lifting off from the Sound and draped me with mist and salt. The taste was comfortingly familiar; the salt on my face saving me a four hundred dollar facial. I creaked open the door to the old café and crossed myself in front of the naked mermaid hanging overhead. She was a beautiful beacon of welcoming light in a cold, gray world. Saint Starbuck.

"The usual, Anna?" The cute barista smiled at me. *Smiled* at nine in the morning. No joke. "Ashley" worked the Saturday morning shift. Ashley, size zero. Dreads, and only five visible piercings. Small tat just above her butt, god I love Seattle.

"No, add two shots please." *And don't you dare mention the bathrobe.* I still felt so foggy, the sun hurt my eyes. "Could I have a Venti water too?" And some Aleve too please. Starbucks made the best water, or at least, I'm programmed to think that about everything they serve.

"Nice day isn't it? So rare in April, are you going to shop for awhile this morning?" Ashley made perky conversation. Black lined lips smiled.

Meaningless barista-small talk did not amuse me. I just smiled and looked at the merchandise. I noticed they had a new seasonal mug, a mug I didn't have yet, a mug I must have. I grabbed it off the shelf and handed it over to purchase. I eyed the pastry case lustfully. Since I didn't have my Columbian lover this morning, I opted for an old fashioned glazed donut instead, does the trick just as well. My total came to $16.81. I didn't even feel guilty. That was only about ten minutes of work-time for me. My Grandpa would roll in his grave if he heard how much it costs one person to have a cup of coffee these days. Speaking of graves...

"One, quad Grande, extra hot soy on the bar! Bottoms up!" So dang perky.

"Thanks Ashley. Have a nice one." I grabbed my coffee from Ashley and headed back to my apartment. I could hear my phone ringing just outside my door, I hunted around in the pockets of my robe for my keys and raced to open the door, careful not to spill my coffee for the "second" time this morning.

"Hello?" I breathlessly answered.

"Anna, you aren't picking up your cell phone."

"You expect me to answer my phone at seven in the morning?" It was Ian.

"This is important, I'm sorry to bother you, but the funeral director called last night and needs to talk about the burial arrangements for the body today. I mean, you know, for your Dad." Ian cleared his throat apprehensively.

"Yes, I *know* who you may be referring to, when you say 'the body,' *Ian*." The phone went dead. Oh, *why do I have to be such a witch?* I closed my eyes and rubbed the headache pounding over my browline. I'm sure he had had it with me. I couldn't blame him. He was trying to be helpful, I just couldn't get over the fact that he was in love with me, and I was too selfish to know how to love him back. So I bit and spat venom, it usually worked in keeping men away, but Ian...Ian hung around (maybe because he was my lawyer and I paid him to, maybe it was the potential for repeat "snogging," as the Brits say). His accommodating and gentle personality often rubbed me the wrong way. He lacked backbone. And I was all wrong for him. He was friendly, compliant and docile. I on the other hand am feisty, controlling and dominant. He lingered in my life like a faithful dog...*now who's the pet?* A St. Bernard, or a wise Golden Retriever, a Husky that barked with a British accent...how would that sound exactly? My mind trailed...

Thanks to the Malbec, I totally forgot that today was the burial. It was going to be small, just myself, a few close friends, no doubt some missionary types, and Dad's best friend Keith, whom he worked with in Africa. I didn't want a show, the memorial service was hard enough with swarms of strangers hovering around, buzzing with forced sincerity. I stood motionless in my doorway, phone still in hand, dial tone pressing me, pushing me, persisting that I make a decision, a decision I was hoping last night's merlot and the nice Columbian man might have helped me with, neither was much of an assistance. I confidently make thousands of decisions everyday. I do so with assurance and arrogance. It's how I make the big bucks at Adobe. But this was a decision I was paralyzed to make.

My body slowly slid down into the hardwood floor, and I whispered to my vintage brick walls, "God, what should I do?" I didn't necessarily believe in God, anymore, but I didn't necessarily not-believe in Him either. Yet it struck me as odd that "God" would somehow find himself on my tongue once again when I was in distress. Banging my head against the wall a few times also did not produce an answer.

I grabbed the wrinkled letter off of my nightstand and read it again. The words jumped off the page in no particular order, *Please. You must do this for me. You're all I have left. The watersource... Utmost importance. Have faith...*

Faith? I was not ready to make that leap. Instead, I pulled out my trusty Eight ball.

"Eight-ball, should I traipse my father's body across the Atlantic, into snake-infested territory, even risking snakes on a plane," I cracked myself up, "and bury him in the Congo?" I shook the ball. That was a complicated question for an Eight Ball, so I shook it hard, spat on it, rubbed it with my rabbit foot key chain, clenched my tired eyes tight and chanted "please say no, please say no." I opened an eye, the ball said, "Ask Again Later." So I asked again. I shook the ball. I read the reply, "It is decidedly so."

It was decidedly so.

I needed to talk to a live person. Not that this ball had ever failed to direct me ever-so keenly with "his" advice and wisdom over the past years, but there was something about a warm human body with a human mind, that, I don't know, offered more. I opened my Mac Book Air. For all the money it cost me, I sure could not tell that the 1.8GHz Intel Core 2 Duo got me onto Facebook any faster. I logged into FB. I noticed in all my 145 "friends," that Becky was online, my old roommate…before she had the audacity to fall in love and get hitched and birth a drooling child. Traitor.

I messaged her: "Bec, are you there? Hello?"

She instantly wrote back. *Oh, thank God, I'm not the only one that doesn't have a life outside of Facebook.*

"Here! Speak!" Times New Roman type presented a cheerful hello.

I wondered how much to tell her, what details to leave out, I opted for being vague.

"Bec, have you ever done anything for anyone else that took great sacrifice? I mean, have you ever done someone a favor, a *huge* favor that cost you time, energy?" I waited for her return comment.

"You mean, besides 46 hours of labor to bear my husband his son?"

She always knew how to make me laugh. Of course, *she* wasn't laughing, 46 hours is nothing to laugh about. I was there for part of it, but fell asleep after 4 arduous hours of waiting in the lobby reading Vogue.

"Ok, that's a good one. Besides that. What if you gained nothing from it?"

Was that the key issue? Doing this for my Dad gave me "nothing" but a headache in return. It wasn't tax deductible; it wasn't a pay-it-forward, Oprah's Big-Give kind of operation. After all, he was dead, he couldn't return the favor. Did there have to be something in it for me? *"...for both our sakes..."* the letter had read. Becky's reply took a while. Then a new comment chimed in.

"I suppose it is those kind of actions that give any kind of beauty to our world that is so ugly as it is. RAK baby. Random Acts of Kindness. Or is it RAOK? Anyway... I guess it's more than that also. That is what I would call grace. Getting something that you don't deserve. Giving something to someone else, who doesn't necessarily deserve it."

He deserved many good things, but not another trip to Africa. If he hadn't taken us all out to that forsaken jungle on his "mission from God," Mom wouldn't have died, I wouldn't have been raised alone in boarding school, and maybe I could have had some stab at a normal life and normal relationships.

'Thanks Bec." I wrote back. Would taking a cadaver to the Congo be considered a random act of kindness? Very random. Very kind, too.

"Funny thing with grace," Becky kept typing, "sometimes when dispensing it, you end up the recipient as well."

What would *I* need grace for? From whom? I signed off, peeled myself from the floor and walked over to the kitchenette. The water inside my little fish tank sitting on the counter was particularly still. I looked carefully inside. Sure enough, Eeyore was upside down, suspended in his plastic, ocean floor tree. I disentangled my beta out from the tree with my bare hands and held him in my wet palm. First Dad, now Eeyore. I was surprised to feel a single wet tear on my cheek. No, wait, good...it was just fish water. I took the slimy blue pet over to my stainless steel compost bin and buried him on the bottom. Maybe his death could be a part of new life. Well, that is a bit too deep for a little fish; I'm just used to composting as a part of my new "green routine."

But perhaps there was some new life that could come from all of this. Did my Dad deserve some grace? How hard could it be anyway? I had already had to make decision upon decision about funeral and burial operations; I had already shelled out thousands of my own dollars trying to put my relationship with Dad to rest, what's one more dollar, one more day?

I shut the door to my bathroom and splashed some cold water on my face and took inventory in the mirror. My light blue eyes seemed to be turning a colder shade of gray. Ash-gray. The youthful cells in my skin were marching me into my later thirties with great enthusiasm. I was in desperate need of a few more highlights in my hair; I had found three more white strands since Dad died. That makes seven gray strands total, at age 31. I felt old. I put my nose right up to the mirror, hoping my two selves could merge into one super human that could produce an answer to my recent conundrum. "What should I do, Anna?" I asked my other self. I made the dreaded call.

I picked up my phone and dialed Marilyn.

"Dr. Ramsey's office," a polite voice answered the phone.

"I need to speak to Dr. Ramsey please, this is an emergency."

"May I ask of what nature, please?"

"The kind that's none of your business. That's why I'm calling my therapist." I rolled my eyes as I waited for her response.

"May I ask who is calling?" The receptionist didn't skip a beat. She was used to us "crazy's."

"Anna Landan."

"Oh. One moment please." I knew that would work. Anna Landan does not have emergencies.

"Anna," Marilyn's voice was sincere, professional and always rather monotone. "What is the problem? Our office just opened."

"My fish died."

"Excuse me?"

"Eeyore, my fish. He is dead."

"Anna... I'm sorry, I don't understand. Your...*fish?*"

"Um...so is my Dad."

"Ohhhh...." I could feel her nodding on the other end of the phone. Nodding, listening, squinting her eyes as she tried to scrutinize, pull apart, understand, and reflect. I waited for the usual, "how does that make you feel?" response.

"Why don't you come in - "

"OK." I cut her off before she could offer me a "slot." I threw my short hair in a ponytail and bobby-pinned most of the stray curls back, leaving a few wisps to frame my face. Calvin skinny Jeans, red Dankso clogs and my favorite J.Crew sweater finished the job and I marched out my door. Never was one for high fashion, but I was definitely a sucker for pricey brands and top quality.

Dad was the first to insist that I see "someone" about my problems. I made a deal that I would if he would. He didn't, said he was over it, but that I wasn't. So the deal was off. My boss was the second to insist that I see a psychologist; she said I was a brilliant programmer, but I had micromanaging control issues and was lacking social skills, or "niceties" as she called it. Since it was either that or lose my job, I reluctantly obeyed. Following her were a series of boyfriends who suggested the same thing, much to their demise. I naturally picked a shrink within walking distance. Just in case of emergencies…like this one. I didn't necessarily see myself pulling a "What About Bob" on her, especially since my fish was dead, but I wasn't one for waiting my turn, standing in line, or being pushed aside for clients who "made regular appointments." Needy people annoy me. "We" were working on this issue. Marilyn calls this "entitlement." Apparently, I have a lot of issues. Screw it, don't we all? I thought of Bill Murray and debated about bringing Eeyore around my neck. Wouldn't that be a hoot?

"…and now breathe out. Envision yourself exhaling all the bad, the negative energies, the toxic self-lies, and breathing in the good, positive, truths about yourself." Marilyn was closing her eyes with her palms up, a creepy smile on her face as she coached me. I just liked to sit in my chair and watch her reach nirvana. It was very entertaining. I wasn't sure if I was at hot-yoga or in a Dr.'s office.

"Very good!" she said, oblivious to the fact that she was the only one doing the exercise.

"Now, let's begin. Anna, you go first." Brilliant idea! I'll remember to tip her this Christmas.

"It's a tad hot in here, Marilyn, can you fix that heater?" I tugged at my sweater around my neck and looked at the old heater chugging away in the corner of the ancient house-turned-office; one of the many on this old street in Bell Town.

"Anna, let's get down to business, I do have a client coming in a few minutes." Marilyn looked at her rhinestone watch and gave it a shake. It fell to the side off of her thin wrist. She was getting thinner every day. I wondered how she did it. Atkins? Green-tea supplements? Sex? Ew. Right, getting down to business.

"Well. Dad died, he wants me to bury his body in the Congo. What should I do?" I was clear and straight to the point. None of that mushy self-disclosure crap, or 'how did you feel about your Father' babble. I needed someone to tell me what to do.

"Wow...that's big Anna. What feeling does that elicit in you?" Marilyn took out her pen and pad, and sat poised, ready to write down anything incriminating, anything that might land me in a straight jacket.

"Really? You're going to with that line? What does it matter how I feel? I need to know if I take this pilgrimage back to Congo or not!" I was getting antsy. Why was I here? I'm smart, I could figure this out. The water fountain in the corner sputtered and splurged, but was unable to produce the calming affect, the water had dried up.

"Interesting that you used the word pilgrimage."

"No, it's not."

"Yes, it is, Anna." Marilyn spoke so calmly it made me want to punch her. The broken fountain didn't help.

"No, it's not interesting, and aren't you going to fix that?" I gestured toward the pathetic machine.

"Not today. Now listen, a pilgrimage is a journey." She didn't skip a beat. I kept flashing my eyes between the fountain and the heater, wishing I had tried the deep breathing exercises. She continued, "It's not just a physical journey, but a mental, emotional, and spiritual one; a visit to the past as well as the future. A journey enhanced with spiritual purpose, it can open new doors and close old painful ones. Do you think there is a painful door you still are working on closing, that perhaps Africa holds the answers too?"

"What do you think, *Marilyn*?" I answered coyly. We had been through this before. In fact, we had been through this every single session.

"It's Dr. Ramsey," Marilyn coughed and shifted uncomfortably. I love making therapists uncomfortable. "Do you want to talk about the funeral again?"

"No."

"I think that burying your Dad in the Congo is bound to open very very deep wounds that you've carried since your Mom's death. Don't you think?"

I sat still and stiff, trying not to breathe. Maybe if I didn't move a muscle, or didn't say a word, it wouldn't be so real, and I wouldn't hear the wailing again.

"Do you still hear it?" I hate it when she reads minds. Is she a shrink or a reader?

"Only when I sleep, but now I take Ambien with scotch and it helps."

"It only masks, it doesn't help." Marilyn prompted me.

"No, it helps. I don't hear the mother wailing, I don't see the baby covered in dirt..." I closed my eyes and shook my head. *It was still so vivid!*

"The baby? You are still recalling the, what did you say the word was for funeral, the Kufa you went to? Isn't it true that there's a different memory you need to be recalling? That you hear a wailing which was your own?" Marilyn poked and prodded at my vulnerable psyche with her Psy.D.

Yes, it's true. But I can't handle the truth! God, I love that movie, Jack Nicholson is at his best. Not to mention Tom Cruise...with his shirt off....

"Anna, what about your *mother's* death? Isn't that more momentous?"

That's one word for it. I closed my eyes briefly, then looked out the window toward the water. *Please don't make me go there.* My mother's death was grotesque and convoluted. I like to remember the infant death of the nearby village because it was easy to consider and to discuss. At such a distance, I could even appreciate the cultural behavior, the methods and customs. Yet that baby's death is but a mere fraction of the severity to which I experienced Mother's funeral. The wailing was deeper, throatier. The grave's dirt was darker and redder. The tears were torrential, saltier. The drums were deafening and ominous. The after-funeral-feasting was more perverted. Her body was foul, the beauty and youth of her face erased with a cursed pale and purple mask, her unblemished skin covered in mud. The scene is forever varnished, grabbing out the colors and sensations of my memory and staining them with a grief too vivid to control.

"Anna? You don't have to recall it all now - "

"They took her hands, and reached them up to my *face*, Marilyn. Her hands touched my cheeks. They were icy cold, rigid, blue. I will never get over that..." *Her hands froze me in time...I could still see my seven year old self standing stationary by her body, touched by her skin, dark hands laying her pale ones back down onto the mat. Her hands froze the tears on my cheeks...they never returned to a warm liquid again.*

"Anna, perhaps we've been looking at that moment all wrong. Try visualizing her hands reaching out to you from the grave, not in morbid fashion, but as a reminder to you that her love reaches to you from beyond death. Visualize love reaching out toward your face and allowing you to feel again. Visualize love allowing you to love again."

"I can love." I stiffened in my seat and lifted my chin.

"I'm not talking lust, Anna. Real love. When was the last time you were in a relationship? And fooling around with Ian doesn't count."

"Didn't you say you had a client? Seriously, Marilyn, you are going to start in on my relationships when the real matter at hand is whether or not I should call my travel agent?" I got up and walked across the office, the old floor creaked underneath my entire 135 lbs. I gave the heater a good kick. It groaned and quieted down. Better. I turned and stared at Marilyn.

"Ok. Let me keep this brief." Marilyn leaned forward in her seat, her pencil skirt tightening around her legs as she scooted up. She took off her glasses. A marked sign of solemnity. Now we were getting serious. I looked directly at her. I am not afraid of the therapist. I am not afraid of the therapist. This was the mantra I'd been secretly chanting for three years.

"You need to go do this. You need to face the actual reality of your mother's death, and now your father's too. Anna, go but don't just face it, embrace it. Go to the place she died. Try to remember everything, as painful as it was. Learn to cry."

"I was traumatized, Marilyn." I snapped back bitterly but inside Fort Knox was shaking.

"Dr. Ramsey. And yes, you were, so much so that you have dramatized the event entirely."

"I have not dramatized it! That is exactly how it was, *Marilyn*." My cheeks were heating.

"Dr. is fine, thanks." We have played this Mariyln/Doctor routine for God knows how many sessions. It was my favorite part. "Anna, what you remember is what you experienced as a seven year old who lost her primary care-giver and then had to leave her father to go to boarding school. That little girl experienced death too close, grew up too fast and moved on without a blink. And because of that, it remains a nightmare. It is left in the shadows, not brought into the light, and therefore it lurks and haunts you."

She had a point.

"Do I have a point?"

"No." I sulked like a small child.

"Wouldn't this just re-traumatize me?" I didn't know much psychology, but wasn't that an acute possibility?

"I don't believe it will. You will face your fears. You will face the memory, and now as an adult, it may not seem so..."

"Horrific? Ghastly?"

"Whatever you want to call it. Cognitively, you understand how the culture works, the way death is handled, it is logical, it makes sense. But your inner-child is repulsed by how it all went down with your mother. Time to let her out and face the scene as an adult. Maybe even try to forgive your Dad, was it really his fault that she died?"

"I knew it would take you five minutes to get to the inner child speech. That is a bunch of psycho mumbo jumbo, *Marilyn.* " I tried to ignore the last part about forgiveness. I've always said, it's best to know whom to blame.

"It's Dr. Ramsey. And you might be right. But *you* are the one... who called *me.*" She looked down with a sly smile and scribbled something incriminating on her legal pad. Wafts of a rubber room paraded my way.

She had another point.

"Am I right?" She prodded as she raised her eyebrows high, looking up from over her notes. She wanted the points. Greedy shrink.

"Hell no, *Marilyn.* " No bone for you. No straight jacket for me man. I shook my head and stood up to go.

But...she *was* right, I had to admit... at least to myself. Maybe now was a good time to take a break from the posh life for a few weeks, show my Father some respect and fulfill his dying wish, even if it was absurd. Perhaps I could bank some good karma from it all. I would go back, tell my "inner child" to buck up, tie my past up in a nice neat bow of acceptance, shed some tears, bury Dad, and, as he said, return to my regular life as soon as possible. My life. Yes, that is what it is...a life, right? Corporate coffee, money, food, drinking, and men. That's as good a life as any.

I wrote another check at the front desk and stormed out of her office. Taking the long way back home, I meandered through the market now invaded by photo-hungry tourists. They all wanted to see where Tom Hanks ate lunch in "Sleepless in Seattle." I admired the beautiful fish displayed on the fresh ice...just waiting to be fried, and tartered. I shuddered. Do we all viciously fight our way upstream our whole life just to find ourselves caught in a net and slung backward? Or worse, flayed open and displayed?

Speaking of display... I grabbed my cell and made the call.

"Mr. Krader? This is Anna Landan, I need to speak to you about James Landan's burial this afternoon."

CHAPTER FOUR

I walked down to the underground garage and pushed the "start" button on my keyless ignition system. Off in the corner I heard my handsome A.J. start up with a throaty roar. Yes, "A.J.", my boy toy substitute. My friends asked about the name. Was it a former boyfriend? In my dreams. Becky was the only one who knew for sure. A. J. Foyt was a dominating Indy car driver in his time. A.J., (Anthony Joseph), blessed the earth and all the women on it with his perfect pecs, lean stature, and classic Hollywood boyish grin; a serious competitor of James Bond's picture next to Webster's definition of "sauve." The Subaru WRX STI was AJ in*car*nated. Sex on wheels; I felt like I needed a smoke when I shut him down. But AJ was not ostentatious. To the uninitiated he looked like a typical sub-compact economy car. That was good for Seattle and all of my tree hugging neighbors. Nobody was going to firebomb my car like the Earth Liberation Front did to those homes on the so-called "Street of Dreams." There was no hood scoop, nothing to expose its secrets, I even took off the "STI" emblem. Nothing gave it away except the 18" red-walled Toyo RA 1 tires and that excruciatingly sweet sound of the engine. But with a turbo'd 2.5 liter four putting out 305 hp almost instantaneously, the WRX was arguably one of the most understated, meanest, snarliest rally cars ever built. It may look green but it smoked nitrous oxide.

I approached AJ like one might approach "Seattle Slew" - the only undefeated Triple Crown Winner thoroughbred - with caution and respect. I like horses too. Anything that moves fast, but gracefully. "Hey A.J," I fondly greeted my sweetheart, ran a hand along the roof line, plopped into the contoured seat, buckled up, and eased out of the garage onto Pike Street, heading to Bellevue. I loved the I-5 onramp. With a little nudging, the turbo kicked in and pulled me back in my seat. I shifted into 2nd, a little sloppy, I admitted, losing a few too many revs. Bob Bondurant would not have liked that. I had taken his one-week high performance driving course last year and it changed my life - I would never drive the same again. I watched eagerly as the tach climbed towards 4,000. The shift into 3rd was much better. I glanced out the side window and realized that the wall along Freeway Park was too blurry and backed off the throttle. AJ liked to run. I liked to run him, especially in the sweet Seattle air. With my window down, I could still smell the saltwater. Even when it rains, I crack open my window. I love the feel of the fresh air and I don't mind the drops of water. The ferries coming and going beckoned me for a ride. No thanks, too slow. I'd rather drive across the Tacoma Narrows, even if they did turn it into a toll bridge.

The I-90 floating Bridge gladly flattened its back across Lake Washington, beckoning cars and drivers to discover the upper class suburbs of Mercer Island and Bellevue. Speaking of ostentatious. Bellevue smelled nothing like dirty saltwater and seagulls; it smelled white and wealthy. I urged A.J. across the island and gently into Bellevue, where he soon ranked below average to his fellow wheeled friends on the road. But I had no envy. Never wanted a BMW. I prefer a car with less glitz on the outside, and more guts on the inside. I suppose that's why we fit together so well.

My stomach felt queasy as I pulled up to the funeral home to meet with the director, Dale Krader. I didn't want to enter and make one more decision. "They" say that decision-making under pressure is the number one leading cause of stress, heart attacks, ulcers, cancer, canker sores and webbed feet. Everything is the leading number one cause of everything. Handling my Father's death and funeral arrangement, just four days ago, was by far the saddest, most psychologically complex situation I have ever experienced. I thought that all would be taken care of swiftly, with peace, and with respect. However, working with a funeral home was more like walking into a Chevy dealership during the summer time sales extravaganza, except the dealers all whisper and the studios are adorned with candles and crucifixes. I heard the same slogans and polished lines like, "I'm sure you simply want the best for your family," (translation: If you loved your Dad, you would pay through the nose), and "This one comes in blue, most people prefer blue." The dead have a color preference?

Having to pick a casket for Dad was more stressful than ordering a latte. Mathematically speaking there are over 87,000 possible drink choice combinations at Starbucks alone! 87,000! No wonder we spend five bucks per cup; we are so overwhelmed when faced with the decision, we'll spend anything to crawl away from the stress. Casket shopping was no different, and a little more morose. Just a little. I began to recall the memory as I sat inside AJ in front of the funeral home.

"Do you think your Dad would prefer metal or wood?" The glib mortician previously worked as a courtesy clerk offering "paper or plastic." *Who cares, do you think my Dad cares if he peacefully decays in metal or wood?*

The mortician smiled morbidly, smelling his prey, and continued waltzing around his show room, "This one is great for carrying, it is lightweight steel alloy, 18 gage unit... This one over here, now, this is our special carrier. This here is our bronze 32 ounce (per square foot), top of the line, heavy-duty home." *Did he really just call it a "home?" Good lord.* He continues, rubbing his hands together, feeling a sale coming on. "This is on sale right now for only $9,999! If you get it now, we'll throw in free cosmetics for the body preparation, and a large bouquet of calla lilies." *Oh well, since you mentioned the calla lilies, then of course...*

I learn all the names of the possible casket choices, names that sound ethereal and earthy like Montrachet Mahogany, Paragon Mahogany,

Pembroke Cherry and Golden Sienna Bronze. There are caskets for everyone and every lifestyle: The Puritan Copper (for the goody-goody two-shoes), The Neopolitan Blue (for the Italians), The Renaissance Rose (for the French), The Woodland Green Honor Oak (for the hippies). The mortician pushes the major players like the Prince African Mahogany, The Excalibir, The Admiral, and The Going Home. Ranging from 1,000-50,000 dollars, the choice for me was easy, the cheaper, the better. In order to stop myself from purchasing the $23,000 bronze, "Going Home" casket, hoping that Dad may not want to "go home" after all, I compartmentalize my grief and heartache (lest I be taken advantage of) and choose rationally. The Prince African is fitting to the circumstance, but I decide to pack Dad in style with the QO2 Earthtone lightweight brown 20 gauge steel for the incredible bargain of 1,600 dollars. No calla lilies.

Four days ago felt already like an eon...

I sat in AJ with one hand on the keys in the ignition, and stared at the front door of "Bellevue's Homeward Bound Funeral Home." *Homeward Bound? Really? Isn't that a puppy movie?* Massive hanging plants and flowerbeds cushioned the building, attempting to portray life. The manicured grass was eerily green. I was seconds away from throwing my car in reverse and heading south down I-5 toward California and leaving this whole mess behind. Maybe my craving for California was a sign that I needed to spend a few weeks in a tropical place with palm trees, except in the Congo instead, with snakes and tarantulas. I turned off the engine and listened to it spool down, putting out my cigarette, so to speak. I loved that sound. Then I headed inside.

Dale Krader turned out to be a nice funeral director. He was not glib and he did not exhibit any kind of vampire teeth when he flashed a smile. But he did look like a Bellevue native. He was young with slick hair, and I wondered how on earth he landed in this profession. Maybe he was drawn to the spiritual aspect. No, it had to be about the money, always is. And he was about to make a lot more money off my Dad's sudden passing. He had better thank me for this later. Maybe he could thank me with a nice steak dinner, a few martinis, a slow dance…

"Miss Landan? I'm glad you are here early! We have a lot to talk about. You want to make some pretty sudden changes?" Dale shook my hand and led me into his office. He didn't have the usual candles and crosses, I was rather relieved.

"Yes," I hesitated, here we go, am I really going to do this? "Yes, Mr. Krader, we have decided not to bury my Father at the cemetery." I tended to talk using "we" when I felt slightly vulnerable; "we" gives the impression that there is more intellect behind the operation than the singular brain knocking around in my lonesome head, making decisions for the Anna-show. I had people.

"Please call me Dale. Is there a particular reason for this, uh, sudden change in plans Miss Landan? You know that the burial service is set for today at 2:00…" Dale looked inquisitive, he looked perturbed, but he didn't look alarmed, so I continued.

"My Father left us a note, that probably should have been found and opened much sooner, requesting that we bury his body in the Congo." I said all of this with a straight face (I think) and handed over the letter, now adorned with coffee stains and fish water over to Dale. I held my breath as he read the letter, anticipating all kinds of responses. Perhaps some laughter, some nervous coughing, and maybe some more laughter.

Dale set the letter down, folded his hands, leaned forward over his desk, looked me in the eyes and said matter-of-factly, "We can help with this." We? Dale had people. Now I was the one nervously coughing, I even let out a faint grunt of a laugh, "You can? That would be great. Is it that easy?"

"It's not easy at all Miss Landan, in fact, this will be a great deal of work, probably more than you anticipated biting off, but we can make it happen. It will be complex and frankly, expensive." There it was. The reason for the immediate "we can do this." *Of course you can do this, for a free-for-all into my savings account.*

"How much?" I swallowed hard. I admit, I enjoy a posh lifestyle, cars, espressos, a typical yuppie I once swore I'd never become. But money came with the job, what was I to do, ask for less compensation? I was paid what the "market could bear" and it could bear a lot. Right now I was trouble-shooting visualization system for Adobe. This year I could expect about 150K - before taxes of course.

"I've never shipped to the Congo before, but if it's anything like Ghana, we're talking at least $7,000 which includes the Ziegler box, paperwork, freight costs per pound, airline expenses, Dr.'s reports, death certificates, government notary, and, well, maybe a few bucks for bribes." Dale said this all with a straight face as if he had done it all his life. I swear I noticed a glimmer of exhilaration.

"Bribes for who? For you?" I said with a flirty smile, trying to crack the obvious tension that came with talking about shipping dead bodies.

"Me? Of course not Miss Landan, I do not accept bribes, I have never accepted a bribe, I have no reason to…"

"Dale, just joking."

Dale looked only slightly mollified. "This is not a joking matter, Miss Landan. This is serious business…"

"Yes Dale, it is, I take coffin colors and Zeager boxes…."

"That's a Ziegler box….

"Whatever….very seriously."

"Well, if you will excuse me just a moment, I will go and gather some of the documents you may want to take a look at, to help describe the process." Dale shoved his chair back, stood up, walked stiffly toward the back of his office. I admired the view. He entered a small room with a thousand file cabinets and shut the door. I looked anxiously at my Gucci watch, we still had some time before the burial was supposed to commence. I needed to begin making some phone calls, but was lured by a pressing curiosity about the "procedures" for shipping Dad. Pulling out my laptop, I connected to "Homeward Bound" wireless and began to Google. I used to prefer Bing, but Google alone was still the best for general search.

The first hit was a "Yahoo answer" site, someone asking how to ship dead grandpa to California. I scoffed, *California? They have it easy, just rent a limo*. I was appalled at my own cynicism, having just lost a loved one I should be more empathetic. However, I was faced with a daunting task, so all defenses were up, my cognitive senses were all in a "dogpile" - cynicism, sarcasm, denial, speeding, jello shots - anything was up for grabs to help me get through this.

E-How was a little more helpful and broke the process down into 6 'easy' steps. Six easy steps? I couldn't even handle six steps for a Mojito recipe. Especially if I was working on the second batch. The next result piqued my curiosity. It was an article written in the Wall Street Journal about funeral directors earning frequent "dier" miles per dead body shipped with an associated airline. No kidding. Dale was probably in the back room on the phone with his travel agent, planning his free trip to Puerto Viarta right now.

Maybe I could go with him. I had to admit he could definitely use a good tan, but was nauseated by the thought of a corpse-shipping perks program. Did that come with a punch card?

I Googled airlines that shipped to Congo. No such luck. I Googled airlines that flew to Europe and then to Africa. Northwest Airlines, in conjunction with KLM, made the cut. I shot off an email to the NW Customer Service that read: "I noticed that KLM makes flights to Kinshasa, Congo. I need information on how I might be able to ship a deceased loved one back to their home in Africa, using Northwest/KLM airlines. Thank you very much for your speedy reply."

Dale came back in with a stack of papers and immediately began explaining the complexity of the situation. With my keen mathematical abilities I counted more than six steps.

"Maybe we should just Fed-Ex him, or try UPS." I muttered under my breath as I leafed through the paperwork.

"Miss Landan, I don't think that Fed-Ex or UPS provides such services, I'm sorry."

I rolled my eyes. "Maybe DHL then?"

He finally gave me a faint smile. "Want me to ask?"

Ok, that was funny. I smiled back.

"Mostly it is paper work. I need to get a doctor to sign that there were no epidemics around here at the time of your father's, ah...demise. We need to arrange with the airlines a bonded area...."

"What's that?"

"We take the ah, ...the casket to a secure area. They more or less make sure nobody tampers with it until it is offloaded in ....where, again?"

"Kinshasa."

He still looked blank.

"In Congo."

"Which one?" He knew his geography.

"Democratic Republic of."

"Oh...ok. In Kinshasa then. We take care of all that. It also has to be a casket that seals shut, only metal, not wood."

"Why is that?"

"Rules, just rules. Keeps the air pure I guess. We will probably have to put him into a Ziegler box inside the coffin."

"A Ziegler. Ok. Of course...ah Dale,"

I hesitated, wondering if my next question was too morbid. Then I remembered what Dale did for a living, "the body, after all this time...is it..."

He laughed. "Don't worry about that Miss Landan. We shipped a body to Ghana once that was here for about a month first. I heard that when they opened the casket in Ghana she looked wonderful." He laughed again. He did have a macabre sense of humor after all.

"I'm sure she did, *Dale*." My game now was to see if I could get him to say "Anna."

We both sat there in silence like two conspirators plotting a heist of some enormous proportion, perhaps a little titillated by the adventure.

"Ok, Dale, God help me, let's do this."

There it was. The decision was made to send dead Dad to Congo. If Dale had just said "it really can't be done" or "this is unheard of" or even "I have no idea how to even begin this....thing..." I would have capitulated. But no, Dale had to actually be a competent professional who apparently knew what he was doing, although, that alone, kind of freezes the blood.

I instantly wanted to take the words back. I hadn't talked to anybody else except Marilyn about it. Ian was actually encouraging me to disregard Dad's postcard from the edge. Funerals and memorial services are really for the living, not the dead. But it was the phrase "for both our sakes" that mesmerized me and called me softly forward. There was also an element of mystery… why the water source? Why *this* gravesite? Why not just some ashes?

Dale was busy adding things up, getting his endless papers in order. "Miss Landan, this could run from between $7,000- $10,000 plus the shipping. I'll need some down payment. There may be some, ah, unexpected contingencies as well."

"How much do you need?" I cracked my knuckles nervously, a habit Ian loathes.

"Half now?"

"Third now?" My years of shopping on E-bay lent itself to skillful bargaining.

He paused. "Ok Miss Landan." Dale still did not budge from his formalities.

"Take Visa do you, *Dale*?"

"Certainly!" Dale shot his cuff and looked at his watch. "I hate to be indelicate, but Miss Landan, you have a bunch of people heading to a gravesite soon…with no, um…."

"With no body? Yes, well, what is the protocol here, Dale, if there is no body at the graveside service, do we still have to have refreshments somewhere?"

He smiled ever so slightly. He was catching on. "I am sure I don't know. Meet you there or do you want ride in the hearse Miss Landan?"

The idea was interesting. I would arrive in the hearse, but it would be empty. Why are we taking an empty hearse? Because I had prepaid for all this.

"No, I'll take my car. See you there."

We both got up and walked to the door. He opened it for me.

"That your car?" he said looking at A.J.

"Yeah." A small frisson went up my spine. A man who noticed...?

"What's with the red-walls, Anna?"

I could tell we had no future together, although he did finally use my first name.

CHAPTER FIVE

I took my time driving over to the Bayview cemetery. But inevitably I arrived. Four chairs were lined up by the hole. A few people were already there, Keith, Ian, some friends, a few missionaries, some vaguely familiar distant relatives that showed up uninvited. Keith was also a Right Reverend and would say all the religious stuff. He and Dad worked together for over twenty years in Africa planting churches, running the schools, earning crowns in heaven. Keith was "Uncle Keith" to me, even though he wasn't related, and now he was the last living kin I had. Maybe I had more family left in my life than I realized...

Keith was sporting a pair of thick square glasses, a button up shirt hugging a bit too tight around his retired mid-section and a flowery necktie that could put a master-gardener to shame. No doubt picked out for him by his sweet wife. I did love them dearly. Keith knew me my whole life, watched me grow up into the lovely young woman that I am today. Indeed. I always appreciated that Keith never put on airs or pretenses; he was true-blue and punctuated his words with a little bit of southern love. I wondered if he would be surprised by James' request....

Keith came over. "Anna, I am so so very sorry about your Dad. We all loved him so much. How are you doing kiddo?" I could barely see his lips move through his hefty white beard, but his warm and loving brown eyes spoke volumes. They looked a little moist, a little red. At least someone could cry for Dad.

I took a deep breath and counted to two. What a question. I had no idea how I was doing. I was technically an orphan. No parents, no siblings, 145 friends on Facebook. I was still angry at Mom for dying when I was seven, and my Dad for dragging her out to the hot zone in the first place, and then after her death leaving me to fend for myself. I was pretty ticked at the God I wasn't sure was there anymore. I was angry with Him for maybe not existing. As of this morning I learned from my therapist that I was incapable of love. I drank too much, flirted too long, and drove too fast. But I was cussing less...

"Fine, thanks Keith." He gave me a hug. Keith was a bit older than my Dad, and carried with him the kind of soul that makes your heart want to jump out of your skin and share all of its deepest burdens, but now was not the time. I was thankful to have a father figure around me today.

I said hello to the others and ended up standing next to Ian. *He smelled so good...*

"How did things go at the funeral home, Anna?" he asked me

"Any epidemics around here recently?" Ian looked puzzled at my response. I resisted the habit of being acerbi*c, adding, like Ebola Fever*. "They need to know in order to send Dad to Congo."

Ian looked at me surprised, "You're doing this?!"

I nodded and kept quiet. I did not feel like trying to explain to Ian my reasons, I wouldn't know how to articulate it. Ian stared at the hearse entering the long drive. "So if you are going ahead with this- and, wait, don't get mad- sorry, *as* you are going ahead with this, what is in that hearse?"

"Dale."

"Dale?"

"The funeral director. It's empty, Ian."

The hearse stopped by the mourners. It was time. I found my voice and addressed the small crowd of family and friends, lovers and lawyers. Ok, just one lover, one lawyer, same person.

"Everybody. Can I have your attention for a moment. This is a unique graveside service. Unique in that there is no body. Dad was transported directly to heaven on a chariot of fire..." I grew up an Missionary Kid, or "MK" as they say. I knew the stories. I didn't know what I expected, a laugh, or an exclamation maybe. No sound. They just stared at me as if to say "really?" *No, not really.* I wanted more Malbec.

"Seriously, Keith, will you just go ahead with the service as if there were a body here? We can still say goodbye and, ah...godspeed to James Landan, right? I mean, what's the body got to do with it? If there were a casket here and the embalmed body inside, would he hear you better that way or something?" I realized I should stop talking. "I might as well tell you. At Dad's request, we are shipping the body back to Congo for burial."

Now that got a reaction. Two people sat down in the chairs. I was one of them.

"Keith, go ahead."

Keith was a veteran missionary to the Congo. Not much phased him. He acted like he did a body-less graveside service all the time.

"Dearly beloved, we are gathered here…"

I watched Keith's words water the people gathered there like an oscillating sprinkler. Every once in a while a splash would hit me. "Promise of resurrection…eternal life…blessed hope…." I was mostly thinking about Friday. By Friday I would be on a plane to Kinshasa with Dad, who should be in this hole, instead in the cargo hold of an Airbus. I didn't want to do this alone.

I knew something of Africa. The "easy" part would end when the plane touched down. I wanted someone there with me. I wanted Ian there…the last person I wanted there was Ian. I tried to imagine this rather formal, fastidious but clumsy Brit dribbling palm oil on his chin, washing in a bucket and sporting big sweat circles under his arms. I couldn't, but the thought amused me.

"Our Father, who art in heaven…" Splash. Just to one side was Mother's grave marker. A nice little brass plaque had the info: Marie Anne Landan. Beloved Wife and Mother. 1940-1984.

Once in the states, I insisted that my Dad shell out some good money for a "real" grave for Mom. He seemed reluctant and confused by the ordeal. I insisted all the more. I wanted more for her than just a dugout pit and a pig-feast. There was nothing sacred about that. Of course, her body was not here, but the little grave marker was enough for me to feel like she was at peace. Somehow I imagined her purple body restless and haunted 9,000 miles away. Maybe this little gesture, this grave marker, helped her. Maybe it helped me.

For the life of me, I had no idea where the real grave was. Dad didn't want me to come to the burial, in fact he didn't want anyone. I remember him wrapping my lifeless mother up in colorful African cloths and carrying her in his arms, out into the jungle. Just him and Keith.

Her little vase-holder had some dried flowers in it, probably from Keith. I felt pangs of guilt for not having visited her more often. A few other relatives were scattered here and there nearby. I wondered how it was that I would end up with two plaques for my parents, with no bodies underneath. I would have to ask Dale about a discount. I had purchased the plot and paid the fees, but didn't bury a corpse. Shouldn't I get a discount? I felt myself getting angry at the Cemetery for refusing me, though we had had no such conversation to date. I just knew they would.

"Ashes to ashes…"

I wanted to go back to Africa. I had never returned in… I did the quick math. 2008 -1991… in seventeen years, since we came back to the States in 1991, I was 14 then. I had taken French in college and spent a semester in Paris, believing that I needed to "keep up my French" for some future rendezvous with my fate in Congo. For a while I hung out with African MK's and that slowed the erosion of my Lingala. Over time I saw them less and less. I had moved on, they all seemed freeze-framed in time.

They loved football, or as we Americans call it, soccer. They told jokes in three or four languages that only insiders could ever get. They went on short-term missions back to Congo, or did the Peace Corps stint, usually in Mali or Niger or somewhere *francophone*. They talked about having visited *Tombouctou*, refusing to say Timbuktu like the plebeians - and *Ouagadougou*. But mostly their missionary faith began to seem simplistic and juvenile to me. I was not one to go and save souls, I was just trying to figure out what was up with my own soul…shouldn't we all just pay attention to our own soul?

"And He will wipe away every tear from their eyes and there will no longer be any death and there will no loner be any mourning, or crying, or pain…Behold I am making all things new. Amen." Splash. Keith turned off his sprinkler and ended the homily. The last one soaked me a bit more than I anticipated and I thought for a moment about a world without pain or death…and sentimentally longed for a feeling of being new again. Botox would have to suffice.

"Thanks, Keith, that was wonderful." I pulled Keith aside and gave him a sideways hug when the service was concluded.

"Glad to help. Don't think you were payin' much attention, though."

That caught my attention. *What was this, actual perception?* "Why do you say that?" I gave a little nervous cough. Pastors make me nervous, I always feel a little guilty about something. Ok, everything.

"Oh, I don't know, just watching you gaze around. So, what now kid?"

"Anna, so very sorry for your loss." Aunt Beth butted in and gave me a hug and a kiss. Apparently, we knew each other well enough for that kind of proximity, although I barely recognized her. All the single women in Congo were "Aunties" to us.

"Thank you." I smiled politely.

"And your sainted mother…." She gestured to her plaque. "Tubercular meningitis, how terrible - went right to the brain. She really suffered for so long. Caught it too late. But so much has improved in modern medicine since then…" she continued to prattle on, oblivious to the fact that I had stopped listening, considering I didn't really need the nightmarish re-cap. Keith caught my eye and shrugged.

Tubercular meningitis. Cerebral meningitis. I vaguely remembered the treatments given her on the field, directed by caring, competent but under-equipped doctors, the smell of the hospital room, the long hours we spent by her bed, and then the "service." *Her icy cold hand…*

Aunt Beth eventually wound down. "Well, we really must be moving along. So good to see you Anna."

"Thanks Aunt Beth." *Thanks for nothing.* "Good to see you too." I was lying right in front of a pastor. I shuffled my feet nervously. Is that considered a venial sin?

Ian, Keith and Dale were still there, now engrossed in conversation. A lawyer, a pastor, and a funeral director… sounds like the beginning of a joke.

Something about their presence put me at ease, but I still was not ready to let down my guard and spill a few tears. Had I yet? I thought back on the past week and realized that no, in fact, I had not cried over my Father. Probably never will. I don't believe I've really truly cried since Mom. Perhaps she really did freeze my tears. Or, as I like to tell myself, crying is a sign of weakness, and I, am not weak. I swallowed hard and inched nearer to the three, who were huddled deep in conversation about the ins and outs of shipping bodies. They all seemed to be overly enthusiastic about the possibility. Gross.

Ian noticed me and put his arm around me. I did not recoil. I was genuinely touched that he came, especially after the way I've treated him.

"Thanks for being here Ian, I…" I hesitated before swallowing an inch of pride, and confessed, "I have been so intolerable, I know."

"Well, you've been through a lot." I noticed he didn't deny it. We both knew that my behavior toward him had little to do with the recent events, but we nodded in agreement to this conclusion, smiling shyly at each other, momentarily finding comfort under the thin shroud of pretense.

"Anna, I would like to go with you." Ian's words yanked me out of the shroud.

"No, I need to go home, be alone for a while. Pack. Get a visa in four days, acquire a butt-full of shots, literally. Tell Adobe I'll be gone for a while but not to worry that all the stuff I have been working on can just wait, no problem, things like that. Throw out the fish water."

"Fish water?…."

54

"Yeah, but maybe you could come by after I get back. Have a drink with me." Was I coming onto him *again*? What was wrong with me? Hadn't we broken up? Or maybe not... I can't remember all the texts, an obviously very effective way of communication. Ian was about to answer but was interrupted.

Aunt Miriam came up. She also was not a real bloodline Aunt. Aunt Miriam weighed in at about 220 lbs. She reminded me of Rosie O'Donnell, except that she had probably never heard of Rosie. She and Rosie would not see eye to eye on anything, of that I was sure.

"James was a great, great man," she offered right off.

"Thanks." I said curtly. I wanted to go home.

"No, really. But he was gone so much."

"Yes, I remember those absences. Evangelizing and such." I shrugged and hoped she would consider the conversation finished.

Miriam continued, "Evangelizing? Half the time nobody knew where he was." Keith looked at me without expression this time. His white beard was a good cover. Aunty was fishing for something. She wanted to know what I knew, which was not much.

"Well, where was he? With you?" I couldn't help myself.

Her eyes got big and her mouth opened wide like Eeyore's. Tears erupted and immediately I was sorry for that barb. For about two seconds.

"Aunt Miriam, I'm sorry, I shouldn't have said that...it's just so...dam- *darned* confusing." I pinched the bridge of my nose with my fingers and squinted in distress, hoping my grieving demeanor could make up for my snide remark.

She flinched a bit but didn't stop, "Anna, maybe you should not go back, you know? Leave sleeping dogs lay."

"Lie."

"Lie?"

"Sleeping dogs lie...never mind. So what happens if a dog wakes up? I don't get what you are saying."

"Well, you will do what you need to do I guess. I have said too much already. Keith, you take care of her." And she marched off.

I was still hanging on to Ian's arm. What was that all about? I'd never even owned a dog. Always wanted one, only got parrots and monkeys and such. Of course, I knew Aunt Miriam was talking about something unrelated to the mysterious world of canine slumber, but what, and for what reason she would start prying certain doors open now, I was unsure. I made a mental note to ask Keith about that later.

Ian broke up my thoughts and steered me by my elbow to look at him. He cleared his throat, "No, Anna, I mean go with you to, ah, mm, ...to Kinchacha." I had forgotten that we were interrupted in mid sentence but Ian hadn't lost the thread at all. I pulled back and looked at him, trying to piece together our broken conversation. I finally realized what he was saying.

"Ian, it's Kinshasa, not Kinchacha. And the answer is No. *Are you nuts?* You have no idea....and Kinshasa is NOT the destination. That is a, a...like a stopover. We will end up in the jungle with a Zieglerized cadaver."

Ian looked at Dale and raised his eyebrows.

"She likes to say 'Ziegler'" Dale deadpanned. He had come a long way in a few short hours. I liked his humor. Maybe I could overlook the car discrepancy and still join him in Puerto Viarta...margaritas, beaches, tequila, dancing, coronas, more tequila...I felt thirsty.

"What's a Ziegler?" Ian asked.

"A special kind of box for cadavers...." I answered, trying to rip myself away from the image of me in my little bikini on the beach. Somehow, Dale wasn't actually in that picture. Maybe he would just give me his frequent dier miles.

"Never mind. Yes, Anna, I know that I don't know what I am saying or what I am getting myself into. But I do know I want to go with you."

Finally I snapped out of it and entered fully into the conversation.

"Ian. Drop it. You are certifiable. You can't go."

"Why not?"

"For many reasons. One, you are white, very white. Two, you are a rich, yuppie, lawyer who probably has never even been camping. And three, well, you are NOT coming to Africa. You wouldn't last a day. You aren't Nate O'Reily."

"Sorry, who?"

"John Grisham's jungle lawyer... *The Testament*? Don't you read?"

I yanked my arm away from his hand, but somehow felt instant regret. Hadn't I wanted someone to go with me, someone I could trust? I am comfortable deep inside my vault, I'll admit that. I change the combination every so often, just to be sure that no one could enter, not even me. Marilyn tells me that one-day, I will hand over the numbers and I won't even know that I did. At 200 dollars an hour, what does she know? I had insisted to her that I wasn't in the least bit lonely or in need of anyone. I wasn't lonely. I had my iPhone and my GPS – navigation voice choice? Hot Aussie male. He talked to me, understood my needs. I don't know how I ever got along without him. I also had *Seinfeld* re-runs, *Ellen* and expensive wine to keep me company every night. And occasionally, I had Ian's warmth and company.

I had to admit, Ian had courage. I admired that about him. Aside from his beautiful Bond facial features, he was a small-framed person who wins the prize for awkwardness. Yet, he could stand in front of jurors, lawyers, judges, and go fiercely to war against the snares of injustice. Okay, so he was a death and tax lawyer, but still, I'm sure he had to do that at least once. He was naïve maybe, suffered from acute romanticism, but he was resilient. However, what good is a lawyer in the middle of the jungle? I then thought about the complexities and trouble that an overpopulated African city like Kinshasa could bring. Maybe what we needed was someone who could be quick and willing to deal out the cash in dicey situations. Maybe what I needed was someone to lean on, even if he was pale and clumsy. I began to reluctantly change my mind, Ian should come, and bring his wallet.

"I'm going Anna. I'm going and *that's* final." Ian must have seen the altered expression on my face and pressed for his case one more time. He *did* have guts. The jurors folded and handed in their verdict.

"Alright. But if you get malaria and die, it's not my fault. Understand? I'm exempt from all blame for anything that happens to you on this trip. You can fantasize all you want about some luxurious, exotic safari type vacation we are about to go on, but if I were you, I'd start writing your will tonight." I was only half joking. The Congo relentlessly takes lives, without discrimination.

My stomach did flips as I thought about the trip. Ian on the plane, by me. Ian, in a bed, near me. Ian in a truck, smooshed up next to me. Could I handle this? There was definitely something electric between us, but now was not the time for more complications in my life.

"Count me in." That was Keith of course. I knew he'd sign up and I was thankful that he did. He and Dad had pounded countless miles of roads over the years. Hit several chickens and goats. Planted dozens of churches, no doubt saved quite a few of those souls. Keith knew a lot of people and had valuable contacts. His wife would see the light and be supportive. She always was.

CHAPTER SIX

The small, mad man with yellow warped teeth smiles knowingly in my direction. His gaze unstitches me, stirs up all my nerves till they are running up my spine and hurdling off the hairs on the back of my neck. His eyes are like a crow's, his laugh - a hyenas, and he has a snake-like wheeze. He has bones dangling out of his ears, and in his hands he carries a potion of coconut juice and leopard's blood. He throws it in the air, and the sun turns into the moon, my shadow takes the form of a dog that melts into two graves. He raises his voice to the night and curdles out a slow hiss, words eek out from between the dark spaces in his teeth, *"Now you know, don't you? I knew you'd come…"* He pounds on the drums that hang around his neck, the reverb grows louder in my ears, restricts my breath and descends into my heart.

The pounding on the drums grows louder and louder. The pounding was not the drums, it was my heart. I woke up, leaping upright, palms sweaty, heart racing, at home in my bed. It was the Larium - the malaria medicine- talking, causing nightmares and hallucinations, I was sure of it. Except, I had had this dream before, I was sure of that, too. I traded my nice Columbian man in for a witchdoctor?

I shook it off and turned over in my bed, opening my blinds to see the waterfront hoping to gain some peace of mind. It was raining. I lived in Seattle, what did I expect? I could barely make out the red Pike Place sign from behind the wall of water. Despite living under a permanent showerhead, I love Seattle. I love that it is gray most of the year round. I love wearing scarves and sweaters. I love the smell of fresh fish, and the hollers the famous Pike Place fish-throwers make at the market as they toss portly salmons to their eager maritime customers. Seattle's shops and streets are not simply to be visited and toured, these are my homes, and this is where I do my living. These places end up in my DNA that I sweat out on yoga mats in the park, perspire away on long walks, sweat that seeps into the sidewalk, rising back up at the first rainfall - a sweet, musty scent that triggers an inexplicable yearning for a five dollar cup of joe.

Seattle is an intersection of the trendy and diverse worlds that converge at Pike and Pine: pink hair, yellow rain boots, Louis Vitton handbags, tattoos, cheek piercings and skinny jeans. We drink breves with sugar free vanilla, eat only organic foods, wear Birkenstocks and North Face jackets, flash our non-conflict diamonds, yet drive Touaregs and Escalades. It's "make it up as you go." We are riddled with acupuncture and free-trade coffee; cafés and spas are more frequently available than bus stops. This is why I belong here. I do not know my value system, I make it up as I go. I recycle, create compost, yet I am an enemy to the environment when I get in my car. I meditate and drink shots of organic wheat grass while I light candles at St. Marks and eat sausage pizza. My own world converges within my spirit and leaves me unidentifiable, unknown, and this makes me a perfect fit for Seattle.

I shut my blinds to the wet world below me, and tried to go back to sleep. But now I was aware of my aches and pains. My butt hurt. My arms hurt, especially my shoulders. Seven shots for one trip to the Congo: Hep A (twice), Polio, Typhim VI, Tetanus-diphtheria, Meningococcal, and Influenza - I better not get sick. I was loaded and ready to go with an armory of Larium, calamine lotion, anti-diarrhea pills, antibacterial hand soap, 100% Deet mosquito repellent and mosquito nets to keep me from getting anything those venomous African creatures might thrust into my bloodstream. Basically, I was now anti-Africa, ready to repel the jungle. It was Friday, time to fly.

I grabbed my yellow legal pad and reviewed my checklist for the last time. Visa – check - just barely. I had paid hundreds of dollars to have the whole thing "expedited" and it sure was. Passport - check. Tickets - check. The airline security and officials were notified and ready to receive us at 10:30am. Flight to New York, then Paris, then to Kinshasa left at 2:00pm. I placed all my important paper work into an official looking folder: the King County Department of Health Non-Contagious disease affidavit, the Funeral Home Statement of authorization (for proper embalming, casket disinfection, and shipping tray) as well as the

Embalmers Non-Contraband Affidavit - which states explicitly that my Father's casket, Zeigler, and shipping container held nothing but his remains. For a moment I happily imagined Dale as the ringleader of a drug-smuggling operation, using dead bodies and caskets as a means to traffic - like Denzel in *American Gangster*. Then I remembered Dale's face, and my fantasy vanished; he only shipped bodies for the miles. He was probably on the beach right now.

I checked my work mail for the last time, and sent a generic, "Anna is... in the Congo, back in three weeks" message on my Facebook wall for all my "friends" to read, in case they missed me. I opened my Gmail and saw a new message waiting for me. It was the reply from Northwest/KLM airlines to the email that I had ignorantly shot off when I was waiting in Dale's office. A little late, but I opened it anyway out of curiosity. It read: *"Dear Anna Landan, Thank you for contacting nwa.com Customer Service. Northwest Airlines has partnered with Sports Express, the premier sports equipment and luggage delivery service, to offer you an innovative travel convenience. Sports Express will pick up your luggage, golf clubs, skis, bicycle or other sports equipment at your home or office and deliver it to your destination."*

I laughed out loud. *Sports Equipment??* Skis, clubs, canoes, dead bodies...I had never really considered caskets or dead bodies as sporting goods, but hey, whatever works. But then again, I was never good at that test question, "Which one doesn't belong."

I needed a good laugh. Just oversized luggage, that's all.

I gave my 3g a kiss goodbye and slid her, along with my Amazon kindle into my little safe under the bed.

My taxi was coming shortly. I had enough time for a cup of Starbucks. I walked downstairs and into the café. Ashley was humming as she was counting her tips.

"Good morning, Ashley." I offered a pleasantry.

"OMG! It's you! Hi! Do you want your usual?" she squeaked. I nodded and pulled out a five. "What are you doing this weekend, Anna?" She was chewing gum and making coffee at the same time, I was impressed.

"Taking a casket with my dead Dad in it and going to the Congo, what about you?" I waited eagerly for her reply.

"LOL, right!?, I love Australia! I knew someone who had a brother who went there once!" She bounced a little as she spoke. OMG, LOL - are these actual words?

I was actually shocked that she knew that Congo was at least across some ocean. She was sweet. I gave her a dollar tip to go toward her college fund, and left with my last good cup of coffee for sometime…My stomach did flips again. Goodbye, Seattle. Be back ASAP.

CHAPTER SEVEN

I slumped down into my aisle seat, already exhausted from the airport stress and security check. I never make it through smoothly. Never. The red light goes off, the beeping begins. This time I had emptied my pockets, took off my shoes, belt, watch, necklace, and sweater. I had placed dozens of 3.7oz lotions, sunscreens, deets, shampoos and conditioners into their baggies and laid them out for all to see that I had no intention of taking the plane down with L'oréal and Estée Lauder. With a dry swallow, I held my breath as I walked through the metal detector. I stepped out and the TSA officer pulled me to the side and said, "Wait here." The gentleman in uniform got really tense and waved for other agents to come over. It was all over for me at that point. There was no leisurely airport shopping and coffee sipping enjoyment; I was stressed out. I looked around for the nearest bar.

"Father, can't I just say ten hail-Mary's and move on?" I asked flirtatiously with a coy smile. The SeaTac guard was not so coy and not so fatherly. After a very thorough pat-down, I asked if it was good for him too, which wasn't taken well.

I prefer the aisle seat. I am willing to take the chance of a good elbow beating in order to occasionally stretch out my legs. Ian was busy heaving our carry-on bags into the overhead compartments. He accommodated me, as always, and took the window seat. I glanced back and waved at Keith all alone in the very back of the plane, by the bathrooms. At least he wouldn't have 90 pairs of eyes on him if he needed to relieve himself. I remembered the last time I flew to Orlando for work. I got food poisoning from the airport sushi bar, and suffered the whole flight. Back and forth to the bathroom, back and forth for five hours.

But today I will suffer in other ways. I was embarking on the longest trip of my adult life. The mature woman in me groaned with boredom, dreading the stiff joints and the lack of sleep sure to come. The adventurous, single girl inside of me was giddy with excitement; she had "People" magazine to read, Sudoku to cheat at, free drinks to guzzle - including wine - a real man lodged in tight next to her, and twenty hours alone with him.

"Headphone, *mademoiselle?*"

"*Oui, j'aimerais bien un ecouteur, s'il vous plait, merci.*" Ian smirked at my attempt at being French. I don't think he got that I actually did speak French.

"Me too, thanks." He reached over me and grabbed his headset, brushing my face with his arm and paying for both of us. He smelled good, for now. His Nivea aftershave was what clinched the deal for me months ago. Something so intoxicating about that scent. I had seen his bottle on his bathroom counter and made a mental note that that was my favorite.

Not sure why I added that to my memory tank; was I going to replenish his bottle in his stocking some Christmas morning? Not likely. At least the upcoming humid hours in the jungle of Africa would alter this aroma. I brushed the thought aside and stared at him analytically.

Our romantic history folded itself over our two seats, wrapping us together tightly like seat belts. As much as I tried to convince myself, and him, that we weren't going anywhere, I feared that Ian and I were stuck together, not just for this plane ride, or the next, but for a longer journey of sorts. I both hated and loved this notion, and surprised myself with the latter. Yet I keep hissing and selfishly clawing my way out of the love scene permanently. I always grimace with disgust when I think about how the praying mantises mate. After mating, the female bites the male's head off and eats him. No cuddling. Saw it on the Discovery Channel once. What a witch, she has her man and eats it too. Yet, I sometimes resemble her antics. I bit Ian's head off many times. I wondered how long he could keep growing another. If he couldn't, he would be in luck. He would find someone else - someone wonderful, careful, sweet, delicate and gracious, with "niceties" and he would live happily ever after. For his sake, I hoped I could keep him out. For my sake, I wasn't sure what I wanted... *but man did he smell so good...*

"Do you want a glass of wine? It's free." Ian was showing me the in-flight menu. I smiled and thought that this might either have a hint of foreplay to it, or that he wanted me to pass out in hopes that I wouldn't irritate him for sixteen hours.

"Yeah, I'll order a glass of chardonnay. Or just to be French, I'll try the pinot gris."

"There are other ways you can be French..." Ian sounded like Sean Connery when he said that. I began to catch on; I thought this was flirting. I took a shot at it.

"Educate me." I said with a smile, and then rapidly wiped it off. Ian noticed, and turned back to his Skymall. *Why am I encouraging this?* I needed to swear Ian off like nicotine. I tried to put him on the Anna-patch in hopes he would quit. I tried to bite his head off and then devour him. What did I fear?

The answer was easy, and any psychologist, or anyone who had known me these last 31 years could tell you that I was afraid of love. Real love plays all the cards, aims for the jackpot, gambles all or nothing in a high stakes poker game, like in *Casino Royale*. It risks hurt, risks heartache, worst of all, it risks coming to a dreadful end. I had seen it all too personally. My mother's death broke my Dad in two. Scratch that, it shattered him into pieces severing his heart from the rest of his body. Meningitis won the gamble he had taken and left him bankrupt with a seven-year-old daughter to raise. He never remarried. Despite various emotional-surgical attempts at removing the hurt, it festered on the outside - an infectious open wound - blinking its yellow light for me to note and observe for twenty-four years. At least, that is how I saw it. A caution light screaming, "Don't take the plunge, it hurts too much. Save yourself, Anna!" I was trying to save myself.

The pinot gris did me a bit of good. "Brilliant," as Ian would say. Love the British. I turned off my personal light, wrapped up in a flimsy Air France blanket and laid my head back, listening to the drone of the engine. It would be hard to sleep knowing that my dead Dad was in the cargo hold just a few feet below my seat, nestled in his Ziegler box. I hoped he enjoyed his flight. *Be careful, shift happens, Dad.*

The tingling sensation in my left arm woke me up from a shallow sleep. I lifted my head off of Ian's shoulder, surprised to find it there, and shook my sleeping arm. It was dead, I could hardly lift it. Needles pricked and tingled every cell from my pinky to my shoulder like bad acupuncture.

"*Excusez moi,*" I grabbed the flight attendant that was coming down the aisle. She addressed me coolly. Snooty French. "*Est-ce que je peux prendre un digestif, s'il vous plait?*" *I needed more to drink.*

"*Naturellement.*" My French was just rusty enough, that I couldn't remember if that meant "naturally" or "of course." If she meant "naturally" I was offended. But who will ever know.

"Your French is great." A male voice across the aisle grabbed my attention.

"Thank you! You speak French?" I ran my hand through my curls, just for good measure, in case it helped my attractiveness. The gentleman was wearing an expensive black jacket that set off his silver hair perfectly. He reminded me of George Clooney. I tried to smile and fidget with my clothes and face. *Oh, who am I kidding? I've been sleeping on a plane for the last few hours, not a pretty sight.* I gave up the bizarre mating behavior and floated back down to earth. He was speaking to me.

"*Un peu. Mais, j'ai oublié beaucoup.* I don't remember much, I lost it once I learned Swahili."

"Swahili? Were you in Kenya?"

"Still am. Well, obviously not at the moment. I teach at a university in Nairobi." I wanted to ask what a man, who looks like George Clooney, is doing in Nairobi when there are so few good looking, straight men in Seattle, but I restrained myself. Maybe he wasn't straight.

"Which university?" I asked, opting for the socially acceptable question over the embarrassing, intrusive question, "Are you single or straight?"

"It's called Daystar. A great college. I love to work there. But my main passion is in working with the young boys in an orphanage, just a few miles outside the campus." I heard Elaine's voice in my head saying, "*Get out!*" I instantly turned the mating ritual back on. This man was unreal. *An orphanage?*

"That's so great! I'm sure they, um, need the help." I couldn't think of many intelligent things to say. I was thankful Ian was still sleeping.

"They do. So, how about you? Where are you headed, to Paris?" He glanced at my khaki pants, Teva sandals, and lack of style, and noted, "Maybe Egypt?"

"Close. Congo."

"That's not even close."

"Thought I'd give you the point anyhow."

"Congo? Are you serious? Congo Brazza or Democratic Republic? What are you doing in the Congo? Some gorilla expedition? No - wait, I got it - you are a medical scientist genius, going to find a cure for cancer in the Ituri rainforest."

"I'll answer your questions. Yes. DRC, not a gorilla expedition, and no, I'm not nearly that genius. I'm burying my dead Dad in the jungle. He's beneath us." I pointed down toward our feet. I didn't know how to eloquently phrase the truth. Perhaps I could have just lied. Should have just lied. Should have said I was going to work with AIDS victims in India.

"I'm so sorry. When did he die?" The gentleman passed right over the morbid part of my answer, and responded like Clooney would have. Smooth.

"Last week. Heart attack. It was totally unexpected. At least it was to me. I wish I had gotten to see more of him before he died."

"Why the Congo?"

"He lived there most of his life. Went out there as a missionary in his early twenties, with my mom. Had me. We lived there till I was 14. Well, Mom died when I was seven, we went back to the states for that year, for treatment, then a funeral. But we returned promptly and stayed until till '91. I left when I was 14." I tried to stop myself from babbling to this complete stranger, but somehow the stories just kept spilling out of me. His eyes drew the words out of my mouth. He seemed to be actually listening.

"What did your Mom die of?"

"Tubercular Meningitis." Smooth man choked at that one, he obviously knew how painful and grotesque the disease was.

"Should be out in the rainforest trying to find a cure for *that!*" I tried to lighten the air.

"I'm also sorry she died, that must have been so hard for you, as a child and all." Was this man listening *and* empathizing? "So you and your Dad

71

returned to Africa, just the two of you? Did he remarry?"

"I went to boarding school near where he worked. He never remarried. Lonesome man as far I knew. We survived, but grew apart for obvious reasons. We were as tight as they come before that. That perfect Father-daughter thing, you know?" I paused but Clooney gave me the "go on" nod. So I went on.

"Anyway, after I turned seventeen I flew the coop to college, Dad got me settled in, but then didn't waste a minute returning home. Africa was all he knew, all he wanted. Although Africa inflicted her death, I think he needed to return to survive his heart wound. Actually, he never did quite survive - return to us - I mean, the way he was before…but he never ceased to amaze me. He had heart. Funny, "he had heart," yet his heart was what failed." I tried desperately to shut-up now and pushed the brandy into my mouth as a muffler. I sipped it. Then I gulped it back. God, I needed another. This poor man, *he* needs another. I thought of the movie *Airplane* and that little old lady who died of boredom listening to "Striker" share his heartaches.

"So, if he was out in Africa since you were…seventeen, and now you are, what, twenty-six?"

I was in love. "Close, thirty-one." I couldn't believe I just divulged my age.

"Not even close!" I liked his humor. "So," he continued, "So, if he was out in Africa, how did he end up dying here in the States?"

"He had returned home a year ago for something." *Oh god! Please stop asking me these questions, I will tell you my whole life story, and then you'll want to switch seats! Can't we just make-out?*

He kept coming back into the ring for more hits. "What did he return home for?"

"What is this, the inquisition?" My sarcasm got the best of me, as did my defenses.

"Oh gosh, I'm so sorry, not at all. Not at all. I just...rarely meet such interesting people. Blondes, no less."

"It's fake, I'm a brunette." He had me making personal, intimate confessions.

"I knew it. Even better." Clooney flashed his pearly whites. I could just lick them.

"Dad came home to ask me to return to Africa with him. He said it was important, that he needed me to come back with him, just for a short visit. I kind of wanted to, but I just couldn't. Africa had meaning to me, it was home, so to speak, but I felt that I would find my mom's ghost, or that I would get meningitis or something. Selfish really."

"Understandable." His blue eyes kept fixated. *Would you at least please blink?*

"I wish I had gone. It seemed he needed to do something with me, show me something, or who knows...he had some strange reason, I should have listened better. Should have been a better daughter, in many ways. So now, I am returning with him, as to his dying wish, but not the way he anticipated. Nor I." My brandy was gone. I felt thirsty. Clooney was drinking Perrier, of course, not a drinker. We also had no future. First Dale, then Clooney. I was back to Ian.

"Maybe you'll make some discoveries after all. Africa has a way of drawing out our true selves... earthy, rustic, strips us of all our usual luxuries and defenses...takes off the shell." I wanted to take off *his* shell.

"You'll be alright," he said.

"Who said I didn't think I would be?" I hated looking weak.

"Your eyes, they give you away. But, like I said, you'll be alright, more than alright. I have a feeling." Clooney was stretching his chair back and turning down his light. He'd had enough. So had I. He pulled his sleep mask over his face and said, "Goodnight."

"*Bonne nuit*," I replied. I leaned my chair back as well, hoping that the person behind me also had their chair leaned. The reclining situation never works unless everyone is reclined, or no one is reclined. I took a glance behind me. The elderly woman was sitting straight, totally upright. I mumbled profanities and only tilted half way. I am a good person, after all.

"I didn't know all that about you and your Dad." Ian's voice crawled out of his mouth while the rest of him still appeared to be asleep. He waited a moment and opened his eyes, grinning.

"I thought you were sleeping! You freaked me out!" I punched the side of his arm.

"Sorry, I tend to do that to women. I didn't mean to eavesdrop, I just, well, tried to listen."

"Pathetic, Ian. I told you all that before, apparently you weren't listening."

"I was listening, you told me about your life and your Dad. You just never told me that he had come home to ask you to go back with him last year."

"It wasn't important. It was personal."

"Personal? You could tell a complete stranger, but not your boyfriend?" Ian kept grinning at me.

"You aren't my boyfriend. I reviewed the texts. And yes, sometimes it's easier to talk to complete strangers than people that you loath... care for... that you *know*. And like I said, it wasn't important." I finally stumbled on the definition I was looking for. I followed my neighbor's example of how to cut off a conversation and slipped my eye mask over my face.

"When the flight attendant comes by, can you order me a cranberry and vodka, please?" I gave Ian my order and pulled my blanket up again. I heard him mutter under his breath, "Sounds very important to me. Your Dad wanted to tell you something."

The plane was dark and there was little noise except the whir of the engine. People were bundled up asleep in pockets all over the cabin, some faces were illuminated by the glow of their laptops, others were fixated on the in-flight movie. Rocky Balboa. An aging warrior back for more. Storyline felt familiar: aging, and returning back for more. But not a warrior. Not in the least. We were somewhere over the Atlantic. I assumed it was early Saturday already. The little map popped up from time to time with arrows and how cold it was outside; -20 degrees. Centigrade I supposed.

CHAPTER EIGHT

Finally the Airbus 330 from Luanda touched down at Ndjili International Airport twenty-eight hours and three changes of aircraft after take off from Seattle. I glanced at my watch. It said 11pm, but I had no idea what day it was, I think it was Sunday. I reeked of stale air-conditioning and blue leather upholstery. I rubbed my eyes and threw back a couple Aleve, without water. I didn't have a headache, but I was about to get one very shortly. I'm all for preventative health care. I gazed at Ian, who was also rubbing his eyes. I offered him an Aleve and he declined. His loss. Ian's presentation was more shambled than his usual tidiness, and I was appreciating the 5 o'clock shadow, no, the 11 o'clock shadow. It suited him better. It suited me better. A few strands of hair flopped over his forehead haphazardly. I wondered if he brought his fifty-dollar hair gel. I liked the falling strands. It was a bit endearing, the way he would stick his lower lip out and blow air up toward his forehead to whisk the strays away from his brow. However, this might not still be charming a week from now.

The complexion of the passengers got darker with each stop. There were a handful of "Mondeles"- or whites. Peace Corps, UN, business, missionaries. I could label them all with a glance. The missionaries were all asleep and only woke up with the first bounce. The others were avidly looking out the window. Nothing to see. The jet landed hard, bounced, landed again and stuck to the tarmac. The engines roared in reverse thrust.

"Bienvenu à *Kinshasa!"* said the air attendant, a tall foxy African. I loved her long dangling ivory earrings. Probably carved from some elephant tusk. Maybe it was *my* former pet elephant. "Remain in your seats," she continued in English, "until the plane has come to a complete stop and the seat-belt sign goes off." Ian was looking out the window.

"I don't see a thing," he said.

"Well, they turned off the runway lights as soon as we touched down. Look out over there, you can see the terminal." I was desperately tired and a little nauseous from the combination of sleeping pills, Larium, and the last shot of Black Label. I shook out another Aleve. The plane taxied forever then stopped. Nothing happened.

"What's happening?" Ian eventually asked.

"Ian, promise me that you won't ask 'what is happening?' all the time. Makes you sound like a virgin."

"You know better than that." Ian was grinning. I punched his arm. Were we *teens?*

He managed a wan smile. He had on a lightweight suit coat and tie. I sighed as he adjusted the knot. Actually most of the Africans on board were dressed to the max. The women wore gorgeous and colorful long dresses and scarves, the men suits of various kinds. Dress was a sign of status, wealth and clout. You needed all you could get. Years ago Zaire had banned neckties, but once Mobutu fell from power, neckties were apparently back. Only the Peace Corps and missionaries dressed down.

Still we sat. I put my head back on the seat and closed my eyes. Finally after about fifteen minutes the engines revved up and we moved forward towards the big sign that said "Aereoport de Ndjili." The engines stopped and within seconds the temperature mounted. Ian loosened his tie.

Again we sat.

"Why don't they open the doors....never mind." He smiled at me.

"Most of the time we aren't going to know what is going on, Ian. So, just go with it."

"I see you are reverting to Jane pretty quickly."

"Jane?" I bit.

"Tarzan and Jane...you've heard of her?"

"Sure. Where is Tarzan, though?"

"Funny."

But he was right. I could feel myself changing already. Even though I had left this place as a child, I was forever imprinted. I had also grown up on a steady diet of Congo stories. The unbelievable ones were the true ones. I craned my neck around to see what Keith was up to. He gave me a little wave; he actually looked refreshed. He probably managed more sleep than I did, being as I constantly worried about accidentally falling asleep on Ian, but then managed to wake up on his shoulder anyway. It's a wonder we lay our heads on shoulders; what a bony surface to intrude upon our soft temples. However,

Ian's shoulder fit like a puzzle piece for my head, I was thankful for the sleep it provided. He didn't seem to mind either.

The door opened and a rolling wave of warm humid and pungent air filled the Airbus. People were already up taking down their luggage and crowding the isles. There was no hurry. I continued to sit. Ian stood up excitably, bending half way over so as to not to hit his head. He looked way too eager to meet his death. I shook my head at him and closed my eyes again.

Nobody moved forward. Minutes ticked by.

"I bet the ramp is in use elsewhere." I offered this to Ian, anticipating his next question.

"*The* ramp?"

"Sure, one ramp. I am guessing that one is broken, and two planes are rarely here at the same time."

Finally the line moved forward and we grabbed our duffels and shuffled along towards the door.

"Au revoir, dames, messieurs" said Foxy. "Enjoy your stay." She said this with a straight face. On Hawaiian airlines, they always smile. Should have buried Dad in Hawaii.

We descended the ramp and began the walk across the blistering tarmac, still hot from the sun's daily scorching. "Don't worry, Ian, it won't be like this inside the terminal."

"I hope not!"

"It will be worse. I'll bet you five that there is no air conditioning."

"Are you always this pessimistic?" Ian was already sweating, the tie was coming off. I looked forward to what other layers he might shed.

"Pessimistic? No. Realistic, yes. Word of advice, Ian, in Africa, always expect the worst, then you *might* be pleasantly surprised, and maybe not too disappointed." I hated to break it to him like that, but it was true. Even expecting the worst doesn't offer much in the way of aid, usually the most unexpected happens, the kind of circumstance you can't dream up, and you go with it. Being type A doesn't fly. Neither does B. Try Type X.

We hooked up with Keith and sandwiched our way through the double glass doors. The passengers piled up before the security checkpoints. Somehow we had already been outmaneuvered and were almost at the back of the crowd. Keith had arranged to have a travel service meet us there, to help us through security and with transportation into town. I didn't see anybody that looked remotely helpful.

I couldn't wait for the encounter with immigration; like a box of chocolates…

Finally we made it to the checkpoint and offered our passports and visas.

A fat, sweating official sat behind a scarred wooden table with a stamp. He thumbed through my passport and couldn't find the visa. I resisted the impulse to find it for him. He started through my visa pages again.

"There, there it is," I pointed it out to him as he went by it again. He scowled at me. I am not so good at resisting my impulses for very long.

"*Livret de vaccination* - vaccination booklet." I handed it to him. He examined it. Then in broken English said "Yellow Fever not good."

"You're right, yellow fever is *not* good, which is why I got my shot." I couldn't resist. Keith swatted me on the arm.

"Not good, not official." The man glared at me from behind his desk.

"What do you mean? I just got the shot. There it is, right there!" I pointed it out to him. I could even show him the bruise on my butt, but opted not to…yet.

"*Oui, mais*…too soon. Not effective. Two more days." He wiped his forehead with a wet, dirty hanky.

I said nothing. Keith was about to get involved. I basically didn't like protective Uncles, so I said in French, "Ok, I understand. Shall we wait here two more days, then?" Keith rolled his eyes.

"Anna, don't," he whispered.

"*What* did she say?" Ian was getting fidgety already, and we were just getting started.

"Ian, looks like we have to stay here two more days in the waiting room until our yellow fever shots become effective." I knew that would get him.

"Ian, it'll be ok," said Keith, "especially if Anna doesn't aggravate this guy."

The "guy" looked at me with a bit of a surprise. "Vous ne pouvez pas attendre ici – you can't wait here."

"Where then?" Still conversing in French.

"You must leave, then return."

"I don't have a ticket."

"You'll have to buy one."

"OK, let me through and I promise to go buy a ticket to return." I was starting to perk up.

The official said something under his breath to the man sitting next him, who snorted in laughter. I caught something about "she can come home with me" in Lingala. Keith caught it too…

"Anna, don't….!"

"*Yango wana, tokenda elongo, donc* - sure thing, let's go together then," I said to him, also casting a glance at his buddy and winking.

This time he really did start. He looked me over, then over at Ian and Keith who just smiled back and shrugged as if to say "I can't believe her either." Male bonding.

I added, "How much does a temporary permit to enter while waiting for vaccine to become effective cost?"

Keith looked away. Ian was clutching his throat.

"24€ " he said. I handed it to him. "For all of us, a group permit, ok?"

"*Ca va.*"

"Ian, hand me your wallet." Ian did so without asking. Good boy. I pulled out our Euros. He stamped our passport and we went through.

"What was that all about, Anna?" Ian was sweating and stuffing his wallet into his back pocket.

"I offered to go home with him but he took some money instead. Put your wallet somewhere safer, Ian, don't be an idiot."

Ian didn't say anything, which was good.

We met the chauffeur from the Travel Service. His nametag said "Kolongo."

He picked up my bag. All we had was our carry-ons. Except for Dad. "This way to the car, please." He seemed nice enough, eager to help.

"Ah, Monsieur Kolongo, we have to get the body first."

I am sure he was not confident enough in his English to think he understood.

"*Comment?* – What? The body? What body?"

"Keith, didn't you tell them that we had some oversized luggage?"

We all just stopped in the lobby of the airport. Taxi drivers were clamoring all over us, gesturing towards their vehicles, insisting on their service.

"Pretty lady! This way! To my car, I help!" Africa is not the place to get titillated by compliments. *Everyone* is a pretty lady. Even the Aunt Miriams.

"*50€ pour aller en ville.* This way! Come! Come!" Numbers of porters made attempts to grab our carry-ons, to no avail.

"*Tika yango* - leave it!" I yelled periodically. It seemed to help. Me anyway. Kolongo waved them all away.

"I did ask Josh Adams from the Baptist mission to arrange whatever we needed with a funeral home here in Kin," said Keith.

"Maybe there is no such thing," Ian said. That was astute. He was learning.

"Well, somewhere out there they are unloading that plane, and, hopefully, Dad is being carted into the storage area, or else he didn't make the transfer in Luanda." That was a thought. Dad would sit there in Angola for who knows how long. I thought about the woman from Ghana and Dale's remark, "she looked wonderful." I crossed my fingers for Dad.

"Monsieur Kolongo, where do you think they would unload a casket?" Among the four of us, he did, after all, know the airport the best.

"*Eh bien*, I know some things that need special attention are stored down there." He gestured with his lip towards a hallway. Finger pointing was offensive.

"We can ask, maybe..." offered Ian.

"Better not to ask, Ian," said Keith. "Always act as if you are sure."

"Should be easy for you, you're a lawyer." I couldn't help myself.

Ian digested this bit of lore, debating within himself if he could act sure.

We started off down the hallway of no return. Any moment I expected armed guards to come running, sirens to go off.

"Ian, walk with more confidence." The target on his chest wasn't fading yet. We picked up the pace a bit. The hallway came to a large door that opened with a sort of crash-bar. A big sign read, "*Acces Interdit*." I didn't slow down.

"Anna!" said Keith. I always seemed to worry these guys. I didn't hesitate. I hit the bars and went through. Kolongo, Keith, and Tarzan had no choice but to follow. The hallway opened into an open-air causeway. Across the way I could see another large double door that was open. A couple of carts from the plane were headed that way. Some were parked just outside.

The QO2 Earthtone 20 gauge was there. All alone on its very own cart. *Hello Daddy.* I breathed a sigh of relief. But even from here it didn't look right. We approached it slowly. It was totally caved in. Made me so glad we didn't check any luggage, or a puppy. I ran my hand over it.

"How in the world did that happen?" asked Ian.

Keith walked around it. "Over here. These coffins have little valves that need to be open when shipped, to equalize the air pressure. This one is closed tight."

Knowing stuff like that was a mark of a true missionary.

But the QO2 looked hideous. Surely the air seal was broken.

"I can make out the shape of the Ziegler in there," I said. Thank goodness for Ziegler. If I got through this trip, I would invent a drink and name it "the Ziegler."

"*Arretez! C'est interdit!*" The angry shout came from behind one of the fast approaching carts. A couple more guys came through the big open doors. One wore a suit and had a clipboard. The other had an AK-47. *Thirty-shot banana clip*. I had heard too many Congo stories involving these. Clipboard faced us. AK-47 stood by and watched.

I leaned in to Ian, pointed discreetly at the man with my lip, and whispered, "Now him, I would *not* go home with." Ian looked astonished, as if suddenly believing that I would have indeed "gone home" with the security check point man.

"You are not allowed in here. This is a serious infraction! Serious infraction! Very serious!" He said, thumping his clipboard. He had sized us up and decided English would work. His English was not bad.

"How serious is it?" I asked nicely. I waited for someone to say "Anna!" Nobody said anything.

"*Très serieux!*" He had trouble keeping his needle in the English groove. "Vous serez arrêté! Go to the police office!"

I felt Keith relax and I knew why. No civilian would ever involve the police. The police were not our friends. It was an empty threat, meant to scare newbies like Ian. Ian did look scared.

I pointed to the imploded casket. "Did you do that to my father's casket?" It was time to regain the offensive. "Maybe I should report *that* to the police."

"*Non, non, pas ma faute* - not my fault!...your father?"

"Yes, my *father*." I handed him the first of a huge file of papers I had carried out just in anticipation of this moment. The paper was a notarized official death certificate. While he was still trying to decipher that one, I handed him the official Funeral Home Statement by Krader Funeral Home. For good measure I added the official Non Contagious Disease Affidavit. I had Dale add some stamps and a seal. Everything was so very official.

"We need to take *mon père* with us," I said.

"C'est impossible! Only a licensed representative from the *funerarium* can remove the casket. There are formalities, fees, permits." At least we were off the subject of our arrest. That was progress.

Keith said, "I called the *funerarium*. They should be here. But, who knows, it is late, maybe there is a problem on the road." I was sure nobody present even knew if a *funerarium* existed in Kinshasa. The civil war had killed, either by outright violence or by consequent disease and starvation, maybe ten million people. The dead were just buried or tossed into the river for the crocs.

"Can we obtain the permit here?" I went to the basics. It worked with the vaccine Nazi back in the airport.

He paused for a moment. "Come inside to my office. We can talk there." He wanted to shed AK-47 and anybody else around. We all moved inside. The huge hangar was piled high with boxes, crates, and barrels. Somewhere in there I heard the bleating of a goat. I was sure that some of this stuff went back fifty years. *Still no permit*? *So sorry.* Some crates were obviously pried open, a few barrels sprung. No wonder he thought I was serious about him violating Dad's casket.

We entered a dingy little 8X8 office with a huge steel gray desk. Papers were piled high. Old Dickinsonian ledgers sat on a shelf above his head. A fan clunked away in the corner. He sat down behind the desk and shuffled some papers. Two backless metal chairs faced the desk. No wires attached.

"*Assayez-vous* - sit down." He gestured at the chairs. I didn't want to sit on those. Keith gestured to Ian to have a seat. Ian would never sit while I was standing. I sighed and sat down, then Ian sat down.

"*Alors*, what shall we do about all this…unfortunate situation? Obviously you can't just put the box in the back of your Hi-Lux."

"Landcruiser," I corrected him.

"Anna."

"Landcruiser, then."

"Actually an Isuzu Trooper," Kolongo corrected us all.

Clipboard aimed a look at him, Kolongo backed up. He was probably the most vulnerable one present. I knew my projected arrogance and confidence came from an illusion that my white skin and money made me invulnerable. But still, these were the only tools I had.

"Monsieur," said Keith, trying to head me off, "We want to fully comply with all the laws of the country, of course." Keith hated bribes of all kind. He knew where I would take this. I didn't believe in bribes either, but I was not averse to pre-emptive tipping.

"Oui, and I am sure there are permits that we need. We are more than happy to pay whatever they cost." If we waited until morning and came back, there would be more officials present, the hassle factor would grow out of proportion. We might actually have to hire a *funerairium*, whatever that was.

He opened a ledger as if to look up the price. He was good at play-acting. We knew he was playacting, and he knew we knew, and we knew that he knew that we knew, but so long as we all subscribed to the same game, it would go ok.

"Well, let's see. There is the import permit...and the storage fee... and the guarantee of burial..." he paused to think of more.

"What about the security fee?"

He looked at me. "Yes, the security fee."

"Can we deduct the damage to the casket?"

"You may, mademoiselle, take that up with the airline. So, there is the fee to expedite all this...*un cas urgent* - an urgent case...."

"How much do all these cost?" Ian couldn't stand it any longer. He was thinking in terms of thousands of dollars.

He jotted some notes on a paper. He was thinking, *wealthy Mondeles*.

"Ok, I am so sorry that it is so much money, but this *cas urgent*..." he pursed his lips in despair. He sighed. "300€."

Ian was reaching for his wallet. I put a hand on him.

"300€!!! That is outrageous! I should just leave the casket here and take the body with us. In fact, that's what I'll do! He is embalmed, he will be fine outside the box! We don't have 300€! One-hundred €," I countered.

We eventually settled on two hundred. Ian paid. He did actually stamp some of the papers we handed to him and returned them to us.

"OK, you may go."

We walked back out to the casket. The Earthtone was so huge and heavy and now damaged, I had no idea how we were going to manage that. We stood by the imploded stainless steel box.

"Let's just take the Ziegler box and leave this here." I was brilliant.

"You can't open this, Anna, no..." Ian began. He shook his head in futile protest.

"Uncle Keith, why can't we do that?"

"Ah, I don't know why not. Sure. Now this Ziegler thing, he is ok in there, right, I mean, it doesn't leak or smell or won't fall apart, right?"

"No, it's all good." I had no idea. I had never actually seen it.

Keith began to undo the bolts. Some were loose, others were bound tight. He looked around and spotted the guy still by the cart. He went over to him. I faintly heard him say "wrench." Soon he came back with an enormous pipe wrench that would tear off the nuts holding down the Space Needle. These gave easily.

"OK, Anna, you open it."

I raised the lid. Nothing happened. The much smaller box was nestled inside. It looked strong and intact. We lifted the damaged casket off the cart, then hoisted the Ziegler box onto the cart. I was soon gazing down, looking directly into my father's face. The Ziegler had a small window. *You've got to be kidding me.* The window was a bit scratched, it was rectangular shaped, and placed directly above Dad's head. His eyes were still closed, he looked alright. Not "wonderful" but alright. Considering. I made a personal vow to never look in that window again, it would simply undue me. I was amazed that my tall father crammed in the short box. It must be uncomfortable, he couldn't even fit in a Mini Cooper.

Then we just pushed him down the hallway towards the open air. Nobody stopped us. We emerged outside, enveloped by the thick humidity.

"The Trooper is over there." Kolongo pointed to a beige Trooper parked nearby. Another man was standing by it. He would never leave it unattended. It didn't look to me like the Ziegler would fit in the back. There was no roof rack. I flashed to Lampoon Vacation with dead grandma strapped to the roof in her rocking chair. Not a pretty sight.

Kolongo opened the back. The box was too long. He lowered the back seats and it fit in about 2/3 of the way, but now there were not enough seats for everyone.

"Jean," he yelled at the Trooper guard, "*kota awa mpe fanda na sanduku* - get in here and sit on the box." Keith shrugged and got in also. The luggage followed and so the Ziegler was well anchored. Kolongo bungee'd the doors partially open. I squeezed in the front seat with Ian and Kolongo. He started the SUV and immediately a blessed blast of air conditioning hit us. The radio came to life with some great Kinshasa Jazz. Madilu Bialu sang *Makambu Ezali Minene* with that unique African rhythm.

We pulled out of the airport and began the long 25km journey into town. For the moment, things were peaceful. The State Department had issued a traveler warning, but Keith's sources in-country said there was not much danger. *Not much. How much is that exactly?* I had expected a dark ride into town. I had imagined that the war had collapsed everything. The roads would be empty, especially at this time of night. It was now 1am But nothing could be farther from the truth.

Traffic on the two-lane road was heavy. The road was a mess, and each vehicle swerved here and there to avoid the deep potholes, meaning, in and out of our lane. Kolongo was not slow to honk and flash his lights. Huge Mercedes transport trucks laden feet above the top of the rack, lumbered along spewing black diesel fumes into the air. Fires were lit all along the road.

"What are all those fires for?"

"Sentinels, Ian. They sit outside the gates and protect the compound." That was the theory anyway. These watchmen could not ward off a real gang of thieves. They were there to be blamed when something was stolen. Scapegoats.

Women were still out selling, squatting in cramped kiosks with small flickering candles in cans. They sold slivers of soap, sardines, matches, cigarettes called *Ami Fidele* – Faithful Friend, and Primus beer.

"Uncle Keith, where are we staying?" My body was giving out, I yearned for some rest.

"There is a guest house for missionaries, called The Welcome Center. Actually pretty nice."

"You arrange that like you did the *funerairium*?"

He laughed. We were all way too sleep-deprived. "No, this is real."

Kolongo hit a huge hole and the entire inside of the Trooper lifted about two feet. Dad slid towards the open door. Keith grabbed hold and with Jean's help, managed to pull him back in to safety.

"He may never rest in peace," said Ian. He was looking at Dad sympathetically, like he truly cared. I tried to brush away the sudden rush of feelings for Ian that washed over me.

We finally pulled up to the Center. A guard opened the iron gates and we drove in. A few other vehicles were parked there. Keith talked with the guard for a moment then came back with the numbered keys. I had room ten. Ian had room fifteen. No chance they were adjacent. I wondered for a moment if Keith had arranged that.

We got our luggage out. I was so looking forward to a shower and nice bed. I was dead, so to speak, on my feet.

"*Mes amis*...the box?" Kolongo was standing by the Trooper. "I need to leave. I can't take this with me."

I couldn't just leave him in the parking lot, or outside on the veranda. The kitchen door was locked. "Ok, put him in room ten."

We separated finally. Ian and Keith carried the box into my room. I thought this would creep me out, but I guess I was too tired. I took a shower, vaguely surprised that there was water, not hot, but still running water. I slipped on a T-shirt, turned on my fan and crawled under the mosquito net. I was really here.

"Night, Dad."
Night, Annie.

CHAPTER NINE

I heard a knock on my door. I glanced at my watch, it was 8am, Monday morning, I thought. Which would mean it was 10pm, Sunday night, Seattle time. The arduous events of the night helped with the jetlag; I actually felt rested.

"Ko ko ko!" It must have been Keith outside my door, using the Congo-way of knocking. Considering that most either live in mud-huts, or have screen doors, knocking is not a useful method of announcing oneself. "Ko ko ko," on the other hand, is.

I threw on some shorts, opened my door and found myself greeting Ian.

"How did you know about ko-ko-ko?" I interrogated him as if he had cracked open some top secret code. I felt ill prepared to greet him, remembering still that he knew me in a more romantic, attractive way sometimes. I hadn't brushed my teeth. I fidgeted with my hair and kept my distance.

"You look lovely, Anna." Somehow he read my mind. "Here, I made this for you, I know how you are without it." His smile was tender. I accepted the steaming cup of Nescafe, instant coffee; we drink only the best in the Congo. An abomination to

Starbucks, but on par with Lilly's Folgers. Tasting the bitter "brew" brought back a cloud of memories, nostalgia overwhelmed me and I felt like I had returned home, and then I gagged. Two tablespoons of sugar would help.

Ian welcomed himself into my room with his own cup of coffee, looked around for a place to sit, decided against sitting on Dad, and plopped down on my bed. In doing so, he yanked the mosquito net off of its hook on the ceiling. The net collapsed all over him.

This time I did spit out my coffee, laughing out loud, as I watched him try to battle the netting with one hand and protect his coffee with the other.

"Oh Bloody Nora!" How come when Ian cusses it sounds so sophisticated? Who is Nora anyway, I always wondered...

"Pathetic - you look like a fish caught in a net, but on my bed!" I was snickering, but not yet helping.

Ian was still floundering and also laughing, "You don't have to snare me to get me in your bed." Ian was all about the innuendos; maybe he thought he was Daniel Craig too.

"Enough Ian, I hate flirting. Cut it out." My mood turned sour instantly. Of course, I remembered that I was all too involved in the last round of flirting. But something about being here, in Africa, my Africa, with Ian, unsettled me. My lives were colliding. Or maybe it was just Ian, and it had nothing to do with Africa. How long could I keep up this battle?

Ian got himself free and stood up, facing me. He stoically put his coffee down and looked me seriously in the eyes.

"No, enough from *you*, Anna." His voice was gentle, yet confrontational. I felt nervous as if I had finally gotten caught cheating, sent to the principal's office. I swallowed hard and tried to maintain his gaze as if I had nothing to feel guilty about. Innocent until proven guilty, right, Ian?

He continued, "We've never once mentioned the turns we've taken together, never once talked about taking in beyond these occasional "dates". The first one I'd hardly even call a date. You adore me for a short spell, and then you're ice-cold. You lean on me, and then you don't need me. You take my arm, then push it away. Need I go on? I'm here with you now, in the middle of nowhere, wanting to help, wanting to be with you. If you didn't want me to come, you should have said so. But now that we're here, I'd like to at least know what to expect. Are you the ice queen of Narnia, or a tad bit warmer than that?"

"You've read C.S Lewis? Or did you just see the movie."

"Don't change the subject." Ian wasn't budging. He held his gaze. His eyes were mesmerizing.

"I'm sorry." I tried to be sincere.

"You've said that before." I was trapped, and my bluff was called. I was playing cat and mouse. I was giving mixed signals. None of it was pretending, I truly was mixed.

"Ian, I don't know what I feel. This trip is not exactly the time to be trying to unravel one another's tangled, relational webs. Especially not mine. You'll get stuck and want out. I promise."

"When is the time then?" Ian raised his voice considerably and moved closer to my face. "You're no more complicated than anyone else. We all have a past, we all have stories, holes in our hearts, and genuine fears. You're not special in that regard. I'm willing to risk getting stuck in your web, and I promise you, I won't want out." Ian set his full cup down on my nightstand and without another word opened my door to leave. I liked it better when he was entering, not exiting. I hesitated for a brief moment, then called after him.

"I'm not Jadis. Not the ice queen. More like the wicked witch of the west."

Ian turned around, "Excuse me?"

"I'm melting, I'm melting!" I said with a laugh, pretending to slink to the floor, hoping the humor would cut tension. If he had read Lewis, he must have read the Wizard of Oz.

"If you're melting, that means you're still ice." My heart sank, he did not understand the peace pipe I was trying to offer. I admit, it wasn't very loaded. "However," Ian continued - *yes - there is more!* "However, if you are ice, and you are melting, no better place to do that than right under the nose of the equator….we're definitely not in Kansas anymore, *Dorothy*. But don't for one minute think I'm your Toto." He grinned his boyishly cute British grin that I could just eat up, and shut my door. I breathed a sigh of relief; he took a puff from my flimsy pipe. I shut all thoughts of Ian aside and began my morning properly.

I changed into a pair of khakis, a short sleeve shirt, and threw on some sandals. The sink tried hard to spit out some yellow-orange water, and I dared to splash it over my face, trying not to swallow. I took a glance in the dirty mirror and decided against any make-up. In the humidity, it would be sloughed off within ten minutes. I admired the glow on my skin, compliments of the equator. I threw my hair in a ponytail and stepped over the casket to the window, opening my drapes. The city was no less busy than when we arrived. This time I noticed all the familiar vegetation. Umbrella sized leaves, palm trees, bushes that looked like paint cans had exploded all over them. Chickens scuffed about comically in the red dirt, children kicked a grapefruit around with their bare feet. The smell of kwanga, dried eel, and fried plantains accosted my nose. I wanted to taste some, but not all at once, and certainly not for breakfast. It felt surreal to be here.

I left my door ajar so that I could keep an eye on Dad. Lest he make a run for it.

"Morning, Keith!" Keith was swatting mosquitoes and stirring up a drink. We were all doing Nescafe this morning, and pretending to enjoy it. Perhaps we'd enjoy it more with a shot of whiskey I "borrowed" from the plane - white Euro-Americans, drinking Irish coffee, in the Congo. Nice tapestry of culture.

"Anna. How did you sleep?" He was looking at a large map folded out on the white plastic kitchen table.

"Fine actually, I sleep better under mosquito nets. What is our plan for the day?" I handed Ian the coffee he left in my room without a look or a word, hoping that gestures could say more.

"Here's what we're thinking. The plane we arranged for through M.A.F. is not here." *Of course it isn't.* "However, Kolongo says that A.I.M. has a Caravan, great plane, turbo-prop that we just might be able to make the weight limit for, and it is available today."

"What's the limit?" I had just layered my baguette with Nutella, and set it down. One more pound could just tip the scales.

"A couple of tons of carrying capacity, more than enough. So, let's see. That's 220 for me, about, 190 for Ian, 170 for you-"

"170? Excuse me?"

"I've never been good with women's…stuff." Poor Keith.

"135."

"Aren't you nearly six feet tall?"

"5'10'' and she's very…svelte." Ian added in my defense. I blushed.

"Ok, so that leaves the Ziegler and your Dad at about 200 lbs."

"And our luggage." I added.

"Um, where are we going, exactly? And what's M.A.F? What's A.I.M?" Poor Ian.

Keith turned back to his map and bent over the table, studying the details. He shoved his glasses back down to the tip of his nose and clicked open his pen.

"We are here," he placed an x on Kinshasa, "and we need to get here, to Gbadolité and then onto Goyongo. That isn't our only problem though."

"*Only* problem?" Ian called another bluff. He was catching onto the plethora of possible snares and problems that the Congo so eagerly offers.

Keith continued, "Gbadolité is the closest real airport to where we want to take James. The Caravan has the range for it. We'll need to get permits to do this, file a flight plan."

I answered Ian's question, "Yes, there will be more problems, but this one shouldn't be too much of a hassle. If we had to, we could also take a barge up the Congo River." I had always wanted to take a boat trip up the Congo. "That's a 200 mile river trip. That's at least a week's journey…unless we end up on a dug-out, then we're looking at several weeks en route."

"We won't go by boat, way too risky." Keith interrupted, wiping his forehead and taking off his glasses again, waving them around in his hand as he talked. "We'll find a driver. The other option is to fly into Gemena, but there probably isn't any fuel there for refueling. There are smaller strips around, the Caravan only needs about 1300 feet to land. It's an amazing plane."

We all stood around the small kitchen table, leaning over, pointing, placing x's on the map and murmuring about the best possible plan of attack. I couldn't help but feel a rush of adrenaline and excitement. We were three people ready to make a great heist as in the Italian Job, learning the ropes, finding the snares, eliminating the worst routes. We schemed and plotted our way from Kinshasa to Goyongo. Keith figured the best bet was to take a flight to Gbadolité, then drive onward.

"From Gbadolité, it's about 100 miles to Bosobolo - very near Goyongo where we want to end up." He placed a big circle around Goyongo a few times and placed his pen down.

"100 miles? So, that's what? Just an hour and half drive, right?" Ian shrugged hopefully in our direction. Keith and I stopped and gawked at Ian, afraid to address his question.

"Should we tell him now?" Keith said. We gave each other a knowing smile.

"Ian, dear - " I put my hands on my hips and turned on my school-teacher voice, trying to be as gentle as possible. "Driving 100 miles is not like what we're used to back home. We'd be lucky to make it out of third gear."

"We'd be lucky to make it at all, especially during rainy season." Keith's approach was less...gentle.

"100 miles - we're looking at about a 9 hour drive, maybe less, maybe more. Don't worry, I brought some Vicodin." Ian laughed. I was serious. He had no idea how bruised his backside was about to get.

"Last time I took that trip, our entire axle broke off of the HiLux. We camped outside in the rain. Heck, it took 6 days to rig it just enough to make it 15 miles to where we were supposed to cross a river. Darn bridge was just clean washed out. We tried to throw some logs on it but - "

It was my turn to interrupt. I could see Ian's eyes getting wider and wider, and I didn't want him to panic...there would be time for that later.

"So, he threw some logs on, they made it across and all was well, right, Keith?" I nodded in Keith's direction.

It took Keith a moment to catch my eye and he finally choked out, "Yeah. Yeah, that's it...we all, yeah... made it." He looked obviously disappointed to not be able to tell the rest of his story. Missionaries and their stories. They tell them at any pause in the conversation and wear them as gospel badges of pride on their shoulder. The more near-death experiences a missionary encounters in Congo, the greater their reward in heaven. Keith had many rubies awaiting him in the upperworld, and he could tell a good story, especially with his colorful words like "darn" and "heck." I guess I would be adopting similar cheesy words. I could tell Keith wanted to try another story, I could just hear him thinking, *I wonder when I can tell them about the one with the elephant stampede of '86 or the army-ant slaughter of '89?*

"Let's go talk to A.I.M about the plane then. Who should keep on eye on Dad?"

"Kolongo can." Keith offered.

"Trustworthy?"

"Always."

CHAPTER TEN

"Taste this." I held up some kwanga to Ian's mouth. We were buying some food for our trip from a nearby market.

"No." Ian tilted his head backward. When a Britain says "no" it always sounds like "new." So annoying.

"Just try it, you'll like it."

"That's what you said last time."

"And… you liked it!"

"No I didn't."

"How could you not like it?"

"It was chocolate covered termites, Anna."

"Yumm…! Ok, this one though, you *will* like, I promise." I started unwrapping a long, thick, twisted piece of squishy food.

"No. Yuck! Does it taste like it smells?"

"Kind of."   I shoved the kwanga further into Ian's face.

"It stinks to high heaven."

"Heaven doesn't stink. Dad said so. Now, just try it."

Ian closed his eyes and grimaced, opening his mouth, I shoved in a bite-full and closed his lips around it. "You can't spit it out!" I held my hand tightly over his mouth. Ian was desperately trying to open his mouth and rid himself of the fermented gummy bread.

"Swallow! Come on!" I was in stitches watching his expressions, surprised at my own ease and laughter.

"Aan I cownt ish goerchs!"

"What? Did you say? Pronunciate!" We were both in hysterics and I finally let my hand off his mouth, and allowed Ian to spit. Gross.

"I can't believe you made me do it."

"It's my favorite African snack. Don't diss it." I chomped down hungrily on the kwanga, wrapped in large green palm leaves. I grew up on this stuff. I admit it had an odor, but it tasted delicious, salty, thick, oily...

"It tastes like old rancid Alpo," offered Ian.

"Really? I'll have to take your word on that. Never tried Alpo...How about these?" I pointed at basket of fried plantains.

"Those, I could eat." We bought a sack full, and ate them as we walked. Ian and I were browsing through a nearby market, picking up some food for lunch and whatever else. We were waiting for Kolongo to return with the truck, so we could take it to A.I.M and charter the plane down at the hangar. We had called them on Kolongo's cell phone and the arrangements were set in motion. The landline phone system in Kinshasa was about as useful as smoke signals.

All the merchants were yelling in our direction, trying to get our attention to buy their goods. Even though I had been here, done this a thousand times, I felt safe having Ian with me. A young white female *mondele* should not be strolling alone through a market near Kinshasa. Ian was tall and was beginning to look more comfortable in his surroundings, a nice companion to have. The market wasn't half bad for a little place outside the city and smelled like old, sweaty pocket money. A large pig snout stared at my right elbow, sheep intestines at my left. The fruit was less disturbing, and in fact, very enticing. The mangoes were in season and shone a bright orange-red. Guava's, bananas and star fruit, filled the gunny sacks on the floor all around us. Water ran down in tiny rivers under our feet, at least I hoped it was water. Sizeable fabrics hung from clotheslines, displaying fine African fashion, patterns resembling the detonation of a crayon box.

The buzz of the city hummed all around us, mopeds, busses, bikes, trucks - all packed out way beyond a natural weight limit, teetering hazardously on broken parts and flattening tires - passengers oblivious to their immediate peril. The vehicles kicked up enough red dirt to give us a free "spray tan," softening our white glow. We grabbed more baguettes, some manioc leaves to make some mpondu, and opting against the snout, we filled our canvas bags with fruit. It was almost like being at Pike Place Market. Actually, it wasn't, not even close, but I liked to picture Ian and I doing something similar back at home. Walking through the market, picking up a few bountiful, five dollar bouquets, eating fresh northwest jam and honey, and ordering a fresh salmon to grill on my patio, toasting each other with ice cold lemony Hefewiesen's.

Ian would give a toast, "Here's to the successful Congo burial of 2008."

"Here's to making it out alive, barely." Clink. We would sit there and talk casually until evening, watching the moon set over Puget Sound, gazing at the ferries and barges coming and going. We would eventually make it inside and be uninhibited, and thanks to the equator melting my ice, I would be capable of true love. I smiled as I daydreamed. But in my dreams I was a pleasant person, open, vulnerable enough to give and receive, to trust. In my dreams, I was capable of love, and fell in love; I was soft and warm. I sighed as I reflected on reality. I was who I was. For me, change was just about as possible as my winning the state lottery…although, I never bought a ticket. Symbolic.

We opened our warm bottles of coke as I tutored Ian in Lingala.

"No - not – 'Botay', say 'Mbote'."

"That's what I said."

"Not you didn't, you left out the M. It's the same as "mpondu" – say the "m" and then add the pone-doo."

"You told me to not to say the "M"."

"*Kind of* say it - just *barely* slip the "M" in there, but don't leave it out altogether!" We were only on "hello," I feared I didn't have the patience to teach him any more words.

We started to walk the half mile back to the Welcome Center when the skies broke open, drenching us instantly; typical of equatorial places, especially in rainy season.

"Did you plan this!?" Ian looked up at the sky, totally bewildered and caught off guard by the sheet of water drenching us entirely.

"No! But it is rainy season!" Ten seconds ago the sun was a menacing force in the sky, now heavy dark clouds brooded and relieved themselves on the unsuspecting, without hesitation. We were practically yelling at each other above the noise, it roared in our ears like a 747 during take off. Ian was laughing, futilely holding a black plastic bag above his head for protection. These plastic bags covered the ground like some rampant eruption of black hives. The wind drove them until they hit a wall or a fence, then they accumulated in vast numbers. If I could figure out a market for them, I'd be rich. Thunder and lightning accompanied the downpour and we made a run for it.

"Grab my hand!" I liked being the leader. Ian clutched the bags, took my hand, and we ran through the torrential downpour. Red dirt tan was gone. Mud splashed up all over the back of our legs and seeped through our shoes.

We arrived breathless back at the center. Baguettes were soggy. Our clothes, now a second layer of skin, did little to cover any secrets we may have been hiding under the cotton. White t-shirts didn't help to maintain any mystery.

"You ok!?" Ian looked at me approvingly. A sly smiled crept into the corner of his mouth.

"Yeah, but I lost my sandal!" The rain battered against the screen windows, spraying onto the cement kitchen floor. The tin roof magnified the pounding.

"Does it always rain this hard?"

"WHAT?"

"Does it ALWAYS RAIN THIS HARD?" Ian was yelling at me with great volume, in order to be heard above the noise. A noise I loved, so familiar, so strong. In Goyongo, I would sit outside on the porch with my Dad, wrapped up in a little sari, watching, listening and smelling the magic. Dad sipped Nescafe, I sipped warm coke. We would sit in silence, talking would be yelling, and besides, we were comfortable with silence around each other.

"It usually rains harder! Help me get the shutters!"

We ran outside for the last time and shut the shutters. Kolongo's truck was still gone. Keith wasn't around. We hurried back inside, dripping like we had just jumped out of a pool.

"I'll go get some towels!" I rushed over to the laundry room and looked around in the cupboards, turned around to race out the door and ran right into Ian. Neither of us moved away.

"Here's a towel." I handed Ian a towel. He took it and began to wipe the water off of my forehead, and from the ends of my hair. We stared at each other silently. I tried to look away, but was held by the force of his long silent stare. The blood in my body had a mind of its own and raced through my veins rapidly, eager to heat up. I instinctively placed my hand over my chest to stop the noise. Why did he have this effect on me? I tried to control my breathing. I mistakenly glanced down at his lips. *Crap, look up, look up Anna!*

"You know, water is dangerous stuff for an ice queen." He tenderly pressed the towel to my eyes.

"Wicked witch of the west." I corrected him and moved closer, ignoring the caution voice in my head. I longed to be the girl in my dreams. I could just barely remember the taste of his mouth…

"Even worse, if I remember the story well. However, still a major melting problem." Ian's towel moved from my face to my neck.

"Not so much a problem, more like…a metamorphosis." I was shaking from the cold, or maybe it was because of Ian's arms around my back. He slid his hand down to the small of my back and pushed me in closer to his body. His breath was hot on my face, and I closed my eyes, heart racing like a sixteen-year-old girl during prom with a senior. I didn't want to talk anymore. He lifted my chin toward his face. My lips parted instinctively and I clenched the back of his neck with my hand, pulling him toward me…

"HOLY MACKERAL!" We were interrupted. "Check out this rain! You kids about ready to go? Kolongo's back with the truck!" Keith's voice was loud and intrusive, he shouted and stomped in the puddles down the hall, obviously wearing large army boots. I was thankful he wasn't sneaky. It would feel like getting caught by my Dad. Which I was always careful not to do.

"We're in here! Drying off! Come on down!" I yelled down the hallway to Keith.

"You're inviting him to join us? A little strange…" Ian grinned and leaned in toward my lips again.

I glared, quickly pulled away from Ian and began to take off my shoes. I suddenly felt embarrassed.

Heat rose to my face and flooded into my cheeks. I hoped he didn't notice. It wasn't just embarrassment, I was suddenly angry, indignant at myself and at Ian's casual, romantic demeanor. Didn't he care about what this could do to us? To me? Didn't he care that this was just the beginning of another very messy ending, causing himself pain? He was wrong, I was not melting; my icy layer of protection was still thick. Keith came around the corner and glanced at us suspiciously.

I quickly offered an explanation for our skin-tight clothing.

"We wouldn't have gotten stuck in this downpour if it wasn't for Ian hankering for some mangoes." Ian glared at me. I shrugged and walked past him, feeling tense. I wished I could sort through my feelings. It would take some unraveling to sort it all out. I could go from 0 to 60 in seconds flat, and then throw on the brakes without a moment's hesitation and only a slight pang of guilt. I needed another therapist.

"Boy, you ARE a mess! Get changed, and let's go." Keith kept a tight ship.

I walked back down the yellow hallway and turned the knob to room ten. I turned around and glanced back at Ian, still standing in the open doorway to the laundry room. He looked beautiful with droplets of water sliding off his hair down onto his face. He solemnly held his gaze at me, then slowly shook his head and sighed so deeply, his entire body deflated right before my eyes. I shrugged and turned around, thankful that moment was behind us. My legs still felt like rubber.

I opened the door, walked in and began to change my clothes. Something was wrong. It took me a second to realize, the Ziegler was gone.

CHAPTER ELEVEN

"KEITH!" I breathlessly ran throughout the center yelling for Keith, I was sure to be the next Landan to die of a heart attack.

"KEITH! Dad is gone! The Ziegler is gone!" I spotted Keith outside on the covered porch casually shelling peanuts into a soup can. He watched me come and tossed a peanut into his mouth.

"Sweetheart! Calm down! He's in the truck!"

"WHAT?" I was livid. No one informed me of this new plan. "WHY?" People just shouldn't be moving Dad around here and there without me knowing it!

"Was thinkin' that it might just be smarter to try and take him with us, to be sure he fits in the plane." I was finally breathing with more regularity, maintaining my glare on Keith.

"I'm sorry, Anna! I didn't mean to scare you sweetheart." *Forget the sweetheart stuff, Uncle Keith.* Ian came up behind me and placed his hands on my shoulders.

"You Ok? I heard you screaming everywhere...Sounds like he's not missing?" Ian inquired.

"He's in the truck. I can't lose him, Ian." I sighed deeply. I wasn't sure what exactly I meant by that.

"You won't." He kissed the top of my forehead like a brother would. I was comforted by his sincerity and turned and gave him a hug. He pinned my animosity against the wall with his tenderness. Zero to sixty.

"Let's go." I ran back to my room, changed, grabbed my bag of valuables and left the center.

We crammed ourselves into the Isuzu like we had done just hours earlier. This time Dad was bungeed in a bit more securely. I sat on top of the Ziegler, just to be sure. It felt nice to be close to Dad, even if it was like this. He knew where we were going, he knew where he was taking us, even if we didn't. We drove ten minutes through the city to the A.I.M center. I soaked in the sights of the city, it looked different during the daytime. I could see how the war had taken its toll, the city had suffered a lot of decay. Billboards warred against each other and vast canopies stamped with Congolese slogans draped the windows, commercial marketing was totally ungoverned. Most of them were cell phone companies - "Modeler. Le futur" - was wrapped against half of a skyscraper, adorned with a beautiful black athletic woman. It could have been Serena or Venus Williams. The ad was for "Celtel." Cell phones, I shook my head in disbelief. When I grew up here, you couldn't make contact with the outside world except by short-wave radio and hand carried letters. Homing parrots never caught on the way pigeons did.

Kinshasa's buildings were old and painted in 70's colors of light pink and light blue. The paint was chipping and overgrown ivy of graffiti sprawled itself along the cracks of the buildings. On every corner was a drug store, carrying the essentials: magazines, cigarettes and black-market videos. Questionably dressed women walked the streets without discretion, earning a living. Dirty Volkswagen bus-type vans lined up along the sidewalk, each carrying a number that would transport a traveler to their supposed destination. These could fit up to thirty people, creatively. Two words to describe Kinshasa: resourceful, busy. The energy was limitless; noise permeated every wavelength. Ian's head was hanging out the window, trying to see all the "sights."

"Take your head in, or when we stop, someone could yank you right out the truck."

"Really?"

"No, not really, but pull it in anyway! One time, I was stopped in my vehicle and someone came up to me, stuck their hand through my window and pulled my necklace right off my neck."

"You're kidding."

"Nope. So be careful. Where's your wallet?"

"In my pocket." Ian said proudly.

"What? Never put it in your *pocket!* Here, give it to me, I'll wear inside my shirt with my travel purse." Ian grinned. Even the thought of his wallet inside my shirt made him happy. What a boy. I pulled out my beige, hidden passport holder and stuck Ian's wallet inside, along with my mom's simple gold band that I always wore. I knew that if someone really wanted to find this, they could, but I'd at least make it difficult. Ian still was halfway out the window.

"What happened to this city?" Naïve, but valid question.

"The war."

"Which one? Wasn't Congo named something else a few years ago?" Again, a good question. At least Ian didn't say "what war." I'm sure he watched CNN for more than the stock market reports.

"Yeah, Congo was first named the Belgian Congo when it was under Belgian occupation. After the war for independence it was renamed the Republic of Congo. Then Mobutu Sese Seko came along and reshaped the entire nation into his personality. He named it Zaire, and renamed all the cities to his liking. He put his portrait on every single bank note, building, and billboard. A humble man. Stayed in office for decades, raped the country clean of all its resources." I said this in a single breath. I had it memorized, had lived half of it.

"Weren't there any elections?"

"Sure! Congo is very democratic," I said with a smirk, "Mobutu held an election where he was the only candidate. It was rigged. Green card meant a vote for him, a red card meant a vote against him. So, how would you vote with soldiers and everybody watching? After years of his presidency, the rest of the world realized how corrupt his regime was. There may have been peace, but the country was deteriorating. He became one of the wealthiest men in the world, his worth equal to Zaire's national debt. The term "Kleptocracy" was coined after his rule." I was thankful Kolongo couldn't hear me, I had no idea where his loyalties lay.

"Sounds like he used aid from the IMF as his own personal checkbook. Did you ever meet him?" A few green clad soldiers with bright red beret drove around us in a hurry. Ian stiffened.

"No. But I saw his palace. Gold-lined, massive thing. Up on the hill in his city, Gbado-Lite, where I think we will be landing. He lived there, so he poured the money into making it a real town. Paved the roads, put up hotels. We would stay there on vacation sometimes, in a real hotel, with a real swimming pool. They served cold pop and ice cream. What a treat. That was the president's city." I paused and thought back, then laughed out loud. "It had one paved road that ran for about ten miles. Some general imported a Pontiac Firebird. It couldn't go off that one road, but it could cover it in about a minute! I'm assuming, it's more like a ghost town now."

"So, that was Zaire, now it's the Congo...what happened?" I felt like I was telling a kid a scary ghost story.

"Conflict arose around 1990. Long story short, he was finally driven out in 1997, Zaire and all its cities, rivers, and the like were renamed again, purging Congo of Mobutu's name. Now we have the Democratic Republic of Congo." I remembered trying to tell people how to pronounce Zaire by drawing a line on my face from my eye to my ear - "Z-eye-ear." I will never do that again, but I wasn't sorry. It was a good change for the country, to be rid of Mobutu.

"And then that is when the great African war began?"

"Yes - very good Ian." Again the schoolteacher, I gave Ian five stars on the blackboard and maybe a few extra perks.

"I have read some of that. I saw Blood Diamond. Child soldiers, absolutely chilling."

"Blood Diamond was in Sierra Leone, but yes, child soldiers, mostly from Rwanda area, were heavily involved. In fact, this war involved eight African countries, lasted from 1998 to around 2003. 5.4 million people died, total. The deadliest war since World War II."

"Yeah, I read that on Wikipedia."

"Wikipedia?"

"I Googled Congo and Wikipedia'd some of its history before I came." I had never used Wikipedia as a verb, but it worked. "I wanted to know some things." So, he didn't see it live on CNN, he wiki'd the history. At least it was something, better than Ashley.

"Most people don't know that about Congo, about the wars. Hardly anyone in our neck of the woods even knows there was a war out here, equal to the likes of World War II. Simply because it didn't involve America." Maybe it wasn't that simple, but I wasn't impartial. I wondered how many of my playmates were brutally raped and murdered. One of them, Mpasi, was actually a daughter of one of the current warlords, Jean-Pierre Bemba, who apparently still controlled much of Northwest Congo. The war was over, but even so, wars in Congo continue to pop up out of the jungle like tenacious, bloodthirsty lemurs. *When will Africa stop bleeding...no wonder the dirt is red. King Leopold's ghost still haunts the land.*

"History lesson over, looks like we're here." Kolongo viewed the stop signs as suggestions and we had made it to the office in seven minutes. He parked and waited in the car.

We exited our car and walked along the burnt orange dirt road, avoiding the black garbage bags, the questionable lumps of dung, and the slew of peddlers pushing kwanga and plaintains in our faces.

"Non merci, pas de bananes pour moi." I say politely but firmly.

"Madame! S'il vous plait! Juste une, ma famille est malade, juste une! Juste une!" He pleaded desperately, breaking off plantains and opening my hand, placing it in my limp grip.

"Non merci, non." I handed it back and pushed my way through, determined not to be had. Besides, one measly banana is not going to save his "malade" – sick - family. This country eats its young for breakfast without remorse, mothers included. A banana wouldn't have saved my mom either. Tant pis - too bad.

The peddler tried Ian next, "My family needs buy you to this banana. My family is sick from banana." The attempted translation didn't go well, Ian was about to pull out some money to buy it until he heard that it would make him ill.

Keith gathered the peddlers over toward him and began to talk, asking about their family, letting them know where they might find extra help, and then buying the entire cluster and throwing it over his shoulder he joined us on the porch of the office. I marveled at his patience and tender care. I don't have time for that kind of love, I'm on a mission from God. Literally. Or Dad, pretty much one and the same.

"Do you really think this cluster will save his family, Keith? Do you really think his family is sick?" I said with a bit of a smile, poking at his soft heart to see what logic might seep out.

"Maybe it will, maybe it won't. Maybe his family is sick, maybe it's not. That's not my call. Let's say this was in fact all the money he needed to afford antibiotics? Plus, sometimes all it takes is a couple loaves and fishes."

I bit the inside of my cheek and nodded. I remember that bible story well. Jesus multiplies the little humble gift from a boy and feeds 5,000.

"Keith, no offense but I don't think you're Jesus. You're too pale." I jested.

"No, no, I sure am not, sweetheart, but He is in me, and He works through me, just as He works through you."

"That's where you're wrong, Uncle Keith. It's just me, myself and I."

"He works through you whether you know it or not... It's not about whether he can, it's whether or not you recognize that he does."

The A.I.M office was decorated in 1960's oranges and yellows, paisley patterns everywhere, velvet lanterns with fringes, and shag carpets. The floor of the old brick building creaked with every step we took. Pictures lined the walls of all the African Inland Missions families, workers and supporters. A dusty, large goatskin drum sat in the corner. Little African market items littered the bookshelves - beautifully carved women with long black legs carried jugs on their heads, ebony elephants - hooked together by tusk and tail - marched along the shelves in orderly fashion.

"You all must be the Landan group. I'm Clara, nice to meet you!" The slight, older woman, wearing a blue prairie dress, greeted us with the usual limp African handshake and asked us to have a seat. I kept one eye on the window where Kolongo sat with the Trooper.

"So, as we discussed on the phone, we will have our Cessna Caravan ready in about three hours for your charter, if you wish. I heard it land a little while ago. It was to head right back out, but the flight was cancelled. It's an extra 500 dollars if you'd prefer the larger aircraft."

"What's our total then?" Ian had his calculator out already.

"2,200 dollars per hour is our normal rate." She hesitated and then glanced at me sympathetically. "I knew your Dad, Miss Landan. His name was kind of known around here on the mission field. I saw him just last year in Mbandaka, as he was heading back to Kinshasa. Course, he always made a stop in Mbandaka for a few days. In fact, here's his last signature." Clara opened the logbook and pointed to his penmanship. She continued, "Anyway, I'm so sorry he died. We can charter the prop to you for $1,600 an hour if that works for you."

"Perfect, thank you, we'll make our way to the hangar then. Who is the pilot?" Keith stepped in, I had very few words. I was finally in my Dad's wake. I was meeting people he lived with, worked with, companions who knew his comings and goings. Each knew something about him, each one had a piece of the James' puzzle. I was piecing together his life. I could see him signing the log, I could see him smiling at Clara. My Dad felt very much alive at the moment, I wondered if the Ziegler had gotten any lighter.

When we arrived at the hangar, surprisingly, we encountered no hassle or kink. We offered no bribes, or threats, simply signed the paperwork. Of course nobody volunteered the information that there was a two-week-old cadaver in that box, and we covered the window with my luggage.

Dan Olson, the pilot, walked around the Caravan checking it over. We were chartered and ready to go. I wondered if Dad would be buried within the next 72 hours. What a relief it would be to quit lugging around that big Ziegler; a relief to leave my Dad's body in peace. Yet, I knew I'd miss his constant presence. Even if he was dead.

The 12-seater was just what we needed. It had seen better days, but I was comforted knowing it had a few miles on it, and preferably lots of practice landing on airstrips. Dan was young but already an experienced bush pilot. These pilots not only knew how to fly, they could rebuild the entire airplane if the need arose.

"Folks, about ready?" Dan asked. He looked to me like a closet tobacco chewer. He spit a few times with questionable expertise from behind his thick red beard, kicked the wheel, and hopped up inside.

Dad fit in perfectly without any hassle or extra bungee chords, and so did we, and our luggage, with weight room to spare. I wished I had eaten my Nutella sandwich. I knew I could use a couple extra pounds anyway. Like Dad, years of running had sloughed off any fat that may have otherwise hugged my body. And these days, I was even thinner, it seemed. Svelte, I amended. We boarded and strapped in. My heart began to pound as I looked out the window at the dismal little N'Dolo "airport." I hoped to be landing back here in a couple of days. I was almost done.

"Keeeeeeebaaaaaa!" Pilot Dan yelled out his window a "be careful" warning with Southern-accented Lingala as he stirred up the engine. The engine coughed and the propeller began to spin slowly like a windmill in just a whisper of wind. I could still make out each individual blade. Within a few seconds I could see right through them, a blur of motion. The powerful turboprop deafened us. I remembered my many flights to and from boarding school in a much smaller Cessna 206. I would pack my bags for ten weeks, stand on the edge of the dry airstrip carved out of the jungle by axes and machetes, and wait for my school bus. The bus looked suspiciously like a four-seater vehicle that flew in the sky. I remember asking Mom when I'd be able to ride a yellow school bus like "normal" children. She turned to me and said, "Oh honey, you'll never be normal." I was not comforted by that response. But now I knew what she meant. I was half African, and coming back to the States at age 17 left me far outside the ranges of "normal" for an

American teenager. But in Congo, I fit into a small peg-hole in the African scaffold, left open for returning MK's. I speak Lingla and French, eat mpondu and kwanga, and mosquitos leave my blood alone for the most part. Here, I am half American.

Dan pushed the throttle in and the Caravan bellowed as suddenly all the thousand horses were released at once. The buildings went by faster and faster. The end of the strip was coming up fast. Then with a slight lifting of the yoke, our plane lifted gently off of terra firma and aimed for the heavens above. I thought of the three-hour flight in front of us, and wished I had gone to the bathroom one more time. The ground beneath us was a mound of gray with spatterings of red and green. Kinshasa's buildings looked small, sprawled out on the red dirt, with pockets of palm trees nestled in between abandoned structures. The dysfunctional yet beloved city became miniature in my tiny window. Soon, we would be hovering over nothing but green, the thick, dense, Ituri rainforest. I would hate to crash there. I would hate to crash anywhere, but especially not in that jungle. Dad jiggled and jostled in the back, but remained secure.

We fastened on our headphones so we could talk to each other over the roar of the engine.

"Everybody ok back there?" asked Dan.

"What's the in-flight movie?" I asked.

"Airplane III." Everybody is a comic.

"We'll be setting down in Bumba to pick up one passenger before we continue on to Gbadolité. Weather is spotty but good all the way, so they say."

"Sounds good." This from Keith. "Who are we getting at Bumba?"

"Not sure. Clara just said there was a Peace Corps guy there looking for a ride back to Kin."

Ian nudged me as we looked out the window. We were flying along the Congo River. Below we could make out canoes and a couple of smaller barges. I remembered Dad telling stories about the time he and Mom took one of the riverboats, the Captain Kongo.

Five thousand feet below us the green jungle canopy stretched forever. It was a sea of green that disappeared over the horizon in every direction. Under the jungle awning, people farmed and hunted and fished. Wars were fought, bodies rotted. The hyenas roamed and endangered animals diminished. But it was enchantingly beautiful. Small rivers sliced through the green, all flowing to the great and mighty *Fleuve Congo* that stretched across the entire nation. Islands dotted the vast expanse of the River. I could see canoes lined up on the beaches.

I must have finally dozed off because Dan's voice snapped me awake.

"Bumba, this is aircraft November 483 Sierra Pappa. Flight sequence scheduled. Arrival for approximately 1300 hours. You copy? Over." Pilot Dan was radioing the small air traffic tower, or what passed for it. They should have been notified of our coming, but one could not be sure. "Bumba, Bumba, over." I could hear the crackling of the static. "No sweat, they are not always there. Just want to check in, get the weather ya know."

Indeed the cloud cover was increasing and rain pelted hard on the windows the further upcountry we traveled. Now for minutes at a time I could not see the jungle below. "You can land this on instruments, can't you Dan?" I joked.

"Sure! But…" he laughed "Bumba doesn't have any signal for me to follow."

"So, then what?" Ian was awake. I could tell he was trying to be cool.

"Well now, it can get interesting. Some hills around there, nothing much. As long as we are above, say, 700 meters, we should be fine. Game is, get under the clouds or go around, land somewhere else."

"Ever have to crash land?"

"Ian, right, is it Ian? We don't crash land. Sometimes we put them down hard, or put them down, shall we say, not on the asphalt! Bent a wheel once. But don't worry, lots of JP1, lots of landing options…"

"JP1?"

"Sorry, fuel…we're ok. We could probably even get all the way back to Mbandaka if we had to."

Sure, *probably.*

Eventually he called in again. "Bumba, Bumba, this is three sierra pappa. We will be on the ground in one zero minutes, over." They had been previously notified of our flight plan…somebody had to be standing by.

Finally the radio cackled into life. "Three sierra pappa we copy." The operator spoke in almost unintelligible English. "You are not authorized to land, over."

"Ah Bumba tower…what do you mean 'not authorized'? *Qu'est-ce que vous voulez dire? Nous arrivons dans sept minutes. A vous* - what do you mean to say? We arrive in five minutes, over."

I could hear the edge to his voice. Switching to French was mildly insulting to the Tower operator.

"November 483 Sierra Pappa , runway not clear, not clear, not landing. Over?" still in English.

"Copy. What is the problem? Over."

"Not clear."

"I understand. Why not clear?"

There was a long silence. "Not landing here."

"We have a passenger to pick up…do you read?"

Silence.

"Dan, something isn't right there." Keith finally chimed in. *Duh.*

"Yeah, I gather that. Well, the weather around here is getting iffy anyway. So let the Peace Corps dude take the boat. Let's head to Gbadolité, save us a lot of time anyway."

I felt the Caravan change course, banking slight left as he settled on the new coordinates. I breathed a sigh of relief. Gbadolité was sophisticated. Heck, I could even suffer to spend the night there, if the hotel still had running water. I pictured myself swimming in the pool, drinking coke. They even had a restaurant. Of course, despite the lengthy menu offerings, they only cooked one dish.

"Be there in about 45 minutes."

Ian and I looked at each other and smiled. Oh well. Ian had caught on, he was going with the flow. I glanced back at Keith who gave his characteristic shrug. I liked our team, the three musketeers on a *Weekend at Bernies.*

My ears popped as the plane descended to Gbadolité. This was a very nice airport... or had been. The Concorde actually landed here once.

"Gbado Tower, this is November 483 sierra pappa. Permission to land in five minutes, do you copy, over?"

"Novermber 483 Sierra Pappa, this is Gbado air traffic control. Do you copy me?"

His English was good.

"Copy," said Dan.

"Three sierra pappa, this is reserved military air space...turn away now. Over?"

Since when was a commercial airport reserved military air space?

"Urgent, need to land, low on fuel. Request permission to land."

"Three sierra pappa, you are in violation of reserved military airspace. Depart the airspace directly or you will be fired upon."

"What the....No, Gbado Air Traffic, we have a filed flight plan from Kin, passengers and cargo to unload." Dan's voice began to crack, I shifted nervously in my seat.

"This is your last warning. We have you on radar."

Dan toggled a switch on the instrument panel and spoke to us. "I don't have a clue what is going on, but hey, nobody down there can hit crap..."

I had never heard a missionary pilot "swear" before. This was *très serieux*.

"We can land, but we could end up in all kinds of trouble. They don't have chase planes or AA down there...."

"AA?" Ian, thinking it was another acronym or a recovery group.

"Anti aircraft fire...What do you want to do?"

Keith spoke up. "Well, we know the people here at Gbado a lot better. I think we can land ok and just talk our way though all this."

"And get shot at!?" Ian's voice raised an octave. I placed a reassuring hand on his, yet inside I was churning.

Dan appeared to think for a while. "OK, no can do. We have to operate in this country tomorrow too...we need to head back..."

"Back to WHERE?" I was starting to feel anxious. This wasn't just a usual glitch in the usual African adventure. We were 5,000 feet high above the very same jungle I had hoped not to crash in.

Suddenly the plane shuttered and turned steeply to the right. I looked out at thin trail of smoke streaming from the left wing.

"Uh oh." Dan said, trying to sound casual. "Maybe no AA but they got big enough guns. Sorry folks." He suddenly banked hard left, then right, and climbed for altitude. "That's Bemba's group down there."

Nothing further happened as he turned the Caravan out of harm's way. "Well, they hit something. Doesn't seem serious...I took a bird into the engine once, that wasn't good..."

"Tell the scary stories later, Dan." I was looking at the treetops.

"Man, probably an electrical fire....everything seems to work ok. Nothing vital...I hope. We gotta diddy-mau outta here though. Back to Bumba, ok?"

Dan seemed to cover his own anxiety up with quick smiles and shrugs of the shoulder, but the sweat pouring out of his armpits gave his nervousness away.

"Dan - I thought the runway is not clear!" Ian said. So much for going with the flow.

"Well, we'll see soon enough. If not, there is a plantation nearby we can land at. I told you there were always lots of options." A smile, a twitch, I watched as his shirt took on a different shade through the neck and arms.

The cloud cover obscured the port-city of Bumba. Dan forced the nose down through the cloud layer. I hoped to God nothing was sticking up higher than 700 meters, and that's a lot of hope coming from an atheist. I guess to be really honest, a fake-atheist. God seems to be an inevitable place of wishing and hoping and praying that I turn to in times of need. Hate that. Try as I might, He's just there, but I won't admit it to anyone but maybe my own psyche. Ian reached over and gripped my hand. I gripped back.

"Anna, if this is the end..."

"Oh shut up, Ian." But I held his hand tightly and thought of words that I too would like to say if this was indeed "the end." This couldn't be the end, not like this. I had a few loose ends of my life to wrap up and some things to get straight before I met St. Peter or whoever tended the Pearly Gates these days. Dad's body was still not laid to rest. I still hadn't found love. I hadn't ordered every drink combination on the Starbucks menu. I couldn't die yet. The rain continued to drench our little plane, only gray out the window. We had to be lower than 700 meters. I braced, white knuckled Ian's hand, expecting to clip a tree any moment. I could hear Keith practicing his gift of tongues just behind me. At least someone knew how to pray. I hoped our plane didn't burst into flames. I wanted out as soon as possible. My stomach was somewhere up near my lungs and was threatening a dramatic exit out my throat.

Then we burst through. Maybe ten feet above the tree tops.

"Jesus!" It sounded like swearing, but I had a feeling it was more a one-word prayer than profanity.

He pulled up just a hair. We just cut across the airstrip at 90 degrees. He could hardly bank without his wingtip hitting the treetops. He gained a few meters and made a long slow bank to set us up for the landing.

"Anybody see anything on the strip?"

"Nothing" we all said at once.

"Maybe some goats at the far end." I thought I saw something there.

More smoke. The plane lined up for a steep landing. He was coming in faster than I had ever experienced it before. He wanted down *now*. The wheels hit the strip about two feet after we flashed over the end. Immediately the engines went into reverse thrust and we were thrown brutally forward against our harness as the brakes began to bite. The plane began to slide far to the left and Dan compensated...too much, we swung dangerously to the right. The buildings were rushing by and I could see smoke pouring out of somewhere. It felt like my ABS on AJ as we shuttered and swung back and forth down the rough runway. Couldn't he just release the drag chute? But we were slowing. We were going to live through this. I was suddenly glad I hadn't made any deathbed vows or confessed any sentimental B.S. to Ian.

Ian's head smashed against the windowpane and I instinctively put my head between my knees so as to not follow suit. From behind me I heard cracking and banging and knew that our luggage was flying about from side to side despite the tarp tying it all down. The Ziegler was also shimmying back and forth. The moment I took to look behind me, the ties securing the box snapped loose and the Ziegler cracked hard against the partition. It broke free from the restraints along with all the rest of the baggage and slid forward at an alarming rate. The coffin crashed along down the aisle way like a log ride reaching its end, fell on its side, and collided with me pinning me down hard. Suddenly I found myself cheek-to-cheek with Dad and only a thin layer of glass between us. His face had turned a bit toward mine; he seemed to be enjoying all this. I stared at his eyelids, and then, I saw them open and smile. He got up, stretched, yawned and said "Hey ya Annie! Heck of a ride!" The surreal situation held me severely frozen in place, easier to do now that the plane had rapidly bled off speed as Dan was taxing to the tower. I let go of Ian's hand, wrinkled and white from loss of blood flow, and shook my head to rid myself of the hallucination resulting in a resounding thump as my forehead hit the Ziegler like a drum. Ian turned and looked at me and gasped.

"Bloody - Shite! Keith! Anna…almost crushed by a coffin!" Ian was using his wide vocabulary and doing all the freaking out that I would have been doing if I hadn't been fixated, mesmerized by my Father's face - white, pale, powdered with make-up, bent and crooked in his tiny tin Ziegler home. *Hey ya Annie. Hey ya.* His voice echoed in my head. I finally moved away from his face as Ian gave the Zig enough push to fall back. I lunged forward and threw up in the aisle.

"KEITH! DAN!" Ian was holding up my hair as all the morning's kwanga and baguettes and papaya ended up in a nasty mess on the plane's floor. Keith came wobbling down the aisle, stepped with difficulty over both of us.

"You guys ok back here? Look at this mess. Sure you're ok?"

I left my head down and hid my face in my hands. Ian stroked my hair and said "shhhh," without the "ite" this time.

Dan killed the engine and yanked off his headset. I could tell he was steamed.

The noise of the engine subsided. I could hear everyone breathing a deep sigh of relief.

"I can't believe it." I finally looked up, everyone was staring at the Ziegler and then at me. It was terribly quiet for just a moment.

"Anna, everybody, I'm so sorry." Dan started to apologize, but lost his words, probably lost his appetite too when he saw my lovely contribution on the floor of his plane.

"Can I get a voucher to compensate me for this inconvenience?" *And some money for more therapy?* I needed humor to break me from the spell I felt I was under. The bile in the throat hurt as I spoke. I needed water. Humor always opens a door. I managed a weak smile toward Dan as I wiped my mouth with my sleeve, avoiding "eye contact" with Dad.

Dan turned in his seat, still looking ghostly serious, but the look faded. Any landing you walked away from was a good landing, even with corpses practically flying loose.

"Anna, the next time you fly with AIM, it's free." Dan joined me in the remedy of gallows humor.

"Goodie - so our trip back is on you?" He laughed in spite of himself.

"No, because you'll owe me for the carpet." That I did.

"Well, let's go face the music. I'll just explain we were shot down over Gbadolité and had to crash here. Shouldn't be a problem…right."

I could see a couple of officials coming out on the airstrip to meet us. They didn't look happy. But so what. We were down, and alive, and little bit closer to…somewhere.

We all disembarked and let Dan lead the way. I noticed a couple of soldiers out on the tarmac now with those banana clips. They looked sérieux and pissed. My kind of people.

Ian took me by the elbow. "Anna, please just let Dan handle this, ok?"

For the life of me I didn't know what he was talking about. For all my faux bravado, I knew we were in deep, as Dan put it, "crap." These AK totting soldiers were not standard issue government troops. These were the Bemba irregulars. They looked to be in their late teens. Not child soldiers exactly, but the next worst thing. Brainwashed, hormonal teenagers with guns.

Dan walked towards the most obvious senior man out there.

"*Je regrettes de devoir attérir ici…*" he started in bad French. With a nod from Senior Official, one soldier stepped up and hammered Dan in the gut with the butt of his AK. Dan doubled over and fell to his knees, coughing badly.

Ian started forward. I put a hand on him. "Don't." He didn't. Keith walked slowly forward with hands held up. He spoke in Lingala. He was one of them.

"*Mbote, baninga*. Hello friends. *Dis, tozali na likambo te*. Hey, we don't have any problem here."

Dan slowly got up with a little moan, clutching his stomach.

Keith said, still in fluent Lingala. He was "*mwana na mboka*" – a son of the village. He threw in all the slang. "I apologize. The plane caught fire, we had to land. Please, look for yourselves. It wasn't in our hands." He shrugged. Everybody seemed to take a step back and relax. Even I knew enough to shut up for a change. It was one thing arguing with a corrupt official in Kin and another facing hopped up (yes, pupils dilated…a sign I knew well) adolescents with lethal weapons.

Senior Official approached Dan. "I told you not to land."

"Sorry. It was either land here or die."

Senior seemed to accept that. He had no doubt seen the streaming smoke from the Caravan. He seemed to come to a conclusion in his mind. Then in French…

"*Ca va*. Ok. I understand. There will be an investigation."

"I understand."

"Thorough investigation."

"Yes, of course."

"Probably some fines."

Now we were all on solid ground. I could sense Ian about to ask what was happening.

"It will be ok, we're talkin' money now." I whispered to Ian. Money was a language that Ian *did* understand.

We walked towards the Tower. Dan was holding his side as he turned and addressed me.

"Anna, we can probably get through this, get the plane fixed, get out of here. You don't have to go any farther, do you?"

Ian just laughed at the notion that I might turn around just because of being shot down and a crash landing.

We followed Senior into the Tower and ended up in a room that for all the world resembled that 8X8 claustrophobic little shake down room at N'Djili airport. *Maybe they just build them that way at every airport.*

Now that we were back on the familiar territory of pure undisguised graft and greed, I felt my fainting spirit revive.

Also in Lingala, just to establish that we were seasoned not-to-be-messed-with vets, I said "Camarade, I feel badly about landing here against your explicit orders not to land. I am sure there is a fine we must pay."

Ian instinctively went for his wallet, good boy, but I had it in my sling.

"*Oui, madame…*"

"*Mademoiselle.*"

"*Pardon. Mademoiselle…*"

And so it went. The forced landing cost us about a hundred bucks. Ian's dollars. Just as we began to exit the Tower Room I asked Senior, "Please, forgive me for asking, but what was blocking the strip when we tried to land earlier?"

"Ah, mademoiselle…" we were almost friends now. "I should not tell you this."

"Nobody else will know, just between you and me." I gave him a little smile for good measure.

"The plane of Marshall Jean Pierre Bemba had just landed here."

"Of course." *Marshall?*

"Who?" Ian took my elbow away and began his questions.

"You keep eavesdropping. Bemba, he is the warlord up here, remember? Apparently, he is here, and this air space is military now.

"Did you know him?"

"Nope. Dad may have somehow. We often ran through the village where his extended family lived, aunts, uncles, kids, etc. I met a few of them once. Back then, no one knew he'd be the warlord that is he today."

"His mommy must be proud." Ian attempted a joke, but I'm sure Bemba's mom probably was proud. He is neither evil nor good; so hard to place a political leader of the Congo in either category. Leading a coup, and donning title "war lord" is not necessarily an honorable picture, but perhaps Bemba had some higher virtue to offer.

Keith walked out to the street and considered the alternatives before him. He noted a couple of autos, actual *cars*...these would never do. He also saw a couple of larger commercial vehicles that were fully loaded and evidently ready to depart. Where, he had no idea. He then spotted a Hilux. These sturdy Toyotas were to the Congo what camels were to the Sahara. Indestructible and miserly on the diesel. He walked over to it and handed out the cash. We were booked.

In the meantime we unloaded the Caravan. Dan was on the radio back to Kin trying to get some people and materials up to Bumba to fix the plane. Soon the Hilux drove onto the tarmac - another ten dollar permit - and we unloaded the Ziegler and our stuff onto the truck while crowds gathered around and watched curiously. Dad's face peered out from behind the glass and I covered him with my shawl. We hopped into the truck, and I felt my body began to relax. We made it through the crash landing and the near soldier-abduction. One more hurdle, one step closer to the grave. Dad's grave, that is. Or maybe mine too. I felt weary and shut my eyes for half a second and wiped the dust off my forehead. Sleep wasn't too far away, it was nearing dusk. I needed a gin and tonic. I hoped they had a full bar. Even a mini bar. I'd even stoop to take a Mike's Hard Lemonade if I was hard pressed.

Keith gave directions to the driver to take us to a hotel in town. I remembered enough to know that this would not be Sandals Vacation resort. But as we pulled up to a group of dilapidated buildings, I was dismayed by its state of disrepair. The war had left ghostly fingerprints everywhere, and this always surprised me. I wondered how little I truly knew about what happened here while I was gone. We drove into the courtyard of what was clearly a hotel and bar. My heart skipped a beat. Captain Morgan or Mr. Daniels was waiting for me. The music of Kin was blaring loudly with its tonal notes and exuberant rhythms. A few customers were sitting in the shade drinking. The arrival of three Mondeles and a casket created some interest. I was getting used to being stared at. Keith "checked" us in.

Once in the "lobby" I sat on Dad protectively. I watched nervously as Ian walked over to the bar and tried to order a couple drinks. He knew the remedy that I wanted for my nerves. I smiled as he stumbled through his memorized phrases from French-for-Dummies. Finally I saw him reach over the counter, grab a bottle and hand it to the bar tender. Good boy. He came back with two Scotch neats. He sat on Dad with me, close to me, and without a word, we both clinked our cups together, silently toasting to our crash landing. I dragged my fingers through my dirty hair and rubbed my temples. I could still see Dad's frozen face such centimeters from my own. I knew it would take years and many dollars with Marilyn to try and erase that moment, and I hadn't yet even made a dent in the fingers-of-my-Mom moment. I was screwed. Dad was suspended in my memory now as a corpse that sits up and says *Hey ya* while waving a hand around rigidly like a Mime. Without a word Ian wrapped his arm around me and pulled me in closer. I slid across the Ziegler and rested my head on his shoulder. My daydream of toasting on my balcony with a "Here's to barely making it out alive," was becoming frighteningly accurate.

"The god's must be crazy, huh, Tarzan?"

"Indeed they are…indeed they are, Jane." Ian hadn't even flinched at the reference to one of my favorite old-time cult classic movies. Maybe we had a future. We both sucked the scotch through our teeth and gulped with a grimace. I smiled.

"No ice, that's good."

"Why is that?"

"Never know what kind of water goes into the ice."

I tilted my head and eyed Ian inquisitively as he drank. He looked tired, but yet alert and ready for more adventure. Maybe he could be Indiana Jones and I could be his Marion. I missed my eight ball. I missed my movies; at least I managed to keep one foot in the MGM world. Kept reality at bay.

Keith returned with our keys. He eyed our drinks but didn't say anything. We all gladly parted ways to get some rest. My room had a single bed with a foam mattress covered with a stained sheet, a table, lamp, candles, and a chair. That was it. A window looked out on the courtyard. I heard Keith negotiating with the Hilux owner about just leaving the truck there for the night and keeping dear old Dad in the back. Money changed hands, the universal lubricant. I watched, feeling uneasy, and sauntered back to the truck. I told Keith that Dad would stay in my room again. And that was that.

Suddenly I was exhausted. The adrenalin that had sustained me from the fly-by and the shoot-down and the crash landing and Dad's "embrace" was gone.

Even this bed looked good. I laid down and said a prayer of thanks to something or someone out there who miraculously protected the Ziegler enough to keep it from breaking open during the crash. A broken seal would be cause for quite an expedited burial adventure. The last thing I needed to see and smell was Dad becoming purple, putrid, bloated and the like. I looked over at him, eyes still shut, and pulled a blanket over my head.

Night, Dad.

Night Annie, sleep well.

I smiled.

No, you *sleep well. Just stay put.*

CHAPTER TWELVE

Bumba was a river town. The place ran on scam and hustle. When the barges came in, the areas around the port were jammed with people who were either buying or selling or stealing, or all three. Lines of sweaty porters poured out of the barges with sacks on their heads while another line entered. Within a block of the "hotel" I could buy a baby croc or have one bbq'd on a stick. Under large parasols, vendors sat by wheeled carts advertising Primus beer and Arctic Ice Cream bars. A terrific pairing. Trucks of every kind and size also made their way down to the river's edge to discharge cargo or take on a load. Women and men and children were knee deep in the river bending over large rocks with soap in hand, beating their clothes against the surface and scrubbing. It was the local laundromat. Just a few yards downstream a man scooped the water up in his hands and took a drink.

It was towards this line of departing trucks that Keith headed. He was determined to negotiate transportation of our special cargo from here to Gbadolité and hopefully on to Bosobolo. That would be a couple hundred miles, depending on detours - and you could depend on some. It took us 40 minutes in the Caravan, it could take a few days on the road. Assuming the bridges were ok and the roads weren't washed out. Assuming the truck was ok. Assuming Dad wouldn't fall out again. Dad always said that assuming makes an ass out of you and me. Ass-U-Me. I was beginning to see his point.

It was about 10 in the morning when I walked out to the little patio area of the hotel. My favorite African tree was swaying in the breeze, we called it the Franzy Panzy tree. The tree had little white perfumed flowers with a small orange center, smelled like honeysuckle and gardenia, smelled like old memories. I think it was the same flower used to get lei'd - as in a Hawaiian Lei.

Speaking of lei'd…Ian was already sitting out on the balcony.

"Morning." He looked up and winked at me.

"Uh oh. No 'good' in front of that?" I said, and slumped down in a small dusty plastic chair.

"Not feelin' so good."

"Too much Scotch?" Ian was hunched over rubbing his forehead.

"No, actually - something I ate last night."

"You ate last night?" I remember I headed straight to bed and crashed, no dinner.

"Yeah, actually, Keith and I stayed up for awhile and ate at the 'restaurant.'" Ian made quotation marks with his fingers.

"What did you have?"

"Mpondu, sheep intestines, the usual. It was nice actually, had a couple cold cokes, yup, COLD."

"You ate the food?" Ian's backbone was growing stronger, more African than I had anticipated.

"Yeah! We ate some good hot food, mostly we just talked for hours."

"You and Keith?"

"Yeah. That guy, I tell ya, he surprised me, he actually really has a way with words."

"Oh, no kidding, he can tell some of the wildest stories about snakes and coups - "

"Not like that, other...words. About life, love, God."

"God." I eyed him suspiciously.

"Yeah." Ian and I just stared at each other. It felt like there was a world of conversation waiting to happen about our thoughts, philosophies, fears and spirituality, or lack of, or of what our relationship was, or was not. But my near-death experience yesterday was enough spirituality to last me for quite a while.

"Speaking of God, I have to go check on Ziegler, he's in my room." Changing the subject was my forte.

"You're using the Ziegler as a proper noun now... interesting. I thought Ziegy stayed in the truck last night?" Ian followed me down the hall.

"Nah, I had him brought in. Was a little nervous about him being out there, alone." Dad had come to life for me in some ways, I couldn't leave him in the truck.

Ian and I headed back down the hall to my room. Ziegler was still there. And so was a strange new friend.

"Did you order that?" I pointed at the stranger sitting on the box.

"No, didn't order it. It wasn't on the menu."

"Is that a -"

"That's a cat."

"I know it's a cat, but what is it doing on my box, and how did it get in my room?"

Lying on top of Dad's small window, a small gray cat was curled up on the Ziegler, peacefully asleep, its little stomach rising and falling with small breaths.

"It must be the hotel cat or something, looks domestic."

"Well, obviously, it isn't a jungle cat, Ian." Lawyers were so literal about everything in life. Of course it's a cat. Of course it's domestic. Of course, Ian. of course. I was starting to like this about Ian, it was surprisingly endearing.

"Maybe he wants to go with you."

"Sure, right away. Wonder why he picked a cold metal surface?"

"Maybe it's attracted to the peace that surrounds death."

"Peace? And death?"

"Sure, Keith said that -"

"I don't care what Keith said about it. What do you know about it? Dad has yet to 'rest in peace,' *that* much I know." My tongue had no rein, heat rose to my face.

"How do you know? Maybe he is, you know, in peace." Ian was still trying to get philosophical with me. *Fine, I'll wade in, to my toes.*

"I just think that the body and the spirit are somehow intricately linked. And yet, here is his body, bouncing around the jungle, bouncing for hours...going from here to there, changing hands, plane rides...flying around in its box, it's awful. It's anything *but* peaceful. Death is not peaceful!"

I was feeling my blood pressure rising. "It's disturbing. His face, right there. It's just...awful. I hate it. I really, really HATE IT!" I kicked the Ziegler with my toes, surprised at my sudden outburst of emotion. But it was welling up in me, and threatening to wash over me like a dreadful tsunami. I couldn't let it. I didn't let it out at the funeral; I didn't let it out on the plane. Yet I couldn't stop feeling overwhelmingly angry and bitter. I hated being blatantly faced with the ethereal divide between life and death and the hereafter. I want to ignore it and walk blissfully and spiritually ignorant through life until my sudden end. I missed my Dad. I hated that he was with me, but unable to laugh, to talk, to smile. Where was he anyway? Was he here? Was he...*there?* And yet I could see him? I couldn't stand the constant reminder of my ambivalent, hesitant spirituality.

I had lost track of my words and my thoughts, put my hand over my eyes and rubbed them, pretending to be tired. I wiped away the moisture before Ian could notice. This trip was wearing me down. I had to get home soon before I cracked. I couldn't stand the dead body around me anymore. I didn't want to sleep with it in a hotel room. I didn't want it in the truck. I didn't want to carry him, I wanted him buried, I wanted to go home. I wished he hadn't asked me to do this…who else would he have asked?

"Anna, love - I'm sorry, we're almost through."

"No we're not. Not even close." *And don't call me love.* Something inside of me said that. Something that instinctively knew there was a lot more to come.

The gray cat looked up and yawned wide, displaying his pointy teeth. He closed his mouth and looked at me with his green eyes. I looked back. *Never have a staring contest with a cat.*

"Meow! Kitty kitty!" I stretched out my hand and offered him a pet. He took it gladly and his big motor engine started up inside his throat.

"He's so cute!" I was smitten with him and picked him up.

"I would have never thought YOU liked cats."

"I don't. What do you mean by that anyway? Why wouldn't *I* like cats? And in any case, there's lots you don't know about me, yet."

"I like that, 'yet.'" I allowed Ian to pull me into him while I dumped the cat back down. I hated to admit that I needed a hug, or a feline for that matter. And that's pretty much all I needed at the moment. Ian wrapped his strong arms around me and held me close. I could tell he was smelling my hair, and I instantly pulled away. Not for fear of intimacy this time, but because I knew my hair couldn't be smelling like peaches right about now.

"I'm going to name him Ziegler."

"You already did."

"No, not the box, the cat."

"You can't do that."

"Why not?"

"Ok, do it, but you can't take him with us. We have enough cargo."

True enough. I loved his little furry company in spite of myself. "Keep Dad company, Ziegler, we'll be back in a moment." The cat curled back down on top of the crate and tucked his head deep inside his paws and let his motor slowly subside. I had to admit, he looked peaceful. The wispy curtains blew in the wind, in and out of the screen-less window. I glanced back and wondered if that was similar to all that hung between the beating of my heart and the "other side." A delicate threadbare cloth? My over-inflated sense of security and pride was shaking. Maybe we would find the fountain of youth somewhere at the source of the Ebola River.

CHAPTER THIRTEEN

I heard the truck a moment before I smelled it. An old Mercedes L323 chugged around the corner spewing some kind of satanic mix of diesel and sulfur. It was at least two car lengths long and wide with a small cab and a vast open tail. A green tarp was fastened over the cargo, some of which was dried fish by the smell of it. A number of people perched on top.

"Well, Ian, looks like our chariot has arrived."

Ian looked at that truck. "It has to be fifty years old."

"At least. Think you can manage this?"

"Anything for you, my dear." Ian stretched his foot up high on top of the tire, and yanked himself up to the top of the truck, turned around and grinned. He was becoming quite the safari man.

Keith climbed out of the cab and signaled me to come over.

"Monsieur Nganago here has agreed to take us as far as Gbadolité."

"I bet we could convince him to take us the rest of the way." I could see the end in sight.

"No doubt. Let's get our stuff."

For some reason I didn't like Dad being referred to as stuff.

We brought our carry-ons and the Ziegler over to the Mercedes, without the cat. A small crowd had gathered to watch. A couple of the working girls from the hotel edged up to me.

"Hello. How are you?" Trying on their English, a favorite past time.

"I'm good, just fine, thanks. And you?"

"We are very fine also, thank you. Where go you?"

"To Mojamboli." Instinctively I gave them the name of some other place down another road.

"Why?"

"*Kosala tourism.*" I switched to Lingala. I didn't really want to answer these questions.

"*Ajali mobali na yo* - is he your man?" one giggled and gestured at Ian, who had hopped back down from the truck and was making his way over.

"No, do you want him?" They both laughed.

"Not after last night." I choked and laughed. Most Congolese women didn't have what I would call an acerbic sense of humor.

"What are you all giggling about?" Ian must have heard his name.

"I offered to sell you to them, but they are only bidding one euro."

"Hey, I'll pay them!" Did Ian recognize a working girl when he saw one, or did he stumble on a funny line by accident?

"You go with them and you'll probably pay the rest of your life."

The Ziegler came out of the hotel. Nganago and his "boi chauffeur" felt the weight and then walked it towards the back of the Mercedes. They pushed the box up onto the back of the truck. Boi jumped up and moved some stuff out of the way, and the box slid in under the tarp out of sight.

"Nini ezali kati na sanduku - what's in the box?" These gals were persistent. Why not just be satisfied with Ian? I had best give some kind of plausible answer. I thought about saying rifles, but who knew what kind of trouble that gossip could cause. I couldn't say medicines or we'd be robbed before we got out of Bumba.

"A dead body." They laughed. The truth will set you free.

"Let's get going. Hope to make Yaseke by evening. Sounds like the chauffeur wants to stop there for the night." Keith motioned us towards the truck. "Anna, mind riding in front with Nganago?"

This was of course the place of honor. It would normally go to Keith, white hair, age, status, male and the like. However I represented the tip of the spear in this bit of cross-cultural jousting. Americans gave the top spot to women who were either too beautiful to get mussed up or too fragile to subject themselves to the rigors the men so gallantly volunteer for. It was chivalry of course, which I don't like unless it is genuine and directed towards me in particular. The cab would be hot and smelly, but it had a relatively comfortable seat and would be in the shade. It was too noisy to have to make small talk. That was good. Riding atop the tarp hanging on for dear life would have the wind and dust and sun and was sometimes dangerous. I feared for Ian's life.

"Uncle Keith, why don't you ride up front for a while? We'll see how it goes, ok?" He actually looked relieved.

"OK, just give me a holler if you want to change."

I fastened my scarf tight around my head and donned my Marco Ricci sunglasses. I had on the wrap around all-purpose sari and Teva sandals. I definitely looked jungle chic. Ian, *au contraire,* was still wearing a sport jacket and slacks. At least he had put on a pair of Converse. I was surprised he owned a pair. His perfect haircut, however, was looking more and more untidy, sweat was a part of his attire now, and his shadow was growing nicely into a beard. Maybe eventually, he could pass for Tarzan's second cousin once removed. Keith was just "missionary" - jeans, kaki shirt, baseball cap. Cubs. Yawn.

I climbed up on top, found a place I could actually sit and hang on the ropes that strapped everything down. Ian fastened himself in place next to me. A dozen other Congolese passengers also climbed on board. With a snort of black soot, the Mercedes diesel came to life and ground into gear. We lurched forward. The rpm built up - my AJ tuned ears always caught such things - and built up higher, then at about 5 mph he shifted into second. That was one low granny gear. I longed for my video I-pod, wished I could sit back and watch some great flick like "Hunt for the Red October" to pass the time. Instead, I knew that I would be popping Vicodin, and gaining bruises on my nicely pilates-toned tush.

"Want to play the alphabet game?" I asked.

"How do you play that?"

"Ian. Seriously. Didn't you take any road trips with your family when you were a kid?"

"We flew to D.C. once."

"What did you do there?"

"Lawyers' conference."

"Of course. Ok, let's not talk about your sad childhood. This is how the game works." I explained to Ian that we would start with A and make our way to Z, stating things we were going to bring on the trip.

I started. "I'm going to Goyongo, and I'm going to bring an axe."

"No you're not."

"Ian. I'm not REALLY bringing an axe, I'm saying I am, for the game. Then you say something like, I'm going to Goyongo, and I'm bringing an axe and a bear."

"Why would I bring a bear?"

"You're missing the point, you repeat what I say, I repeat what you say, and we make stuff up - it's supposed to be a challenge for our memory. Ok, I'll go again. I'm going to the Congo, and I'm bringing an axe, a bear, and a candy cane."

"It's not even Christmas." And the game ended before it even started. It was useless.

Ian looked so confused, I felt sorry for him. I had flashbacks to *his* sorry childhood, and it wasn't pretty.

We jostled along in the truck in silence, watching the scenery. We were almost out of town. The shops were getting smaller. Some children ran after us waving and yelling something in our direction. It was a favorite past time, to yell after the vehicles. What the heck, I waved back. A boy ran by whipping a stick on top of an old iron bicycle tire rim as it rolled along. I unwrapped my scarf and wiped the sweat off my head. The crowded truck added at least ten degrees to the already thick, humid ninety-degree weather. At least we had some wind in our hair. One man peed out the other side of the truck. Better outside the truck than in. I closed my eyes and tried to at least rest, I knew I wouldn't sleep. Ian took his hand and pushed my head down upon his shoulder. Amazingly comfortable.

The shadows were getting longer as the sun began its rapid descent. A few painful hours had passed. A bit of edge was taken off the sweltering heat. In an hour it would be pitch black. I hoped that the headlights worked. The horn sure did. The road was narrow and badly eroded. The Mercedes was back in first gear, grinding gamely away. As the road levels changed, we swayed dramatically from one side to another, not unlike riding a camel. The jungle closed in around the narrowing road and the overhead branches almost met at places. We came to a hill and began the descent towards a small river at the bottom. I could see that the log bridge was more or less intact. We were sure to stop and arrange a couple of the logs before passing over it. There was some activity at the bridge, looked like a bamboo pole blocking the road. Then I saw a small shack and couple of soldiers there. It was inevitable, I supposed, to have to pass through roadblocks, but we had come so far from town with nobody stopping us that I was beginning to hope. No doubt it would be another hassle, shake-down, *une infraction grave*, and a permit of some kind to continue on.

The Mercedes shuddered to a stop by the pole. These guards were not teenagers. There were four that I could see. Two approached the truck, two others were alertly watching the scene. All were armed with the ubiquitous AK-47. I could see an antenna running from the shack to the nearest tree.

"*Descendez* - get out." A tall very thin guard with a white streak of hair across the top of his head like a Mohawk gestured at Nganago. The other guard was his complete opposite, short, fat, bulbous nose – a bit like Shrek. He already had unslung his piece.

Nganago got out and showed them whatever papers he needed to show. Mohawk looked through them with little interest. Then he looked into the cab and saw Keith, then up at the others and us.

"*Qui êtes vous*? - who are you?" I didn't like the sound of his voice.

I knew that Keith preferred Lingala but he responded in French to show respect. "I am Keith Carlson. We are heading to Gbadolité. We are missionaries." *Bloody right we are*, I thought. But now was not the time to argue the point.

"Passport."

Keith handed it over.

"Get out...everybody, get off the truck, stand over here." He pointed to the tire.

Ian said, "Anna, I don't like this. Is this normal?"

"How should I know? I left here when I was 17 before the war, before kids had AK-47s instead of toy trucks they made from balsa wood. Sure, this is probably normal for a bandit ridden, war-torn country."

"Take it easy, Anna. Just asking."

We all got down. Shrek pushed one of the men hard against the truck. He cried out but didn't struggle. Nobody reacted. The other two soldiers climbed up on the truck and began to cut the ropes, intent to see what was underneath.

"Capitain, s'il vous plaît…" began Nganago, "I have an invoice here of everything. No need for that!" Capitain turned his AK around and cracked it on top of his forehead. Nganago gasped and sank to the ground.

One of the passengers had been slowly edging towards the end of truck. Suddenly he flipped out of sight of Shrek and around the corner, running hard for the brush. He only needed three more steps before he would disappear into the lush undergrowth. He raced out of my sight. Then the clatter of the AK. Silence. Nobody moved. Nobody was heard thrashing through the brush.

"Don't even move, you guys," Keith muttered under his beard. He didn't need to tell us. I was rooted in place, petrified. This was not the Africa of my childhood. My knees were shaking, my blood had turned to ice and I was unashamedly gripping Ian's arm.

"Silence! Get up."

Nganago struggled back to his feet, but still bent over.

A shout came from one of the soldiers up on the truck. He threw down a burlap bag, then another. Several more came after it. They weren't heavy.

Some kind of produce. Suddenly, in my gut, I knew what it must be. Drugs.

"Keith, Ian, that is hemp in there, I am sure."

"Hemp?"

"Hemp. Mary Jane. Weed, Ganja, whatever you want to call it. We hitched a ride with some mules."

"Mules? You mean, drug trafficking?" Ian always took a moment to process.

"Silence!" This time Ian was hit hard in the stomach and as he doubled over the butt caught him on the forehead and down he went. I went for him only to be grabbed by my hair savagely yanked back and flung against the truck. Keith started to move, but I shook my head. We were all going to live through this if we just didn't provoke them. I was wrong. He slammed my head again, hard against the truck and I saw stars. For the first time, I was frightened for my life.

"*Salope blanche* - white whore." Well, he had the white part right anyway. I used my Lingala again hoping that could help.

"*Boni, tika ngai, nasaleli yo mabe te* - What is this, leave me alone, I never did you any harm." I tried to sound tough and confident, but I know my fear gave me away, I had never experienced this kind of total terror before in my life.

The last thing I saw was Mohawk's ugly face an inch from mine. Yellow broken teeth, bad breath. The last thing I remembered was he pulling me back for another slam against the truck.

CHAPTER FOURTEEN

I fought for consciousness. My head hurt, my whole body hurt. I could hear voices, but they seemed far away, dialects I didn't recognize. Laughter. Sounds of tin dishes, eating. I slowly opened one eye then the other and groaned as terrible pain racked my body. I didn't move a muscle. I knew better. I didn't see anybody. I was on a dirt floor in what was obviously a round mud hut of some kind, but it looked solid and the door was made of lumber. I wasn't tied up. Nobody thought I could free myself and escape, and they were no doubt right about that. Light trickled in from outside. It was daytime. By the heat it felt like maybe mid morning or later afternoon. I had no idea how much time had passed. My watch was gone, so were my Marco Ricci's. That really ticked me off on some level, although I knew I had greater problems to consider. My hand went to my forehead and felt the bump. I sat up an inch at a time until I was leaning against the wall. The room was empty, not a bed or a cup or a chair. I was alone.

I faded in and out of awareness. I vaguely remembered seeing Ian on the ground, then being dragged by his feet. Thirst began to work its way into dominating my thoughts. My tongue was dry and a bit swollen. Where was Dad? Keith? Ian? Oddly enough, though afraid, I realized I was not terrified. If they had wanted me dead, I would be dead already. I figured somehow or other being white and rich and something of a local gal would win the day. They weren't going to kill us. They wanted something, they always did. I just hoped it wasn't what I was most afraid of... I don't know how I would ever recover from that kind of raw abuse. I fell asleep in spite of the thought.

I awoke in the dark. It was pitch black inside, not a flicker of light. It reminded me of spelunking the inside of Carlsbad cavern when the guide turned the lights off. It was disorienting. Without eyesight, all my other senses were heightened and every nerve was on edge. I waved my hand in front of my face and saw nothing. I was on the ground, back to a wall. My head still throbbed fiercely but the edge was off. Now the thirst was the tormenter. I tried to summon up some saliva to wet my mouth and swallow, but there was nothing. Slowly I sat up and felt around. Nothing. I remembered the door was to my right. I inched my way up the wall until I was standing, swaying, leaning against the mud wall. I kept one hand on the wall and began to walk around the hut.

I felt the door and groped for the handle. Tried it gently. It was firmly locked. I finished the tour and came back around to the door again. A few sounds from the outside reached through the wall, an occasional bleat from a goat. A snore. Probably the watchman. Some scuffling in the thatch roof overhead. Whining of mosquitoes about my ears. But not many, thank God. I was all alone. *Where was everyone else?*

Sinking back down to the ground, I felt despair begin to wash over me. How could this be happening….to me? Just a few days ago I had been just fine, thank you! Great job, big money, fast car, great condo, some friends. Bored a bit with life already at age 30, well ok, 31. Well, I wasn't bored anymore. I kept up with news from Africa, more or less. Atrocities were always headliners, genocide, burning of villages, rape, displacing whole populations, corruption, violence, economics fueling tribal hatreds…the usual. Maybe I *was* in real danger. Maybe we'd all disappear into the "heart of darkness." *My God.*

Now that was a thought. Prayer. But somehow along the way in my life I had grown out of faith, or something like that. Religion had become irrelevant. God didn't matter, or we didn't matter to him perhaps. It felt wrong to begin to pray now just because I was stuck in a hard place. I don't suppose God likes being used as a magic blue genie. But hey, I'll try anything once. I started to pray.

"God…" I began, "If you are, I mean, if I am, *merde*….never mind." I can't even pray to God without swearing! Even if it was in French. This just wasn't working. Is there still something left to believe in, when there is nothing left to believe in? These words of my favorite postmodern cynical author, David Coupland seeped up into my head. He described himself as a broken person, pushed off the edge of loneliness, and when he climbed back up, his world never looked the same. I don't really know exactly what he meant, but it sounded deep, and I felt that I understood. Coupland, however, recovered somehow from brokenhood. Claimed he found God. So much for a fellow cynic. I wondered what Ian was thinking right now.

Ian…my mind reached out toward him. He was probably in a place like this one, or worse. I wanted him to be OK. I just really wanted *him*.

Sleep must have overcome me once again, as I awoke with a start when light filtered in. Smoke from the campfire reached me along with the aroma of coffee. What I would give for a cup of coffee… My muscles pulsed with a profound ache penetrating to my bones.

The door opened and in stepped Shrek again. My heart started racing. I wasn't used to the feeling of being afraid of anything, or anyone for that matter. But I was, I was terrified.

"*Telema* - stand up."

I stood up uneasily. I mustered up some of my old self and courage and spoke confidently, "I could use a drink. Maybe some of that coffee I smell, with sugar."

That got me a backhanded slap that snapped my neck around, accompanied with more insults. The "white slut" thing had better go. I felt blood dribble down my chin. He grabbed my arm and pulled me outside into the cool early-morning air. A light ground mist hovered here and there. A couple of women looked up from the fires, then quickly back down to their tasks. A quick glance around told me that we were in some kind of run down semi-abandoned town. It used to have operating stores.

There were a few cement buildings with eroded porches here and there, covered in rusting metal roofing. Didn't see the truck or any sign of anybody else. Great.

I wiped off the blood with my arm.

Shrek dragged me over to one of these old buildings, opened the door made of aluminum siding and pushed me inside. I stumbled but didn't fall as I collapsed onto a wall of packed-in people. The room was jammed. The hum of conversation died down instantly when they saw what had just been thrown in. Most were standing, a few were sitting around the edges, leaning on the wall. Most of those slouching against the wall were men. The women tended to be gathered on one side, the men on the other. A few children cried. Infants suckled. The stench of manioc and unwashed manioc-eating bodies and sewage was overwhelming. Flies droned about our heads. I wanted back in solitary confinement.

The other prisoners obviously didn't know what to do with me. The feeling was mutual. I sensed curiosity and not hostility. I gently pushed my way through the crowd towards the back corner. A way was magically made for me. Nobody wanted to get too close. One woman gestured at her spot against the wall. I smiled gratefully, not sure whether to give away my language secrets yet or not.

"Merci beaucoup." I sat down with my knees drawn up and leaned my head against the wall. The decibel level rebounded to the pre-entry level.

Dad had told me about jails like this. He visited them frequently to bail out a worker that had fallen afoul of the law in some way. I never expected to be in one. These little rooms were in every town of any size. People ended up here for debts, offending a chief, minor theft, failing to do *Salongo* - the obligatory Saturday morning labor required by the State. Of course rape was endemic in places like this. I opened my eyes and looked around again. There didn't seem to be an imminent threat. The women were gathered like circled wagons, the biggest mamas on the outside perimeter. The men seemed lethargic and somnolent in the stifling heat. Everyone was sweating profusely adding to the permeating odor. I wondered briefly what Al Pacino would think of *A Scent of a Woman* in here. The cement walls and tin roof formed an oven. There seemed to be one hole in the cement floor in the other corner. That was most certainly the "latrine." I would have to watch and see how that bit of protocol worked. I felt a lump rising in my throat, yet, oddly enough, being here gave me some hope. Anything could happen to me in some isolated ward. Here, there were people. They wouldn't have put me here had they wanted to disappear me. *Where were Ian and Keith and our driver? Where was Dad? I need some water or I will die.*

"*Pardon, madame, pardon, êtes-vous malade?* - excuse me, ma'am, are you ill?"

"*Mademoiselle...oui, je suis très malade*, et vous? - Miss... yes, I am very sick...thank you for asking. And you?" I extended the conversation. The ripe smell was intoxicating, but not in the way I frequently enjoyed. My head was spinning and my stomach was turning.

A man urinated in the corner. No big deal. That wasn't the protocol I was interested in.

"I am not bad." She was possibly about my age and had an infant snagged on one breast. She smiled and her white teeth almost sparkled. Her eyes were bloodshot though. She looked tired.

"I speak some French...finished 5th year in the secondary school...so I am the one to talk to you. Understand?"

"Yes."

"You are not French. You are American."

She deflated my pride. She could tell from those few words I had spoken? I needed to buy the Rosetta Stone for French and work on my accent. Or I just needed to live in Paris for a few good years, shopping and eating, drinking, and working on my accent.

"No, Canadian." I lied. Everyone likes Canadians. "Do you have any water? Some aspirin?"

"Aspirin. No. You have money? The guards will get what you need." She pulled out a small plastic bottle with a few ounces of liquid in it and gave it to me. I hesitated. This was hers, for her and her baby. She pushed it at me again. I took it and swallowed it gratefully.

For the first time I felt for my secreted money pouch. Not surprisingly it was gone. Ian's wallet too. I felt in the pocket of my shorts worn under the sari. There were a few bills. I thought I probably had fifty dollars there.

"Yes, a dollar maybe."

She said, "A dollar. Perhaps. One dollar for the aspirin, one for the guard. OK?"

"OK. What is your name, *mon amie*?" I was surprised she didn't demand a dollar for herself.

"Sombo Yakoma."

"You are from Yakoma?"

Her eyes widened. "How do you know about Yakoma?"

"I'll tell you after you get the aspirin."

"Hey hey…open up you idiots…." She pounded on door and shouted again. "*Fungola* - open up!"

Idiots? She didn't seem to have a lot of fear or respect for these guards! Sombo then shuffled over to the bars and shook them with her one free hand. She had no shoes on. No one did. I looked at my feet and noticed my Tevas were still securely fastened. Thank God, I do not have African feet like I used to, they were soft and flimsy from countless spa pedicures. A world so very surreal and distant to me now. I wished for some good hard calluses.

Sombo pounded some more. Finally an idiot came and opened it a crack. I figured we could all rush the door and push it open. But we didn't.

I couldn't hear the hushed negotiation, but my money exchanged hands, the door slammed shut. Sombo came back.

"It will take a while. So, Yakoma?"

"*Nakoli pene na Bosobolo* - I grew up near Bosobolo." That shook her world. She shook her long tresses. The infant became detached and gave a whimper. "How old is your…daughter?" I guessed. "She is certainly very cute." The baby had quite a head of curly black hair. It's a shame white babies are mostly born bald.

"She has six months now...you grew up at Bosobolo!" She lapsed into silence. "What is your name?"

"Anna Landan."

"Landan, yes, of course!" *Of course?*

"You knew my father?" Suddenly my headache diminished.

A woman made her way to the hole. A couple of others followed her. As she stepped over the hole, the others modestly sheltered her. The men paid no attention whatsoever.

"No, but I..." then she gestured at the group in general, "...we know about him. He started some churches up here. How is your father?"

"*Morte* - Dead."

She put her hand over her mouth. "I am so sorry to hear that. I did see him sometimes. I heard him preach, but I was just a little girl then, I don't think I knew what he was saying."

"You heard him preach." I just let that wash over me. I also had memories of his preaching. Fluent, without notes, persuasive, judging by the hundreds that always came forward. I wanted to tell her why I was there, but I wasn't quite ready to tell her the whole blessed story just yet. The thought occurred to me that she was some kind of a plant, a spy.

"Why are you in here?" I asked her first.

She laughed. "My husband had me thrown in the *geole*." She shrugged. "The first wife accused me of stealing some of her money."

"Did you?"

"Sure. I'll be out soon. He needs me."

The door opened and a little bag was passed inside. It was passed from hand to hand until it reached Sombo, who handed it to me. I opened it. Five white pills were in a piece of paper.

"How do I know these are aspirin?"

Sombo laughed. I loved her laugh. How was it that she still had a vivacious spirit, being a second wife, or maybe third, locked in a jail with no shoes on her feet?

"They probably aren't. But whatever they are, they will kill your pain. You must understand, he wants you to deal more with him. He wants your money."

"So why not just steal it."

"He would have, but somehow they missed it. Now you are here. It's ok…for now."

"Any water?"

She shook her head, then shouted something in another dialect. One of the women came over and produced a plastic bottle from somewhere in her clothing.

"Here."

I swallowed one, not sure what they were or what effect they might have. Didn't care. I'd see what effect it had before I tried a second.

"Please, Sombo, tell me about this place. What happens next?"

She paused. "Well, it always depends on money and who you know. If you have people on the outside, they will feed you and eventually get you out…for a price. If not…" she pursed her lips and shrugged, "you can be here a long, long time. Who is out there for you?"

"I really don't know." I wondered where Ian and Keith were, and tried not to think about the possibilities.

"You are not traveling alone?"

"No, there are two mondeles with me…but I have no idea where they are." The white pill was helping. It wasn't aspirin.

"How did you get here, Anna?"

I told her the story of the roadblock and the blow that knocked me out.

"Those *cochons* - pigs. The soldiers just turned around and sold the *bangi* - the hemp. They killed somebody?"

"Yes."

"Well, that could be a problem. They don't really want witnesses to that kind of thing."

Oh great. Where was the witness protection program?

"But, Anna, they will let you out sooner or later. Don't worry. You are here, that is good." *Good? Being in here is good?* She put her gentle hand up to my cheek and brushed the hair out of my face. Her hand was warm and tender on my face; I wished I remembered my mother's last touch the same way. Sombo looked at me compassionately and thoughtfully and said again, "Ne vous inquiêtez pas, fille - don't worry daughter." She held my face in her affectionate hands and then gave my cheeks a motherly pat and turned back to her baby.

In spite of myself I felt the tears well up. These tears were a long time in coming. They were being collected and pooled in a black swelling cloud somewhere inside my soul, if I still had one. All it took was a motherly touch I had missed for 24 years, a little sympathy and I was rapidly thawing. Also, of course, a jail, a very public latrine, the fear of rape, and the possible loss of all the genuine friends I know. I was stripped bare. I had no resources. Money, humor, skin-color, sarcasm, not even my she-devil defensive system could give me a little rescue; nothing could cut the pain of loneliness and fear. Was I at the edge or over it? I reached up to my face and felt where Sombo's fingers stroked. I visualized my own Mother's beautiful slender hands. Reaching up and touching my face in love, tenderness. I felt the blanket of helplessness swaddle me up and carry me to a place where Anna Landan cries. And I cried. The cries turned into wracking sobs and I wasn't even embarrassed. Sombo came closer and just held me. Little Sombo's eyes were about an inch from mine. I looked into them and she looked into my watering eyes, and tears formed in hers too. Baby Sombo's thick little hands reached up and grabbed my nose. I held her tiny hand in mine and closed my eyes, letting the tears fall where they may. I too was at the mercy of other people, in some one else's hands, even if it was "just" God's.

I finally found some rest on my corner of the floor. The white pill was great. I took another. The tears had worn me out, but *God,* it felt so good to cry. I dreamt about a cat named Ziegler and a man that looked like George Clooney, and about Ian and I alone in his apartment. He was painting my toes. I made a promise to myself to finally tell him how I really feel, once I figured it out. I dreamt loud and hard about witch doctors, my Dad preaching, a strange beautiful black woman - all while I was eating fried calamari and cob salad and sipping a cold Mac and Jack's with lemon. It had to be valium. But valium was yellow, right?

CHAPTER FIFTEEN

"Mondele! Levez-vous! - Whitey - get up!" I cracked open my eyes and felt around my mouth with my dry tongue. What I would give for a Perrier, or a venti frappuccino. My heavy lids fell back down. I had three more white pills. I'd save them for later.

"*Mondele!*" I heard the clanking of keys against our door and opened my eyes again. I finally focused and saw an enraged guard looking, pointing and yelling in my direction. Sombo nudged me in the ribs, and I began to stand up. My stomach growled with hunger and I felt light headed. Sombo stood up next to me and held my arm for support.

"You! Come here!" The guard opened the door and motioned for me to come along quickly. I looked around for my things to grab, and realized I had none. Heart racing, I walked nervously out the door, hoping that wherever I was headed still included being around other people. I looked back at Sombo who smiled helplessly. *Please do not put me in solitary, please do not rape me, I beg you, I beg you.* Sombo's baby gave a cry, I turned and waved. What an angel, I wish I was wrapped up close to my Mom, safe in her arms like that. I sauntered timidly out of the prison gate, got kicked in the leg like a horse, and was told to hurry up.

"You are done. Out. *Get - Out.*" The guard punctuated his last two words and handled me roughly, pushing me out of the makeshift prison yard. I stared blankly at the guard. I figured this must be some trick right before the end. I braced myself for the worst and put my hands up. I just hoped Dad and I might miraculously be buried together. I was suddenly sorry for the way I'd been handling my life, but didn't know who to confess that to. I momentarily considered asking for a last meal or a priest, but thought better of it. What he did next unnerved me more than anything I had encountered yet. He handed me back my passport sling, as well as Ian's wallet. Both still had some weight, so they had not been completely emptied.

"White whore. Are you stupid? Put your hands down. Your truck is there." The guard came up close to my head and gripped my hair between his fingers, turning my neck painfully in the direction he was pointing. There was a Hilux, with the Ziegler in back. My heart stopped. He turned my head back toward his ugly yellow teeth. He needed dentures badly. And mouthwash. His bulbous nose was touching mine as he whispered in my face, "If I had it my way, you'd be mine, *mondele.* All just for *me.*" His tongue hung out and he let his other hand slide down my neck stopping at my throat. He was panting heavily, I nearly threw up right in his face. "But I have orders - at least for now, things change you know, and you - you have, let's say, the right friends." His let his hand slide off my throat, across my chest and down to my waist. He yanked me into his body, thrust his hips toward me one inch closer, and then hurled me backward, taking a handful of hair with him.

"There will be another time. I am a patient man." He looked down on me with a mixture of rage and lust. "This is not over." He spat on my sandals and said *"Abientot,"* and walked away laughing menacingly.

My knees gave in, I buckled over and I knelt on the dirt, staring at the empty Hilux. *Oh good God.* I said that prayer, if you call it a prayer, and then proceeded to curse my Dad a couple times under my breath. What a grand idea. *That's the last time I'm even going to so much as open someone's last will and testament. I don't care if it bequeaths ten million dollars to me. I don't want to know what their last dying wish is, and I definitely don't want to be responsible for fulfilling it. Damn you.* I hoped he wasn't damned, I really hoped he was somehow very much alive and working overtime with Peter, Paul, and Mary - not the band - and the angels in this rescue operation. I glanced again at the Hilux. Still in disbelief. Lusty guard was a good few feet away. I hoped he would be eaten alive by army ants, starting with his privates. I really did.

Were there keys in the ignition? Who on earth did I know that could pull this off that happened to be the *"right"* people? I had so many questions, but definitely wasn't going to ask the friendly prison staff.

I got up off the ground and decided it would be best to hurry my ass out of there as soon as possible, before the guard caught another glimpse of my legs and changed his mind. I approached the Hilux cautiously. It had what I supposed was a machine-gun mount in the back, but minus the machine gun. I looked around and didn't see anyone else. The guard was watching me, so I hopped in the cab, and sure enough, I saw the keys dangling in the ignition. Was this a dream? As soon as I turned them, the passenger door opened and someone got in and shut the door.

"Drive." The pale African woman stared straight ahead and pointed in the direction away from town. A couple of armed men also jumped into the back of the truck and sat down on the edge.

I shouted a bit hysterically "Who *are* you?! What is going on?"

She replied, "Your friends are waiting." I stared dumfounded at my passenger and all I could manage to say was, "Hold on." I jumped out of the driver's seat and ran around to the back of the Hilux. One guard stood up and unslung his rifle, but didn't point it at me. I guess I startled him. I was about to drive off into the jungle with a total stranger and I was paranoid, scared, and needed some reassurance about one thing. I jumped in the back and looked in the window. Dad was there. Eyes closed. He looked a little more jarred, and was even more crooked. I didn't mind, it was him. I had a friend with me. I needed to know that throughout all the captivity, prison goings and the like, that Dad hadn't been traded in for a bunch of pot or someone else's stiff. I breathed a sigh of relief. It occurred to me that it might not be wholly normal to have nicknames for a casket. I didn't even mind seeing the dead body anymore. I was getting accustomed to everything, sexually charged guards, drug smuggling, corpses, plane crashes, emotional meltdowns. *C'est la vie.* Living the dream baby, living the dream. I looked around, astonished to see that our bags of clothes, and other strange belongings, including some tents I had never seen before, were also thrown in the back of the truck.

I jumped back into the driver's seat and looked at the gearshift. It was a five-speed manual, as if the last three gears were of any use around here. But a stick was a stick even if it wasn't AJ. I slammed it into first, popped the clutch and threw up some gravel and mud from our spinning tires, spewing it all over the guards standing watch. Eat my dirt, or something to that effect, raced through my mind, but with a little more profanity. Just a little.

We drove in silence for nearly a minute. I glanced nervously in the rearview mirror every other second.

"You drive fast," said the woman. "My brother has a fast car."

"*This...* is *not* a fast car," I returned.

Finally we began introductions.

"Now, once again, in heaven's name, who are you, what do you want?" I wasn't sure if I should be thankful, or careful, or witchy. I opted for the latter, because it comes naturally, even in French.

"*Je m'appelle Mpasi.* I rescue you."

Yes, she did that, alright. "Nice to meet you, I'm Anna...and...thank you." My defenses disappeared too quickly. I wasn't sure who this friendly, needy version of me was, but I was kind of liking her better than the edgy one. I took my hand off the clutch and reached out my right arm toward the girl. Mpasi shook it limply. I wasn't sure what to say, or how to thank her properly. I was more disturbed by the fact that a total stranger, a woman, managed to free me out of prison, no questions asked, including a getaway vehicle and my belongings. I tried to shake it off while I just kept driving away from the compound. I had too many questions, like *"Why I am driving? It's not my truck!"* But that one could wait.

"Where are my friends?"

"Just beyond the log bridge, over the water. They are ok." Mpasi anticipated my next question.

"How, why did you - ?"

"Later, I tell you later. For now, just drive."

I couldn't argue with that, but I had one more burning question.

"Do you have any water, bananas, or food of any sort?" I was starving, thirsty, about to pass out from fatigue along with a dizzy spell, and I could feel a migraine creeping up my neck. Great recipe for driving across a log bridge in the Congo. Mpasi immediately reached into her sack and pulled out a dirty thermos, poured me some tea with sugar, and handed me a kwanga. She held an open papaya in her hand, realizing I couldn't hold all the food and drive at the same time. It was a feast for my eyes and I immediately began to take in the nourishment. I finally glanced at her. She was beautiful. Her hair was softer, less coarse than typical Congolese hair. She had much paler skin, was obviously part of some white breeding, who knows how many generations ago. She looked about twenty. Her lips were smaller, her nose was longer and her cheekbones were exquisite, the kind typically only created on Nip/Tuck. Although I really doubted that she'd ever seen that appalling show, much less had any work done. She saw me looking at her and smiled wide. She had perfect teeth. I smiled back, at least, half of my lips turned upward, the other half was stuffed with kwanga.

"Is that your Dad?" She tossed her chin towards the truck bed.

"Yes, it is. I had to be sure, you know." I had seen Mpasi staring out the window into the back as I cleared Ziggy's window to look inside.

"I'm used to bodies." Mpasi offered freely.

"Sure. Mpasi - right?" I over pronounced the long *a* and took off the slight *m*, just to be sure I wasn't ruining the pronunciation.

"Yes! Mpasi."

All of a sudden her name struck a chord in my memory box. *Mpasi*. Mpasi – I had known this name. I had met a toddler once, Bemba's daughter, her name was Mpasi. Could this be her? It wasn't an uncommon name though. But something in this woman's look was familiar.

"You related to the Bemba family by any chance?"

"I will tell you."

"Ok." I waited. *I will tell you? Alright then, tell me!*

"More later."

"Fine. Mpasi, means pain, right? Why are you named pain?"

"Yes, I think it had something to do with the manner of the birth."

"Ouch. I have no idea, never had kids, but I hope to have a C-section."

"A what?"

"Never mind. So, she felt a little pain, and called you 'Pain.' Makes sense." I kind of laughed.

Mpasi didn't laugh. Apparently plays on words were not funny. "Yes it does. She died at childbirth." I immediately regretted my sarcasm about birth. I shut my mouth and simply drove. I would probably do a lot better in life if I just shut my mouth. I could see the bridge ahead of us. I scarffed down my food, gulped the tepid tea and felt a little revival seep back into my tired veins. I noticed bug bites on my arms, mosquitoes were liking my sugary American blood. That's ok, we were old friends.

"Who are those men in the back?" I kind of half pointed with my lip over my shoulder.

"Bodyguards." *Dad needed guards*? Then I realized she meant her bodyguards. Now, that brought up a whole lot of other questions.

I looked up and noticed we were at the bridge. But I didn't see Keith or Ian.

"Stop here, I help you." Mpasi got out of the truck and ran in front of me. She surveyed the bridge. As did I. It was perilous, as usual. I had seen my Dad and Keith cross these bridges numerous times. They would get out, try to roll a couple logs in at a better angle. One of them would stand in front and wave the driver to and fro until each tire was "securely" on the correct log. I usually got out, walked across, closed my eyes, held my breath and watched. Keith usually prayed first. Didn't seem like such a bad idea. Nothing I learned in high performance driving school was going to help this performance. The ravine below did not look like a nice place to camp for the night. Mpasi gave me the thumbs up – *where did she learn that?* - and started directing me. A little to the left, a little to the right. I eased onto the bridge following her directions and held my breath, but kept my eyes open for good measure. Maybe I'd do better with them closed. The truck revved high at the first shot at getting the tires off the road and on top of the thick wood logs. Once I got the first two over, I prayed the last two would follow suit nicely. Mpasi walked backward and kept waving her hand in her direction. *Don't look down. Don't look down.* It didn't take long to get across, and I finally let out my breath. Mpasi hopped in, and said "Ok."

Ok. *Ok, what?*

"Where are my friends?" I was hungry for some more answers.

"In the village, just after this bridge. Ok? Go." I finally remembered that in Africa, things are not so black and white. *OK, that's funny...* "Just over the bridge" could actually mean half a day's journey. "Be there at 6," could mean 7, 8, 9 or tomorrow. Time and distance were relative. I let out a long sigh and slumped my shoulders. I wanted to see Ian so bad, it hurt. I tried not to think about it and held back my tears welling up. It hurt my throat to keep them there. I swallowed hard. Once the tear-duct-dam had broken, they just seemed to keep rising up as they pleased.

"Don't worry. I really mean, just beyond. See - right there!" Mpasi must have read my body language and was pointing at a small village I could see now. I could even see two white men standing awkwardly by the edge of the road, looking very out of place. I didn't care anymore who Mpasi was, or what she wanted. She did, in fact, rescue us and bring us back together. All four of us. I grabbed her hand and squeezed it and said a big "Merci," my eyes brimming gratefully. I would have bear-hugged her if I wasn't driving like a maniac. I floored the truck and skidded toward them over the bumps and ditches. We were flying around inside the cab, probably looked a little silly, but I didn't care. Mpasi took a hold of the handle above the window and held on tight. Once close enough, I barely pushed it into park before I was already out of the cab. Without the consent or permission of my obnoxiously over-cautious mind, my legs were running as fast as they could toward Ian and Keith. I must have looked like a schoolgirl, running to her beau. Ian probably would like that image, too.

He was also coming toward me now and met me half way, although he was limping quite sorely. As I got closer I had residual instinct to slow down, play it cool and greet him with a hand shake accompanied with "I'm hard-to-get" flip of my hair. But the ice queen was pretty much defeated; she had melted, laid down like a little dog in that dark prison overnight. Good. Forget her! I did not want to be that person anymore. I needed Ian. I *needed* and it was good to admit it. I remembered Sombo's face. I couldn't save myself. As I got closer I could see Ian's face was etched with great emotion, wiping his eyes with the back of his hand as he limped as fast as he could toward me. I could see relief, joy, exhaustion, pain, and maybe even love written all over his expressions.

"Ian!" We finally collided and I threw my arms wide, allowing my throat and eyes to finally let go of the tears they were holding. I wouldn't be able to play it off as dust in my eyes anyway, might as well let them show. I didn't mind; I had about 18 years worth of tears stored up and needing out.

"Anna - " Ian grabbed me tight, wrapped his strong arms completely around me and whispered my name softly into my ear through a mouthful of my hair. And then he said it over and over and over again. With each whisper of my name I pulled him closer and closer to me. It was nothing like the way he had ever said it before during our sorry, selfish, train-wreck or a 'relationship'. It was tender, full of affection and worry, promise and future. I buried my face in his neck and let the ache of my heart come out, wetting his skin mercilessly. He responded even more to that, and held me till I hardly felt like a singular person; I felt like part of his own skin, but barely able to breathe. I finally looked up into his face, he bent down and firmly kissed me, inadvertently picking me up off the ground. My feet hovered a few inches above the dirt while we kissed, and finally I came back down to earth, suddenly all too aware of the spectacle we were creating. The little children in the village were yelping with glee and whistling in our direction. I wished we were alone.

"*Baisez-moi, baisez-moi!* Kiss me, kiss me!" A little boy ran out and made kissy gestures with his lips. I blushed and turned quickly to Keith and gave him a huge hug.

"Anna, I'm so sorry. I'm so happy to see you. Are you OK?" Keith took me by the shoulders and stood me at arms length examining me. He looked grave and concerned, also wearing moisture around the eyes.

"I'm fine. Alive. Untouched...still a virgin." Ian blushed. I attempted a smile and some humor to downplay how close that call was. Years from now, I will still know the face of the guard, and his trembling body will still haunt my dreams. I saw Ian's shoulders relax and he breathed out an obvious sigh of relief. I could tell he had been wondering, but afraid to ask.

"What about you two?"

"We are OK, too. Ian got kicked around quite a bit - thus the limp - I was hoping you might still have some Vicodin for him. I got more the gut-punches, our things were taken, including your Dad, and then we were just holed up inside this empty dirt room until about three hours ago. Someone came in, told us to get going, threw us into the back of another truck and told us that they had orders to dump us here. So we were dumped. That's all we know. How did you do this?"

"You think *I* managed to do this?" I was shocked at the assumption. Of course, it stroked my ego a little. "Not my doing. She did it." I pointed to Mpasi. I told Ian and Keith all about my imprisonment and about Sombo, how she knew about Dad, the mysterious exit and Mpasi. I described the guard in some detail. I pointed toward Mpasi and the truck. She was leaning against it, watching us with her two bodyguards next to her. Smoke from a cigarette curled out from between her fingers. She made a comment to them and they laughed. *What could be so funny?* She took a deep drag on the cigarette and blew it slowly out her nostrils. That looked so tough. I admired the panache. I wanted a smoke too. She noticed us looking at her and waved.

"Who are those guys with her?" Ian asked.

"Her bodyguards."

"What?"

"Bodyguards. That's all I know, sorry. I think I knew her as a kid, but she doesn't seem to know me."

"What do we do now? Do we pay her?" Keith, for the first time in his African career was at a loss. It surprised me; I had hoped that Keith would know exactly what to do.

"Maybe? I actually was given your things, believe it or not - doubtful there is any money in there." I gave Ian his wallet and Keith his passport. Ian opened his wallet, it was empty. He fingered a small fold inside one of the slits, and pulled out a bill, folded up to about the size of a fingernail.

"You freaked me out with that necklace story, so I hid this in here." It was 200 bucks.

"Let's give her one, and see if she'll tell us about her magic powers." *And her motive.* I thought, *I don't care how she did it, I want to know why.*

CHAPTER SIXTEEN

When I offered Mpasi a Benjamin, she held it up to the guards and said something I didn't catch and they all laughed.

"No thank you for the monies." She then returned it to me and told me that she simply wanted to travel with us to Bosobolo. That was all. She refused to speak about the prison break at all. She wouldn't answer questions, and remained evasive, yet friendly. Though I knew the stories would come out later, it ate away at me. I didn't like the burden of owing someone, owing them for my life, but I guessed I have to get used to it, and accept that she had simply rescued us, and I would know why later. Those were exactly the kinds of words that came out of my father's mouth when he preached. Something about sacrifice for my life without merit. Something about grace and mercy. Something... I kind of wished I had listened better.

We filled the Hilux tank with a few of the plastic gas cans in the back, Mpasi spoke kindly with the villagers hanging around and managed to buy us some hot dinner. She wrapped it up in her bag for later. It was hard to wait, we were salivating just looking at it. Broiled chicken in palm oil, nuts, and pilipili pepper, pounded mpondu with crushed peanuts, also with pilipili pepper. Some sour fuku - a bread-rice type dish with the pungent smell of sewer, the consistency of wet Playdough. My favorite. She also had with her a chicken, and a basket full of eggs. I wasn't sure what the chicken was for, but I didn't ask. Mpasi befuddled me. I couldn't help staring at her most of the time, making up stories in my head that would put the pieces together that made up the whole of who she seemed to be. Nothing worked. She was kind, quiet, yet decisive. She gave orders and instinctively we all obeyed: "Keith drives, I sit in back, we drive till eight and stop for night and eat." She had great English, although she often messed up her plurals and was minus a few filler articles like "the" and "and." When she smiled at me, I felt strangely warmed and at ease. She looked like someone I knew, or at least someone I thought I knew.

As to Mpasi's orders, the three of us huddled inside the cab. Mpasi hopped in back with Ziegler and the chicken. Keith insisted on rigging up the tarp having noticed the black clouds threatening above us. Mpasi agreed and snuck in underneath it with Dad. I noticed her staring at him through the window. I wondered what she must think of that.

Keith suggested we say a prayer before we start. I was about to scoff and crack a joke but flashed to the guards, the guns, the prison...I guess it couldn't hurt, right? Like fire-insurance? I immediately bowed my head and said, "Go for it, Keith." I opened one eye to glance at Mpasi while Keith prayed. To my surprise the tough-girl demeanor was put on hold. She had her head bowed and her hands clasped together near her mouth. Her lips moved and whispered as Keith spoke. Her eyes shut tight in earnest. She "uh huh'd" and "amen'd" as Keith called on God for mercy, protection, safe roads, and encouraged spirits. He thanked Him for our release from prison and I saw the corners of Mpasi's mouth curl upward as she nodded and gave a big "amen" to that one. *What secret is she hiding?* Keith wrapped up with the Lord's Prayer, and I found myself able to say a few words, albeit somewhat robotically; I was raised on this stuff, I might as well be a part of the group therapy.

"...thou preparest a table before me in the presence of my enemies..."

Now that's more like it! God can go ahead and prepare a big feast for me and let the prison guards hungrily watch from hell as I eat with pleasure! I had a feeling that somehow I missed a theological nuance or two, but I spoke the phrase loud and proud anyway. Ian just looked around at everyone with wide eyes. My guess is that he had never heard it before. He probably wondered why everyone knew the secret handshake but him. I felt sorry for Ian and stopped "praying."

"Amen." Keith turned the ignition and we continued from where we left off... but not quite. I was not exactly the same person that left from Bumba, something had shifted within me but toward whom or away from what I wasn't sure... and now we had a secret weapon with us: Mpasi.

Keith began to hum classic Willie Nelson, "On the Road Again," and in spite of myself, I joined with the rest of the lyrics which came easier to me than the

Lord's prayer, "...just can't wait to get on the road again, the life I love is making music with my friends, and I can't wait to get on the road again." True. The grind of the truck was music to my ears, Dad was one foot closer to the grave. He'd be pushing up mangos in no time. I cracked myself up and imagined a muffled laugh from the Zig.

The small village disappeared behind us, and as usual, the kids screamed and ran after us until we lost them going a whopping 20 kmph. Keith drove with one arm out the window. That left arm had a crisp distinctive tan wrapping around from wrist to bicep. As to Keith's prediction, the rain pummeled us without mercy, a busy percussion concert on top of the steel roof. The jungle canopy muffled the sounds of the old Hilux as it labored through the mud. Ian sat loosely in the passenger seat, allowing his body to sway with the rhythms of the journey, one wrist hanging limply through the overhead grip. I curled up next to him and he kissed me tenderly on the forehead. I managed to doze off and on. I have always needed the rain, it seems to offer a cleansing to the earth and somehow a magical cleansing of my spirit, too. All the dirt and filth of the day gets washed away in the peaceful melody. All the wretched things we do and say suddenly seem to be gone. The rain is a forgiving presence. Especially African rain, because it is so dreadfully powerful.

Darkness settled in on us. Only the dim headlights brightened the dark funnel ahead. The slender yellow crescent moon overhead could be occasionally glimpsed through the trees; the palms wiggled their fingers rapidly through the rain.

Thousands of brutal miles driving the unpaved roads of Congo had long ago taught me the futility of bracing myself for each bump or sickening plunge. I swayed with Ian. The rainstorm slowed and the humid heat of the night poured through the open windows. It felt like running a blow dryer in a sauna.

I glanced to my left at Keith, he was still humming and had a perpetual smile on his face. He actually seemed to relish wrestling with the wheel while doing the endless shifting. Up a gear, down a gear, never higher than third, always in four-wheel drive. If he wasn't careful, he might break the gearshift, again. That was Keith and Dad's favorite story to share; it made Keith seem like a muscle man, and it always made my Dad laugh.

A few hours passed and I heard a loud knock against the windowpane. I turned around to see Mpasi lifting off the tarp, the rain had stopped. She was trying to open the cab window. I opened it the rest of the way for her. She stuck her head inside the cab to talk.

"We stop here, yeah? Might be a good place to sleep for night." She was right, it had been a long day, and sleep was necessary for all of us refugees. The road was getting hard to see and it would be even more dangerous to drive. We were in the middle of tall *sobi* grass, grass up to the level of our chest. It definitely seemed to be safer camping in the grasslands than in the thick of the jungle. We pulled gently to a stop. Stretching my legs was a luxury I enjoyed immensely. So did Ian. The guards and Keith got busy unloading our stuff, and Ian started setting up the tents that Mpasi had brought. Mpasi pulled out some of her baskets from the back, and unloaded the tin pots with lids.

"We eat." She sat down on the ground and opened the pots of mpondu and fuku.

"I'll make a fire." Ian limped off to find some dry brush, I smiled at his attempt to be the jungle man. Tomorrow he'll be beating his chest and saying "Me! Make fire!" Like Tom Hanks in *Castaway*. Love it.

"Don't wander too far!" I couldn't help it. He's a white suburban lawyer, for Pete's sake.

"Yes, *Mom*." Ian quickly disappeared behind layers of grass.

Much to my surprise, he returned a few minutes later with a few random sprigs of wood of a decent size and some dry grass, which had managed shelter from the rain. He set up a fire pit then poured a little gas on it from one of the cans.

"That should start it up ok." When all else fails, douse it with gas. The fire roared up and we scooted in closer. We sat down on blankets and ate with our hands. The food was delicious and the oil stained our palms and mouths orange. I felt like a child again, recapturing some of the lost magic of youthful joy. I almost felt at home. I almost felt happy. Ian sat near me and kept his hand on my leg, occasionally circling his thumb around the top of my knee. Every gesture of tenderness he offered I gladly accepted.

"Mpasi, tell me about your name." Keith smiled at her across from the tin pots, some green sprigs of mpondu stuck to his teeth.

"My name means 'pain.'" She said matter-of-factly.

"Her name means pain, Keith. OK? So - Mpasi, how did you rescue us?" I didn't want Keith to fall into the same trap I did with the childbirth and pain situation. Plus, rescue was still the question of the night.

"Tomorrow. I will tell you tomorrow." She smiled, and ate. I wondered if this was tomorrow African time or American time. I hoped for American time.

We ate silently. I thought about the three tents. I think Ian was thinking about the three tents too. Obviously, I would have to share a tent with Mpasi, and Keith and Ian would take the other two. The guards would probably sleep in the truck. I felt disappointed in the arrangement, yet a little relieved. We finished off the food in a hurry. Mpasi pulled out a pack of cigarettes and offered them around. The guards took one each. Keith and Ian shook their heads no. Ian was watching me. I was not a smoker. Well, the occasional cigarillo. I took one and lit up, smiled wide at Keith and Ian. I tried the exhale through the nose. Not good. But the immediate buzz was beautiful; an adequate replacement for the little white pills which were gone.

"Mpasi, Anna, why don't you two take this big tent, Ian and I will take the one-man tents. Should we get some rest? I think we all need it." Keith stood up, brushed his hands on his pants, stretched and yawned...as if to drive the point home. We did not argue.

Mpasi wanted to sleep outside, but Keith insisted on the sleeping situation, a lot. Ian caught my grimace, got up, and motioned for me to come over behind the truck. My heart skipped a beat like a silly eighth-grader with a crush. I hoped for another kiss. The kiss I shared with Ian earlier that day still lingered on my lips, as did all other thoughts that tagged along with that. Do I love him? Does he love me? I needed a flower with petals, so I could test my theory: He loves me, He loves me not. I needed my eight ball. I needed a drink. I needed to drive. Not drink and drive though. Never.

"Ian - we are sleeping in separate tents and that's final." We stood behind the truck and I scolded him as if he had stepped out of line, playing the schoolteacher. He playfully grabbed me and pushed me further behind the truck, completely out of sight.

"Of course it is final, Miss Landan. I just wanted to say goodnight. I actually want my own tent." Ian's smiled played across his lips flirtatiously. I wanted another kiss.

"You want your own tent? Fine. Me, too. It's for the best anyway, isn't it?" I played along.

"Yes it is." Ian tried to run his fingers through my hair and quickly gave up. It was a mess. His fingers were stuck. He gently touched the bruised knot on my forehead and kissed it compassionately.

"Ian - do you ever wonder - that perhaps our embrace earlier today was simply due to the fact that we both almost died, and that's all? We were scared." I desperately wanted to believe that I was falling in love, but needed exorbitant amounts of reassurance. I felt like one of the final contestants on "The Bachelor," hoping to get a rose, hoping to get picked, but worrying about not getting the rose. Dumbest show ever. I never missed it.

"Sure, I was scared. Scared I would lose you, doesn't that count for something?"

"A little. Did you ever see the movie *Speed*?" I could not deal with how close we were standing but not really touching, so I just kept talking.

"Yeah, but I doubt we could catch a flick at this hour." Ian smiled again and inched nearer to me. I exhaled deeply…God I loved his accent.

"Very funny. Remember the end where Sandra Bullock and Keanu Reeves are laying on that small metal plank, having just narrowly escaped death by that bomb - "

"On the bus."

"Later, after the subway derailed… and they are laying there, kissing, and Bullock says 'I've heard that relationships, based on intense experiences, never last.' Then Reeves smartly replies, 'Ok, we'll just have to base it on sex then.' Remember that scene?"

"Yes? Where are you going with this? Do you want to base our relationship on sex?"

"No! I mean, yes, no - do you?" I suddenly felt confused, and lost track of my thoughts, I was trying to go somewhere else with that story, and I wanted Ian to follow me there.

"Yes." Ian smiled, then shook his head adamantly. "Nope, no. Not in the least. I want to base it on much, much more than that." He went back to the hair stroking, with much futility. "What's in your hair, anyway, Anna?"

"Prison will do that. But me, too, what I meant was that it was an intense circumstance, and Bullock knew that it would never work, it wasn't real.

Relationships kindled in the fire of abnormal life never work."

"Very poetic."

"Thank you. What do you think?" I was having trouble concentrating. I was reaching out pathetically for a rose. *Just give me a rose, Ian! Is this real or not?* I had to know. Before I totally caved and let myself open to another human being I had to be totally sure. But are we ever totally sure? Do we just have to take a leap of faith now and then? Does it have to be a leap? Maybe just a little "twitch" of faith?

"Anna - for one, you have *got* to stop living in the movies, and two, I think our life will never be normal. People will always die, and naturally, they will all need to be buried in Africa and it could go on like this forever..." he continued to smile and kiss my cheeks, "...and ever...and ever..." I couldn't help but laugh, but then got agitated.

"Are you taking me seriously?" I pushed him back, just a bit.

Ian sighed, wiped his smile off, stepped back and examined my eyes. "Anna, this *is* life," he said, "intense, abnormal, or not. It will go up and down. It will never be predictable, and there will always be uncertainties as well as certainties." He stopped and waited for me to respond. I was stuck on the "uncertainty's" part. But Ian continued playfully again, "I'm also hoping for some more down moments - where we can sit on the couch together. I can paint your toes - " he leaned in and kissed me. *Toes? Did he watch my dreams?* Another kiss - "while you do a crossword - " *I hate crosswords.*

More kisses " - while we watch *Antiques Roadshow* - " *I love that show* - "While we drink malbec - " *bullseye, that's my favorite, dang it Ian, stop!* - "Whether I'm crashing planes with you, or surviving prison camps, I just want to be with you. I know that now more than ever." Ian kissed me as he talked, and it occurred to me that his words sounded an awful lot like someone's cheesy self-made wedding vows. I hated it and wanted more of it at the same time. My own uncertainty drove me berserk. Part of me was certainly melting like I had during our emotional roadside reunion, but the whole idea made me nervous, risk was something I was still hoping to avoid. Couldn't it all just be certain and easy? How does anyone ever know for sure?

"Maybe, Ian - " I tried to talk while he kissed, he gave up and paid attention - "Maybe somewhere in our twisted Darwinian-Freudian psyche two people are drawn together because of some programmed instinct to hook up and procreate to carry on our name and leave our seed on the earth." *What was I saying? Did all of that just come out of my mouth? Really?*

"What happened to the poetic side of you? You think that all of this between you and me is just some impersonal primal link in evolution? You're crazy!" Ian twirled his finger around his head for affect. "This is your theory, is it? All this crazy talk because of our kiss this afternoon? Must have really been a good one." He leaned in to repeat it.

It *was* a good one, I thought. So good I almost said the dreadful, forbidden three words. I felt there must be another reason for telling another human being that you love them, other reasons for tears and embraces. I knew I was sounding crazy as I tried to avoid saying, or even feeling what I feared. The lessons I learned in Sunday School also invaded my thoughts. The great Genesis creation mandate - "Go and subdue the earth, be fruitful and multiply." Maybe that is the only reason man and woman get together; they were simply doing what they were told. However, I was certain I did not survive prison and near-rape just to puke for nine months and then push a tiny person out of my body, to uphold my part of Genesis chapter two. It must have been something more.

"Ian, I just wish that we hadn't gotten so negatively tangled up in the first place."

"I'm sorry it got that way." He was so sincere. "For me, I've always been in love with you, nothing less. Hasn't been too complicated on my end."

"Love? We're talking about love here?" I grimaced that he obviously pointed the "complicated" part toward my doing.

"I am. Aren't you? Do you love me, Anna?" *You did not just ask me that!*

"Not yet. Maybe. Sometimes. Ian, I just don't know, OK? I don't know! I'm tired. I need some sleep." I pressed my fingers against my eyes and sighed. *Why do I do this? Why can't I just experience...leave it... Why must I push?*

I kissed Ian briefly to soften my words, and began to walk away. Poor Ian. He turned around and rested his tall back up against the truck, shook his head, folded his arms, and watched me leave. I gave a little wave behind me.

My defenses had come back, but not full blown. I just needed to rest; I had too many things to think about. Getting Dad buried was one of them. Trying to keep us all alive was another, and of course, digging around the mystery of Mpasi. Falling in love with Ian could wait. Our "relationship" had started simply as a result of a Chris Issak concert and cheap gin, who wouldn't "fall in love" after that? But Ian had never faded away like every other casual relationship. Ian must just think he's in love, trying to match it all up.

Love is like a three-legged stool my Dad used to say. It requires precise balance. All sides need to match each other - physical, emotional, spiritual. When one side gets higher than another, it's impossible to equalize. Months ago, my body had jumped in with Ian long before my heart did. My heart was protected at first, and naturally defended itself thereafter, punishing me for my fast track behavior, at least, that's how I saw it. If the physical side takes off first, the mind tries to convince itself that it must feel a certain depth of love that it really doesn't, trying to catch up, but winds up disappointed later when the love isn't actually there. Or, the mind tries to back-pedal so fast, it denies any depth that may have actually been there, ruining a chance at love. I was the latter, usually was. Ian wasn't the first. Ian was one of those rare people who were simply open to all three facets of the stool. I could see why people would wait for marriage – so the physical act of love matches the level of commitment - the stool is balanced. Next time, I should wait.

Then again...I looked back at Ian as he walked away from the truck and ditched that last thought.

I crawled into the two person orange tent. Mpasi was sleeping quietly, hugging the very edge of the tent. The rain started to pour down on top of the tarp that was covering all three tents. Dad had great timing, dying during rainy season. Maybe next time he'd be more considerate. The sound of the rain was so melodic and peaceful. I felt rocked to sleep inside an orange rain cloud that abandoned its place in the heavens and took a rest with me on the earth. I could hear Keith snoring. Dad was sleeping next to us in the back of the truck. He wasn't snoring. Tomorrow we would hit Gbadolité, home of president Mobutu. I wondered what our secret weapon might have in store for us next...

CHAPTER SEVENTEEN

The next day we made it as far as Gbadolité. One moment we were slogging along in first gear down a washed out dirt road, then with a bump, we were on pavement. As we picked up speed and shifted into third, then fourth, the Hilux began to vibrate.

"Out of alignment!" I shouted to Keith.

"No kidding."

People stepped off the road to let us pass. A few waved, some stared, most ignored us. Hiluxes and men with machine guns in the back no doubt were a common sight.

"Turn left up here!" Mpasi shouted from the back.

Left took us up a long driveway towards what I remembered to be the *Présidence* or the residence of President Mobutu. It was a two-story building, huge in fact, surrounded by what were once well-manicured grounds. Some empty ponds surrounded the entrance. Three guards stepped out at the gate. Mpasi jumped down and walked over to them. One swung the gate open and we went through. She had a few words with them and got back in.

"*Allons-y,* let's go!" she commanded.

I was pretty sure that she was the Mpasi of my childhood, the daughter of the local warlord Bemba. It would explain the bodyguards and her air of authority. It explained in part how she could pull us out of jail and why these gates opened for us. But how and why she had been there to rescue us was still unknown.

A young man in a lightweight white suit came out to meet us. We looked incredibly grubby after these last several days.

"Welcome to Gbado," he offered. He looked us over, then smiled at Mpasi as she came over and gave him a double-eared air-kiss. She noticed us watching and smiled.

"My *ndeko*." *Ndeko* could mean brother, cousin, anybody in the family.

"Come in, come in!" He ushered us inside. Two more servants rushed out to take our belongings.

"Ah...Mpasi...the *sanduku* - box....?" I delicately phrased it.

"Don't worry. We'll take good care of Dad."

...of Dad? Where does she get off...

"I am Pelendo, first son of General Bemba. You must be Anna." Sure, he knew my name, why not?

"Nice to meet you." I nodded to Pelendo.

"Keith Carlson." Keith offered his hand.

"Ian Price." Ian did the same.

The interior showed signs of wear but was obviously well maintained. Leather chairs and a deep sofa occupied one corner. Some local art adorned the walls. The floors were covered with thatched matting. The servants took what remained of our packs up a flight of stairs.

"Perhaps you'd like a shower and to change before we eat, yes?"

Oh yes yes yes.

The shower was hot. It ran and ran and never ran out. Reluctantly I turned it off after a half-hour and stepped out of the shower, back into the room. Some new clothes were laid out for me. Khaki pants, a pullover embroidered shirt. It was good. I didn't care whose they were. I slipped on the clothes and left my hair down and wet. I descended the steps to the men sitting below. They'd already cleaned up. They all looked up at me as if I were making some gala appearance.

"Don't get up," I said, just in case they weren't. I plopped down in one of leather easy chairs.

"*Un boire, mademoiselle?*" A servant stood ready to take my drink order. I glanced at Ian who smiled and shook his head.

"*Un coca, merci.*" I smiled at Ian. "Please add some rum."

Ian just rolled his eyes. Keith pretended not to hear all this.

"Anna," said Pelendo, "Mpasi says you know how to drive."

"What, you never met a woman who could drive before?" This was irritating.

"*Non, non*, I did not mean it that way…all of my sisters can at least steer a car. No, she says you can really *drive*, know what I mean?"

"How many sisters do you have?" My drink arrived and I sipped it gratefully.

He thought a moment. "Many."

I added, "Yeah, I can in fact really *drive*, if you get my *drift*?"

"Drift, I don't know that word."

"It's hard to explain, but I can show you. Mpasi says you have a fast car. How fast is fast?"

"Fastest car in the Congo."

I had to laugh. Surely that was his attempt at humor. "I'll bet it is. I would love to see it." Pelendo stood up and motioned for the door. I smiled, downed my coke, and followed him.

We left Ian, Keith and company and walked out the back door, across the little plaza centered on a fountain that dribbled water to what looked like a garage. A guard saw us coming and ran to open the door. This was not just a garage, it was a hanger. It contained several machine-gun mounted jeeps, what looked like a Bradley fighting vehicle of some kind, a couple of Unimogs…and a Pontiac Firebird probably driven by Jim Rockford.

I was not a big muscle car fan, but I had respect for the genre. Muscle cars were just big heavy blunt instruments that handled like pigs. As the 70's wore on, they faded away to wimpy copies of their former selves. I wasn't at first sure where this Firebird fit in. It was just surreal enough to find one in the middle of the Congo.

It was painted black with gold trim. Tires looked good. It was spotless. Somebody was taking good care of this machine.

"Is this a Ram Air IV?" I asked Pelendo. I doubted if he knew the various distinctions.

He laughed. "Sheet no. This is a V."

I'd have to teach him to pronounce some words correctly.

I stood in awe. This was a collector's car. The V was to the IV like the Challenger was to the Sputnik. Few were ever made. It had a specially modified 500 hp engine, solid lifters and tunnel port heads. It would rip the quarter in under 13 seconds - almost as fast as AJ. I ran my hand over it.

"Let's go for a ride. You drive." He handed me the keys with that irritating smile. He was baiting me. He figured I'd jerk and kill the engine right at the start. We slid into the seats and I buckled up. Pelendo did not. He was not in the habit.

"Better buckle up," I suggested. He ignored me.

With a turn of the key the engine throbbed into life. The whole car vibrated smoothly with kinetic energy. I shivered. I looked at the gearshift. It was a Hurst four speed. I pushed down the clutch, shifted into first and let it out gently, not sure what to expect. The clutch was stiff but it caught nicely as I let it out. The Firebird snarled out of the garage feeling like a lion out for a kill. I played nice as we went around the plaza, getting the feel. It was heavy and cumbersome, rear-wheel drive - not agile like AJ, but mean enough. Mpasi and my two white friends were now watching from the door as I came by.

"Anna," said Ian as he came over to my window, "I know what you are thinking. Please don't do this!" Then he smiled. "I had to say that. Don't scare him to death."

"Can't promise a thing, Ian." He backed up a step then, crossed himself with a broad smile.

"Why did he do that? He isn't Catholic, is he?"

"No, not Catholic, just British. Used to be Anglican."

We headed down the driveway. Snicked into second, smooth. The sound of the engine carried well ahead of us like a fighter plane and people got off the paved road. I knew the airport was about a klick down the road and headed that way. Snick into third, not pushing it.

Pelendo smiled. "Very nice, isn't it?"

"Sure, nice car to take shopping at the market." Pelendo laughed at that.

"I wish I could drive in America. I am tired of driving this only in Gbadolité."

People lined the road and waved. Children hid behind their mothers. As we began to leave the town, I picked up speed. Up ahead a sign with an arrow pointed to the Aéroport de Gbadolité. I didn't slow down.

"This is the turn, Anna."

"I know. Just hang on."

We hit the corner just hard enough as I snapped it down into third and we fishtailed into the turn. I was not used to the rear wheel drive, but already I had learned something about the oversteer.

The guards at the airport knew that sound and waved us through. *Probably the same guards that shot our plane down.* No planes to worry about. There were a couple of small jets and smaller prop planes lined up. We tore by them toward the main strip. I set up for the turn, hit the strip and spun the wheel. This time the rear wheels broke loose just right and we did a very nice 45-degree turn onto the main strip. Pelendo was indeed hanging on. That made me smile.

Into fourth. The revs climbed. I desperately wanted a fifth. We were doing about 150 when the markers for the end of the strip started the count down. I slowed…some. The end was coming fast in more ways than one. Pelendo was making little noises but I couldn't understand what he was saying. Slowed a little more. A tad more.

Here we go. Shift into third, keep revs up. Clutch, a flick of the wheel into the corner, pull the handbrake. Feed it some gas. The rear tires broke loose, then the front, smoke, squealing rubber, more noises from Pelendo, we were sliding sideways around the end of the airstrip. A little more throttle to control the angle. I popped the clutch to revive wheel spin. As we lined up facing the other way, I let off a bit of power and released the handbrake. We tore back down the strip the other way.

"Should have buckled up. Click it or ticket, you know."

Still he said nothing. We motored calmly back through the town. Finally he spoke.

"Ah, Anna, what in *kuzimu* did you just do? I have to learn that!" Pelendo was all jazzed up and throwing around some Swahili slang.

"That, my *ndeko,* is a drift….another time, maybe. We really have to move on." I had one more idea in mind. We crept up the palace driveway until we came to the plaza that surrounded the little fountain. It didn't take much. I hit it one more time and did the same tricks. The Ram V broke loose and we spun around the fountain with the nose pointed at the center. Twice. Filled the air with the sweet incense of burning rubber. People were at the doors and windows. Ian was just shaking his head.

I stopped by Ian and got out. It took a long moment before Pelendo got out. He might have to order new rubber.

"This really makes me miss AJ."

"Who's AJ?" Ian sounded jealous.

"No one you know." I smiled. I liked to keep AJ to myself, and so far in our "relationship", I had had no reason to introduce the two of them.

We needed another night there, time to unwind, repack, re-energize a bit. Gbadolité is like a mirage in the dessert. It can fool you into thinking this is life in Africa, when just a jungle block away, reality bites.

Later that night we were sitting around just outside the back door, watching the dry fountain not burble, sipping drinks and casually chatting. A meager fire crackled to life in a small metal pit. We sat circling the pit and listened to the nocturnals begin to wake up for their evening romp. I wondered what animal might find me alluring enough to eat for the evening if I wandered out of the courtyard. If I had to choose, would I rather be eaten alive by a hundred ants, or swallowed whole by a snake? I turned to Uncle Keith with a pressing question.

"Why did you choose this, Uncle Keith? Out here, the center of the equator, danger at every turn. Torrential rainstorms. Tarantulas, mamba's, flesh eating army ants… who would choose this?"

"Are you questioning my sanity?"

"Sort of." I smiled at him across the flames. He looked like part of the fabric I was gazing at. He seemed to possess a symbiotic relationship with the jungle.

"Well, I suppose it must be more than an over-inflamed boy-scout infatuation." I was poking him now, for good measure.

"Maybe it's just an overdose of testosterone."

"Maybe."

"Ok, I'll try to explain." The prodding worked.

"Long time ago… "

"Oh, I love stories that start with long, long ago, in a land far away…" I scooted up closer like a little girl about to hear a fairytale, covering my legs with my blanket, holding my knees. The more I knew about Keith and the way his mind worked, the more I knew about my Dad. And at this point, that's all I truly wanted out of this journey. Whatever possessed Keith to live out here was similar to what spurred my Dad.

"Are you going to let me tell this?" Keith said with a smile. "Well, long ago, I felt I nearly imploded on myself. You see, when I was young, I did not have much responsibility. I did whatever I wanted, when I wanted. I had no sense of self 'cuz I had no sense of others. Does that make sense?"

"Keith, you've never really had a way with words, but somehow, it's making sense, go on." I smiled. I could see why Dad chose him as such a close companion. Or maybe Keith chose Dad.

"Well, as you know, I became a Christian, and everything changed for me." I grimaced. I forgot that this might come around to Christ, but I couldn't cut Keith off in mid-story. I listened. He continued, "It wasn't this dramatic spiritual transformation moment.

For me, it was just comin' 'round to common sense. If we spend ourselves on ourselves, we eventually become so self-consumed that we eat the world - as if it lives inside our body - but is too large to contain - so we combust."

I looked at him quizzically. He was losing me.

"Ok, let me try that part again. I ate the world. Meaning, I swallowed all the lies, I lived for me. I wasn't all messed up on drugs you see, not a total 'worldly' person as you might expect" - *don't worry Keith, never expected that* - "but just a person, whose sole life was 'bout their own life. Like any other. But in this way, I just swallowed all that was around me into my mind, actions, goings and comings and gave out none of it."

"So you wanted to do good works? Practice self-denial?" Now I was tracking with him.

"No, I'm not talkin' about 'works.'" Nope, I wasn't tracking. Keith continued, "Anytime we try to 'do good works' for ourselves sake - to feel good 'bout ourselves - to 'do time' for others, so to speak - even if it is truly in our desire to help - it backfires spiritually - it's still so selfishly motivated - don't work - at least not in the full capacity that it could. Doesn't appease God either, and He doesn't ask to be appeased anyhow. Not talkin' about works. Talkin' about faith. I had to have faith that the power of God was indeed inside of me and that only His power could work through my person to keep me from eating poison - to keep others from poison."

"Poison?" Definitely not tracking.

"Yeah. Poison. Lies. The great big lie, the lie that God doesn't love you." I took a moment to inhale that one. Keith continued, "Without God, a person's whole life is toxic. I know this. May not look like it, lives may look so pretty, don't they? And sometimes, we don't even know we're on a slow and steady diet of poison. We eat up other people and step all over each other, meanin' to or not, in driving our way capitalistically through life, because, we are taught, that 'it's all about me.' Gratifying your own nature at every turn, turns a person in on themselves. And there is a darkness in there too deep and cavernous - no one should look upon that. You've heard the whole term 'look within yourself' - well, every time I tried to glance 'within myself' - I got plum freaked out I did - sometimes the soul can look mighty dark without the light of God."

"So, what you're saying, is that you recognized that inside of yourself is God - your inner deity. In my case - my inner goddess, right?"

"Not even close."

I threw a pebble into the empty fountain. Is a wishing stone still a wishing stone if there is no water? These were the existential questions of my life. Keith was far deeper. "Well, dang, throw me a bone here, Keith, I'm not inclined to be spiritual. Meditation is about as far as I come, and that alone does little for me."

"Good. That's why this isn't 'spiritual' - it's not about that. You're still looking in. You're looking at what *you* can do to be spiritual and what can help *you*. True faith isn't about *your* inner goddess, no matter what way you say it; you're still yakking on about yourself. This isn't about some divine 'That' - that breathes a stream of spiritual smoke through your soul. This is about finally, finally, looking out and up. Discovering who are you. Your Heavenly Father's child. A wondrous creation from the Creator. Beloved one of the Lover. It's an identity issue." Marilyn always said I had identity issues. But this was a different kind of identity Keith was referring to. Something I had never heard of before.

"Should I go on?"

"Yes," I surprised myself how quickly I answered in the affirmative.

"Once I really saw who I was, or rather, Whose I was, I then started lookin' to Him. The more I know about my creator, the more I know of my purpose. Jesus, God in the flesh, well - he taught me about humility, abundant love, graciousness, sacrificing yourself entirely, dying to every single thought about yourself, every desire of your own, and giving it all to the One who made you and to others."

"Sorry to be blunt," I interrupted shaking my head, "but that last part just sounds horrible. Aren't we made for pleasure? To be happy?"

"Well, it's a funny thing, Annie. It's actually what brings the most ultimate joy, and yes, pleasure too. We are meant to seek pleasure, but our problem, as one writer said, is that we don't seek pleasure hard enough. We are easily pleased with the small stuff: sex," I coughed uncomfortably, "movies, vacations, money, whatever. These things are all great and pleasurable, but we stop there and think that that is all there is. But the real, deep, never-ending pleasure comes when we serve, know, and love God and others."

Keith stopped for breath. It was definitely time for bed, he was making sense and I could feel my spiritual jaw begin to chew on this bone. Who knew where this kind of salivating would lead me. Out of my comfort zone, that I knew. And I loved comfort.

Keith continued without my prompting.

"Honey, only the One who created you, can know your every inner working well enough, to know exactly what you need. Like you and your computers. You create these systems - or at least you help them work - you know how they work, what makes them tick - only the creator can aid the created. God showed me that His aid is really in giving and pouring myself out through Christ. Sounds selfish don't it?"

"Selfish? Hardly. How is giving to others selfish?"

"I mean, I knew that if I wanted the best for my life, I had to turn and surrender. See, selfish. I still was trying to do what was in the end, best for me. But in this case, I realized that in looking for what was for my best - I finally found it *outside* of me, not inside. I also realized that that ain't so bad after all. God does want our best, He wants us to enjoy life, He wants to give us good gifts. But usually His gift comes in packages we don't recognize or usually give two thoughts about. They ain't wrapped up neatly with big ol' bows. They are packages that come in the faces of the needy, sick, and hungry, and those without knowledge of faith and God, the hurting and the broken hearted. God gives us hurting people for us to share life with, and share ourselves with - and in return, as we think we are healing something missing in *them*, God is actually healin' something missing in *us*." I remembered what Becky had said about sometimes when we offer grace we end up the recipient as well. *Is grace something I even need?*

Keith looked at me for any comments. I had none. I loved to hear him speak and yet hated it. It turned and twisted me up. I could see why Ian was feeling so tired that one morning after talking to Keith. Somehow this rough woodsy cave man of a person was speaking a beautiful language I could sit and listen to for hours. I was close to replying with a, "that is good for *you* Keith, but not for *me*. To each his own" - but instead I just wanted to listen to more, plus I questioned the profundity of such a subjective statement. Was there really no absolute moral truth?

"So that's why I went out here." Keith continued. "I asked Him where I could go to see His love and to feel his grace. I asked Him where I could go to serve Him and be his hands and feet in the world and one day I met your Dad who was headed out to Congo with all the zeal and enthusiasm of, well, someone with zeal and enthusiasm, and, uh - here I was. Here I am. Doin' His work. Ain't aimin' to just be pious or to throw hellfire and damnation down any one's throat. I'm aimin' to tell people about faith in God, remind them that He came to them first, He sent his son to die for them, they don't have to try and try to *be* or *do* to get their way to him - they just have to have faith like a chil' that He came to them first. So, I just try to tell people about that, that God is available to all in this manner - without exception, without favoritism - and that in findin' that faith - your insides are changed."

Insides. I think Keith had ran out of ways to say why he was here, and his language was turning a bit earthy. Plus, it seemed the conversation was starting to turn more and more toward *Jesus* and that is where I get squeamish. Something about that name...

"Makes sense, Keith. Thanks for telling me, I guess that helps me remember why Dad was here too. He was a good man."

"He was. Sometimes he wasn't, and that was O.K. too, right honey?" Keith laughed and also threw a non-wishing pebble into the fountain. In that very sentence, I felt he was telling me that I was OK, too.

"Right. G'night Keith." I kissed him on top of his head and turned to leave.

"Annie. Jesus loves you. I pray for you everyday, Annie," Keith said just above a whisper as he threw another pebble. I stopped and felt my body shudder a little. *Everyday? Jesus loves me?* I kept walking and shut the door. It was time to sleep. Dad used to call me Annie...I missed him more and more. I wondered what Keith meant about Dad not being a good man sometimes. I pondered what he said about pleasure, and being a child of God, about the great big lie, and about not having to try to do or be. I couldn't quite swallow all of it, and yet it sounded like a pure melody, a melody that I wanted to join in and play... I just didn't know if I had the gift to play it.

In the morning we began to load up the truck. It didn't take long. Backpacks, bodyguards, a couple of trunks from Mpasi, and Dad. We said goodbye. Pelendo stood on the porch and watched us leave. I waved, and he waved back with a broad smile. It was already late afternoon and we would not get far before we had to stop.

We drove mainly in silence until it was past dark and then set up camp. It began to feel like routine. I was trying not to think about my conversation with Keith. I was trying not to think about Ian. I was trying not to think about prison. That left little else to think about so I occupied my mind with reciting the entire movie of Groundhog Day by heart, in my head of course. What if I had to live *this* day over and over and over again for the rest of my life?

CHAPTER EIGHTEEN

"I am Bemba's daughter."

Keith and Ian and I sat around the ashes from last night's fire and leaned in to hear more from Mpasi. Dawn was being lifted up gently over the horizon by pink hands of time. It was not yet 6 am.

"I am Bemba's daughter. Sort of. More like, his niece. He calls me his daughter."

"Bemba is your Dad, or Uncle?" I said.

"Yes. Uncle." She stared at us. We waited for more. She waited for more questions. Silence prevailed.

"That's how you got us out? You had powerful connections?" Keith pointed out what we were all thinking.

"More or less. I got news of roadblock and the drug smuggle, and the arrestings. Of course, news got around that there were three *mondeles* with them, we learn your names. Tata, that is General Bemba - he like to keep up appearance with other foreign relation. He want to be Vice President someday, maybe even President…after Kabila that is…don't misunderstand… he needs to be well liked. Incarcerating, that is the word, yes? - three white Americans on his territory may not be best...appearance." We nodded as if we understood all that she was explaining. How could a man be comfortable with coups and militia, but not imprisoning three white people? The system was befuddling.

"Why did he send you?" I asked. *A woman?*

"He didn't *send* me. He wasn't sure what to do with you. I told him I must have to go and get you. He allowed, assigned a bodyguards and sent word to the prison, along with a few threats. *C'est tout."*

"That's it? You asked, he said yes. You got the truck..." - *by the way - whose truck is it?* "...and got the body back in more or less the same condition, all our passports and then freed us. *C'est tout?*" I mimicked her. "Why did you care?" We were no longer nodding; we were baffled.

"Yes. That's it for now. We move on, yes?"

"Yes. Mpasi, by the way, did you know that we used to play together?" My suspicions had been confirmed. We were childhood friends. A long time ago in another world.

"Yes I did. We move on." Mpasi said this with a straight face, and not a glimmer of excitement. *She doesn't find that...coincidental?*

Mpasi was obviously finished spilling parts of her story for the morning. She got up and wiped her hands on her *liputa* - African sari. She walked back to the tent to grab her sack. The rest of us stared at each other, more confused.

"Bemba's *daughter*? I knew it!" I choked out the words in a half-whisper to the boys.

Keith took off his glasses and rubbed his eyes. He seemed to do that frequently when he was trying to process something. But he didn't say a word.

"Niece. Or something. What interest would she have in our predicament? What does she want? She obviously wants something?" That was Ian, catching onto African pragmatism.

It wasn't that people acted on someone's behalf just to get something out of it - it was the way of life. Not just greed, it was survival, mutual dependency. But what did she need? She was surviving just fine as a daughter of a wealthy, well-armed "diplomat"/warlord.

"Maybe she'll tell us more later. She'll let us know. She does know who I am after all, she remembers playing with me..."

"Do you think it has something to do with James?" Ian asked.

"Dad? Why - why would you think that?"

"Just thinking out loud. He still has a story to tell us, too." Ian was staring toward the truck.

"I suppose he does." I glanced back toward the Ziegler, wished that Dad could wake up and sit down with us by the cold fire, and explain everything. On the other hand, that would freak me out, just a little, and it was time to bury him, and head back to Seattle.

"The rains are doing a good job washing out our roads, we need to keep moving on while we can." Keith started packing up the tents, and we headed out. I didn't like the sound of "while we can." As if on cue, a great Congo rain poured down on us as we lumbered along the beaten path. My butt and back were aching and turning a nice shade of blue and purple. Everything was sore from the bouncing. If I was fatter, perhaps I'd be better cushioned. The ditches were getting worse, deep ravines in the road that the tires battled with in every rotation. The chicken squabbled in the back, unrelenting noise. I crossed my fingers that we would eat chicken for dinner tonight.

Another day went by sitting in the sticky cab, sweaty legs stuck to the vinyl seat, or standing in the windy back or sitting on the steel wheel well. All my insides bounced around so much, none of them were in the right place, I was sure of it. Maybe my appendix got shoved around, who needs those anyway? I was not a person anymore, I was a piece of meat put through the truck blender. From time to time I fell asleep despite the bouncing, but I soon learned this was dangerous as I would wake up being splashed with a puddle because I didn't notice it in time to put my window up, or crashing my head against the window, a very rude awakening, a very big bump. Breaks for shade, snacks, and a stretch. Idle chitchat. We saw an occasional antelope and one place where either buffalo or elephants had crossed the road, nothing to fear though. I changed my clothes a couple times in the bushes - thankful for our mysteriously intact bags and some new duds from Mpasi. I changed underclothes too, but kept my same bra. I had hidden some cash, sewed it along the bottom as an under-wire. We had plenty of money, no one knew that though. I was saving it for the worst-case scenario. Perhaps that was back in prison, but I ended up not needing it. I glanced again at Mpasi. *How odd...*

The day was long and arduous, Congo terrain and weather were brutal. The rains came and went. The tarp went on, the tarp went off. We played the alphabet game. Ian was getting good at it even. Maybe we would take a road trip together again some day. Maybe to California. Wine Country. No, somewhere cold. Whistler. We'd ski all day in the powder, and then at night snuggle up with hot buttered rums, sit in the hot tub while flakes gently landed on our steamy skin. Yes. That is what we would do, as soon as we got home. We changed games.

"Let's play, 'would you rather'." I said to Ian.

"How?"

"I'll start. Would you rather eat honey with your fingers, for two hours straight? Or, change your own brakes on your car?"

"What? They aren't similar at all!"

"True. That's the point." Ian looked at me with his eyebrows all askew.

"Ok. I'll try another one. Would you rather lose a court case, or be the most inflexible person in the world."

"Court case. That was easy."

"Your turn."

"Would you rather," Ian took a deep breath, I could tell he was thinking too hard, "would you rather drink a rum and coke, or a gin and tonic?"

"Boring. That is *boring* Ian! Think outside the box, will ya?" Tall order for a tax lawyer. "Rum and coke. Ok, try this one. Would you rather solve global warming, or have free Starbucks and gas for you and your family for the rest of your life."

"You are nuts."

"Yes I am. Would you rather lose all your toes to frost bite, or be forced to only breathe through your nose, forever."

"I'm done with this game."

"You're no fun." No road trips for Ian and me. We'd fly to Whistler. Maybe he'd buy us a plane, and we'd get our pilot's licenses.

"What do you think her story is?" Keith began a new conversation. Whistler faded away quickly. I entered in, anxious to hear everyone else's ideas. The look on Keith's face said that he had a few ideas of his own.

"I have no idea. Bemba's daughter, rescues three white people, for no political or personal gain? I don't know." I hated not knowing. Even worse, I hated admitting it.

"Maybe she was paid too. Maybe she is actually taking us somewhere, she'll get paid for her delivery." I added. I looked behind me at Mpasi sitting in the back of the truck, holding a chicken between her skirt, without any AK-47. No, she was not dangerous, just strange.

"James knew Bemba, you know." Keith said.

"Yeah, I know. They weren't buddies or anything though." *I hoped not anyway.*

"No, but maybe Bemba felt obligated." Keith kept trying to connect the dots.

"But how would he know we were James' company?" Ian asked.

"The body, got a good look, knew who it was, and placed us appropriately," I said. "None of this makes sense. Plus, Mpasi said that it was her idea.

So it would have been her obligation I suppose, not Bemba's. It doesn't work...I guess it doesn't have to. How much farther to Bosobolo?" I was tired of the puzzle.

"Maybe one more day. We could be there by night fall tomorrow." I could feel him shrug in the dark. Keith didn't sound too sure, especially as he was driving in first gear. It was getting very dark.

I sighed, unable to hide my fatigue and impatience. I had forgotten Africa's cruel roads, and cruel weather. I closed my eyes for a minute, and everything went silent. But I wasn't asleep, the truck had lurched to a sudden stop. I hit my head on the dashboard.

"Ouch! Keith!?" I looked at him a little ticked off, rubbing my head, trying not to swear in front of the missionary.

Keith was leaning over, staring over the wheel out the window. The wipers flung rain back and forth.

"Look."

I elbowed Ian in the ribs, using my nonverbal communication skills, telling him to get out of the truck. Ian opened the door and I fell out behind him, wading through the puddles to the front of the truck. I looked down, and down, further down, and then across. There was no bridge. There were no logs, only a small river beneath us. The wheels of the truck were just inches from the edge. The bridge had been washed out. This was the only road to Bosobolo. Just a few feet between us and the other side put a stop to our travels. Keith, Ian, Mpasi and myself now stood at the brink in silence, looking down at the river. No one dared to speak.

CHAPTER NINETEEN

"We're done." I offered. We had stood still for more than enough time to reach the natural conclusion. There was no way around it. We're finished.

"Anna - we don't have to be. We can figure something out." Keith answered quickly.

"Sure we could, there's always a way. But I don't want to. Whatever way it is, it's difficult and strenuous. I am done in. Nothing left in the tank, you know." Why bother? Dad didn't need a specific gravesite; he just wanted to come home. The river was as good a place as any to say goodbye.

Keith still insisted, "If we drive back to Bumba, we can take another route here via Lisala…

"Or we could make a bridge." Ian's comments got a few smirks. He persisted, "I'm serious, how hard could it be to throw some logs across…"

Mpasi remained silent. She seemed more stunned and paralyzed by our dead end than we were. I ignored her, it always seemed to be the thing to do.

"Stop with the suggestions. It's final." This was enough for me. I turned from the ravine and hopped up into the back of the truck. The tarp was off, the sun was out, and we were sweaty, hungry, and tired.

I sat down on the Zig and as if it were alive, I stroked the shiny metal. *Dad, I'm sorry. Is this close enough? This is close enough, it has to be. I'm done with this journey. Whatever you intended for me to discover in Africa, I've discovered. I left some of my pride at the prison, I think I'm in love, I've realized a lot about perseverance... I'm done. I'm sorry.*

I whispered my apologies and let those incriminating tears well up one more time. I wasn't Jane of jungle. I missed my yuppie life, the comfort of familiarity...I couldn't imagine a second leg to this journey – to retrace our steps back three long days, then another long trek, and who knew, maybe yet another bridge out. We'd catch malaria, all die of Ebola...not an option. Dad did say Goyongo, a little village near Bosobolo. He said *"a mile down the path heading past the water source...."* What did it matter? Nothing, he should be glad I got him this far. I looked in Ziegler's window. He didn't look glad.

I noticed that the three of them were looking up at me in the Hilux. I stood up, as if I were a preacher on a platform about to begin a long sermon.

"We have gone as far as we can. Dad will be buried here. Don't argue please, this is what he wanted. To be buried in Africa, to bring me back with him. I came back, he will be buried. This is close enough, it's as far as we go. We have a home to get back to, *this"* - I swung my arm dramatically around the jungle - "isn't it." I sat back down on Ziegler. I wasn't feeling well. Maybe it was my "speech," but I felt light headed and slightly feverish. Maybe I was hungry. I scratched at my mosquito bites and waited for a response.

"Ok Anna. You call the shots. I think you've done great." Keith affirmed my decision. He was looking haggard himself. He missed his wife.

"Let's find a place to bury him." Ian looked around and scratched his head, as if Peaceful Palms Cemetery would instantly reveal itself.

"No. We go." We all turned and stared at Mpasi. Her greenish-bluish eyes were gleaming, her soft skin aglow with sweat and she looked almost mad. She looked so familiar, especially when she was determined. I opened my jaw, but not a word came out. I didn't know what to make of her comment. Was she joking?

"Mpasi. Did you understand? We are not going further sweetheart." Uncle Keith stepped up first.

"I understand. We go on to Bosobolo, then to Goyongo."

"No, you don't understand. We are not going on to Goyongo, Mpasi, it's impossible. We can't cross the ravine. I'm so sorry we can't take you there. Can we take you back to Bumba?" I tried to offer another alternative.

"Yes. There is no bridge. But we are so close. There has to be a ways." Mpasi looked at Ian for support, after all, it was his idea.

"Mpasi. I can't go on. This is *my* journey. I'm done." I was getting frustrated. Mpasi kept staring straight at me, she hadn't blinked yet. It was unnerving me. Her liputa-skirt waved around her in the soft wind, she still looked kind, but she also looked like she would snap me in two if I disagreed one more time.

"This my journey too."

"I know you wanted a lift. I know you rescued us, but you won't tell us why, and we don't know what you want. I don't know how this is your journey too. We offered you money, what do you want?"

"To go to Goyongo."

I looked at Keith bewildered. *Your turn.*

"Mpasi, what alternative is there?"

"This is not my journey." She was turning me in circles.

"You just said it was your journey." Ian gave his two cents, also looking a little impatient.

"Not *just* mine. Yours, and yours, and his -" she pointed at us, and then at the Ziegler. *What did she care about my Dad's burial for?*

"His journey was to be buried in Africa. Here he is." Ian persisted.

"That's not what he said is it? He said Goyongo, down the path past water source, right? Didn't he? Right? We are not there yet." She pursed her lips and placed her hands on her hips.

We stared at her, bewildered. She obviously overheard some conversation somewhere along the way, how else would she have known the details? But for the life of me I couldn't remember talking about that will.

"He's dead. He doesn't know the difference." Ian's mad lawyer skills stepped up to bat.

"But we will."

"We will know that we didn't make it all the way. But we will also know that we tried hard. We came very close. No one could blame us." Ian worked the invisible jury with his plea: we did all we could, we fulfilled his wishes, do not convict!

"But - " Mpasi began her plea again and I stood up to interrupt. I was through with this conversation; it was obviously going nowhere. She either needed to reveal more of her intentions, or get on board.

"This is my decision. *Mine*." I attempted to sound as commanding as she was. "I'm sorry. This is *my* Dad. I am his family. I am his only family left. I am his daughter - I decide. Unless you have something else to tell us. That is final."

"No you aren't." Mpasi's voice fell down a decibel. She seemed frightened by her own words. Ian and Keith remained fixated on her mouth, wondering where the words came from. What was wrong with this girl?

"I'm not? I'm not, what?"

"You are not his only families."

"Well, sure, he has cousins, and a few others back at home - " I stopped and looked at Keith - "Oh! You mean Uncle Keith! He is not really my uncle - we just call the men uncle - "

"Not meaning *Keith*."

"Who the *kuzimu* do you mean then, Mpasi?" I hissed, trying on some of Pelendo's Swahili to make my point. I felt nauseous and confused.

Mpasi looked at the ground and shuffled her feet. She took a deep breath. My heart was pounding, somewhere inside I knew she would say something monumental or totally crazy. I was hoping for crazy.

"Me. I mean, me." Crazy.

"You?"

"I am family too."

"Because your Uncle knew my Dad?"

"Because your Dad...is also my Dad." Mpasi looked worse than me, maybe. She nearly choked on her words. Mpasi wiped her forehead with her skirt and kicked the rear tire, shuffling around with useless actions...stamping the words into the silence. She pulled out a cigarette and tried to light it, but her hands were too shaky. She eventually leaned against the tailgate of the truck, with her head between her hands, on her lap.

I sat back down on Ziegler and tapped my hand on the window - as if to waken Dad. *Um, Dad... you there? Can you help us out here? Explain please?* I felt shell shocked and defensive. She was mistaken. She was in it for money. There is no other explanation. She heard we had a white man, who lived here for years. It made sense, of course this could be her story. She didn't want a small sum of money, she wanted *inheritance*. Maybe she needed it to get out of some situation. A poorly arranged marriage...maybe she wasn't Bemba's daughter but some kind of slave. My imagination could come up with a thousand different scenarios. They all concluded that she was lying.

"You're a liar. " I looked down at her and enunciated my words. I couldn't help myself. She was visibly shaken, but a great liar. She was taking advantage of my Dad's death and me. I hated her for that.

"Anna. Please." Keith put his hand out toward me as if to clamp it over my mouth.

"Keith. You take care of this lying nonsense. She wants our money, or something worse, and you know it. Get her gone. We have enough problems." I turned and jumped down from the Hilux, yanked the cigarette and matches out of her hands, grabbed the toilet paper and headed off into the thick for some privacy. *Liar. What an innocent act. Who did she think she was?* As I walked away lighting her cigarette she called after me.

"Ok. Right. I go."

I turned around and stared at her. I called her bluff. I knew it.

"You'll go? Good. Bye." I waved her away with the back of my hand like she was a puppy dog. Shoo. I took a drag and waited for her reply.

"I'll go. Get help to cross the river."

"Ok! Cross the river, make it to Goyongo. We're going the other way. Have a nice trip!" *Shoo! Shoo!*

"I'll come back and tell you how to cross." She jumped off the tailgate and started to walk quickly toward the village with her sack on her head. The two guards scrambled to catch up. I stared in her direction and cursed her under my breath one more time. Her hips moved gracefully as she rapidly disappeared from sight. I looked at Keith and heard him mutter something about her determination. Ian was ignoring her, slapping mosquitoes and lathering on more bug spray and sunscreen. The combination of the two topical lotions was making me even sicker than I already was. I turned and headed into the jungle to smoke and relieve myself, getting away from the deet and spf 40 sauté.

After finding a "bathroom," I found a small patch of low grass under a large leafy tree, and sat down, putting my head between my knees. I listened to my breathing and my heart beat, allowed my body to calm itself. I could hear the various birds and rustlings in the bush. Darkness was thick now; I knew this wasn't smart. I tried not to imagine a visit by a green mamba, or a cobra. Not even an ant. Maybe I would do some meditation. Maybe not. It was too hot, too dark. Maybe I would pray. I didn't know how. I decided to talk to my Dad. I closed my eyes and returned to a favorite memory...

Hey Dad. Remember our move to Goyongo? I was not even five. It was scary to me, so many new noises, new animals. I remember the hyrax screeching as it climbed down from its perch in the trees. I was frightened to death every time. I would lay in bed wide-awake and wait for it to come and lunge down for me. I would wait under my mosquito nets for the flesh-eating army ants to come and invade our house, like they did so often. Invade and eat, eat our parrot, bite my toes. I would wait and hold my breath for morning, too scared to fall asleep. I would wait while the rain-storm shook my shutters and drummed on our thin tin roof. I would wait for you. I lay in bed with my eyes fixated on the bottom of my door. You would usually wake up close to four a.m., and you would light your kerosene lanterns. I could see a glimmer, a flicker of soft orange light leak between the bottom of the door and our cement floor. It was just enough light. Just enough to know you were awake. If you were awake, I knew I could fall asleep. I had to wait for you to be up, in order to find some peace. I knew that you would keep watch over me, and then I could close my eyes. I did, and I'd sleep for a few precious hours, deeply, peacefully. It was always your light that I looked for. Where is it now? Can I close my eyes now?

"Anna! Anna!" Ian was shaking my shoulders. "Wake up! Are you okay? We were worried sick, you've been gone for about a half hour."

"I must have fallen asleep." I shook my head and felt the stiffness in my neck. I was awkwardly leaned up against a tree.

"In the middle of the jungle?! Brilliant. Good God, come on." Ian grabbed my hand and helped me up. I was feeling so faint and weak, so tired out. We walked back to the truck together; we were further away than I thought I had gone.

"I'm sorry for scaring you. Didn't mean to." I apologized.

"Glad you're fine. We are going to camp right here, no use trying to back up any, and it's starting to get dark. The tents are up."

"All three of them?"

"Just two."

"Good, I could use some company." I still felt like a part of my five year old self was with us, scared and alone in the jungle. Waiting for a light. We returned to camp, Keith was already snoring in his tent. Ian gave me a couple hard-boiled eggs with some salt, and some peanuts he shelled. I ate in a daze and then we crawled into the one-man tent. I snuggled up close and laid my head up on his chest by his neck.

"Ian, if I sleep, will you stay awake?"

"Absolutely." Ian muttered, with his eyes closed. I smiled as he visibly slipped into sleep. He wrapped his arms around me, and I was out.

The light flickered along the bottom of my tent. *Dad is up.* It flickered again and shone brighter. *Kerosene lamp.* A few of them, and footsteps. I sprang up. Ian was already sitting up with a protective hand across me.

"Don't move." He whispered. "I'll go check."

"NO! Wait, I hear a voice." We listened quietly. I thought I could hear Keith's whisper, and a female voice. We crawled out of our tent. It was wet everywhere, cold and dark, sometime in the early morning. We had company.

CHAPTER TWENTY

"Just there! About two miles."

"What is she saying, Keith?" It had taken me a moment to gather myself, to wake up and realize that Mpasi had returned and was talking to Keith, pointing wildly west toward the jungle. She had some other people with her, carrying flashlights and long bamboo poles. It was all very confusing.

"What is going on?!"

"Anna, Mpasi says she asked the village, they told her that this bridge has been washed out for months, but there is a shallower crossing point just upstream a little ways. They had to be able to get into Bosobolo for the market." Keith was also pointing west.

"Great. So what kind of solution is this?"

"We walk."

"Walk?" I looked at Ian and Keith, waiting for some kind of acknowledgement that this was a crazy idea.

"Anna, we are only about 20 some klicks from Bosobolo. We could get there in a couple of days on foot," Keith said.

"He's right, Anna, let's not quit now." Ian was looking at me intently. He knew that was possibly a hair-trigger statement. He was right. Normally I would have taken that sentence and beaten him on the head with it. *"So Ian, now the rah-rah jungle-Jim are we?"* But I didn't. I dialed it back a bit.

"And then two days back, and our truck would still be sitting here, full of gas, waiting for our return?" I thought of how Mpasi was able to rescue us and suddenly realized the scenario didn't seem too outrageous. Nothing did anymore.

"One step at a time," Ian said, buttoning up his shirt.

I paused, ready to answer. Ready to say, that, no, we are going to stop. But the words didn't come out. I thought of being able to see my home again for the first time in years. I thought of Dad's ultra specific letter, as creepy as it all was. I thought of Mpasi and needed more information. WWMD? I wondered…what would Marilyn do? No. That was no good. But we had one pressing issue.

"How will we get the body across?"

Mpasi had been following this conversation pretty well. Mpasi pointed to the strong group of men, holding the bamboo poles. "We can sling the casket under the poles. They say the river is pretty shallow just upstream." She shrugged. Obviously, we would hire them. Sure, they could carry this body for miles, would be nothing new. These people had been trekking back and forth throughout the jungle carrying bodies slung from bamboo poles for decades.

Somewhere inside of me the light had flickered under my door, and gave me a small answer. Dad was up and ready to go for the day, ready to move on.

"Ok. We'll go…. At first light…Mpasi, it's not a casket. It's a Ziegler."

"A what?"

"She just likes to say Ziegler," said Ian, relieved that he had not been eviscerated.

I crawled back into my tent and regretted my decision. Mpasi's chicken squawked. So did a rooster. She had now acquired a rooster, it hooted and hollered like it was morning. Was she planning on breeding them along the way? I fell asleep for a few more hours to the noise and the shuffling around. They were strapping Dad in. Flashlights created strange dancing silhouettes against the sides of my tent. I was alone, Ian was helping the jungle men. Would he ever be able to go back to being a lawyer?

The smell of coffee woke me up. I struggled out of the tent and into the smoke of a little fire. Mpasi had a small pan on the fire with bubbling coffee. The smell itself jolted me awake. The rooster was crowing on schedule. I zipped open the tent and threw a rotten papaya in its general direction. Mpasi glared at me. I glared back and zipped the tent back closed and flopped back down in to my sleeping bag. I did not trust her, even if she was making coffee. I still did not want her company, I believed she was manipulating us, but couldn't figure it all out. She made me mad and uneasy, I was hoping to ditch her as soon as possible. Her and her feathery friends.

The sun had not yet crested the top of the giant trees all around us, and a light mist was rising from the ground. The smoke of the fire rose lazily straight up, there was not a whisper of breeze anywhere. I clumsily got changed in the tent and stumbled out into the open. Already my shirt was damp and sticking to me. Ian and Keith were busy with packing up all that we needed for our hike. A couple of other men from the nearest village were squatting around the fire. The men stared at me, in fact, most everyone was staring at me as I exited the tent. Some tongues clicked in my general direction.

I walked over to Keith and whispered, "Why is everyone staring at me?"

"You slept in Ian's tent. This is not...customary. They are wondering about your, um... new marriage."

"Marriage? I'll send them an embroidered invite from the states." I sneered, and walked off into the jungle for my morning "routine." I felt embarrassed that I had made a public statement about myself. However, I did not regret having company last night through all the commotion. Of course, Ian on the other hand, might get a pat on the back. The guys around the fire just figured Ian had acquired a woman - me. I, however, was not yet feeling very acquired. If there was any acquiring to do, I would do it. Now, I would wear a scarlet letter, "A," except nobody there ever read Hawthorne. An "A" was overkill anyway, we had just kissed. Just a little. It was nice. Maybe I would wear the letter "K" for kisser. Or "B" for *"baiser."* Now with a whole gang traveling with us, I figured my secluded times with Ian were mostly over. Just as well, I needed to focus on the task at hand.

I came out of my "bathroom" and sat on a log by the fire. Mpasi handed me a steaming mug. The first sip scalded my mouth and I almost spilled it all over myself.

"This is hotter than McDonald's…I ought to sue you."

"What?"

I laughed in spite of myself. "Never mind. This is good. Fresh roasted, I bet."

"What?" Mpasi scowled with confusion.

I laughed again at my own little inside joke. All the coffee here was fresh roasted. She probably just pulled the beans off the bushes from the overgrown abandoned coffee garden we had just driven through. Green beans made a potent brew. The coffee drunk in the village often was not aged at all.

I took a deep sip and closed my eyes with contentment. This kind of life wasn't half bad. No traffic, no cell phones, no noise. It wasn't just that it was quiet; the jungle was far from quiet. Something was missing… I took another swallow and figured it out. No hum. Coffee makers, microwaves, lights, TV's, phone lines, water coolers, computers…everything hums with electromagnetic activity. I didn't miss the humming. There was a new tune to listen to out here. In spite of my aching back, leaves for toilet paper, monsoons and creatures of death…there was a part of me that liked it here, even loved it. Cherished it would be a better word. It was once my home.

"Feels good to be home." I muttered.

"Home? You call this your home?"

"In a way, I suppose. I lived half of my life here you know."

"Yes, I know. But it's not your home." I didn't know what to make of her remark, so I let it pass over. Mpasi passed around some peanuts in a leaf and some crispy fried plantains. I sighed deeply. This was good, very good. The aromas and mist, the birds coming to life overhead, my men working hard while I sat on a log...why move on? I was somewhat content, aside from my questionable company. Mpasi and I stared at each other from across the fire; neither of us had much to say, and I was out of coffee jokes. There was a lot of smoke between us.

"Ok, I think we are about ready to go." Keith came over. The Zielger was lashed onto two long bamboo poles with some vines. Two men could carry it but four were ready to go, each taking an end. Ian had dismantled the tents and locked them into the truck. We each had a small backpack with a few items in it. As long as I had a mosquito net and some Larium, I was set to go.

"What about the truck?" I asked.

"It'll be ok," said Mpasi. She gestured to one of her bodyguards, he smiled back, raising his rifle. "He'll sleep in the back. Don't worry."

"I am not walking back to Bumba."

Mpasi gave some kind of imperceptible signal and the four men hoisted the bamboo poles to their shoulders. Another villager started into the jungle and we followed. Mpasi's other bodyguard followed us close behind. The brush is always the densest closest to the road, as the sunlight manages to get through there. It was hard going for bit, but the guide seemed to either find a way through or cut a hole with his long machete. Then we were through and onto the jungle floor. There was surprisingly little undergrowth. The awning of the trees overhead allowed in only spotty light and the shadows and sunspots danced here and there around us. It was cooler and darker, which was good since I was still ticked about losing my shades. Occasionally a troupe of monkeys off in the distance would hoot and holler and move through the treetops. The men would always look up, tracking their progress. They were hunters…but not this time.

I was in my own movie, circa 1940, that showed rows of sweating black porters and the white hunters filing through the African jungle. All I lacked was a pith helmet and a rifle. I shook my head and laughed out loud.

"What's so funny, Anna?" asked Ian behind me.

"I've seen this movie before…the hunting party never comes back. The natives run off and abandon us."

Ian laughed too. "Ever see Crichton's *Congo*? They all die there also."

"Hey, you are supposed to balance my pessimism - not jump on board with it! All we need is for the porters to start singing."

The trek through the jungle to the river crossing did in fact bring back some memories. Dad had taken us up the Dua River from Businga in a canoe a couple of times to one of the villages, where a new church was just starting to grow. We would come to the river's edge, disembark, then walk a mile or so in to the village. Everybody knew we were coming, of course, and ran out meet us. The children loved me. They loved to touch me and feel my hair. I didn't love that so much. I remember watching the Jesus film on a large white sheet hoisted up on sticks against the night sky. We taught the kids Sunday school songs in Lingala, most of which I still knew by heart. I hummed along to the words in my head. The longer we were in Congo, the more I felt like a part of me had come home. Did I belong here somehow? Yet the inconsistent emotions did not escape me. I also longed to be back in civilization.

The guide veered to the left and a few minutes later we came to the river's edge.

"This is a better place to cross?" I asked in amazement. The bank was steep down to the river. I envisioned Ziggy sliding right off his bamboo poles, right down into the murky water, and disappearing around the bend. Bye-bye Dad. Like a dead Viking on his ship, we could light arrows and shoot them onto Ziegler that would go gloriously up and up in flames. Aside from the fact that it was metal, and Dad wasn't a Viking, it would never happen. I still longed for a short cut out of this Congo "vacation." Not to be confused with *Lampoon Vacation*.

I could see ripples across the river indicating that it was not terribly deep. But it was wide and fast flowing.

"The bank on the other side is a gentle slope, that should help," offered Keith.

Our little group gathered at the top of the bank. The guide and Mpasi were arguing about something or other. Finally Mpasi seemed to make up her mind.

"Let's send the …ah, Zaglhair, oui? The Zaglhair with Tata over first. It will float, non?"

"Yes, it will float," I assured her, "but if it is floating that means it is going fast downstream. If Tata, *my* Dad, floats away, well, *c'est dommage* - that's too bad."

"Yes, it would float all the way to Bumba!" All the porters hooted. Mpasi thought that was funny. I never really got African humor. They didn't tell jokes exactly, like "Did you hear the one about the guy who walked into a bar…" and their stories were not funny like we think funny…but when there was irony or a reversal in the story they would crack up. Apparently Dad floating back to Bumba from whence we had come was a real knee-slapper.

The porters stood up and hoisted the poles once again. The first guys went over the edge backward. The Zig was sliding along the ground and tipped over the edge, but they had control of the poles. Then slowly they began to slide it down to the river. It was actually easy. They slowly moved out into the river, feeling their way. The Zig was indeed floating but firmly tethered to the poles.

"Ok, our turn." Keith went over, then Ian. I think he thought he would be there to catch me on the way down. That was gallant but chauvinist. Ian slipped himself and slid the last few feet on his butt and into the water feet first. Mpasi covered her mouth but was laughing her head off. She was having an extraordinarily good morning. I unwound my liputa skirt, exposing my kaki shorts underneath. I am sure they were all disappointed. Mpasi did too. She had on sort of knee-length culottes.

"*Après-toi, mademoiselle*," she said laughing.

I turned around and faced the bank and slid over the edge, my shoes digging in as I grabbed for the few roots there were along the way. I slid to a stop right at the edge and stepped into the river with some aplomb.

"Nine point five," said Ian.

Mpasi did about a nine point zero and ended up right next to me, covered in mud. I couldn't help but want to like her. I shrugged it off, reminding myself of her lies. The first guys were about half way across the river. We watched them make slow progress. They were about waist deep and the flow of the river was threatening to detach them from the bottom.

Then one of the porters slipped and lost his footing and the Zig began to swing out of control. The other porter let go to extend a hand to him and the Zig swung directly into the current. The other two tried to hold on but the force of the swing also lifted them off the river bottom, they were being carried downstream fast, and had to let go of the poles.

"*No no no!*" I shrieked as I tucked in my shirt and dashed into the river. It was a lot colder than I had anticipated. Strange gooey things moved beneath my feet. *Don't look down, don't look down...*

Mpasi shouted after me "Non, Anna...wait....!" But I was in. I was not walking back to Bumba to find Dad. Not on your life.

Keith and Ian and one of the bodyguards were way ahead of me. Without hesitation they had plunged in and were after Dad with all their might. The Zig was not going to get far, as it was headed for a tangled pile of tree limbs and debris hung up on something in the river. But the river had gotten deep fast. The bamboo poles hit the logjam and the Zig held there. Ian got there first, then Keith and then the rest of us. We all hung on to the logs. The undertow was pulling us down but it was manageable. I closed my eyes and tried not to look down into the water; I could not imagine what swirling creatures lurked in the deep. I imagined the eyes of a croc examining us from the shore.

"Well, here we all are," said Ian.

"Don't worry, Dad's a good swimmer." No one laughed at my joke.

"So, now what?" I asked. It didn't look possible to somehow detach the Zig and swim the whole contraption to shore. I looked downstream. It only looked worse. That's probably why the villagers crossed here. That was a clever deduction on my part.

Dad was looking at me through that wretched window. Well, his eyes were shut of course, but his face about two inches from mine was unnerving. Yet he was serene. Nothing disturbed the sleep of the dead.

"Enjoying your float, Dad?" I smiled and tapped on the glass. I was becoming all too comfortable with the dead. Maybe I would find a new profession when I got home, work with Dale at "Homeward Bound."

We heard some commotion along the other bank. The porters had scrambled along and were now just across from us. I saw Mpasi emerge from the river and run in their direction also. We were about twenty feet from the shore but the current was pulling us back towards the center. The porters were talking and gesturing with some vigor...*this is where the porters abandon the white hunters*...I couldn't help but think.

We could all make it to shore, no problem, but the Zig was the problem.

"This is as good a burial as any. Keith, want to say a few words?" I said jokingly, but there was a part of me that was a tad serious. Mpasi just glared at me.

A bodyguard came up with a long vine. He handed his rifle to Mpasi, who slung it over her shoulder with just a little too much familiarity. She looked around at the jungle periphery. She was one alert girl. The guard tied the vine around his waist and waded into the river, then began to swim towards us, allowing the current to carry him right into our jam-up.

Keith helped to untie him and then tied the makeshift rope onto the Zig's poles. The porters on the shore began to pull. We helped by pushing with what little force we could muster and finally got it unstuck and into the current. They pulled it to shore with us kicking and hanging on until our feet hit ground. We all emerged from the river and sat on the bank.

I thought I'd try my hand at African humor. "Well, at least the Mamiwata didn't get him." The Mamiwata was a mythical, at least I hoped it was mythical, river god. Keith chuckled. Nobody else did.

"That wasn't Mamiwata, mademoiselle," said Bodyguard with a bit of reproach in his voice.

I know that! I don't even believe in Mamiwata! I wanted to shout at him. *Joke, ok?* I sighed and let it go.

"Well, the hard part is over. Only twenty klicks to go." Ian was now the official cheerleader. At what point exactly had he started to actually enjoy this adventure? I would have to think back on that. He was a long long way from Legalzoom.com and spreadsheets or whatever the heck lawyers worked with.

We took the opportunity to rest and eat some more peanuts, kwanga and plantains. We passed around a bottle of water. *Where did they fill this bottle?* I hoped it wasn't from the river.

We got to our soggy feet and headed up the embankment and back into the jungle. We quickly veered left to intersect the road on the other side of the washed out bridge. Progress was rapid and made mostly in silence. The afternoon heat was becoming more oppressive. Mpasi walked with the rifle slung under her arm. Another dip in the river sounded pretty good. This time, without clothes. My socks and shoes were damp and extremely uncomfortable, stripping my skin off little by little. By noon I was biting down hard on my lips to redirect the sting of painful blisters. Hiking in a jungle with wet feet is no walk in the park. No one complained. Far be it from me to be the first to whine. I could be just as tough as Mpasi. She could even smoke and hike at the same time.

"There it is!" shouted Mpasi and we stepped back onto the road. I immediately looked back across the river. The Hilux was there. The guard waved. We all waved back. So far we had averaged about 200 meters in a hard days slog. We'd have to pick it up a bit.

"We have about five more hours of light. There should be a village not too far up ahead where we can stay the night," Keith outlined the afternoon agenda.

The porters picked up the poles and we headed west down the road.

We hiked a good distance, it only down-poured on us once. The humidity and the mud added extra friction to our hike, a much better workout than my elliptical. I hate the elliptical, I'd much rather run. The pallbearers looked tired, so was I, and I wasn't carrying Dad on my shoulders. My blisters oozed. I was sick of iodine-drugged, orange-flavored water. I had also exhausted my brief liking for kwanga and bread. As long as Ziggy moved, I moved. I just kept my eyes on the shiny metal in front of me, hovering in the air, and put one foot in front of the other. Like the Israelites in the dessert, led by a gray cloud throughout the day, we were led by shiny gray steel. I looked at Ian, drenched in sweat, not complaining a bit, but I'm sure he was cursing himself for having ever fallen for me and asking to come out here. He was probably missing his central air-conditioned condo on Queen Anne. This wasn't what he signed up for, or was it? I don't think he had a clue. Maybe he was in it for the elephant ride. I walked over to him and put my arm through his arm.

"You do know you probably won't get to ride an elephant, don't you?" Ian looked dumfounded. I shook my head never mind. "A few more steps… then we'll rest." I tried not to come across sounding condescending.

"I know. I'm doing pretty good, I love this stuff, we should do this again."

"Do *this* again? What part of this do you want to do again?"

"Well, not bury your Dad obviously…"

"Obviously. So, you're already talking about a re-run and we haven't even finished the show yet. What is wrong with you?"

"Nothing, I just, I like this. You know, the adventure with you."

"Ian, if we were to ever 'adventure' together again...I'm thinking more like something along the lines of Italy. Cappuccinos, tiramisu, Chianti. Lots of it."

"How about after this?" He pulled me in closer and kissed me on top of my head.

"Sure." I was pretty much serious. I smiled up at him.

"Yeah, but you have to admit that this jungle stuff is pretty awesome. Far cry from Queen Anne."

I shot Ian a "give me a break" look. Part me felt the same way, loved being African again. However, I was tired to death and hoping Africa would put a leash on the surprises we were being dealt. My feet hurt so bad.

"By the way, you're looking kind of hot."

"Thanks." I smiled.

"Not that kind of hot, I mean... not hot."

"Not hot?"

"No, ugh, sweaty-hot...you exasperate me. You are looking *worn out*." Ian clarified.

"Exasperate? Who, me?" I tried to keep up the banter, I did not want to admit how I was feeling, something was taking over me, but it was slow. I figured it was just pure exhaustion. I did feel hot, a little dizzy, and my stomach couldn't be soothed.

"Do you want to talk about Mpasi?"

"No."

"Ok."

"We can't sleep together tonight." I changed the subject.

"We didn't sleep together last night."

"Not 'sleep together' - sleep together. I mean - really *sleep* together."

"You're confusing me."

"No, I'm not. Stop it. You know what I mean. We can't *tent* together."

"I know." Ian's smile was so contagious. "We didn't bring the tents."

"You like to push my buttons, don't you?"

"Yes I do."

"You're good at it."

"Do I? Do I push them well?"

"Yes. What? No. Are we still talking about buttons?"

Ian kissed my hand and said, "Tell me all of your woes, slowly, starting from the top going down."

"Woes? From the top down, huh?"

"Yes. What hurts... Tell Big Daddy." He was in a flirty mood, I liked the banter.

"Ha. Ok, 'Big Daddy' - I'll tell ya. My head is pounding. Caffeine withdrawal, sun, et cetera. My hair is a total disaster also, does that count as a woe?"

"Indeed. Go on." He looked at my hair, shook his head, and clucked his tongue in disapproval.

I smiled, he was being so cute, sympathetic, and he was listening..."My nose hurts because it's very sunburned and red."

"Yes, you could even say it glows."

"Thank you for that. Also, my eyes, I forgot my eyes, they feel so very dry and ready to fall out of my face. My arms hurt still from holding onto the handle in the truck. My neck hurts, from sleeping on the ground most likely. My stomach from kwanga overdose, I have felt nauseous for a few days now…"

"Maybe you're pregnant."

"That's not funny. Not at all. Sore muscles, blisters, hunger… ok, I think that's about it. You?" I downplayed everything. The truth was, I was so irritated that Ian wasn't feeling a bit of pain. Did he workout? He must hike Mt. Si every weekend, in the snow, in order to be in shape for this. I tried not to limp even though my feet begged me to.

"Me? I'm fine. I'm Tarzan." Ian grinned in reply and thumped his chest, yet his eyes revealed a good deal of fatigue. We were all suffering. I changed the subject.

"If you could be anywhere in the world right now, where would you be, what would you be doing?" I was saying this between massive breaths. We were hiking up a small hill before we descended down into the village. Maybe Pilates wasn't the way to go. I should take up running again.

"If I could be anywhere in the world huh? Well, I guess I'd be right here."

"So funny Ian… C'mon, really! *Anywhere.*"

"I'd be here, with you, burying your Dad. I'd be wherever you are, Anna."

"Are you *trying* to be cheesy, or does it just come naturally?" I caught the total sincerity in his eyes, but it made me so nervous. How could anyone speak like that without being sarcastic? Who talks like that these days? Without another word Ian pecked me on the cheek and moved forward to talk to Keith. I blew it again. He'd forgive me, again...Love makes me so uneasy.

Towards evening we came to the outer edges of a village. The jungle had given way to some gardens and a few little huts, visible now as we crested the hill. The village was small and dotted here and there with round mud huts with thatched roofs. Wisps of smoke flew upward from pockets of small fires in the dirt. Coffee beans sun tanned on burlap sacks. Chickens and roosters pecked around. The small children were a delight to watch, not that I would ever want one of those things, but their high-pitched squeals and laughter was musical and refreshing. Free from typical adult burdens. Of course, they carried deeper ones. A young boy's stomach protruded far out beyond its natural means; malnutrition captured many young people's lives. Women were walking toward us with at least two children strapped to their bodies in some ingenious fashion, while they carried oversized jars or bundles of wood on their heads. Their black skin glistened in the sun, defining the toned muscles on their arms, muscles one doesn't get from just doing occasional yoga.

"Where are we exactly?" I turned toward Mpasi for the answer.

"We are near Dubulu" said Mpasi. That name rang a faint bell with me. I let the memory slowly percolate to the surface of consciousness. Dubulu....Dubulu....yes...there had been a Catholic Mission there. I had been here before. Dad had stopped here with the family to have lunch with the

Catholic "pères" For no good reason I could think of, tears welled up in my eyes. Memories.

"Mpasi, can we stop at the mission?" I asked her. I was imagining the big soup tureens of hot potage and a nice bed...like we had before.

Mpasi was silent.

"What about it? We must be near the Catholic mission."

"Anna," said Keith, "the, ah, mission...isn't here anymore."

Not here? It had a large brick church and number of very solid looking brick homes and schools. Where would it go? Silence still lingered as I waited and looked back and forth from Mpasi to Keith.

Finally Mpasi spoke. "The rebels destroyed the mission. Everyone there was killed." She stopped and took a breath, turned and faced me. "This not the home you knew." She pointed off into the *jamba*. "The ruins are back in there, in the bush. Skeletons too, Do you want to go see them? They burned them alive in the church."

Alive...in a church...kids too? I swallowed hard, unable to comprehend.

"Shall we go take a *picture*, Anna?" The sneer on Mpasi's face was not favorable.

Why was she angry with me all of a sudden? What did I say? And who was she calling rebels? Johnny Yuma was a rebel. Bemba was a rebel according to some.

As if reading my thoughts she said, "The Rwandan rebels, Anna, not mine."

Mine? She had rebels, was a rebel? My mind was reeling.

"We fought them all the way to Gemena, then went into hiding. I lived in the jungle in a war camp for years. Want to go see it? We moved constantly, always being pursued, hunted down. But we did some hunting and killing of our own, you understand?" Mpasi was inching closer to my face.

"Yes, I think so," I croaked out. *We fought them, we hunted and killed?*

"No you don't understand! I killed people, Anna. Look."

She un-slung the rifle and in one smooth move switched off the safety and let loose a burst that stitched a tree from top to bottom. The village got very quiet.

"See that? I can shoot. I can kill. You can't ever understand. You come back here like this and think it is home to you because you still speak some bad Lingala and can throw out a word like Mamiwata that you don't really even know about." She safetied the rifle.

"My Lingala is not that bad!" I deflected with humor. Marilyn tells me I do this often.

"Anna," said Ian, "What's the matter?" All this had been in Frangala, the local mix of Lingala and French. Keith was following and was probably about to step between us. Ian hadn't understood a word. He was looking at the smoke curling from the barrel. The smell of cordite hung in the air.

"Later, Ian, it's ok…" Then to Mpasi I said, taking a deep breath, "You are right. I don't fully understand, I don't belong. I haven't paid my dues in blood and suffering like you have. But I have paid my dues too! This dreadful place took the life of my *mother.* I have seen blood too. I just haven't taken it...yet. Like it or not, this is partly my home too. And there is a part of me, Mpasi, that is *here.*" I pointed to the Zig and continued. I couldn't help raising my voice, although it came out a bit shaky. "What do you have against me anyway? What have I done to you? You rescued *me*, remember?"

"I had to rescue *Tata*. What do I have against you? You are reason he left Africa in first place. You complained long enough about boarding school and missing Mommy, and so he took you home to America. And that was it, he came back four years later, and everything was different! We survived in the jungle, without him, just barely!"

"We left *together Mpasi*, we both wanted to go back to America*! C'est n'est pas ma faute - this is not my fault*!" My anger and confusion were rising rapidly into my face and I switched to French to get my point across clearer. "It was tough just the two of us, without Mom. I was in boarding school, by myself, from when I was eight till 14, without my mom, and a Dad who was gone all the time on mission trips, supposedly, and never around. But *I* wanted to stay; it wasn't me that made us leave. It was *your* war. We left because we had to, because of the evacuations. And who are you to accuse me of what, I don't even know. For calling Africa my home? And how do you know any of this anyway?"

"You aren't *listening* Anna! He is *my* Dad!"

"That is B.S. *Mpasi!* For one, you aren't old enough. When we left Africa, I was 14 years old, he returned when I was 17, and you are definitely not 17 years younger than I am!"

"You're right, I am not. He was my Dad many, many years before that."

"What are you trying to say? That my Father had an affair when my mother's brain was slowly decaying and *rotting*?" I was nearly hyperventilating. We were in each other's faces with fists clenched. I couldn't believe I was even having this conversation. Ian tried to stroke my arm to calm me down, but it only pissed me off further, I shrugged him away and moved in closer to Mpasi. Years of yoga had not prepared me for hand-to-hand combat, but I was ready, she was slashing my family to bits.

"It was after she -"

I interrupted her before she could finish. I had had enough.

"Enough! C'est fini! Keith, fix this situation." I said with as much force as I could. I quieted, backed down, shook my head and went into the thick of the jungle, again. It seemed to be my usual hideaway.

"Do you always run from everythings? Anna!" Mpasi was calling after me. I turned and looked at her.

"No, just from liars!"

"She's not lying." Keith's low, solid voice came slicing through the tension in the air. His words froze me in mid stride. A third party had entered the debate, an authoritative source.

"What?!" I snapped at Keith, whirling around, hardly able to believe my ears.

"Anna, I'm sorry. I wanted to tell you more about it later, when it was the right time - but..."

"When exactly did you think it was going to be the *right* time, Keith? Maybe a few days ago would have been nice!" I was so livid and suddenly grieved. I wanted the earth to swallow me. I wanted to climb inside Ziegler and hide, forever...

"She's not lying." Keith repeated. "Your Dad, well, it was after your Mom died...when you were seven...then you went to school." He was having a hard time with his words, so I was having a hard time making sense of it. "He was grieving, Anna. You were at boarding school by then." Keith fidgeted and kicked the ground with his feet. He was quiet. "She is eight years younger than you." He looked at me earnestly, waiting for a reply. I said nothing. I had nothing to say. I shook my head in disbelief and then threw up my hands.

"Ok then." I said.

"Ok?"

"Whatever. I'm done Keith. I don't want to talk about it anymore. We need to go eat." I hated being wrong, ever. I could not, and would not accept that my Father had an entire other life apart from me and my mom. Other loves, other family. I felt betrayed and abandoned. *Who all knew about this?* I wondered. I looked at his pale, dead face in the window and something inside of me suddenly hated him...but I wanted to wake him up and hug him, all the same. More than anything else, I wanted to get moving and get done with this. Shrug it off...head back to my less thought-provoking life of Lost and Grey's Anatomy. Numb it out. I looked over at Mpasi. She had also deflated. She didn't look like Miss Che Guevara anymore. She stood there for a long time. Nobody moved. Ian knew enough to stay quiet. Mpasi spoke first.

"I am sorry, my *ndeko*...this has not been easy, seeing Tata and you and..." She put her hands to her face and turned away. *Ndeko*-sister, family... Though I wasn't sure how she meant it, it wasn't bad. It was a good word, but I would not extend the olive branch back.

We all gave it some more time, allowed the words to hang in the air and evaporate a little. Then Mpasi gave the word and the porters picked up the poles and we hiked down the hill into Dubulu. I was happy to be moving. I needed to think.

The village was still very much awake. Campfires were just being stoked and pungent aromas were wafting around our nostrils. The dogs didn't bark. They kind of yodeled. This had always been an oddity to me, these silent basengi hunting dogs. They were smart enough and could make various sounds, but they didn't bark.

"What bloody kind of dog yodels?" asked Ian.

Mpasi laughed. Ian must have accidentally said something funny.

We stopped in the yard of the biggest hut, one with a tin roof and several smaller huts around it.

"The chief's hut," I informed Ian. "These other huts are for his wives." I counted six.

"Busy man."

"You jealous?"

"Not in the least." He steadied me with his eyes and gave me an approving look. I was tired of blushing so I tried not too, failing miserably.

Soon the wives were all in the yard with about a gaggle of children, some still latched on and nursing while the mamma walked. The Chief came out and never missed a beat when he saw three mondeles in his yard. He looked us over though. Mpasi was talking to him in a low voice. I could only hear "Landan" and a couple of other words that leaked out. He nodded and came over to the Zig and looked through the window at Dad. He looked at him for a long time. Then he looked closely at me, his eyes shifting over to Mpasi, then back to me.

He barked out some orders in what I supposed to be Ngombe and the place came to life. The wives scattered, but the kids did not. They stood around and watched our every move with utter, complete fascination. They had all been born since the evacuations and had never seen a mondele before.

Before long, pots on fires appeared and the work of cooking was underway. The Chief Mama came over to me. I could tell she must be the chief Mama. She was older, huge, and was doing no work.

"Mbote, Anna Landan." She smiled wide.

"Mbote, Mama."

"I am glad you still speak such good Lingala after all these years." *See, Mpasi, not that bad.* "You don't remember me do you, Anna?"

"No, I am sorry, Mama, I have forgotten so very much. I was only 14 when we left."

Yes, my daughter was your *mobateli*-caretaker, so many years ago now. Her name was Ngolu."

Ngolu, I remembered Ngolu. Or maybe I just remembered her from the pictures in our family albums. She had carried me around on her hip or slung me on her back just like an African baby. We played on the grass in my yard. She bathed and washed me and coiled my hair like hers.

"Yes, yes, Ngolu, so very tall and beautiful," I said. "Where is she? She is well?"

Mama became very sad. Her whole face changed into a look of utter sorrow. "She is dead."

"Oh, I am so very sorry." I didn't dare ask how she had died.

"They killed her when they came to your *Mfumu* mission in Bosobolo." Mfumu was not a swear word but it was not nice way to say it either, it meant basically "protestant." "They killed anyone who had worked for the mission." Mamma sighed deeply and started pounding her manioc.

I sat down heavily on a bamboo chair that had been dragged into the fire circle. *They had killed Ngolu...because of me?* My existence here had resulted in the murder of another, my own *mobateli?* How could that be? It wasn't my doing, I was just a kid, running around, having fun, eating mpondu and kicking an orange with the other kids. What did this have to do with me? No, she was killed because of their evil, the rebels were evil, it was their sin, not mine, right? I had no blame in this, no part. Most of my memories here were warm and golden and happy. We had a pet monkey and mom made me special birthday cakes. My nanny, my Ngolu killed like a chicken, bleeding out on this red earth ...because she...had loved me? Was there some way to take responsibility? It was a burden I couldn't bear. Even if her death had nothing to do with me, am I still to shoulder some of the weight of injustice? Are any of us? I was oh so tired. Tired of these kinds of questions. Tired of deciphering truth from lies. Tired of hearing about death and blood. Tired in my bones.

Mama sat down next to me and I put my head onto her ample bosom without reservation, as if she was my own Mom. I shut my eyes tight, again trying to keep back tears. Ngolu's face appeared vividly now in my mind. She smiled and waved at me to follow her as she ran down to our favorite climbing tree. Her braids bounced against her long back. I ran after her and jumped up into her open arms, only to fall right through them. She was gone. Only a vapor of her presence remained. I began to cry…it was the least I could do for her. Cry for her, cry the beloved country. And it was something I was getting all too used to.

Tomorrow we would come to Goyongo. The closer I came to home the harder the journey was becoming.

The mamas were still making dinner. I hugged Mama, got up and walked over to Ian. He was staring at the production.

"Anna," said Ian looking at the amount of food being prepared, "we can't let them do this…they can't afford to feed us all. And I smell meat!"

"Didn't you hear the goat bleating when they cut its throat? Just believe me when I say this is just the usual self-sacrificial, generous, open-handed hospitality…" I was touched that Ian was sensitive to this issue.

"Maybe we can do something for them."

"Maybe. You can leave your pants here or something." I smiled, trying to lighten the subject. "Someone here could probably use them."

"Maybe something else."

"We will invite the chief to the burial."

Ian and I went on a walk to kill time. I filled him in about the conversation with Mpasi, but did not want to process any of it. I simply told him what went down. He listened, sensed my hesitancy, and did not ask questions or try to offer solutions. A rare breed of a man indeed. We roamed around the village holding hands, taking in the news of the mission, Ngolu, Mpasi's story, my life that was unraveling - or maybe being re-woven - before my eyes. How could I have been so blind, to everything? I held Ian's hand tighter and felt a wave of gratefulness wash over me for his presence. He was the only one right now not connected to a web of sad and confusing tales. He was not Africa; he was a part of my other life, my real life, back in Seattle…where I did belong. Or did I?

We ate well that night. In the pitch black, it is impossible to be choosy about the food. We ate what was on our plate, we couldn't see what it was, and that helped. It was delicious and salty. As a kid, I remember Mom would always serve us dinner and then tell us afterward what it was we ate. Monkey, snake, termites. The fire was roaring and I noticed a few men dancing with shakers and rattles attached to their legs. The pounding of their feet on the dirt and the percussion was hypnotic. We joined them by the fire and sat and watched the activities.

"You gonna go dance with them, Ian?" Keith kidded.

"Now this I want to see." I laughed in Ian's direction.

"I know enough to respectfully decline. White men can't dance."

"What about white women?" I shrugged as if I was interested in joining.

"White women can't either." Mpasi got up, shook out her skirt and went to join the festivities. Within seconds she had caught the beat and the moves and was off and shaking. Her body danced with natural precision.

A local brew was passed around, the first drop of the hard stuff I had seen in a few days. It was about time. I gladly accepted and took a few gulps out of the communal bottle. Oh well, I'll risk germs and getting Ebola for small pleasures, not that I hadn't already by simply coming here. Immediately the sharp milky fermentation slapped my tongue with its bitter bite and I almost spit it out.

"What is it?" Ian wasn't about to try it until he saw me swallow.

"Coconut alcohol I think, called Bako. Bleh - it's disgusting. But it burns going down, so that is good news to me. Here." I handed him the bottle. A man watching us was grinning and laughing as he saw our expressions. Ian took a swig and managed to swallow without spitting as well. I was so proud. We slowly got used to the taste. I wanted to drink until I at least felt a little warm and numb from the day's unveilings. I watched Mpasi move some more. She was mysterious and vexing. She raised in me feelings of such anger and disgust along with compassion and something along the lines of admiration, that had never been stirred before.

The flames from the fire licked up the wood and created dancing shadows on the dirt. It hissed and cackled as the flames hit some moisture. Keith was reading the bible to someone a few feet away. I wondered what everyone here went through during the war. I thought about our evacuation and what that must have seemed like to the villagers. Did we have to leave? Yes, I knew that we had to leave. But I *was* also anxious to do so; I was lonely without Mom, and without Dad basically. I was alone for six years at boarding school. I only saw him every 10 weeks or so. I wondered about Mpasi's life, and tried to allow her tale to hit my consciousness, as more than a tale, as reality. *Is she my sister?* Was she a result of one night, or was it more than that? I couldn't imagine that kind of behavior from my Father. Was Dad in love with her Mom? Did Mpasi know him well? If so, what did she feel like to know that he left in the middle of the night? What was it like when he returned? How did Keith know? How could I not have known? And here I thought that Dad never recovered from my mother's death...I thought he was permanently scarred by love lost. This whole perception is partly what added to the trail of failed relationships in my wake. How could I have been so mistaken?

Most everyone had gone to bed, but Keith and I remained, sitting by burning coals. Ian was leaning against a log looking very sleepy, or tipsy. I didn't mind him being there, but I had some talking to do with Keith. The 40 proof had opened my mouth and my courage to ask. We both knew we had a conversation waiting for us. The jungle murmured and cooed with happy-hunting lullabies. I tried not to think about it. Keith poked the fire a couple times for good measure.

"I want to know everything, Keith." I broke the ice.

Keith shifted around and raised his eyes, looking at me from underneath his bushy eyebrows. He sighed long and hard. "It's hard to know where to start, ya know, sweetie?"

"I know. Just try. Please. I need it." Keith, the constant oracle.

He took a deep breath and exhaled slowly.

"Your Dad, he... well, your mom's death really shook him up hard. He could hardly raise you on his own, what with the mission work and all, but you were the age to go to boarding school, so it seemed to work out in his mind." Keith poked the fire some more.

"So..." I prodded him along, he seemed reluctant to talk about the hard stuff. He needed to drink some of the hard stuff. I held up the bottle toward him as a joke and wiggled it back and forth in the air. To my absolute astonishment Keith leaned forward, took a swig and handed it back nonchalantly. *Good, maybe now we can get somewhere...*

"You were gone at school, and he and I went to Modiri one day, nearby village to Goyongo. We visited there often, ya know? Lots of work. Built a church, built a school. Most of our days and weeks and months were there. We had such strong favor from the Spirit. He just worked, ya know? A movement. People wept, repented, believed, were filled with faith. One night, when we showed the Jesus film, there was such a response..."

"Keith. Please." I had to interrupt; he was obviously on a tangent that had no significance to me.

"Oh. Sorry. Ok, so, at the village...I don't know how anything started, but almost a year later, he came to me and told me he met someone."

"Mpasi's mom. What was her name?"

"Her name was Nzala Sombolo. He simply begged me to keep it confidential, told me he loved her, wanted to marry her."

"*Marry* her?"

"Yup. So he did. Paid a bride price and everything. She was costly - he had to pay a lot for her. 'Course he still stayed on a lot in the mission. But he stayed in her village often too. Shortly after, she was pregnant."

"Keith. You are serious? This is so hard to take in."

"I bet it is sweetie, I bet it is. That's why I was hoping we could just get on by without divulging it."

"So he lied to the church. He kept his life in the dark. What kind of person does that?"

"But it's not like that, sweetie. He was true, through and through. You should know that. You see, at first, I was the only one who knew. But after awhile, you just can't hide these things. And he didn't want to. He was in love, he had found a wife, he was going to be a Dad - " I coughed uncomfortably - "again," Keith added. "He went to the church, you don't want to know the details of all that went down, but basically to make a long story short, everyone did know, and he settled into his life. It wasn't in the dark. Your Dad always wanted to live his life in the light - "

"That can't be. If everyone knew, so would I."
Naturally...

"Well - " Keith hemmed and hawed and poked at the fire a bit. I handed him the bottle. He declined.

"Well, what?" I waited.

"Well, I guess you can say, we all kept it from you. I know, I know, sweetie. It sounds harsh... but you - "

"What? I was too young? That is crazy! Why would everyone, every missionary, keep it from *me*, his *daughter*?" My voice was unsteady with passion and nerves.

"No. It wasn't that, sweetie. You were, well, you were so traumatized about your Mom." Keith stopped and looked up at me, trying to gage a response. I stared back. I had no defense to that.

"The whole awful sickness, her death, how you found her that day, then the funeral..." *how I found her that day*... I had almost forgotten. I closed my eyes to try to block the memory, but like the memory of Ngolu it attacked me and flattened me... *She was so sick. She couldn't move her neck anymore. She had been vomiting for four months. Sometimes she was mentally present, sometimes she wasn't. Her fevers came and went, spiking and falling dreadfully low. She had become intolerant to light and noise, remained in her dark room for most of the day. I could see my hand opening the door to her room and calling for her. She didn't answer. I opened it wider, she still didn't answer. I moved in toward her bed one small footstep at a time calling her name softly, "Mommy?" She was so still... I don't remember how long I stood there frozen, just looking at her and crying. I didn't yell for help. I didn't move. I just stood still and cried.*

I shook my head and opened my eyes. This wasn't the subject at hand. Dad was.

"He didn't mean to lie to you."

"You mean, you all also didn't mean to lie to me?" We were like a family, all of us missionaries. During break from boarding school we would all go to Lake Kwada. Play games, eat dinners. No one said anything then?

"Anna, we would have, but we all thought it was best. Like I said, the trauma of your Mom left you almost comatose inside. You really didn't speak for about a year! You kept to yourself. You did your work, you cleaned your room, you followed the dormitory rules, but you made no friends, did not talk to a soul, never asked for help for anything. Your Dad wrote you once a week, but didn't hear back from you - "

"What are you getting at? I was a mess? So I was! Wouldn't you be?"

"Absolutely I would be." Keith said with all gravity. "We all would be if we were in your shoes, which is why your Dad, and the rest of us, decided that you could not handle one more piece of news like this that would upset your world. You were so fragile, sweetie."

"Well, I'm not now, am I, Uncle Keith?" I bit down on my lip. It made sense to come to my own defense. So I was a wreck. So I was a traumatized child. Look at me now! *Look at me now...* I sighed and shook my head.

"Let's move on. So, you all knew, you all kept it a secret. But weren't some of you upset? Didn't he break a thousand biblical rules for knocking her up?

Don't you Christians have some stringent puritanical laws about that?"

"God didn't give us laws just to restrict us, Anna. He did it for our protection."

"Don't preach at me, Keith." I snapped at Uncle Keith, and immediately felt horrible. "I'm sorry, I didn't mean - I'm sorry. Go on please."

"Well, anyone can see it how they choose to, but that's the story basically. He fell in love, got married, *then* fathered a child." Keith made careful emphasis on the sequence. "They raised her for six, almost seven years together, the same time you were at boarding school. And then you left Africa, when you were, what, 14? Mpasi was seven. The war was especially hard on your Dad. He knew he had to get you home, out of harm's way, protect you...but he missed his family."

"His family." The words hissed out from behind my clenched teeth.

Keith coughed uncomfortably and went on. "Plus, ya know, the church and basically the government ordered all ex-patriots out of the country. We had to go. Your Dad was heartbroken. He was sure that all would be lost, sure that he'd come back to find them dead."

"But he did come back. He went back after my second year into college."

"Yup. It still wasn't too safe then, but he insisted anyway. He left and spent all those years out there, almost ten more years."

"With Mpasi. She was what, eleven years old? He was with her till she was 21?"

"Yup, living in the village."

"Was he still… a missionary though?"

"Yeah, after we all came back, then he continued on with me and others. But still lived in the village a lot. He did more developmental work at that time."

"Keith. I just don't. I don't know. I don't get it." I sunk my head into my hands. It felt so heavy.

"Sometimes me 'neither, Anna honey. Me neither. But he did love her, he loved them both."

"She had him as a Dad for, what, a total of *seventeen* years?"

"Can't quite figure out all the years and the math, but that sounds about right."

"Why didn't he tell me." It wasn't really a question toward Keith, just a question for Dad. Keith had already explained what he could. But the question still suspended over me.

"Don't know. Couldn't do it I guess. Loved you and your Mum too, ya know?"

Seventeen years this girl knew my Dad as her Dad. Her whole first seven years. And then from when she was eleven years old until just a couple years ago. She is grieving the loss of *her Dad*. My whole body shivered and I swallowed a lump in my throat. Did she know him better than I did? I almost imagined so. I was away at school and I had stopped living. What was their relationship like? Do I want to know? A part of me felt resentful and jealous, another part of me felt like I wanted to give her a hug and tell her that I know how hard it is to lose your Dad. What a paradox of emotions. I needed more coconut booze.

"It was just two years ago when Dad came back to the States, to get me." I muttered this quietly to myself, but Keith was still tuned in.

"I know. He told me."

He came back to get me...to take me here...to tell me. My slower wits had finally put a few puzzle pieces together. He begged me to come back, he said he needed me to come with him for something. Did he know he was dying? He wanted me to meet my...family. Did he just suddenly think that I was old enough to understand, once I turned *thirty?*

"He wanted me to meet her."

"I reckon so. Yes he did. He knew he made a mistake with the secret, or so he thought. It was time."

"He did make a mistake. A big one. Can't be undone." I muttered. "Keith?"

"Ya?"

"A part of me would like to have never known. Even if Dad told me himself. Can you imagine if I had gone back with him? He brings me to this village and says, 'Here is your sister'? He wouldn't have gone through with it, and I wouldn't have believed him. I still don't quite believe it, and I'm not sure how I should respond."

"I know, honey. I guess the thing is...Mpasi came to rescue us, to rescue James. She needs to bury him too, some closure."

"Did you know it was her when you saw her?"

"Not right off the bat, but when I learned her name I knew who she was. I wasn't sure how this was all going to go down. I'm sorry, Anna, I should have said something, just didn't know how. It's all very…"

"Confusing."

"Yeah."

"What about her Mom? How did they meet?" I just barely dared to ask. The details seemed important, but the more I heard, the more it stung.

"Your Dad and I went to a village near hers to show the Jesus film. One thing led to another."

"Ha! You left a lot out there. Yada yada yada…that yada is the best part. Something about the Jesus film aroused some romance? Go Jesus."

"Not quite! I'll tell you more details later. But there was a great dramatic event with everything…your Dad met up with a lot of opposition about his evangelizing, she ended up on his side."

"Then what happened to her?"

"Sombolo died awhile back. It broke James' heart, but he also knew it was just the way of life around here, it was less traumatic than your Mom's death, but none the less tragic."

"Mpasi lost her mom *and* her Dad. Wow."

"Yup. Just like you."

"She's nothing like me." I was not sharing the sentiment.

"She could probably use a break, Anna." Keith ventured into the danger zone with his comment. I bristled defensively.

"Really?! Do you realize how all of this makes *me* feel, Keith?"

"I can't imagine, honey, but still, …Mpasi - "

"Shhh. Keith." I spoke quietly and waved my hand at him, trying to find my words. "I feel pretty alone out here on the fringe somewhere. I don't even know my Father anymore. I don't know who he is or what he's done with his life. I thought I did, but I didn't. He's all the family I had. He was the last bit, the last strand I had of somehow identifying *myself* as part of a family. If I don't know who *he* is, how do I know who *I am?* Who was I to him? And now I meet this chic, who basically holds the same place in his heart, part of an entirely different life that he led with an entirely *different family!* I *resent* her! She doesn't need a break, Keith, *I* do!" I shook my head and hung it low between my knees, realizing how selfish my remark must have sounded. But that's how I felt. I tugged at my hair. My throat got sticky. I couldn't take any more of this story, and I couldn't share any more of my emotions, I didn't even know how I truly felt. Did I resent her, really?

"I'm going to bed, Uncle Keith. Thank you for everything."

I got up and wiped the dust off my pants and wiped my eyes. Ian, who had been sitting quietly with his eyes closed, probably for Keith and my sake, opened his eyes and stood up to follow me. I quickly held out the palm of my hand, and shook my head, warning him, now is not the time. Keith nodded at me, and I walked to the hut I was to sleep in tonight, alone. Very alone. I laid in my hard little reed bed with a mosquito net dropped over me and wished with all my might I could conjure up some sleeping pills and a bucket of tequila. There were so many questions. I had opened Pandora's box. It shouldn't have been opened. There shouldn't have been a Pandora in the first place. I listened to the hyrax outside shrieking as it rushed down from the trees to forage for food. It screamed to scare off predators, but it was really easy prey. Like me. I fell asleep counting mosquitoes and wondering if I could ever forgive my Dad. I figured my Eight Ball would say, "Outlook not so good."

CHAPTER TWENTY-ONE

The parrot outside my hut was crowing, impersonating the rooster. The rooster was cockling proudly. Between the two of them, it was an all-out six am wake-up call, jungle concert. I woke up stiff and sore, having rolled over at some point in the night, onto the hard dirt floor. Today we would reach Goyongo. This was it. I could see the light at the end of this dark tunnel.

"Good morning, Mama!" I greeted my host in Lingala as I came out of the hut. Today was a new day. I was determined to do more than just survive it.

"Good morning, Miss Anna! Hold please." Mamma handed me her baby so that she could better wrap her liputa around her hips. I held the baby with two hands straight out in front of me. He looked at me cautiously. I held him a bit further out, seeing that he was naked. *Please don't pee on me.* I had never been one for babies.

Ian was already sitting by the fire drinking coffee from a glass. He had to hold it on the top and bottom to keep from burning his fingers.

"Want some?"

"You know I do."

"Too bad. Your hands are full."

"Today we get there, Ian. Hard to believe."

"Yes, but there is a small detour. Mpasi wants us to stop at Bongalo first. It's pretty much along the way, she says."

I frowned. "What for?"

"That is her village. I guess she needs to see a few people."

I groaned. That sounded like an all day affair. I couldn't bear it.

"This is her family, Anna, it's important to her." Again I marveled at the change in the order of the universe. Ian sipping scalding coffee, telling me what's what. I glared at him for good measure. *Traitor.*

Mpasi's village was on the edge of the Ituri forest. Every hut had its own path that led back into the forest to gardens and hunting huts. We passed by fishponds fed by several small streams. The water poured over the dam and splashed on the rocks below. Palm trees surrounded the village.

A handful of Mpasi's relatives were nearby when we entered, and only a few of them ran to greet her warmly. There were a few embraces, a lot of gesturing toward us and the Ziegler, and some uneasy looks our way.

"I wonder what it's like to be the daughter of a white man; is it seen as something negative, Keith?"

"Not as much as you may think. In fact, sometimes just the opposite, there is a little bit of prestige with being more pale skinned. There is also prestige in being the daughter of a rebel leader."

"Your Dad was a rebel leader, Anna? Wow!"

"Very funny, Ian." But at this point, what did I know? Maybe he was.

"Do people like Bemba?" I ventured.

Keith took his time in answering this. "I suppose they feel the same way as they do about many other rising leaders, a bit of hope for the future...the word 'warlord' is our word for men like him, and it is a bit misleading. True, some warlords are vicious tyrants and petty brigands. Bemba is a local hero, his father is a huge *commercant*, known throughout the country. He is a member of the royal family of the dominant Ngbaka tribe. Bemba has a Masters in Sociology from a school in France, don't remember where. He is, how do we say it, *sophistiqué*..."

I prodded. "I have heard stories of atrocities here though..."

Again Keith took his time. Finally he continued. "Don't get me wrong. Bemba is also a strongman, a ruthless leader, but he does have the good of the people in mind and his soldiers are highly disciplined, at least compared to the Rwandans that came through here. The Rwandans slaughtered and pillaged indiscriminately, and when they left, Bemba filled the void. All that carnage stopped. He is loved, but also feared. As usual in Africa, he is a good friend but a terrible enemy to have around here."

"Is he *our* friend, Keith?" Ian inquired.

"Obviously, or we wouldn't have gotten this far."

"Is she welcomed here? They look a little uncertain." I was watching Mpasi and her family. She was still motioning around and voices were rising. Many more people started gathering around her, some shaking their heads, many pointing at Dad. A few

273

curious children gathered around the Ziegler and peered inside. Angry moms raced toward them, and dragged them away from the dead body.

Mpasi came back toward us. "Come inside. We will have tea with my Aunt."

"Your mom's sister?"

"Yes. Come inside."

"Are we welcome?" I still did not see many friends out in the crowd, but a lot of furrowed brows.

"Yes, yes. Come!" Mpasi turned and walked in front of us. We followed her into a dark hut that smelled like a sweet musty mix of rain and dirt...and something else...hemp, a form of cannabis. We sat on a few wooden benches around a little makeshift table. Mpasi's aunt put a pot of water over the fire, and walked out, leaving us alone.

"Mpasi, is there a problem? Maybe we should head on to Goyongo." I asked.

"No. This is my family." She said decisively.

"How long has it been since you've seen them?"

"Just couple years past. I see them when I visit Tata in Goyongo." It was so weird to hear her call him her Dad. *My* Dad.

"They seem...upset." I dared to mention what we were all taking note of.

"They are sad about his death." Mpasi shifted uncomfortably in her chair.

"Really? I doubt it." I was starting to pick another fight.

"Why?" Mpasi looked defensive, but I knew she was bluffing.

"My Dad, or 'Tata' as you say, is the reason Nzala died. At childbirth, right? I'd assume that her sisters and brothers, would not be too happy about that." Mpasi turned and looked away. I always tended to err on the side of being too direct.

"Ok. You are half correct."

"Half?" *Dang it, only half?*

"Yes. They were upset with Dad, upset about the whole thing. They appreciated the nice dowry he paid for mom though, and accepted him, mostly. After her death, well, not very so happy any more. It was easy blame him for her death, after all, he gave her pregnant. But they had me and raised me, I was gift."

Sure you were.

"When did your Uncle…Bemba…when did he take you away?"

"When I was little. But that is also not the issue." Mpasi glanced back outside toward the Ziegler.

"What is the issue, Mpasi?"

"They are upset about the body." We looked at her, waiting for more information.

"Can you explain more, sweetheart?" Keith was prodding her now.

Keith didn't know? We glanced out the hut's open doorway and saw a great number of people arguing around the Ziegler. Something was up, and it sent chills down my spine. The tone and tenor was way beyond the usual hubbub. The men were around now from the fields, obviously called toward the commotion. A few rather important-looking older men were speaking the loudest. Some were tapping on the window, knocking even, as if they were trying to wake the dead. Did they know it was a dead man? Had they ever seen such a coffin type thing before?

275

Most likely not. The window must be part of what was stirring up the crowd. Little children were trying to climb on top and get a good look. I shifted uncomfortably as I watched Dad become a spectacle. I wanted to shoo the birds away and scream *leave him alone!*

"Mpasi - please."

"I don't know exactly the story, but they say, he is not welcome here, and they are scared."

"Scared of a body? Don't you people see these every day?" *Never one for tact either.*

"It's different. I really don't know. I'm sorry. My aunt said something about bad luck. She wants us leave. They all do. We can't stay here tonight." Keith coughed uncomfortably as Mpasi said this and put his head in his hands.

"Then why are we in here, invited to have a cup of tea?" Nothing makes sense. Lost in translation I suppose. If I was freaked out about my visitors, I would not invite them in for tea. We were all peering out now, leaning way over to see through the doorway together. A bunch of mondeles huddled together inside a hut, peaking out at the growing mob.

"It would be impolite to not invite us for tea."

"Impolite? But then she'll ask us to leave after we have tea?" said Ian.

"Yes."

Mpasi's aunt came back in, as she walked through the streaming light I caught a better glimpse of her face. She had kind eyes; she was strikingly tall and beautiful. I could see immediate resemblance in Mpasi. She wore her hair in tight ringlets on her head, and adorned herself with a lot of bracelets and

276

earrings. She had a smaller nose than most, but magnificent Angelina Jolie lips and long curly eye lashes. She was voluptuous. I suddenly wondered how much she looked like Nzala. *My Dad fell in love with a woman just like this. Fell in love and married her. Fathered her child. And she died... in his arms?* I felt a lump rising up in my throat again. I stared at Mpasi and asked her a thousand endless questions that she would never hear, that I would never vocalize, and I received no answers.

The tea was rich and saturated with generous helpings of sweetened condensed milk and spoonfuls of sugar. It was dessert in a cup and managed to soothe my nerves...and wasn't even spiked. The drink was comforting and reminded me of many, many days and nights of drinking this with family and friends, in dark huts, or cement mission houses. We drank in silence. Afterward we thanked Auntie and headed out. The bodyguards and hired help were still around the Ziegler, half protecting Dad.

As we came out of the hut, everyone stared at us in silence; a few clicked their tongues and shook their heads. Many took a step back from us as if we carried some contagious disease. It felt eerie, very vexing. Ziegler was soon hoisted up on the shoulders of the strong men, and we followed after it, suspended in the air like the Ark of the Covenant. We took our beloved ark and left the hostile territory. Mpasi was walking next to me, and I noticed her eyes welling up with tears. Something possessed me at that moment, something very foreign to me...I reached out and grabbed her hand. This was wrong, somehow. Her aunt, her village, had not welcomed her or us. She squeezed it back a little too hard.

"Tata came here often, Anna. This was his second home. These people never thought they'd see Jacques, Tata, again. This is very strange for them."

"They seemed angry."

"Yes, very. This is very *makila mabe* - bad luck- but we are very close now."

"I know." *I like the sound of "we." I am not alone...*

CHAPTER TWENTY-TWO

Goyongo slowly came into view as we trekked on through. Ziegler led the way and we mostly walked in silence. I had lost track of how many days I had been in Congo now. It felt like forever, like I had never left. Seattle became more and more a strange distant memory. I didn't even look like myself anymore. My skin was tanned and tight from the sun, my hair getting blonder, or perhaps grayer, it was hard to tell. Africa was turning and twisting me up and spitting me out slowly as a new creation. I didn't recognize the tenderness in me that snuck out when I wasn't watching. I didn't recognize the smile that crept across my face when I saw the mugs of my Three Musketeers. I didn't recognize the girl who cried and hugged strangers. I was also very unfamiliar with the pain that continued to pulse through my joints and muscles. Sometimes my legs would cramp up so bad I would have to stop and rest. I hated this. I hated being weak, but the more it happened, the more I noted that the world wasn't spewing disgust and judgment in my general direction as much as I anticipated. Sometimes I choked on the attention it conjured; sometimes I reveled in it. Ian would rub my back, Mpasi would make me a snack.

After awhile though, I felt less and less alone in my weakness. Keith needed more breaks than me, his breathing was heavy and he was sweating profusely. Mpasi, however, maintained a lovely glow. Ian was also fading. As much as he enjoyed being jungle man, he had slowed his gait and was popping aspirin as often as *Dr. House* took Vicodin. Never missed an episode. But these days I started to wonder if living my life in the movies and in my shows kept me from fully living the shows of my own life? What episodes have I been missing? Were they good?

"Starting to look familiar, Anna?" Keith interrupted my introspection. I was grateful, deep thoughts make me twitch.

"Yup. I remember this road very well. Dad and I would get up early in the mornings and put on our bandanas and run up and down. I was only four."

"Tough kid," said Ian.

"Tough Dad. He made me do it. I remember stopping at the *nzando* – market - and eating *makatis* - palm oil fried bread-dough, tasted almost as good as Pike Place Market donuts."

"Did you run home after eating that?"

"Merde, non! We waddled." I snickered at the memory. It was good to be on this road again.

I heard Mpasi laugh in front of me. My memories of Dad were stories about her Dad. How bizarre. I fell silent again and watched her walk. She stood so tall; she seemed so brave. I felt a tinge of pride to be related to her. Two totally different girls...or were we that different? Two totally different Dads though, that's for sure; same name, different personnas. So it seemed. I wondered what her Dad was like. Did he tuck her in at night? What kind of nighttime stories did he tell her? Did they go running? Somehow I doubted that. Was that the one thing unique to my Father and me? I wondered if my deep anxiety about Mpasi was really just a selfish sorrow. Dad was all I had, and now I had to share him. I felt stripped of any notion I held onto of being special, of being someone that mattered. I had always mattered to my Dad, even if to no one else. But now, I was not his only daughter; I had to share my memories now, too. My African memories of my Dad were the warmest and best years of my life, before I shut down and shut him out. I felt the strong grip of regret pulling me back to live in the past where I gave him the love he deserved. No wonder he went looking for a new family…

I wondered if I would ever dare ask her about her memories. Asking her would mean finally opening the door permanently to the reality of who she was, the beloved daughter of James Landan. I had only half accepted the truth. It would have to digest slowly, and take its time approaching my mind and heart. I felt Truth reaching cautiously out to me with an open hand, lest like a scared horse I spook and run from it, and hide away forever.

As we entered the village I examined the mud huts that lined the road leading up to the mission station. A woman was fervently sweeping the dirt outside her hut, goats bleated and meandered around the chickens. I wondered what the crew on "While You Were Out" or "Trading Spaces" would do with these homes. A two-story hut? A deck? Wallpaper and some Kohl fixtures? I laughed to myself as I pictured a commercial of that wealthy couple approaching the Kohl president and saying, "build a hut around this," while setting down a fancy faucet.

"I can't wait to go to bed tonight." Ian siddled up near me and started chatting as we walked. He was so overly perky these days. Maybe it was the Vicodin. Maybe it was the first time out of Seattle, who knew.

"I know. Me too. I'm so tired." I commiserated.

"No, I mean it's the most exciting time I've had in a long time."

"Excuse me?" I didn't know if I should feel curious or insulted.

"Larium."

"Larium?"

"Yup. Larium dreams. They are the *best*, isn't that what you're taking for malaria?"

"Yes, but I don't have dreams as exciting as yours."

"I bet you don't. They are something else!" I heard Keith chuckle, listening to our conversation.

"So, Uncle Keith, do you have great Larium dreams too?"

"Oh heck yeah! It's the best!" I tried not to think what kind of exciting dreams Keith had in his sleep. He kept on smiling and shaking his head.

"Care to share?"

"Nope. Some things are better left unsaid." Keith said.

"Let sleeping dogs lie." Ian said.

Ian's words were suddenly injected coolly into my mind. *Where did I hear that before? Aunt Millie?* I remembered my very odd conversation at the "funeral" just weeks earlier. Days I guess, but it felt like weeks. *Did she know about my Dad and Nzala and Mpasi? I guess she did.* Let sleeping dogs lie. Yes, let them. I still half wished the dog was lying, quiet, asleep, keeping his secrets to himself. I hate dogs. I took a deep breath and kept walking.

As we came into the mission compound, I noticed that we were not just our small group and our pallbearers. More and more of the Goyongo villagers were slowly joining us. Keith was chatting with little kids casually in Lingala. They were fascinated by this native-tongue speaking man, caressing his pale skin and then shrieking back with a mix of giggles and astonishment. Mpasi was greeting some Mammas and hugging a bunch of people as if they were old friends. Were they old friends? Did she come here when I was in boarding school? To see Dad when he was not with her and her Mom in the village? Those sleeping dogs had all the answers. But they were slowly twitching and hungrily waking from their comas...

"Anna, these people remember me and your Dad well. They were practically family. You would probably remember a few of them, many remember you. Do you remember your cook, Botoko? Your old yard man, watchman and other field workers would like to see you." Keith prodded me along the social arena.

"Um. Ok. I think I remember a lot of those guys."

"Do you remember what they all called you?"

"No. Was it mean?"

"Not at all!" Keith laughed, "They affectionately named you Gbado, the name of their own village.

You were born here. You are child of the village, you are one of them."

Mpasi turned and looked at me while Keith said this, listening to us talking. I wondered if she resented this somehow, that I was a part of her country, that I had a small claim on this life. Or did she want to share it with me, but was hesitant, testing my loyalty? I knew I had not suffered as she did. I knew she thought I took her Dad away from her She must have little reason to embrace me, as I did her. Yet she did rescue me. She could have just taken Dad's body and moved on, leaving us in jail. She probably wished she had. I was reminded to be grateful.

"Gbado." Mpasi repeated my "name" and smiled. "I like it."

"Me too." I smiled back. *Were we making peace?*

"Means toad," said Mpasi.

"It does not!"

"You don't know what it means, do you, *ndeko*? It means "cloudless" - much better than 'pain,'" Mpasi said this with a smile. I laughed, she was right about that. I pondered the meaning of a life filled and lived without clouds. I was sure that didn't describe mine. Especially not in Seattle.

A short, powerfully built man was coming down the road to meet us. A number of men and women followed in procession.

"Pastor Ndumba," said Keith. "The welcoming committee."

"How did they know we were coming?"

Keith and Mpasi just laughed.

"*Bien venu à Goyongo!*" boomed Pastor Ndumba. "We had hoped you would come back some day, Anna Landan! This is your home. Welcome to you, Mpasi Bemba…Landan."

That was the first time I had heard my name attached to hers. My eyes traveled to hers and she met my gaze. We both offered a tentative smile. The dogs were awake and barking.

Ndumba looked at the Ziegler and bowed his head. He put his hand on the window and whispered "Welcome back, Brother." Tears formed and he took a deep breath and spoke a few words I was unable to decipher. Ndumba finished his speech. Some young girls brought us a little bouquet of flowers and eggs. Finally we were led to our house. Dad was deposited on the porch.

It was not quite what I remembered. It was smaller, resembling more of a shack than the pleasant home I cherished in my memories. The screens were torn and the roof was rusted. The rattan chairs on the porch were not from Trident Imports.

The three-bedroom arrangement was once again awkward. Mpasi commandeered one, Keith tossed his pack into another. Ian and I stood there. I walked into the remaining room and put my pack on the bed, turned and looked at him. A long time he stood there, then slowly he walked into Keith's room. I plopped onto the mattress. It was thin foam, but it cushioned me from the boards. I was exhausted and let myself sink into sleep.

The conversation on the other side of the wall eventually roused me. It was just muffled enough that it was hard to hear, but I heard my name. More than once. I painfully got up and walked out into the living room. It grew quiet. Keith, Ian, Ndumba and some others were there.

"Hey, what's going on? Heard my name, you know, got me kind of curious."

More silence.

"We are getting married," said Ian barely suppressing a smile.

"You and who, exactly? You just got here, you couldn't have met anybody that quickly."

"Funny. You and me, babe."

"Keith, what is he babbling about?"

Keith laughed, so did Ndumba. *When did all these people learn English?* "Anna, they want to make an honest woman out of you."

"Out of *me*? What about him?" I pointed at Ian with my lower lip. "He is the one who took advantage of me."

Ian laughed too. "Nobody has ever taken advantage of you."

"Everybody knows about you two..." Keith began.

"Knows what exactly?"

"Well, sharing the tent, your ah relationship..."

"Ah, that." *Now if I only knew about it.*

Pastor Ndumba joined in. "*Mwana na mboka* – child of the village - let's celebrate a *libala* - a marriage here this week!"

"So fast? We hardly know each other. Who arranged this marriage anyway?" I asked, getting into it a bit.

"It seems as though I have to buy a goat and give some money to your family for you," said Ian with a wild grin spread across his cheeks.

"One goat? I am a ten goat woman, not one goat less, you cheapskate." I was enjoying the banter, as long as it was still just banter.

"At least ten, but apparently they only want one."

"I have nothing to wear."

"Then wear that." All the whites laughed. Keith translated for Ndumba who then didn't laugh.

"My wife has a cloth for you," he offered.

"Well, then, I guess this is the big one, the day every girl dreams of. Thanks for taking care of all the details, so much less stressful this way. Shall we send out the invitations by drum?" I decided to play along. After all, this was my village, these were my people, and they saw me as their daughter. As long as there was no real ordained pastor or judge, it didn't count. I would please them, give Ian a good story to tell back at home, and get on with the real mission. Wouldn't hurt to be the center of attention for a moment; after all, I wanted to matter to someone…

CHAPTER TWENTY-THREE

"They want to do a what?" I questioned Keith. Another bomb had dropped. As if the marriage ceremony wasn't enough.

"Hold a church service for James. They want to honor him, and say a few words. Nothing big. Is that okay? After all, it is Sunday, and they will be having church anyway, so they thought they'd include James." Keith was explaining to me what all the commotion was about. People were surrounding Ziegler, tapping on the window and motioning toward the chapel. A few groups had already started singing. Their deep baritone harmonies saturated the sweltering air around us. As long as there were just a "few" words, I had no problem with the service. I glanced toward our old house up on the hill, and then tried to see a couple miles northeast...where we would burry him, once and for all. All in good time.

"That's fine. That's what Dad would have wanted anyway." I gave Keith an answer.

"What's going on Anna?" Typical Ian form.

"We're going to have a short service, they just want to say a few words for Dad. This was his home village after all. He is well loved and remembered here. I had kind of forgotten that this is not just...you know, about me."

"What do you mean?"

"Dad wanting me to take him back here. This is also for the rest of his life and friends he left behind. A whole village needs to mourn."

"Still would have been easier just to take his ashes."

"Thought of that myself! But Dad always hated the thought of that. Freaked him out. Not a true Viking after all."

"A Viking?"

"Never mind. But it wouldn't have been the same to the Africans. A body is significant. A burial is significant. There is much more consequence and meaning to a dead body here, more reverence, and it's needed for the after-life."

We made our way to the black painted chapel. A long skinny white cross hung on the doorway, welcoming all who entered. There were no windows or doors, just open sides. The children all gathered there, sitting on the wall one after another, one leg dropped outside the church, the other inside.

"So, just a short service?" Ian quickly took note of the small round logs about the width of my leg, and realized that those were the "pews" we'd be sitting on.

"I hope so. I know, it's terribly uncomfortable. Sit here." We were ushered to the very front of the church and sat down hard on our logs.

As the service began I again was yanked back to the past about twenty years ago, sitting on these logs, listening to my Dad preach in Lingala for hours on end. Nothing seemed to have changed at this moment, other than my age and the pace of my Dad's heartbeat. The women's clothing was still just as bright, a beautiful palate of swirling color mixed together all over the fabric. The palms still gently swayed in and out through the church walls. I closed my eyes and appreciated the breeze. The children giggled and threw sticks at a scorpion they had discovered. Children under six walked around naked, all dirty and dusty. Everyone crammed in tight into the "pews." Congolese do not have an invisible personal-space bubble surrounding them like Americans do. The familiar smell of body odor, manioc, and soiled money invaded my senses. I turned behind me as I heard a low rumbling of voices. A processional of men was shuffling down the aisle, singing a soulful and penetrating melody.

"*Sanjola ye, sanjola ye*," they sang, "Praise Him, Praise Him, Amen to his throne, Amen to the resurrection."

Behind the singers I could see Ziegler hoisted up high on the shoulders of many others. Dad was slowly making his way forward, one inch at a time. The mood was somber and intimate. The longer I stared at the casket, and the longer it took, the deeper my pain became. I saw Mpasi hide her face in her hands. I swallowed hard and looked forward. After nearly five minutes, Dad was up in the front of his church once again. I imagined him smiling inside, ready to get out and shuffle along with the best of them in rhythmic African motion. Who said white men can't dance? He would stand up and greet the church with a big smile, "Mbote!" "Mbote!" the crowd would shout back. "Mbote mingi!" "Mbote!"

again, this time a little louder. I missed that. I missed him. Mpasi's head was still down, she was still shaking gently.

"When I was a kid," I turned and whispered to Ian, "I just loved listening to my Dad's sermons." The choir was still singing as we spoke.

"You *liked* sermons? They always make me feel guilty."

"Yeah. Me too. But I liked his. They were full of heart, and humor. Authentic, real stories of life and God. A loving God He really knew well it seemed..."

"Did you?"

"Did I what?"

"Know Him too. You know, the Big Guy." Ian prodded and pointed his finger up to the roof of the chapel, as if the Big Guy was hanging from the rafters.

"Used to, I guess. Who really does though? Anyway, on the way home, we'd walk up that hill right there, to my house," I turned and pointed out the window toward our home, "I would ask him every question I could think of about big topics. Even as a six year old. I always wanted to know if I was saved."

"Saved?"

"Ian. Seriously, didn't you ever go to church?"

"Yeah. But I just haven't heard that term in a long time. It's rather, archaic, don't you think?"

"Maybe. Anyway, I'd always ask him if he thought I was saved. I was so worried about the end times. Dad would always convince me that yes, I was saved, despite my dreadful fear of being sent straight to hell some day because of my great sin."

"You sinned that bad as a six year old? Wow." Ian smiled curiously at me.

"You have no idea." I smiled back, remembering all the trouble I got in. "After that, we'd discuss topics such as post-millennialism and pre-millennialism."

"You lost me there."

"I'll explain later. Or not. Anyway, basically I wanted to know what my Dad thought about the end times. I wanted to think like he did. He would tell me that it doesn't matter when Christ comes, it's going to shock the hell out of us one way or another, so to speak."

"You talked about these things as a kid?"

"Yup. I even started learning Greek."

"Wow. Why?"

"To translate the bible for those who couldn't read it. Duh." I smiled.

"Anna. What happened to you? You seem a million miles away from that path, if you don't mind me saying." *What happened to me? God abandoned me when my mother died... or was it the other way around?*

"Yeah. I suppose so. The closest I am to knowing Greek is from my phi beta gamma sisterhood." I sighed again deeply and sat still on my log bench, just like I used to do, but without my crayons and paper. The choir was now up front, standing around the Ziegler, shuffling and singing. Everyone was standing and joining in. I remembered the Lingala songs, but didn't feel much like singing.

"By the way, the service will be more like three hours."

"Are you kidding me?" Ian looked at me in disbelief.

"That's a *short* service. Sorry about your butt, it'll go flat."

"You won't mind."

"I might. It's your best feature." Talking with Ian helped keep my mind off the pang that kept creeping up into my heart. I wondered if I should try to cry, to keep up with Mpasi. I couldn't. Ironic, when I wanted to the most, I couldn't cry. Not now. I felt disjointed and misplaced, confused... like a guest intruding on a family dinner. Everyone knew the inside stories, and I didn't, yet it was oddly enough, my own family.

A man I didn't recognize began the service. He started out simply, and casually, but with every breath he got louder and more animated and sweaty. He spoke of Jesus' death and resurrection, and the promise of the after-life, a concept I rarely give a second of my time to. My ears perked up when he began to speak of James Landan.

"Pastor Landan," he said in Lingala while he pulled out a white handkerchief and wiped his forehead, "was one of us." A mumbling of "uh-huh's" was murmured in the crowd. He went on, "He was one of us, he was with us, he is with us now." The lanky black man pointed at Ziegler. All eyes followed.

"We followed him, we learned from him, we prayed with him, we ate with him, we sang with him," I wondered how long the list would go on, yet I really wanted to hear more, *what else*? What did he do? "We lived with him, we hunted together, we married off our daughters together..." *Married off our daughters?* I looked down at my left hand instinctively. Yup. Just as I thought, *no* wedding ring. I looked over at Mpasi. She was looking up toward the speaker, tears streamed down her face, she was clutching her left hand. *Did Dad officiate Mpasi's wedding?* He was still talking. "We buried our loved ones together..."

Was he speaking of Mom, or Mpasi's Mom? Both?

"James Landan is in heaven with Jesus. We will meet him there!" A shout rose up from the crowd, a shout of "Amen's" and "Yes's!" Some weeping began.

"It is our loss, not his." Amen. *Amen. Yes. Uh Huh.* The crowd's response rose on the waves of the speaker's intonations.

"We are grieved. We have lost our brother. We have lost our pastor. We have lost our friend." *We have lost our Dad.* I glanced at Mpasi again, she was looking right at me. I quickly turned my head.

"But he has not lost! He has gained! For he sacrificed everything on earth, to gain that which is stored up in heaven for him. We will meet him there!" Again, the gravity of the intonation pulled up a wave of voices that swelled in response. The little chapel began to get very hot, loud, and spiritual for my comfort. Would *we* meet him there? I looked up at the rafters. It didn't make sense to me. Why did faith feel so complex and alien to me, but so natural to others? I needed a distraction from these thoughts...

Pastor Ndumba then came down to the floor and looked us over.

"It is now our sacred privilege to share in the Lord's Supper."

I then noticed the altar covered with a white cloth. Communion.

"...body and blood of our Savior Jesus Christ..."

I can't take communion. I am not clean before God. I am not even sure about God himself. I can't sit here alone if everybody goes up. Merde. Can I say that in church?

"...come, the feast is prepared for everyone..." *did he say, "everyone?" Even me? I need to confess first, right? Confess what? Why? Aren't I always saved if I was once saved? No, probably not. Dad always said faith was a two-way relationship. I wondered if God was still in some way trying to "relate" to me, even if I wasn't relating to Him...*

One by one the rows got up and went forward to receive Communion. Keith went up. Mpasi went up. *How could Mpasi go up? She is a gun-slinging female Rambo.* Ian started to get up but I grabbed his hand. He hesitated, then sat back down. Neither of us spoke. A few people looked our way. I just lowered my head. This was not very seeker friendly.

As the last communicant sat down, Ndumba shouted "Glory to God! May the love of God and the grace of the Lord Jesus Christ and the fellowship of the Holy Spirit be with you all. Amen!" The final words were powerful. I wanted them, I wanted to reach out into the air and grab them and stuff them down into my pockets so I could keep them there when I needed them. Love, grace, fellowship...I ached deep inside. Then my stomach gurgled. Good. It was just hunger.

Then we were out the door. Down to the tables set up for more food and feasting. No *bako* though, this was a mission station. I watched and ate and declined conversation all around me. *Why did I not go up for communion?* I looked up the hill at our house and reflected briefly on the years I had spent in and around that house. We used to have a monkey tied to a log out front. Joey, his name was Joey. One day he was gone. Either he got free or was a free lunch. We played Pit and Uno endlessly. Watched the geckos eat the bugs on our screens. Played Bible charades. *Now who was playing charades?*

Finally we made out way back to the house and fell into the seats as we closed the door behind the last mourner. Ziegler sat in the middle of the living room floor. Dad was finally home. But he was not kicking off his shoes and reading us bible stories by kerosene lantern light. The whole afternoon and evening had felt so surreal. The wailing and mourning still echoed in my ears. Isn't this what I had craved and longed for when I was sipping champagne in Lila's apartment? Who knew I'd get my wish. It was indeed an eventful day. I met old friends, I got "engaged," I went to church, and I went to a real African wake. I was exhausted. I scooted over to Ian and cuddled up with him on the couch. *Hi, Fiancé. Should I acquire this man?* Mpasi and Keith sat across from us. The bodyguards sat outside on the veranda laughing and telling dirty jokes. Passing the coconut concoction all around that they had smuggled in somehow. I had no desire for it.

"Ok kids. I'm going to bed."

"Not yet Uncle Keith. Please."

"You want me to stay up?"

"For a bit. We need your help." I was in no mood for another long conversation with Keith, however, I believed that he knew something about the mysterious situation with Mpasi's village and her neighbors there. We hadn't got a chance to talk about it last night, and it hadn't occurred to me that he knew more. But today, I was convinced, that if anyone knew all the answers, it would be Keith...Dad's constant companion.

"Funny, isn't it Keith, how Goyongo gave Dad a proper funeral, complete with tears and sackcloth...so to speak. And yet the village he married into commanded us to leave as soon as our tea was cold." Keith said nothing. Mpasi looked at me, and seemed to catch on to my questions.

"Do you know why they were afraid?" she asked.

"Maybe I know a little." Keith looked caught.

"Uncle Keith. I can't understand why you keep hiding things from me, and now from Mpasi too. You wished you could have told me earlier about her being my sister and all," I noticed Mpasi half smiled at the word sister, "So now is your chance to tell me more, before it's too late. Does this have anything to do with the opposition to the evangelizing situation you told me about earlier?"

"In a way. Yes it does. I will tell you. But it's really nothing, and it's not important, ok? That's why I didn't tell you. This *may* be the reason they didn't want us there, but it may not, I really don't know."

Keith settled in deeper into his chair and took a deep breath, he kicked off his shoes. It smelled, I wished he hadn't, but it looked so familiar. In a way, we were about to get our bedtime story. The African bugs and crickets were busy scratching their way around the house, finding easy ways in. Kerosene lamps flickered and cast strange beams of light over our faces. Dad lay between the four us. Is it disrespectful to rest my bare feet up on the casket? Keith began.

"We tried numerous times to work in that village. It was small, relatively unknown and hidden away in the forest. No one had shown the Jesus film there yet, no one had preached, no one had witnessed to them. James and I knew it was time. So, we went in one day. We hiked in, mind you this was nearly twenty years ago. There was a great deal more water and mud, and it was thicker. No trails were cut from Goyongo to Bongalo yet. It was difficult and we were carrying a generator, our film equipment, projector, sheets, ya know...the works...to do the whole thing. When we got there, there was a lot of confusion as to who we were, what we wanted...you can imagine. Finally the chief met us and welcomed us in. Apparently the news started spreading around that we were missionaries. Some people were curious, others were hostile. One in particular was a man named Zema. He was a witch doctor."

"A what?" Ian was sitting up straighter now. A cool breeze blew in the screen windows. We all shuddered in unison.

"Witch doctor. A *nganga nkisi*. They do a lot of black magic, medicine-man type healings and work.

They conjure spirits, and are respected to some degree. They are feared in the villages, depending on their history of success. They work against God."

"How do you know it's against God?" said Ian.

"Ian. Please, let's not get theological, I just want to know the story." I said, annoyed with his questions.

"Well, actually that's a good question. Leads into the next thing. Zema knew we were Christians, men of God, ok, our God. He did not want our faith to spread, he did not want God in his village. That night as we were about to set up, he drew up a crowd of people who were not too sure about our presence there. He got them all riled up about it and then proceeded to work up some prayers, dances, God knows what else he does with bones and feathers and the like, to get us to leave. At that moment, a mighty thunderstorm struck. It rained and lightning struck for hours on end. We couldn't set up. In the morning, we had to head home, we weren't welcome."

"So his black magic worked then?" Ian said.

"No."

"But you had to leave."

"Yes, but...only for a while...well, anyway." Keith started shifting in his seat again, but continued on. He had our rapt attention. Mpasi was sitting up close to the end of her seat, elbows on her knees. "So, then, we tried again the next month, hoping some time would help things out. We were greeted in the same way. Half the village was excited, they wanted to see this thing called "film" and the others were hostile. The witch doctor did his thing...again. He prayed and chanted and got a mob going about it."

"Did you leave again?" Ian kept interrupting.

"Yeah. Thunderstorm came. Big rains, we spent the night there and then left in the morning. Couldn't show the film, again. We went back and realized that there was a major spiritual warfare going on here."

"Spiritual what?"

"Ian, I will fill you in on these things later. But to summarize, spiritual warfare is basically what Christian's call the unseen battle going on at all times between Satan and his army and God and his. Good vs. Evil. Dark vs. Light. You know...You've seen Lord of the Rings, Star Wars..."

"Like 'The Force?' Guess I never really thought of all that. Unseen? There is really power on either side?" Ian's questions were like that of a small boy asking his parents "why" about everything – "Why is the sky blue, Daddy?", "Why is there evil in the world?"- although, those questions are not rudimentary in any way. The question of evil in the world has an answer shallow enough to splatter in, deep enough to drown in.

"Uncle Keith, go on, please." I couldn't discuss why bad things happen to good people right now. *But I'm curious as to who classifies as "good people" though*... I wanted to know what happened next.

"Good questions, Ian, we can talk more later about it. But yes, absolutely. There is power. I have no doubt you have seen God's power in some way in your own life. And the enemy's power is always at work. Always working to take away from that which God gives and lives for - like love, faith, joy, goodness..." Keith was preaching again.

"Okay. Okay," I was getting more and more impatient, and had had enough sermons for the night.

"Anyway," Keith glared at me slightly and moved on, "So we realized there was a battle being waged for people's souls. So we prayed harder and harder. It seemed it was our prayers against his."

"But his kept winning." Ian would not shut-up; he was way too ignorant and curious about these things. I was ignorant and not so curious. Note to self, no bedtime stories for Ian.

"For awhile, yes. We tried to go back three, four more times. And each time we tried, even in dry season, the skies would open, the rains would pour down."

"He was more powerful than your God?" Mpasi was now asking. We were all beginning to see it that way.

"No." Apparently Keith did not see it that way. "Temporarily, the enemy displayed his power. The tragic side of this was that Zema was gaining more power each time. And more and more people believed in him over God. More and more people flocked to him as their leader, they were convinced he was all-powerful. But God's side always wins. We prayed some more, and finally one day, we came. Zema shook and stirred and prayed, but the sky did not open. The night was still and clear, every star could be seen. We raised up the sheet, started the generator, showed the film. That night there was a major revival in the village. People saw who Jesus was and what he did for their lives, how far God would go to save people -

"And..." I interrupted.

"And - that was it. It was over. We were welcomed in the village, by a good majority at that point. But…but Zema was so mad that he had fallen so hard. He took quite a beating that day because we overcame his powers. We never saw this part, but the story goes that he put a curse on us from that day forward." Keith stopped and rubbed his forehead.

"What kind of curse?" Mpasi asked.

"What kind? Well, apparently he just straight out cursed James himself. Not even so much me. But it was about Zema vs. James somehow. He put a curse on him that James would lose those dearest to him, that James would be a bearer of death and an enemy to Africa somehow. I don't know the exact words or curse, but whatever it was, it had many people who believed in Zema's power very wary of James. They kept a lot of distance. They believed that as long as he was in Africa, he would be a curse to those he encountered, and to the land." Keith coughed and shifted uncomfortably. All of our eyes fell onto the casket. Keith continued, "After awhile, people who believed this could basically find any reason they wanted to, to believe that he was cursed. A child would die, and they would blame it on James. A drought would come and they would believe it was Zema's curse on James that brought it. They even at some point begged Zema to remove it. But he refused. Said it couldn't be reversed."

"What about the people who didn't believe? The people who came to faith in God?" Mpasi was the most interested at this point. This was her family we were talking about, after all.

"They shrugged it off. They knew that God was bigger and more powerful, as the starry night had proved. They had faith and thought Zema was a bunch of B.S. Pardon my language." Of all the people in this room, I thought, you are the most pardoned, Keith. "In a sense, the village split, some even moved apart. Your mom was one of them. Nzala. She was saved, and her and her family believed in God. She fell in love with your Dad." It was hard for me to hear Keith talking to Mpasi like this, but I was riveted on the story.

"Yes, I know. She did. She loved him very, very much, so Bemba tells me." Mpasi dropped her eyes to the floor. I could almost feel the weight of her heart.

"They married. Your Dad stayed with her in the village often, sometimes she'd come to Goyongo. She was dearly loved, a sweetheart of the villages. Even those who didn't like James, loved Nzala." Keith stopped for a moment and kicked the cement cracks with his bare toes. "When she died, after a long hard labor with you, many, many people mourned. James was there. But he couldn't stay and grieve her. They asked him to leave. Those who believed in the curse, believed that she died because he was cursed. Even those who didn't believe, like your family members, were nonetheless starting to think that he brought this on somehow. He was blamed. He was heartbroken about it too. He had only known your mom for a short while, and was looking forward to many more years. The village, your family, allowed James to see you and help raise you for many years, your childhood years you can remember. He was there often, but only outside the village, and mainly here in Goyongo. Like a split family or something, your aunt and Bemba insisted that he had some kind of visitation rights. And he demanded it basically. He wanted to be with you, and Anna was at boarding school."

"Bemba took me to Bumba to live with him." Mpasi stepped in and continued the story. "Tata visit me there often, and I come to Goyongo to see him. Sometime I see my family, my aunt, but not too much...Tata was really my only family to me. And Bemba. Tata did promised to someday take me to America with him. I wanted to go. Then he had leave...because of war. When he returns I was older, but we did much time together. He again told me he would take me to America. But first, he said, he must have to go to home for something, and then he would return. I do think he did return..." Mpasi stared at Dad's head in the window of the Ziegler, and her eyes filled with tears again.

I clutched Ian's hand and tried to shift through this conversation reeling in my head. I was at boarding school, and Dad was parenting another daughter off and on. He wanted to be with her, he lost her mom, he had basically lost her, too. They had a relationship...they were close and clung to each other...and I was absolutely clueless the whole time. Doing my homework, memorizing bible verses, remaining in sorrow over my mom, holing up inside. I had not moved on. He did. For all intents and purposes he lost me too; two wives, one daughter. James died very much alone, no family that gave him the love he deserved, or needed him, except one - Mpasi.

I sensed blankets of bitterness lifting off from my spirit. I felt sorrow that I had not known. I felt upset with Dad for not telling me about Mpasi now for another reason...*I could have known her.* I could have had a sister. He could have had two daughters. That's what he wanted, that's why he asked me to come back, and I wouldn't go with him. But I'm here now, he still got me here to meet her, even in his death. Does she still want to go to America? I shook my head at my father lying quiet and motionless, "watching" and "listening" to us talk about him. Didn't he trust me enough to include me? Why did he leave me out? I wish...I wish I could have shared in this life with him, this life he had with another woman and with another daughter. I wish I had. And then, we could have shared this grief together, *could we still?*

"Uncle Keith. Why didn't you bother to tell us about this curse?" I couldn't believe how much Keith knew. He was our oracle. Without him, this would simply have been a safari. I hate safaris.

"Meaningless. That's why. Don't mean a dang thing. It's all a bunch of nonsense. Faith always wins out, so there's nothing to be afraid of." I flinched as Keith said dang. The missionary was slipping. In my day, we couldn't say dang without getting detention.

"But didn't you say there is power on both...sides?" Ian was still trying to patch together twenty years of theology that Keith and I had on him. But he was right about that. I had witnessed plenty of supernatural, miraculous events. There is power...on both sides, but it is always uneven.

"Yes. There is. But God is bigger. The curse didn't mean anything. Mpasi's mom passing was simply due to a prolonged labor and complications.

There was nothing to be done. Witch doctor has nothing on God, or on James. So it wasn't worth mentioning. Like a folk tale, kid's ghost story."

The word ghost hung in the air a little too thick. We all scuffed our feet around. It was pitch black outside. Our companions had now passed out outside, breathing out sweet coconut aroma. We could hear crickets and hyrax, the noises of the prowling jungle. Kerosene lamps were getting low. It was definitely time for bed, and some protection to be found loosely under the mosquito net.

"Well, on that note, it's bed time. One more question, Keith..."

"Yah?" He yawned as he spoke.

"Do you think these people who are wary about this...cursed man..." I pointed to Dad, "would have some issue with him being buried here? You know... the curse hasn't entirely left, it's being buried, do they believe it's gone at death?"

"I'm not sure. It seemed to me, the way I heard it, that as long as he remained, the curse would remain...especially on those closest to him, but it didn't clarify if that meant dead or alive. Maybe there's more to it, I don't know. Some think it has to do with his daughters and childbirth, considering Mpasi's mom, even your mom's death. Some believe it has to do with everyone that is near him or comes across him. I guess that could mean those who come across his grave too. But I doubt it."

Mpasi shook her head and grabbed a pillow off the couch and a blanket.

"I sleep outside. I am more comfortable there. I will keep watch."

"For what?" I asked.

"Anything. Ghosts maybe. Good night." The screen door creaked and slammed shut in increments behind her. Clank-Clank, clank. I heard her yell at the bodyguard.

"*Pesa ngai monduki na yo.*" I laughed right out loud.

"What?" Ian.

"She just commandeered a rifle to sleep with tonight."

I heard her open the breach and check the rifle. Apparently it was ready to go.

Keith got up and turned right into my parent's old bedroom. I was flooded with more memories as I sat on the couch against the wall to my parent's room. I could see my old room down the hallway, the bunk beds…my parents had hoped to have a large family. Never happened. I always got the top bunk. The walls were cracked and paint was peeling, but otherwise not much had changed. Even Dad's old books were still on the shelves. Anything valuable was gone, of course, and the Ndumbas were living here, but they moved out for the night in honor of James, allowing us to stay here until we left. Which I hoped was as soon as possible. Everything seemed eerie and gave me the shivers now. Something unexplainable had passed over all of us. The story was indeed a ghost story. And I was hearing it without a shred of faith to hold onto, unlike Keith, who was already snoring peacefully.

"Do you believe this story Anna?"

"I guess so. I've seen some pretty crazy stuff in my life here." Ian grabbed my feet and swung them over his lap and rubbed them.

"I've never heard anything like it in my life. But somehow, I believe it."

"Well, what's not to believe, I guess. People believe in some pretty primitive stuff. I'm sure that they do believe he is cursed. I'm sure they do believe that Zema has power. I'm sure they are not happy that he is back, and bringing this dark cloud back with him, to be buried right under their feet."

"Yeah, but do *you* believe it." Ian prodded.

"I don't believe in anything. However, what *they* believe makes me nervous."

"I find that hard to believe, you don't believe in God anymore?"

"Nope. Not since he took my Mom. Didn't like Him much after that." I looked away, unable to maintain eye contact when I said that. Maybe I wasn't so sure...

"How can you not like something you don't believe in? I don't believe in unicorns, but I never say I don't like them, it doesn't make sense. And if you believe in a God, shouldn't you, shouldn't we figure out what or who He is, or ask God to reveal it? Would hate to be wrong about it too late..." Ian's voice trailed off as he chewed on his own profundity. He had a point. But I wondered if whether believing in God, and having faith, was something more than just hedging your bets. *Maybe I do believe in a God, but I'm just not sure I believe Him...*

"Ok, philosophy major. Aren't you supposed to be a lawyer, not a pastor? I'll simply say this, I'm not sure if I believe in God, but I believe that others believe. And as long as they believe that he, Dad, is cursed, then they will continue to see anything bad that happens as a sign that it has never left, and never will. We need to get this over with fast."

"But then our vacation will be over." Ian smiled and tickled my toes.

"You sure you want to touch those?"

"You're my wife, I can touch them if I want."

"Not yet you know. *Fiancée*!" I corrected. "Ian, this whole wedding thing... we're just going along with this for fun, OK?" I tried explaining to him one more time. Fun! Pretense! Appeasement! It was like telling a three year old why he can't have another cookie.

"I know. But I like it. I like the idea of it." Ian interlaced his fingers with my toes, and bent down to kiss the top of my feet. He was grinning boyishly and eyeing me with mischief. I glanced away, my heart instantly pounding wildly. I hated the effect he had on me, eliciting an array of physical and emotional responses I was typically unwilling to offer.

"It will be a nice gesture to the village leaders, long time friends of my Dad," I continued the conversation, looking away from his smiling face. I think that they just want to believe that I am married, would make them feel better. I'm too old to not be married."

"Would it make you feel better?" Ian continuously nudged around invisible boundary lines. Maybe it was the hazard of being a lawyer.

"To what? Be married? Marriage doesn't fix anything."

"Never said anything about something being broken, Anna. But you're right, it sure doesn't fix anything. That's not the point of it…but it can create great things."

"Like babies? No thanks."

"Yeah, like families. Trust. Love that lasts forever. You know, that kind of stuff." Ian looked down shyly, a little red sneaking into his cheeks.

"You believe in those fairytales, Prince Charming? Didn't your parents divorce?"

"Yup. That's why I believe in it even more." This time Ian gazed directly into my eyes.

"You'll have to explain that another day. Besides, I don't want a family."

"I think it's too late for that." A small smiled played on his lips.

"What do you mean?"

"You have a family, Anna. You have me, and Uncle Keith, and you have a sister, and probably a brother-in-law."

"Is she married? I think she might be." I remembered the pastor's words earlier that day.

"I think she is. I heard her use the word *mobali* – *husband* – in conversation with some of the others with us. She's so young to be married though." Ian said.

"No, not out here. She's old."

"So what does that make you?"

"An old hag."

"My hag. I love this hag." Ian leaned in and kissed me gently on my lips. I wanted more, and kissed him back. We folded into each other, using every limb to embrace all that we could. It felt right.

I felt loved and protected. Ian's kisses were sweet and tentative, not hasty and careless, but a little urgent nonetheless. Making out on my old couch was a weird experience. This is where I used to play with dolls...okay, bugs. This is where Mom would comb the tangles out of my wet hair, patiently, one strand at a time, and read to me from the Janet Oke, *Love Comes Softly* books. I never thought love would come so softly to me now. *Was this love?* This couch was where I used to sit and listen to sermons that we would play from our old stereo. The ancient tapes would screech out the voices of Swindoll and Billy Graham during the hot, buggy nights. We would sit still and listen. And then pray. One night a snake joined the service, hanging above my Dad's head as he amen-ed along to Chuck. The snake met the Lord that night - Dad baptized him in the name of Jesus with his sharp machete and we ate him the next day.

I cuddled up close to Ian and we listened to the rain begin to drum down on the tin roof. It was deafening and beautiful. I closed my eyes and breathed in the cool air that drifted through the window screens. Something about a thunder and rainstorm always makes me feel giddy inside, like something exciting is about to happen. My heart quickened in anticipation, I couldn't help but let out a smile. I did indeed feel home.

We retired to my bedroom. We kissed goodnight and whispered in our bunks, in the dark, under our nets and played with our flashlights. I felt like a little girl at a slumber party. I felt happy for the first time in a long time. Something was shifting in my spirit, and I liked it. The dark, hurting side of Anna tried to fight it and remain defensive and cynical, and it was a powerful side. She would sit on my shoulder and tell my good self that she would just get hurt in the end. "Be strong, be firm, be confident. Don't be soft," she whispered in one ear. The Anna that glowed like my mother whispered in the other ear, "Be soft, open up your life, forgive, it's ok. It's time. I'm right here." The argument went back and forth, one protective of my spirit, the other protecting me from losing spirit.

That night I listened to my mother and told her a prayer of thanks in my top bunk. Great things were about to happen, I could feel it. I closed my eyes and waited to see my Dad's light flicker underneath my door at 4:30 in the morning. But something was keeping me awake. I kept shifting in my bed. I felt itchy and annoyed. The rain outside had turned into a sort of scratchy pitter-patter. My toes started tickling. Something was keeping me awake... Was Ian tickling my toes?

CHAPTER TWENTY-FOUR

"Kids. Get your shoes." Keith flicked on his flashlight and immediately I grasped the situation, or I should say, it grasped me. Ants. Ants everywhere, crawling up the sides of our beds. Keith was fighting them off and Ian was slapping himself like crazy trying to kill them. I lunged off of the top bunk and we all made a dive for our shoes as our bare feet hit the floor, but we could hardly feel the floor. We could feel ants, moving under our feet, climbing up our legs, biting hungrily, and it hurt.

"What the kuzimu kind of ants are these! They are huge!" Ian screamed at an embarrassing decibel for a grown man. The ants were about the size of my toe, so I forgave him.

"No Seattle ant, I can assure you. They are African flesh-eating army ants!"

"What?!"

"They'll eat anything that stands still long enough."

"Including HUMANS?" Ian was still screeching and we were already running out of the house. Mpasi was already half way down the hill along with our other traveling friends. We were trying to get our shoes on still, as we ran away from the invasion. I had done this countless times as a girl. Invasions were common during this season. The ants came looking for food, and they usually cleaned out every cupboard and nook and cranny in our house. If we were still enough, they would eat us alive. We would always remember to save our African Gray parrot from a terrible fate.

"Did you really say flesh-eating?" Ian squeaked as we continued to run down hill into the village.

"Yeah. And they're organized too. Run a tight ship those ants, they have guards and chiefs, the works. A real army! They move in columns, place sentries along the sides to make the desired trail. They spread out and disperse in military fashion. Real warriors!" I said this with a mix of disgust and reverence.

"Do you think they could get into the Ziegler?" Ian said this loud enough and both Keith and I stopped in our tracks. Mpasi stopped too and looked behind us. We turned and stared up at the house. Even in the dim light of a flashlight, we could see the ground moving all around it like waves on a black sea. A black sea of ants.

"Nope!" Keith answered hastily and confidently. Oh well, all the best, Dad, we have to save our toes! I half imagined the Zig being carted away on a black sea of ants. I wouldn't put it past them.

The teachers down the hill in the Goyongo seminary found places for the displaced and we settled in for the night. A student kept watch on the direction they were taking, but it seemed as though they would head across the road and back into the jungle.

The *kalekba*, or reed bed, they gave me was too short. It was also curved so that lying on my back worked ok except my legs hung off the end. Soon I began to lose feeling in them and tried to roll on my side with knees up to my chest. By the faint light I could look around the room. It was about half the size of my condo but had ten times the people in it: several children, a mom and Dad, and various other unidentified individuals. Many were restless, one snored like an old dog. It was hot and stuffy and smelly. No doubt they objected to my smell as well. They said we smelled like milk and cheese. Well, they smelled like fuku and mpondu. The windows were tight shut. No mosquitoes, which was a relief, since I had left my deet behind in my mad flight.

Tomorrow...it would all end tomorrow.

CHAPTER TWENTY-FIVE

Today should be the day of Dad's actual burial. After these many long days, the end had come. I looked forlornly out the window into a thick sheet of rain blurring the jungle scene before me. The rain had not stopped for the last three hours, and there was no sign of it letting up. This was no Seattle rain, not a soft light mist, or something you can still walk in without an umbrella. No real Seattleite uses an umbrella, we are so accustomed to being half wet, it doesn't faze us to run in and out of a grocery store in the pouring rain without some kind of head covering. This makes it easy to spot a tourist, or someone fresh from California. They use umbrellas in a light mist. This, however, would warrant an umbrella, or, rather, a roof. An umbrella would be torn to shreds or whipped upside down within seconds in this kind of torrential storm. This kind of weather was also not conducive to peaceful burials and grave diggings.

We stayed inside and bided our time. We taught Mpasi how to play gin, and then gin rummy, then poker, but not strip poker, of course. Mpasi taught us how to play Mancala. Ian wanted to play "Would you rather," and then it was "have you ever," and then we played, "I never." That last one was a real kick in the pants. Mpasi won most of the time.

"I have never been to Starbucks." This was after a long conversation explaining Starbucks to Mpasi. It boggled her mind.

"I have never seen a movie in a theater."

"I have never had a milkshake."

"I've never worn a bikini." She went on and on all the while laughing hard at herself and our massive losing streak. Of course, we came up with a few good ones too.

"I have never been a rebel in an African war." That was Ian's favorite. He would laugh and snort. Mpasi didn't think it was funny. Of course not.

Mpasi was beginning to feel like family. We enjoyed each other, laughed hard, and made fun of each other, the way a family should. We hadn't talked about the big issues, or the massive elephants in the living room, of course, but we would someday. For now, I was still adjusting to the fact that I actually liked having her around, and that she was my relative. Sister. Zena, warrior princess. I was adjusting to the fact that I no longer resented her, much. Instead I still lingered in more of a realm of disappointment that I had been kept in the dark. I liked her. I really did. One couldn't help but like her. I loved her demanding personality, her "large and in charge" demeanor. I admired her courage and bravery. She had a contagious laugh and a beautiful smile. She could spit venom and bite just as well as I could, and I liked that about her. Yet we were both laying down our weapons and calling a truce. I even saw physical resemblance with one another. We had the same eyes.

"Would you rather bury Dad in a downpour, or bury Dad in sweltering heat?"

We all agreed on heat and waited impatiently for the rain to stop. Dad would have to wait another day. We ate mpondu late that night, thanks to Phillipe, our old cook, and we even had a few cups of the local brew that he offered us. Everyone except Keith, of course. But he looked tempted. After sharing stories and candid conversation around our dinner, we broke out into a timeless tradition for missionaries - bible story charades. The idea was, shamefully, mine. It was something Dad and Mom and I did for years and years, in this very house, and I couldn't resist. We would find the most obscure passages in the bible and act them out without words, trying to stump the guesser. Who knew that the bible could be so much fun.

Keith and I against Mpasi and Ian would be too unfair, so Ian and I teamed up against the two of them. I immediately vetoed David and Bathsheeba, Abraham and Hagar, and any other racy stories that were not meant for children; that didn't leave much. Of course, Ian had no clue what I was talking about. Finally we, I, landed on acting out the story of the murder with the tent peg through the skull. It is always a crowd pleaser. Keith guessed it right away.

Our other companions were down in the village huts that night. It was just our small "family" of five, including Dad. Finally we retired for the night, our smile muscles worn out. I hadn't laughed like that, or felt so free, in longer than I could remember.

Tomorrow, tomorrow, we would bury Dad, and head home. But I didn't feel as anxious to leave anymore; Seattle wasn't beckoning me home. I wasn't even sure if I would fit there anymore. Tarzan definitely wouldn't. What would become of us there? Who would we become? Would we be, a "we" back home? Maybe we'd get a pet monkey.

I brushed my teeth in a bucket of water in the bathroom and looked in the old tarnished mirror. The girl who stared at herself in the glass in Seattle was not the same girl looking back at me now. The one before was cold and tired, half dead to the world, turning a slow shade of gray from every angle. This one looked younger, more alive, with a little pink in her cheeks, tanned, and hair even more bleached from the sun. She even had more freckles. I liked her, and I smiled at her and said Hi. I felt foolish doing so, but I also felt that I needed to greet her and welcome her in. She was a mix of a young Congolese child and an older, broken and yet slowly healing adult American woman. Her identity was such a mixture of uncertainties and questions, fantasies and realities, freedom and fear. It was just starting to peel away and reveal itself to me, one glance at a time.

I remembered a story my Mom used to read to me from C.S. Lewis, one of my all time favorite authors. It was from *The Voyage of the Dawn Treader.* A young hot-headed, rude and selfish boy magically turned into a dragon. In order to return back into a boy, he had to shed his dragon skin, layer by layer. But he couldn't do it himself, try as he might. Aslan, the King Lion, came to his aid. He clawed the thick dragon skin off with his strong paws, one tender outer layer at a time. It was painful, and took some time, but finally the dragon shell rested on the shore of the beach, and Eustace was a boy again, free. I wondered how many snake-like layers I had been shedding, one step at a time in this jungle, and who was helping me.

The morning greeted us with more rain. But it was not as hard as yesterday's. It would make the trek a little more precarious, and slippery, but one mile past the water source, about two miles due northeast was manageable either way. By 10:00 we had loaded up. Ziggy was back up on his poles, and marched before us once more. We had more visitors this time. The news had gotten around that today was finally the day. Friends in Goyongo joined us, as well as a few unfriendly faces from Mpasi's village. She pointed them out to us. I wondered what they were doing here. Would they try to stop us? Were they simply wanting to be sure that James was dead and buried, and therefore everything from the past was over? I had also heard rumors all morning that Mpasi's guards had been telling our whole story to various groups. The plane crash, the prison, the river, the ant invasion. From the looks of it, one who even didn't believe in curses, could easily believe that something in the way of bad luck was shadowing us. I kind of did. I glanced around uneasily as we began the march toward the designated gravesite. I saw a face in the crowd that froze my blood. It was ugly and suspicious and exactly like the face of the medicine man in my nightmares. His teeth were yellow and broken; he had bones hanging around his neck. He disappeared in the crowd. I stood staring until I could see no glimpse of him.

"You OK, Anna? You look pale." Keith prodded me along the path by taking my elbow in his hand.

"Keith, is Zema still alive?" I felt light-headed; the blood had drained from my face.

"The witch doctor? I suppose he could be, he wasn't that old, just looked like it."

"Would he come here, do you think?"

"Hard to reckon. Who knows, I doubt it. This is a funeral procession, Anna. These people care about James. They are here to say goodbye."

"Hmm. Not all of them. Did you see the ones from Mpasi's village? I wonder why they are here?"

"Maybe just to catch a glimpse. Make sure he's dead... although...we never did figure if that negated the curse or not. Anyway, it doesn't matter, Anna, remember? All of this is nonsense to James, and to God."

"His God."

"God." Keith swung back, but then changed the subject. "Anna, it has been a long time for me. A long time since we buried your Mom." He paused. He continued. "And I never came back to visit. I'm not sure, but things are looking familiar. I think we are headed to where she is buried."

"I had wondered the same thing, Keith, a long time ago when I read the note."

"Yeah honey, me too. It makes sense, of course." He squeezed my hand. "This is the end sweetheart, you did it, and we made it. God got us this far."

"God did? I thought *I* did, Uncle Keith." I smiled as I poked at him just a bit. Yet I had to admit, at least to myself, the fact that Dad was not lost, stolen, or drowned, and neither were we, was a bit supernatural. All things seemed to point to a canopy of protection around me. And sometimes I could almost physically feel it. Perhaps life is meant to be a cooperative effort between God and humans.

"Just an hour or so and we are there, honey. Hang tight."

I was. Tight. My muscles and nerves felt tight, my palms were clenched. I felt truly nervous for the first time in a long time. I looked around for Mpasi. I needed her.

I found Mpasi and we walked together, single file of course, on up through the thick jungle. The rain came and went in short showers. The animals serenaded us as we marched onward. I couldn't help but contemplate the vast difference between this funeral, and the one at Homeward Bound. No hearse, no perfect small square hole in the ground. No chairs set out on a perfectly manicured lawn. No one was wearing heels or wide brimmed hats. We had no funeral director. And this time, we had an honest-to-goodness body. Well, I suppose honest was a matter of interpretation.

Mpasi's hips swung to and fro, and I admired her figure again. We had been walking for about an hour, we were getting closer. The writing on the page of Dad's letter to me floated in front of my eyes. I could read it as if it were in my hands, word for word. As if I just opened it. And yet it felt like a decade ago that I was back in the condo on Alki, snapping at Ian, pushing French press and opening that fateful note. *Of course it's addressed to me, Ian, I'm the only family he's got!* I remembered my careless words, my certainty about who I was. How things had changed.

Did I know more now? About who I was? Or Whose I was?

Mpasi's guard and pallbearer stopped and spoke to Mpasi in Lingala. She turned and translated.

"We are here." Just ahead was a clearing.

"How do you know?"

"This is the *mayita* - gravesites." I wondered who else was buried here. I thought about my Mom. Could this be the place? Wouldn't Keith know?

"So what now?" I turned and asked the question into the air. Keith? Ian? Mpasi? Anyone have an answer? I supposed I was the one everyone would look to for an answer. I didn't have any. But I had to use the bathroom.

"Start digging I guess." I did not want to look around for Mom. I didn't want to be disappointed. I excused myself from the large gathering of people standing around in and out and around the trees in the jungle and walked off. *Who are you people!?* I wondered. I had no idea what was supposed to happen next. All of this madness, near-death experiences and emotional trauma were suddenly coming to this anti-climactic halt? We bury him, we say a few words, and what…go home?

I turned to walk to find a place to pee where no one could find me. This cemetery was quite overgrown. People didn't come here to place flowers and nobody manicured the lawn. But I could see the outlines of the clearing and here and there, the mounds of earth. A few had some crosses and rudimentary gravestones. I pushed through some growth into another clearing. Something suddenly caught my attention to the right of where I was standing. It was a rock, another headstone. It was a smooth square stone, large, very wide, but half covered in weeds. I walked over and yanked some vines off and brushed it off with my hands. *A headstone?* It did look suspiciously like a tombstone. I took off my sweaty bandana and used it to wipe away the mud and dirt. There was an inscription etched rudely into the stone. My heart picked up speed. What could this be? I couldn't keep myself from hoping...could this be Mom?

"Ma bien-aimée - Nzala. Je vais te rejoindre ici. Rien à craindre. Merci pour notre Mpasi." *My beloved, Nzala. I will join you here, nothing to fear. Thank you for our Pain.*

CHAPTER TWENTY-SIX

Mpasi bent down and stroked the stone with her hands.

"Mamma." She whispered over and over again. The way she said it carried all the pathos of her life. She hung on the stone and began to weep. We all cried, too. Even me. I blamed it on the fatigue. And part of me wished it were my Mamma. We all stood some distance back, allowing her some time. Dad buried her here, Mpasi's Mom, his second dead wife. Why did he not tell anyone? Did he have to fight the village for rights to bury her? Did he do it in secret? As usual, so many questions, so few answers. Would I ever know? Why wouldn't he want to be next to *my* Mom. The familiar taste of bitterness salivated in my mouth once again.

"You knew, didn't you Keith." I whispered to Keith.

"This time, honey, no, I sure did not." Keith shook his head slowly back and forth. I believed him. He looked as stunned as I did.

Mpasi's villagers mumbled and huddled close, many were Nzala's relatives. This was obviously a discovery on their part as well. Confusion seeped back into my head. Nothing makes sense out here, so much for an easy, anti-climactic burial. On the other hand, it did make sense. Dad told her he'd join her. He wanted to be buried next to her. Why didn't he want to be buried next to Mom? *My Mom*?!

"Anna, this is making sense." Ian read my mind.

"What do you mean?"

"Your Dad, the letter. He wanted you to come out here, bury him here near Nzala's stone and put the pieces together."

"Wow Ian, it sounds so National Treasure, one clue after another. No. He simply wanted to be buried next to his second wife...his wife. This wasn't for me. Besides, we put the pieces together long before we came here."

"I know. But your Dad had no way of knowing that we'd get imprisoned, and that Mpasi would hear about it, and find us, and that you would find your family that way. He banked on *this*, that you would burry him here where he instructed, find the headstone and perhaps it would make you wonder, and go looking for Mpasi."

"Maybe, but for all I could have known, it could have been a weird coincidence that this was here. After all, I could have translated this, "thank you for our pain," not, "thank you for our Mpasi.' As a *noun*, and not a proper name, and it would have never connected. Or we would have never stumbled across it." I felt irritated.

"But he could have asked anyone, for that matter, to come and bury him in Africa. Why did he ask you? To come by yourself? A young single woman? Not too rational, unless he had other motivations."

"I am so rational."

"No, I mean, his plan wouldn't have seemed too rational, unless he had some bigger purpose...a vision, a plan for your life."

"Thank you, Rick Warren." Ian furrowed his brow. Oh lord, did I have to explain everything to him? He didn't even know who Rick Warren was? *The Purpose Driven Life?*

"Sure, maybe Ian. Maybe he did this to lead me to my family. Did he really care that much that I meet Mpasi? Why? What does it matter that I have a sister, or not?" Aggravation rubbed up against me, purring for a pet. I bent down all too willingly to comply. I was ticked about my Mom. *Did she mean nothing?*

Perhaps Ian could be right, I wondered, about the "treasure" hunt. Was my Dad so sad that I was all alone in this world, no mother, no father, no husband, no children, that he went to such great lengths to introduce me to my sister? I somehow doubted it. It could have worked though. If I saw the headstone, it would have bothered me, I would have thought about it, and I would have asked Keith about the stone, and I would have discovered the whole story... one way or another, I was meant to know. *Oh Dad. Why couldn't you have just told me in person? Why couldn't you have just told me? Why this wretched treasure hunt?* I scratched at my bug bites, cursed the mosquito's that bit me. What a waste of my vacation days. My mood flip-flopped again. Zero to sixty.

I glanced over at Ziegler and walked toward Dad, away from that woman's memorial service going on. I could see my Dad's head through the window. I thought I saw him move. I looked closer. He seemed to be smiling, and talking to me, again... Larium didn't touch my dreams, but it offered magnificent daytime illusions. What a magnificent drug.

"Treasure Hunt? So, Anna, you found some treasure after all?" The corpse sat up and talked.

"No. No treasure, just a big Pain." I answered back,

"No, you said it was a treasure hunt."

"I guess. I guess I did."

"Store it up, where moth and rust will not destroy..."

"Quit preaching, Dad."

"It's what I do."

"Apparently, you did a lot more than preach...Why didn't you tell me?"

"I wanted to. I tried a few times, I couldn't do it. I wanted you to know, when I asked you to come back here. I wished you had come."

"Why?"

"So you could know me, so I could know you again, so you could know you weren't alone."

"I didn't know. I didn't know what you wanted." I paused. *"Dad, did you love them more than me?"* I scolded myself for such a childish question. I felt foolish, but it was THE question I had wanted to ask. I felt tears menacingly sneaking up into my throat. *Go away, this is not the time*, I tried to tell them. Dad didn't scold me, he only motioned me closer, and I did. He sighed deeply and took my hand and spoke softly.

"Your Mom was my first love, you are my first born. No one could love you, or she, any more than I did. No one can replace you. I'm proud of you, Anna,

and I love you, more than you'll ever know. I'm fortunate to have found love, not once, but twice. Try it just once, for me? I don't love them more than you. I love you all. I love you. I'm fortunate to have two beautiful girls; no one is more blessed than I.

"You're dead. How is that blessed?"

"I hope, one day, you will see how what happens after death, can be a blessing."

"You're dead. Why am I talking to you?"

"There is one more little treasure yet to find..."

"Anna!" Mpasi was shaking me. I was leaned up against Ziegler with my head against the steel. I wiped my eyes.

"You sleep?"

"I guess. I'm sorry." I stared at her hard and decided to hand her an olive branch. Or maybe just an olive.

"Mpasi, Dad meets me in my dreams, does he meet you?"

"Yes."

"What does he say to you?"

"He tells me he loves me." Mpasi shrugged as she spoke, as if Dad told her that everyday.

"Me too. He tells me that, too." I smiled at her. She ate the olive and smiled back. Should I warn her about the olive-pit?

"Of course he does. Come. Let's bury our Dad." Mpasi smiled at me and offered me her hand. I took it, and she pulled me up. We embraced for the first time. I tried to hide my tears. I did a poor job, the jungle was turning me into a total sap.

My father's casket was clumsily, precariously lowered into the ground, a rough, shallow hole, dug with ebony arms and inhabited by thousands of red ants. The muddy crimson earth poured over the wood, one shovel load at a time. I lost track of time, staring as the hole filled. The hypnotic rhythm of the digging, the hollow thump on the steel crate, and the roar of the rain, left me numb, in a convoluted trance of grief, relief and a great deal of fear.

"*C'est fini.*"

"*Madame, nous avons finis.*"

"*Madame!?*"

"*Oui?*" I came up for air and managed to respond in French. Oui, always seemed to be the correct thing to say in French.

"C'est *mademoiselle*!" I had to make the correction once again. I am not married, I am not a madame.

"We are finished." The men pointed to the haphazard pile of dirt. "Bury dead," a man said in broken English, wiping the dirt off his hands. He threw the shovel on the pile and stood there. I smiled at him. "*Merci mingi mpo na mosala*...thanks very much for the work." I forgot the word for "to dig" so just said "work..."

"*Boye, likambo nini sikawa?* - so, what now?"

I was confused. I understood the words just fine but the implied meaning escaped me. I had given the thirty francs for payment to Ndumba to give him. It wasn't about the money. I think he was wanting some words here, some assurance that the ghost in the darkness, the curse, was gone.

He continued to fix me with his gaze, then turned away. I took a deep breath.

Ian took my arm. "Let's go, Anna. It's over."

Yes. Dead. Done. Finished. Buried. It's over. *J'ai fini.* I realized I had been holding my breath, and let out a long sigh. I finally felt the cold, the rain dripping down my nose and soaking through my socks. I had been holding my breath for four months, and now I stood literally in the middle of Africa, staring at my father's grave, and I truly realized, just now, that he was dead. I had granted his wishes; however, I knew my real journey had just begun.

Mpasi and I stood still together and silently said goodbye to Dad. Ian stood behind me with his hands on my shoulder. Keith had his head bowed. Was he going to say a few words again? It didn't look like it. Not this time. We were just thankful it was over. Mission accomplished. I found the rest of my family, unraveled the story, buried Dad next to a great love of his life, and now it was time to high-tail it out of here, and settle back into the routine of...life. I anticipated a feeling of relief at the thought, but instead it sickened me. Routine? Life? My tiny cramped apartment, my dead fish, my Venti coffee's, my romantic escapades, my high-paying boring-as-hades job? Who cared about Adobe visuals? That is what I get to go back to? But the money, oh yes, the money....

Keith said, "Wait just a bit. Let's look around. There are number of graves here, a few have markers but they are all over grown."

I sighed loudly. "Sure, why not."

We all moved through the area, pulling off weeds and scraping away moss from those with obvious markers. There were many mounds with no markers. Some markers had been defaced.

"Anna, Mpasi...come here for a moment."

Something in his tone caught our attention. We got up from our knees and walked over to him. He pointed at the headstone he had just righted.

I gasped and bent down to see more clearly.

"Marie Anne Landon. 1940-1984. For the love of Africa."

Mpasi and Ian both knelt now, each with a hand on my shoulder as I began to sob involuntarily. This was her actual grave. I thought of the marker at the Bellevue cemetery and the emptiness there. It's just a body. But I needed her; I needed her to be truly present to me somehow, an imaginary memorial did not suffice. Thinking of her six feet beneath my hands, I clutched the dirt violently and brought my face down to it as close as I could.

"Mom? Mom? *Oh...God*!" I just wept, sounding much like the women at those kufas I had attended. "Here you are! I found you!" I laughed as I wiped my nose with my dirty hand. I shook my head in utter disbelief. Why was I surprised? Of course Dad had this planned for me.

Finally I got quiet but didn't want to relinquish my hold on her. Well, this was evidently going to be the official family cemetery. James and his wives. Room for more.

I then turned and looked hard at Keith.

"I really didn't know...I know, you don't trust me anymore, do you? Honey, I knew she was buried somewhere around here, but it has been so long, and the jungle thickens so fast...I just suspected..." Keith stumbled around his words. He looked pleased with himself, yet also genuinely surprised. I let him off the hook and turned back to Mom and Dad. The rain picked up some enthusiasm and so we said our quick goodbyes.

"I'll be seeing you again soon, Mom... thanks Dad." I said out loud and turned and walked away.

We marched back toward Goyongo while the rain washed away our path. We were quite the crowd. The four of us, plus a few of Mpasi's guards, a few pallbearers, and a whole half a village. I still wondered about their presence, their looks, the way they shifted uneasily. I marveled at their superstition. What a hoax! A little toothy old man makes up some kind of curse on my Father, some bad things happen - which isn't abnormal out here to begin with - the whole village believes the evil - and now that my Dad is back, they are spooked? Even though he's dead? Stupid superstition. Or was it faith? Does any kind of faith not look stupid? I could hear whispers behind me; I didn't trust them.

We entered my old house in silence. We took off our muddy boots. We took turns in the bathroom changing out of our wet clothes. We never said a word, not one of us.

A dramatic shift had taken place. A cold new wind blew in through the screen windows and across the cement floor, vacuuming out the sweetness in the air we had become accustomed to. James' presence was finally gone. The box was gone. I missed it; I missed him. I wrapped my arms around my sides and held myself tightly. It hadn't felt real until this moment. Our familiar Ziegler was not sitting in the middle of our living room anymore, not hoisted up on poles anymore, not slipping and sliding along with the best of us through the jungle...anymore. Ziegler, the great pillar of fire by night, and cloud by day, the trailblazer of this journey had departed. It had provided a mysterious presence of peace and united our bizarre group intimately together with common purpose. Now it was far away, alone, and buried under six feet of earth. I wondered if Ziegler was OK in his new home. Was I thinking more about a strange metal casket than I was about my Dad? A few weeks ago a casket was disturbing; now, my life felt empty without one.

As I lay silent and still on my top bunk I couldn't speak and felt rather paralyzed, shivering from the cold rain that lingered in my bones. Ian crawled up the ladder, laid down next to me and wrapped his arms around me tight. I kissed him with wet cheeks and then turned my head. I still wasn't used to letting people see me cry. We fell asleep without a word. Hot tears continued to quietly slide down my cheeks and land on Ian's hands under my head. He didn't say a word.

I wondered, now that our mission was over, would we just go our separate ways? What would become of Ian and me? Could we fit together in Seattle, the way we fit perfectly together now? I felt the gentle curve of his body against mine, a magnificent puzzle piece, completing the picture. Would Mpasi go back home to her rebel Uncle, pick up her gun, and work for the cause again? Had our glue dissipated when we buried it? I listened for sounds of life in the jungle. I wondered what creatures of death we were lying beneath. Plants were feeding on plants. Animals were feeding on animals, or maybe even people. People feeding on animals...again with the self-devouring jungle. I cried until I fell asleep. I didn't really even know all the reasons why.

CHAPTER TWENTY-SEVEN

"Anna! Psst! Yaka awa!"

I rubbed my eyes and looked at my glowing watch - it was 1am. A flashlight blinked under my door. I was waking from a deep sleep.

"Anna! Yaka awa! It's Mpasi!"

"Mpasi?" I rubbed my eyes again. One minute I'm a Dutch immigrant picking blueberries with Ian and my Dad in Russia, and then, *bam*, I'm awake listening to Mpasi banging on my door. Oh, the mystery of dreams…

Ian sat up on his elbows, rubbed his hand through his messy hair and looked at me. *He looks so cute when he's sleepy.*

"What's going on?" He yawned. He needed an Altoid.

"Heck if I know. Too early for breakfast… Mpasi? Just a minute, ok?" I climbed down from the bunk threw on my jeans lying on the floor and opened the door.

"Come with me! Now! No time to talk." Mpasi handed me my sweater and my shoes and pulled me by my arm. I glanced around nervously for ants. No ants. Ian was struggling to put on his clothes and followed out the door. We frantically chased Mpasi out the screen door and into the dark. The parrot greeted us kindly in the night air, "Mbote! Mbote! Shoo, chicken!" He squawked. *Who you callin' chicken?*

The rain had stopped and it was mysteriously clear out. The moon shed just enough light on the land and the rocky path that we were hurrying along. The wet sobi grass scissored across our legs as we ran. I was still trying to get my breath and figure out what exactly we were doing. Aside from blindly following orders from Mpasi without question. *How does she make people DO that? I have to learn...*

"Mpasi! Hold up! What is going on!" Ian was still trying to button his shirt as we ran down a hill.

"I saw them - just through there. They going back!" Mpasi yelled over her shoulder.

"Who is, Mpasi?" I asked.

"My family!"

"Your family? What do you mean? Your Dad is here?" Were we joining the war? I guess I could quit my job...learn how to shoot a gun...

"NO!" Mpasi stopped and turned around to talk to us. "My aunts, uncles, my village people are here!" The village people are here? Wasn't that a Stephen King movie? I held my tongue, no time for sarcasm. I was still trying to wake up. Where is my latte?

I stopped and thought about what Mpasi just told me.

"Mpasi! Stop! Come back here right now." It felt good to try my hand at barking orders again.

Mpasi surprisingly halted. She turned around breathing hard, her hair was not cared for in the tight braids as usual. It was a frightening sight, sticking out every which way, and against the moonlight it looked even spookier. But that was not the issue at hand.

"You mean to tell me, that the medicine man's people are going back... back there? To the grave?"

Mpasi emphatically nodded, "Oui, Mon Dieu! I saw them. I saw their lights, and heard their footstep - I follow for a ways to see where they were go. They were going back up. A whole crowd of them. They were carrying kinds of things...some expedition...Anna, I fear they go to take him, or..."

"Take him!? Take him where? Why?"

"Haven't you been listen! They believe if he is here, if he lays in this ground, the curse continue..." I stopped listening to Mpasi explain the whole gambit again. It sounded like make-believe. A medicine man, a curse, grave robbers... *are you kidding me?* Was I still dreaming? I felt like a main character in the *Blair Witch Project* 5, or an *Indiana Jones* movie: The Curse of the Missionary's Grave...

"Aren't you listen?!" Mpasi was frantic.

"Mpasi, yes," Ian spoke calmly. Someone had to be sensible. "We aren't exactly near any other countries, continents... there is no place they can bring your Dad, Anna's Dad, I mean - y'alls Dad - where he would not still, somehow, be buried here, in Africa. Don't you see? The, uh, curse, would never stop. It has to be something else. Let's just go home and forget about it."

"Are you coming or not?" Mpasi did not respond to Ian's nicely crafted logical statement. She turned on her heels and started to run. It was then I noticed the rifle slung across her back. Ian and I looked at each other, he waited for my move. The sickening thought of shovels and spades hitting Ziegler, of dirty hands pulling out my sweetly rotting Father made me nauseous. It couldn't happen...it wouldn't happen. I ran after her. As expected, Ian followed. What a story he has to tell around the courtroom water cooler.

Mpasi was a natural hunter and tracker. And she was right. A few yards from the gravesite, we all slowed down. I could see lights flickering in the brush, and the murmur of voices.

"What now?" I whispered at Mpasi.

"Shhh! We wait and see." She put the rifle down beside her.

"Wait for what? We should confront them! Stop them now!"

"With what, all of your guns?" Mpasi was starting to grasp sarcasm. She was right, again. I realized that we had nothing. Just one gun and GI Jane here, and two skinny white people.

We ducked down low and scooted quietly closer so we could see. Ian was in an all out Marine Corps crawl on his belly. Stealth lawyer. I couldn't help but let out a little smile. No, we would never be the same...we could never go back to what and where we were before. The mud squished and gave way beneath our hands and knees. I was sure we were crawling over poisonous snakes and scorpions, just like Indiana Jones and the Temple of Doom. Maybe Ian would fry the critters up later for dinner. I wondered what kind of wine pairs well with snake? Chianti? No...too dry. Maybe a Merlot. Merlots go with everything...tasteless, boring, uncomplicated... My mind was a schizophrenic cavern of thoughts:

sometimes dwelling on the Seinfeld topics of life, meaningless, insignificant issues...sometimes chewing on the profound issues of the soul. Ok, maybe not chewing. Licking.

With a flick of her hand General Mpasi gave us the order to stop and lay down. So we did. I snapped back to reality. I could see the gang pretty clearly by now. We were back at the gravesite. Perhaps we were laying on Mpasi's mother's grave, or my mother's. I felt a bizarre streak of comfort surge through me, it was nice to be near a mother figure. Dead or alive. My therapist was going to rake in the dough when I got home.

We watched and waited. Minutes felt like hours. We tried not to sneeze or twitch as we peered through the trees. I could see the freshly dug mound of dirt, and the pile of palm fronds we had placed over Dad's body. A small wooden cross was hammered down on one end, behind a large flat rock we had found in a nearby stream. We had used a knife, and shallowly had carved out the words, "Tata - You are Home Free." Home? That was Mpasi and Keith's idea. I couldn't figure out whether they meant home as in Congo, or home as in... somewhere up there in the clouds, a place called heaven. Dad always used to say, "Heaven is my home." I never understood. He hated the harp, what would he be doing up there all day?

Poor Dad. He *was* finally back in Africa, but was it now more like a brief layover, before his final stop somewhere else? Would they really dig him up and carry him out of Congo? Or burn him? I imagined myself on my hands and knees scooping up his ashes and pouring them into an Urn I would name, appropriately, Ziggy, and then transporting Dad all the way *back* home and burying his ashes in his empty slot at Homeward Bound. All of this, for nothing… I shuddered. I watched as they all bustled around the dirt mound. How could they have so much fear in something so intangible and supernatural? I couldn't wrap my mind around it.

I gripped Ian's hand tightly, and Mpasi grabbed my other hand. It was then that I noticed his face. The face that haunted my dreams, the one I had glimpsed earlier. The yellow teeth, the bones around the neck, the red eyes and low-hanging ears…

"Mpasi! It's him - it's Zema!" I could barely mouth the words, my heart was hammering and my breath was short. I broke out in a cold sweat and willed myself to peel my eyes away from his. He seemed to be looking right at us, directly through the bush. I ducked down lower. I hadn't felt this afraid since jail, but this was a different kind of fear. There was an evil presence here. I could truly feel it. I shuddered and began to panic.

"*What are we going to do*!?" I yelled within my whisper, pronunciating each word poignantly. "How are we going to stop them? We can't let this happen! Mpasi! *Do something*!" I hissed in her face and slapped her on her arm to get her attention. She was the warrior after all. She could take them, couldn't she?

"We pray." Mpasi whispered.

"What?" This was not the answer I expected.

"We are outnumbered, so…let's pray. I don't know - it's always what Dad would do."

"He did, didn't he..." I wondered if Mpasi would still suggest prayer if she *wasn't* outnumbered. I was secretly anxious to see how she would take down the witchdoctor.

"Ian, pray please?" Mpasi asked.

"Who me?" Ian choked. But Mpasi had already closed her eyes. I couldn't help but smile again - and nudged Ian in the ribs.

"You pray!" Ian whispered back at me.

"No way! She asked *you*!"

"Fine!" Mpasi still had her head bowed, her eyes closed. She was breathing calmly, and had a small smile on her lips that were moving. I believe she was already praying.

"Ok. Um, Dear Jesus. God, I mean. Or both. Not too sure about how that works, does anybody really? Ok, I mean - ahem -" Ian quietly cleared his throat and kept on whispering, "God, we need a hand here. Please do not dig up James. We mean it, please. We need your help, we aren't good at this whole... death thing, or life for that matter, I guess. Please let him stay where he belongs." Ian paused, "Put us all back where we belong, always. Amen."

Put us all back where we belong. Ian's words invaded my ears. It was the simplest, worst, best prayer I had ever heard. Isn't that all that we really want in life? To belong? I knew I belonged with family and I knew I belonged with this strange wonderful jungle lawyer man. I swelled up and as a wave of emotion surged over me, I opened my mouth and inched close to Ian. He smelled like manioc and old spice, surprisingly enough, it was intoxicating. I was in love.

"Ian." I whispered close into his ear. He turned his head toward me.

"Yeah? Sorry, I didn't know how to pray, you should have done it."

"Ian. I love you." My lips parted into a smile as my eyes took in all of his face just an inch from my own, "I love you ,Ian." I said again and let my lips brush his.

"What?"

"No matter what happens tonight, I want you to know, I love you so much. I really do." I didn't even choke on the words, they flew out of my heart with ease.

"Nothing is going to happen to us tonight." Ian smiled back and gently kissed me. Mpasi coughed uncomfortably and let out a snicker.

I didn't need to hear the L-word back from Ian. I already knew it. And it would be cheap if he had added, a "you too" back at me. He has loved me since the day we met. I've always known it. Why did it take me so long? Why did it take me until here, in this moment, lying in the mud, in the middle of the Congo, at 2am, watching my Dad's dead body about to be abducted… why would it take all of this, to get me to love? I also knew at this moment, that my Father loved me, wholly and truly, even if his love was imperfect and misguided at times. He loved me, he loved Mpasi, he loved her mom, he loved my mom, he loved this country, he loved the people, and he loved God. He was a man of love, and he almost had a daughter who didn't know how. Almost. If it wasn't for this trip…

I remembered asking Keith way back at the dawn of our trip, if he ever wondered what was the point of taking Dad's *whole* body to Congo. I tried to get him to talk me out of it, and into just taking a part of his body, his heart, or his ashes, or something "easier," after all, he never gave us an explanation for *why* we had to take his *whole body.*

"Anna," Keith had said. "Sometimes short-cuts are just that. They cut us short."

I responded with, "Of course! That's the point, cut the trip short!"

"No, Anna. Not *the trip.* It cuts *us* short. Don't ask why. He has a reason, we don't know about. He always does."

"Does? You mean, he *did* have a reason..."

"Depends on Who we are talking about."

Keith confused me most of the time. Now I think I understood what Keith was saying about a short cut. Dad's body, though seemingly an extra burden, was in fact an extra blessing. The trouble, the heartache, the discoveryies, the journey, the long walks, the looming presence of the large box, the burial, the hiking, swimming, mosquitoes, prison, family, all of it...was meant to cumulate in all of these rare and precious moments. Especially these moments of raw and unadorned, unadulterated and unpretentious prayer.

The long-way around, the road less traveled, or I should say the road *never traveled,* led us to a higher height, a greater vista, invisible to the naked eye, but now visible through the heart - my heart, that had melted under the heated belt of the African equator.

"Mpasi, let's go. It doesn't matter. We did what we came here for, what Dad wanted."

"Anna! Shhh! Watch!" Boy, was this girl good at giving orders.

I turned toward the grave. The crowd had formed a large circle around Dad's grave. No dirt had been flung, no shovels were raised, the cross still stood up straight. I couldn't see the witchdoctor anywhere.

"What are they going to do?"

"How I know that? I'm watch the same thing you are!"

Men and women began to sway, and hold hands. One by one they placed little strange ornamental objects onto the grave. A small piece of a doll, a shiny rock, a makeshift cross, something that looked like a pig snout. I couldn't make all of it out. Then they began to sing.

"What are they saying!?" I couldn't help it. I had to ask questions. Just like when I watch movies, I have to ask because I always feel like I'm missing something that everyone else gets. It's tough to go through life like that!

"Shhh - let me listen." Mpasi stopped breathing and turned her ear. She was concentrating.

"They say, 'Oh light of dark and dark of light, take away our afraid... With - power...'"

"What? Light of what? I don't get it!"

"Anna! Shut up, let her listen!" Ian snapped. I was so antsy and wound up tight, I could have just leapt out of the bushes and shouted at all of them, "Will you speak up! And speak English! The rest of the world does!" Mpasi went on as they continued to sing and sway around the grave.

"With ancient power...something...something, I can't hear good....we call it back... we denounce...

something... and all is well. No more... something...
no more dark, we call it ...back...curse,
something..." Mpasi paused when they paused.

"What on earth does that mean, Mpasi?"

"How should I know!" We were hissing at each
other loudly when they seemed to have finished.
They stood silently, until one old man raised his
walking stick and pointed at the grave. Everyone
began to sing again and the man pointed back toward
our path.

"What did they do? It sounded like they were
doing a chant?" I asked.

"I think, yes. I think they came to, how to say in
English, to ...stop? Cancel...maybe cancel yes,
cancel...the curse that was done ago. Not to dig up
body! No dig!" Mpasi got excited as she talked and
started skipping her definite articles again. "They
came pray peace over curse or something, so maybe
could feel released!" Mpasi all but clapped her hands
together.

"Does that work? Can you do that?" Ian asked
dumbfounded. *As if he knew so much about curses...*

"Ian - what are you talking about! It's all about
what they believe. If they believe they can reverse it,
pray for peace, then they can! And I say, let them!" I
felt giddy with relief, and maybe a tinge of belief too.
Dad would remain in peace. Forever. I would never
have to have haunted dreams about leaving him
unattended only to hear that he was dug up and sent
off in a raft down the Congo River, or shipped back to
the U.S. I could just see Dale Krader signing for the
over-sized package now. Would he earn flyer miles
for that? I could not afford another plot in Bellevue.

"Psst! Go! Go! GO!" Mpasi was scrambling down the hill on her belly. I looked up and saw people coming toward us, just a few feet away. We had to scram, fast.

We tumbled down after Mpasi and took flight again. We probably ran for just a couple miles until we stopped and walked the rest of the way. The sky was getting slightly lighter, the moon was disappearing. It must have been nearing five in the morning, and the eerie air had turned sweet again.

We were far away from the crowd, and had nothing to worry about. As we walked we chatted vigorously about the night's events, adrenaline coursing through us. We laughed at Ian's wonderful child-like prayer. I made fun of Mpasi for freaking out so much, and had to explain to her what "freaking out" meant. That was even more fun. I chastised Ian for telling me to shut-up just seconds after I confessed my love to him. The three of us were like Jr. High school students, giggling and frolicking around after we had all snuck out of our houses, re-telling our stories to one another in our own creative versions. Mpasi was laughing especially hard at her own jokes, how we "had only one gun." For some reason she loved that bit of humor. She was in stitches over her new found humor. We slapped each other's back and held nothing back. We were relieved beyond belief. Ian chased me through the grass like a brand new boyfriend would. Mpasi hooped and hollered as she watched us play. When Mpasi laughs, all the happiness and laughter spills out through her wide smile and her voice. I wished I was more like her. I was so proud that she was my baby sister. Yet I continually felt like the baby. I had so much to learn from her.

The three of us enjoyed a kind of light-heartedness and joy that can only be found upon the rarest and most unintentional of circumstances...or maybe, it was very intentional, on my Dad's part. Did He know how this would all turn out? Did He know the ending, and that is why he initiated the beginning? *Thank you, Father.*

The morning sun was rising slowly. The dirt and grass smelled deliciously fresh, everything glistened and glowed, every drop of water on every small wavering leaf beckoned and hastened in the new day. The palms waved good-morning, and the animals hummed an enchanting chorus.

Keith was waiting on the porch with his hands on his hips like an angry mother, about to scold her children. We couldn't help but smile, even if we were in trouble. We sat down and all three of us at once chorused the story. He poured us tea, he listened intently, squinted wisely, and somehow, did not seem surprised. When we were through, he got up and helped us all up one by one.

"Well, children. Mission accomplished. Shall we go home now? I miss my wife."

"You have a wife?" Ian asked. *Will Ian ever get a clue...?*

We mostly napped the rest of the day away, and that night we feasted one more time on the most incredible foods. Mpondu cooked to perfection, soaked in the most savory of palm oil juices and roasted peanuts. Ian finally ate some kwanga. I soon realized that I had an aversion to kwanga breath. The boiled lamb, stuffed inside large Manioc leaves and dipped in a tomato peanut sauce was delectable. We ate, and laughed late into the night with Pastor Ndumba and his wife, the bodyguards and others from the village. We shared everything, our stories, our friendship, our food, our laughter... my spirit felt illuminated within me, my heart was strangely warmed...

As I sauntered sleepily back to the house for our last stay, I heard giggling and girly noises following me along the way. I turned to look at a pack of young girls, teens maybe, smiling and nodding in my direction, turning to each other to whisper, and laughing some more. I looked at my feet. Nope, no toilet paper attached to the bottom of my shoes. My zipper was good.

"*Bozali koseka nini, bana?* -What are you snickering at girls?"

"*Lobi okoyeba mobali* -Tomorrow you know a man!"

Were they serious? Tomorrow? I thought perhaps with the funeral and the burial that the village had moved on to more important matters; my fake wedding was not one of them.

"*Asili kosomba ntaba?* - Did he already buy a goat? *Malamu bojonga ndako sikawa* - good time for you to all go home."

I mused this over in my head. Tomorrow I become a fake bride. Fine, I'll do it. No use whining about it, it'll give everyone a good laugh, make the village happy that their Gbado is bought and sold...and Ian has yet another story to add to his Tarzan tales. I looked around for Ian and saw him still laughing and eating with everyone around the tables and lanterns. He was enjoying himself immensely; I admired his attempts at Lingala...and that he didn't mind being the butt of the jokes when he tried. His skin had darkened and his hair had also lightened. Ian looked young and fresh and alive; his cheeks were pink from sun, food, and smiles. The new tan enhanced the sky-blue spirit of his eyes. His African attire, which hung loosely on his body, suited him much better than the staunchy coat and black tie he always wore. Ian, the young frisky puppy freed from the pound. Would he ever return to such confinement in the field of death and tax law? I shook my head and smiled. I did not need an eight ball to prophecy the answer. It was decidedly...no.

He seemed to be forgetting that he was getting hitched tomorrow, I thought. My stomach suddenly did flips. What if he didn't want to... you know, play along? What if he wanted a finer, better, more gentile wife? Maybe an African wife? I reminded myself that this *wasn't real*. I needed to go to sleep. The bride needs beauty rest. I took one last glance in Ian's direction as he turned to wave at me. I waved back. He smiled flirtatiously, took out his left hand and charaded slipping a ring over the finger. *He remembered!* I scowled and with the back of my hand "shoo'd" him off and walked away.

I lay in bed and tried to shake the thought from my head, reminding myself over and over again that this was *just pretense!* But like a bride before her big day, I lay awake dreaming, smiling...nervously tossing and turning as my stomach lurched in anticipation. Or maybe it was the goat...

CHAPTER TWENTY-EIGHT

I awoke in the morning to the rude interruption. A gaggle of girls had let themselves into my room and threw off my covers. Ndumba's wife, Mama Bolingo, addressed me respectfully, smiled and held out a traditional dress in my direction. It took me a couple eye rubs, yawns and a few questions to remember that today was my "wedding day." I smiled and tried to play it all off very causally. I suddenly remembered that this was Ian's room too and looked underneath me at the bottom bunk. He was already out. I inquired about Ian to Mama Bolingo. She told me that Ian was already out acquiring my bride-price...a goat. I burst out laughing. I couldn't help it. Was he for real?

Mama Bolingo helped me down from my bed and into the bathroom. She stood me before the mirror and clucked her tongue, shaking her head, as she fingered my hair and pinched the skin around my face. I got the general idea that she disapproved of my appearance. With a loud whistle she called the other girls into the bathroom, sat me down on the toilet and began to mess with my hair. I couldn't fight it, I couldn't resist the six or seven hands that now tugged and tightened my hair. I hoped to God that I did not come out looking like Medusa. I saw one girl enter the bathroom with arms full of something that looked like hair. *Oh dear God, extensions!?* This could take six hours!

"*Mama, limbisa ngai, nasengeli café liboso na kobanda* - forgive me, could I please have some coffee before we start? *Makasi? Strong* coffee?" I was going to be sitting here for a long time. I was either going to need a strange little white pill or a carafe of coffee. Within a few minutes, a strong piping hot brew of sun baked African coffee arrived in the palms of my grateful hands along with a plate of *makembas*. I was scolded not to eat too much, or I wouldn't fit into my gown. *And what gown would that be?* I closed my eyes and enjoyed the petting I was receiving. I saw long pieces of hair began to fall around my shoulders and down to my waist. It was a bit darker than my own natural color, but surprisingly a good match. I closed my eyes and let myself sway to the tugging and pulling. I did not try to resist the entirety of the day's activity. *Did I even want to?*

By midday my hair was finished. I wasn't allowed to see it until after I was properly dressed. Mama and several other women came to dress me. They managed to fit me into a traditional dress that wrapped around me at least three times. The colors were vibrant and beautiful; color patterns I would have never chosen - oranges, blues, and reds. They swirled tightly around me, accentuating my best features. A younger girl, probably six, entered into the bedroom with a beautifully woven crown of white and yellow franzy-panzy flowers. I bent down low so that she could place it on my head. I felt an undeserving queen. She looked directly into my eyes and smiled wide. I kissed her on the cheek and said, "Merci."

"*De rien*," she offered back, "It was nothing." Yet the details in the crown betrayed her. It was something. She worked hard on it all morning so that I might be a bride today. I flashed to Sombo's baby and tears welled up in my eyes. The basic care and tenderness that a single human soul can exhibit overcame me. Where did this kind of love and generosity originate? An old Sunday school song came to mind, "for love is from God, and everyone that loveth, is born of God..." Did I have it within me to truly love? Does that mean I am born of God? I wondered if everyone was originally born of God, and depending on what direction they take away from Him, finds their way back to their origin? And yet I was not the one doing the finding and seeking...was He seeking me? Like a lost daughter that belonged to Him? I wondered again about love. I told Ian I loved him. What did that mean? Could I do this thing, this love thing? What have I ever given back to the world in this manner? Had I not lived my life entirely in the service of my best interest? And to what gain? A nice income, a dead fish, and a car for a best friend?

I heard my Dad's voice in my head, I heard him preaching gently and sweetly, *"She who seeks to gain her life will lose it, but she who seeks to lose her life will find it."* Was this what he meant? If I lost my life, giving it as a gift to the world around me, would I find life? Would I find some peace? And yet here I was gaining a life even though I did not attempt to lose it first. What was that called? Was that grace?

"What is your name, little one?" I realized I had been staring at her while my mind sifted through my spiritual state, I needed to break the anxious silence.

"*Kimia* - Peace." She answered softly. Before she could have a moment to turn and run away from the mesmerized, sentimental bride, I reached out to her and heaved her into my arms, holding her tight. I couldn't help the tears. I told myself this would be the last time… in Africa… that I would cry. I said her name over and over. Kimia. Kimia. I loved this little girl Kimia with all my heart, all of a sudden. If she wasn't careful, she may find herself being checked as my over-sized luggage; I would bring her home with me.

"*Ozali kitoko* - You are beautiful." She whispered in my ears. I looked at her and said, "*You* are beautiful." Peace. I squeezed her one more time and then let her out of my vice grip. Mama Bolingo clucked over me one more time as she wiped my face with her liputa. She was not happy about my red and puffy eyes. Oh well…get used to it. They finally led me to a mirror so that I could look at their craftsmanship. I took in a quick breath and covered my mouth with my hand. I was definitely not staring at Anna Landan. The woman before me was radiant, tall and bright, shining almost. My hair was long, in a thousand braids laying down my back, my shoulders, and my chest. Half of it was braided around the top of my head in a crown; a nest for the flower-wreath to sit on. Mama Bolingo had rubbed some palm oil on my cheeks and they glistened with a bit of sheen and color. I smiled bright and wide, turned around to my audience and gave them a big applause. The women hooted and hollered, eating up the recognition I gave them for turning me into a bride. A fake bride, that is.

When we heard the bleating of the goat, I was finally escorted outside. I wondered if Ian had extensions in his hair too. I walked outside of the house and the women stood me on the porch, instructing me not to move. Ian and Keith were leading a goat up the road towards the house. Ian was also dressed in native attire. The beautifully embroidered shirt hung around his body, clinging in all the right places. He was donned in purples and blues. I smiled to myself noting that the outfit did not suit him, but he seemed pretty at ease in his new duds. He smiled at me widely as he ushered a beautiful female goat up the hill. Ok, she wasn't that beautiful. Scrawny and spotted, but it seemed to be a fitting bride price. The entire village of Goyongo was following Ian and Ndumba as they marched. When they arrived at the top of the hill near the front of the house, Mama Bolingo came forward and led me and the other women out into the yard to meet them. I looked up at Ian and gave a little shrug of my shoulders, raising my eyebrows as if to say, *well, this is it...what do you think?* Ian looked me up and down approvingly and mouthed, "WOW." I blushed.

It suddenly dawned on me that we were actually getting married. This was no game to these people. They were literally marrying off a child of the village to this mad jungle lawyer man. I wiped my hands on my dress and suddenly felt faint and queasy. I took deep long breaths and tried to come up with a thousand excuses to get out of this. *Ok! I played along! Can we stop now?* I wasn't ready to get married, or was I? I was so conflicted. I didn't deserve Ian, but I wanted him. Would we last forever? Who does these days? My heart pulsed obnoxiously fast; my skin became clammy. Mama Bolingo took me by the elbow to steady me. Ian and entourage stopped a few feet away. Ndumba stepped into the middle and in a loud powerful voice, began the ceremony. *Oh merde, was he ordained?* I crossed my fingers behind my back. Just in case. Then I uncrossed them, then crossed them again. Merde! *Get a grip, Anna!*

"In the beginning God created the heavens and the earth…"

Oh my God. He is going to literally start from the beginning and work forward to the present. Ndumba took his time, explaining all about Adam and Eve and God's intent for marriage, the whole one-flesh thing, leaving and cleaving. Ian now started shifting uncomfortably. I wondered if he was thinking about what I was thinking about. At least I wasn't the only one getting nervous. Ndumba talked about family, the need for children, for love and respect, obedience and submission. Ok, as long as I didn't have to sign anything, but really, did he have to mention children? And where was Mpasi? I looked anxiously around at the crowd. She had been absent all morning for my grooming. I realized I missed her greatly. She is my sister! She should have been there for all of that!

I finally got a glimpse of Mpasi at the edge of the crowd. She looked very somber. *Where have you been for the last seven hours!* Oh the mysterious life of a rebel leader's daughter.

Ndumba finally said "Amen," and everyone muttered "Amen" in agreement. He indicated to Ian to come forward with the goat. Ian did so and handed the tether to Mama Ndumba and said in Lingala,

"I give you this goat in payment for the wife you give me. I pray God will bless you and us." Ian's voice sounded a little high and nervous, but he spoke fluidly nonetheless.

In Lingala?? He said that in Lingala? Where did my old Ian go? He had memorized that line and did pretty well. He looked up, teasingly raised his eyebrows a few times, turned up a sweet half-smile and shrugged his shoulders, all to say "so there you go, what do you think? Your turn."

My turn. Ndumba gestured for me to go to him and I did, leaving my Goyongo family and standing next to Ian. He took my hand. I felt someone stand close behind me. I turned and saw Mpasi. She had made her way through the crowd and had come up to put her hand on my shoulder. I gave it a squeeze and smiled at her. I turned back to Ian and held his hands in mine.

"I now declare that you are husband and wife!" Everybody shouted and applauded. I waited for "you may now kiss the bride" instruction, but it never came.

Ian kissed me anyway. This got another shout from the crowd. He kissed me again.

"Ok Ian, that's enough." We hadn't even had the DFR or "define the relationship" talk yet. Good grief. We were *married* already? Legally bound to one another in holy matrimony? Matrimony…it sounded so old-fashioned. Somehow I couldn't recall an Ian and an Anna in Leave it to Beaver…

"Yes dear." Ian quit the kissing and whispered in my ear, "You are a beautiful wife…I am very lucky." He said this teasingly yet when he backed up to gaze at me, his look was sincere. I felt absolutely stuck between this pretend-wedding game we had just played, and the hope for the reality. *Please be real…please don't be real…* I couldn't decide. Maybe it was time for the DFR. "Honey, are we married, or aren't we?"

Directly after the ceremony there was a small feast down in the village where we ate the goat and a few chickens, as well. As much as I liked the feastings, I was pretty sure that I could not force one more ounce of food past my lips. It was time to go back to my Luna bars and non-fat lattes. The dancing began, yet again, and I couldn't help but think we had basically been feasting and partying since we arrived. All over a memorial service, a burial, and a wedding! Sounds something like *Three Weddings and a Funeral*…but different, more like *Three Funerals and a Wedding*. There was no way I was going to be able to move in the dress, wrapped tight around me like a mummy, so I opted out of the traditional wedding dance. When the crowd expressed disappointment, Mpasi came to my defense, sort of, claiming yet again, that white girls couldn't dance. I mouthed "thank you" to her, and sidled up next to Ian on a bench to have a little relationship talk.

"Ian, this…what we did today…it was a drama, an act…symbolic, you know, the village giving me away. It is not a real marriage." I decided to take the cynical-humorous route as opposed to the vulnerable-transparent route. I wasn't about to open with, "Ian, is there a part of you that really does want to marry me?"

Ian took my hand and jested, "No? Really? What makes a real marriage? I paid a lot of money for you. I bought you, I own you." He grinned. *Such a boy...*

"Ian, this isn't funny. It was nice, it was great, a real memory maker, but there wasn't any cake or champagne, how could it be real?" As if cake and champagne clenches the deal.

"But we killed the goat...and you said you would leave and cleave."

"I did not." I pushed back.

"You did so, you said, 'I do.'"

"Why do you think people get married anyway, Ian? Do two people really need a legal piece of paper that "binds" them together to say they are committed to each other for life? A piece of paper? That is so...flimsy...so fleeting."

"I know. That's why I think a real wedding, a real marriage of commitment is binding only if it is done before God and friends. God is not fleeting or flimsy, He is not a piece of paper framed above our bed reminding us to stay faithful, He is the heartbeat of marriage, the covenantal glue that binds and ties two people together into one."

I paused with my mouth wide open staring at him in disbelief. *Are you kidding me right now?*

I finally nodded and smiled, I got it. "You've been talking to Keith, haven't you." Ian looked shy as though he had just got caught with a naughty secret.

"You got me. Yes, that was all Keith."

"But it sounds good, doesn't it," I ventured.

"Sounds about right to me."

"So what do we do now?" I couldn't bear to be the one not in control of this situation, to be subject to whatever Ian wanted to do with "us" and our marriage/non-marriage situation. We were beating around the bush. The elephant in the room was starting to stomp and snort. China would break.

"Anna Landan. For the last year, I have admired you, adored you, loved your tenacity, your ferocity, and your...

"Venom?" I offered. I know I had been a snake.

Ian laughed, "Yeah, kind of. Your bite. I liked that part of you too. I had a crush on you since the day you came to me for help with your overdue taxes...the way you stormed into my office with your pretentious quad-shot latte, acting like you owned the place, the world, and me. I constantly looked for excuses to call you, 'needing' more information in order to process your forms. Your voice on the other end of the line made my heart flip. And then..." Ian kind of coughed and squirmed..." And then we came here..."

"You skipped some parts, " I teased.

"I know," Ian blushed, then continued. "I got to come with you to Africa. I counted myself the luckiest man in the world. I knew it wasn't going to be easy. I did not expect all that we encountered, of course... to make a long story short..."

"Long indeed..." I shook my head, flashing back to the last couple of weeks, which truly seemed like a year.

"...I got to see other sides of you. I have been able to witness the unraveling of your relationship with your Dad. I see how much you loved him; how much forgiveness you are capable of...and how much love you are capable of for your parents...and now for Mpasi...maybe even - " Ian paused. I stared at him, wondering where he was going with all of this. Was he breaking up with me? Could he even, if we weren't even together? Or were we truly married...was he divorcing me already? Or was it technically an annulment? I panicked and clenched my jaw tightly. Of course, he could not want me. He is trying to let me down easy. Oh God!

"Anna, you are strong and beautiful, tough yet gentle, cynical yet vulnerable...and you are the woman I would be more than honored to spend the rest of my life with. Will you marry me?" Ian spoke evenly. His voice didn't crack once. His eyes did not peel away from mine for a minute.

My mouth jumped ahead of my brain, my jaw quickly unlocked and I answered outside of myself urgently and confidently, "Yes," simultaneously breathing out a great sigh of relief. Ian leaned in, took my face in both of his hands and kissed me firmly on the lips, as if for the first time. I smiled through most of it. Elated. And then I cried. I think they were tears of joy. No. They were tears of everything. Ian wiped them with his kisses.

I was engaged... Now, where was my diamond?

CHAPTER TWENTY-NINE

"Mpasi, are you sure you won't come with us?" We stood with our bags packed on the freshly cut grass on the Goyongo airstrip. We waited for Dan the pilot to land, safely, pick us up and take us back to Kinshasa.

"I'm sure. I need to stay. This is my home."

"But Dad was going to bring you back, I thought..."

"He wanted to, I never did. It sounded glamory - is that the word?"

"You mean glamorous?"

"Yes! It sounded glamorous at first... he thought he offer me better life in the States. Away from war, and heartache. But I think he was wrong. I think better life, is here, for me anyway."

I couldn't help but nod, and slightly agree with her. In the U.S. we live in a world of isolated communities - bonded together merely as bystanders of shared experiences such as *Lost, Gilmore Girls, The Office, Greys,* etc. Do we actually experience life together in the United States, or do we just chat about what we experience alone at home, sitting on our own leather thrones, in our tiny kingdoms? But on the other hand, Congo offered guerilla warfare. It was a toss up. But I didn't want to go home. I had let my drawbridge down, the enemy of love invaded my kingdom along with the enemy of vulnerability and need...and maybe a little faith. Would I naturally be inclined to draw that bridge back up? I doubted the strength of my crumbly fortress walls, and was thankful they were only made of clay, after all. My night in shining armor had rescued me from the tallest tower. I glanced over at Ian. He was a little too skinny, a little too pale for a knight, even with his farmer's burn. He was too naïve, yet somehow smart enough to be a lawyer. He loved too dangerously, without reserve, yet could level me with his eyes when need be - the oddest-looking knight I'd ever met. I was indeed conquered for good. But he didn't conquer alone. It took an army of four. Dad, Keith, Mpasi, Ian. Maybe five...if you count God. I wasn't sure if I did yet, but I was thinking about it. But I think He counted me.

I took Mpasi's elbow and led her away from the gang.

"Mpasi. I don't know what to say...how to say good-bye." *I will not cry unless she does!*

"It's ok. I don't either know."

"We'll be back you know. Maybe even next year, as soon as we can. And I want you to come visit sometime, please?" I meant it, and smiled at the thought.

"I will. I know you will be back. Maybe you even stay."

"Maybe, but you're going to have to end this war of yours first, okay? And be safe out there."

Mpasi smiled, her beautiful white teeth flashed in front of me, a smile I was very used to by now.

"I'm sorry I gave you such a hard time, I'm sorry I didn't believe you, I just..."

"It is ok. Anna, will you to write me, tell me everything you knew about Tata, what was he like, what did you do together, what made him laugh..."

"I was just going to ask you to do the same, I want to know what he was like, too." We smiled at each other, smiling at the irony of it all. A pen pal; letters I would cherish. Maybe I would quit my job and write a book about my Dad's life.

"I love you, big sister."

"Love you, lil' sis. See you." I hugged Mpasi tight and tried not to cry. She wrapped her ebony arms securely around me, I could tell that she was at least twice as strong as I was. I had some working out to do. Somehow I figured 24-hour fitness wouldn't offer me the same kind of work out that Mpasi gets.

I could hear the Cessna landing. Mpasi had sent word to Bemba who had "his people" contact MAF and arrange a safe passage for this landing. It seemed so simple, now, hearing the drone overhead. Why couldn't we have just landed here in the first place? But then...what would I have lost?

"Oh! I almost forgot, one more thing." I took out my "secret" passport holder from under my blouse and opened a small pocket on the inside. Soldiers did not look that thoroughly, thank God, Mpasi didn't give them the time. I pulled out a thick gold band.

"This was Dad's ring. The funeral director gave it to me before they, put him... you know. I want you to have it."

"Thank you." Mpasi took the ring from my hand and put it over her thumb. It was the African way to accept and be matter of fact. An American sister would have pretended to feel too overwhelmed, would have hemmed and hawed, and said, "No! I can't - it's too precious, you have it!" And we would have argued back and forth until the end result was the same as it was now. I loved that about Mpasi. She had no airs. I hoped to take that quality with me back home. I wondered if Mpasi had or was hoping to take anything from me, aside from my wicked sense of humor.

We let go of our embrace and I headed back toward Ian. Ian and Mpasi hugged tightly, Keith also said his good-byes. Fluent Lingala poured out from between the two of them, I couldn't keep up with all that they were saying, but they seemed to know something we didn't. They laughed and patted each other on the backs as if they had just finished a project.

We were distracted by the sound of a truck pulling up. We all turned to see what was happening. A rooster-tail of dust washed over it and for a moment we could not see anything. A couple of men emerged from the dust and came resolutely toward us.

I gasped and grabbed Ian's arm. "Ian..." I felt myself slipping. So close. So close to leaving happily ever after. It was just not going to be that easy, nothing has been so far...

Ian, alarmed, "What?"

I pointed, I could not talk. Then finally, "It's them...from the jail..."

Immediately he understood. I could feel his muscles tighten. *Where was Mpasi?* How could she disappear so quickly? I didn't see her. Where were the bodyguards, always so evident, but now where were they? Ian took a stop forward.

"Ian, don't…they'll kill you."

"I'll kill him first."

I was impressed, but still, that wouldn't do. "Ian, don't. Please."

They were near now. *Why were they here? Didn't they know whom they were crossing? Mpasi, where are you!?*

Lusty guard was leading the gang. He took his time sauntering toward us with a resolute sneer on his face. I stopped breathing and inched closer to Ian. He glanced at Ian with a smirk, and then back at me. He smiled wide with his yellow teeth. I shuddered with the memory of his breath.

"*Bonjour, mademoiselle,*" he said with exaggerated formality.

"F-off," I said in exaggerated English. He understood well enough in general if not specifically. I didn't care if I was too brazen or bold. This creep was not about to steal my newly found happiness. I had to defend it for all that it was worth…it was worth everything.

"Leaving us so soon, white whore?"

I was getting really tired of this nickname. Oh well - what did I have to lose? He wouldn't hit me or kill me here in public, would he? I stepped up and gave him the most viscous slap I could muster. It caught him by surprise. Some blood began to ooze from his nose. His gaze riveted on me, then on Ian.

Ian moved, and Lusty pulled out a big ugly pistol and pointed it at his temple. Ian stopped. Lusty pulled the hammer back. My heart stopped. *What have I done!* God would not take him from me now, would He? *Please God...Please God!*

"Now, mademoiselle, I ask again, leaving so soon?"

I mustered up some confidence...

"Hear that plane? That is ours. You, however have to stay here." I remained calm and assertive...on the outside. My fiancé had a gun to his head. I didn't know if this was the time to be tough, or vulnerable. Two qualities he admired in me, which do I choose to save his life? My knees trembled. Keith stepped toward me to help talk us through this. But at that moment I saw movement behind the soldiers, and I smiled. My courage just grew. So did Ian's, who smiled at him.

"Put down the gun." Ian hissed.

Lusty looked at me. "Quoi?"

I said in Lingala, "He said put the gun down," then added just softly enough for him to hear, "you black dog." It wasn't the same as white slut, but I tried. It was about the worst dehumanizing racist comment I could muster. I got the reaction I wanted just when I wanted it.

His eyes widened. Blood effused his face. His face turned into a snarl. He turned the gun on me and pulled back the hammer. Then a cough sounded beside him as his lieutenants tried to get his attention. He turned slightly. "What?"

Silence. He turned more and saw several AKs pointed at him and his little gang. The barrel of

Mpasi's gun was unwaveringly aimed at his torso. One gun was enough. She stepped up.

"You know who I am, you pig?"

He was quiet. Then finally, faintly, "Yes."

"This is my sister, you pile of dung." Dog, pig, dung...the names got more and more interesting. This was just not going his way at all.

"What is she saying?" Ian said to me.

"In a minute, Ian..."

His face blanched, eyes moving between us.

"Your sister?"

"Yes. She said you hit her, tried to rape her..."

"I never tried to..."

Mpasi moved closer, her rife a foot from his head. "What's that?"

"I didn't know, I am sorry."

"So, if she wasn't my sister, that would be ok, to rape her?"

He was now confused.

"Yes, no...?"

"How many of my African sisters have you raped, you monkey?"

Monkey...that was the worst possible insult. It shocked me to hear it. Mpasi was trying to goad him into doing something stupid, something maybe fatal. But he knew that. He swallowed hard.

"None, nobody, really...."

"Put down your pistol." She looked at his group. "All of you, put them all on the ground. Now!"

They all did. As soon as his gun was in the dirt, with all of that power I had felt in her earlier embrace, she hit him with the butt of the rifle right between the eyes and he went down hard, head hitting the red earth. She said something to the guards and they hauled him off towards the truck. The lieutenants kept their eyes down.

"Go," she said to them, and they went.

I smiled at her. "Thanks, sister. I enjoyed that."

She smiled back. "Yes, sister, ok. So did I. "

"There was a woman in the jail who helped me...name of, ah, Sombo..."

"Yes, I know."

I hesitated. "You know? You know what?"

"Sombo is my cousin."

I stood there for a long moment. The hot wind blew around us. I shaded my eyes and looked intently at her.

"So, she didn't steal from her husband?"

"Probably did."

I smiled. "OK, you were watching me."

"Yes. I didn't know for sure about you. I wanted to find out. I wanted to know what you were like, who you really were."

"Well, say hi for me."

We looked at each other for a long moment, then embraced. I couldn't let go. My throat closed and the heat and moisture in my eyes pushed through my many barriers, I let the tears fall. Willingly, submissively. After all, tears mean I have something worth crying over, rather, someone.

The plane circled overhead, then cruised down, landing gently and taxied over to us. Still we embraced.

"Gotta go."

"I know."

Ian, Keith and I finally separated ourselves and walked toward the plane. We went around the prop and I turned back to wave at Mpasi one more time. She cupped her hands around her mouth and yelled at me,

"Invite me to your wedding!"

"Whose?" Did I hear her correctly?

"Yours and Ian's! Invite me! I will be there!"

I smiled and waved her off. *How did she know?*

We flew into Kinshasa. The next day our plane took off from Ndjili airport and headed to Brussels. I didn't care where it was going, just out of Africa. Secretly, I was hoping to convince Ian to hop out in Brussels and head down to Italy like we had joked about. Tuscany was calling me. Chianti was calling me. But as I looked out the window at my country, maybe for the last time, I felt torn. So much of me was "down there" in the jungle, in the red mud, in the villages, at the gravesite. But Mpasi was right, it was not home.

"Mesdames, Messieurs, we are needing to spray the cabin for insects. This will not harm you, but you may wish to shut your eyes and not breathe."

Just in case it is harmful, right? Left over Agent Orange. The stewards came down the isles spraying some kind of aerosol into the air. I shut my eyes and held my breath. This was a rite of departure from Africa. Fumigation.

I had a couple of "digestifs," the French euphemism for hard liqueur and put my head back on the headrest. Closed my eyes.

"Didn't we meet on the way here?" The voice was vaguely familiar. I opened my eyes and looked across the isle. It was Clooney with the pearly whites.

"Odd, isn't it, that we are leaving together. What are the chances?" Seriously, I thought, what *are* the chances? I was still trying to put it all together. Didn't I meet this guy last year? No, it was just a couple weeks ago, back when I was a different Anna.

"Huge." I finally managed to answer, and pretended not to be so thrown off. Clooney didn't look that cute to me anymore either.

"What?"

"The odds against this are huge."

"Oh, yes…well, how was your trip?" Clooney tried to look flirty, I had no interest.

My "trip." I laughed out loud and Ian looked over, I took his hand.

"Well, they buried my heart in Africa but my body is returning." I *had* buried my heart in Africa, I thought, my old one. And I had acquired a new one, one that made room for others, and was starting to make room for the quintessential Other; after all, He made room for me.

"For sure." Clooney looked at me intently.

"I determined never to stop until I had come to the end and achieved my purpose."

Clooney thought for a moment then said, "David Livingstone, right?"

"Yup. Time to go home." I smiled at him, pulled my sleep mask over my eyes, and went to sleep. I would never be homeward bound.

ABOUT THE AUTHOR

A little about me: I was born in Zaire, Africa, now The Democratic Republic of Congo, and lived there for most of my younger, formative years. This exotic and lush tapestry of my life is the canvas on which I compose my writing. My affection for African culture found its way into my studies, and I completed my last credits of college at Daystar University in Nairobi, Kenya, focusing on African theology.

I was blessed to be able to travel back to post-war Congo with my family in 2003 and visited the villages and sites of my childhood. I experienced a great dissonance between my memories and the reality before me, especially due to the devastation and cultural tension left in the wake of war. These themes that are at once heartbreaking as well as profoundly healing find their way into this story, as our protagonist searches for family, faith, and meaning-making amidst beauty and brutality.

My own faith and identity journey has been complicated: riddled with questions, failures, rebellion, many doubts, as well as peace in the forgiveness, transformation and redemption given to me by the grace of God.

I am now a mother of two, and currently live in Seattle, Washington - the most beautiful city on earth. Go Hawks!

- Rebecca (*facebook.com/RebeccaJWorl*)

SPECIAL THANKS

My husband, Robert Worl; my champion, biggest fan, and incredible artist who created the cover. Ben Cassidy, a top Amazon Kindle author, my brother, and the one who applauded me and pushed me the most to "get this book out there." My Mom for all of her multiple edits. And finally, Justin Key, if you were here with me, you would already be a best selling author, you inspired me.